ABBY NORMAL

SAMUEL THOMAS FRASER

To learn more about the author, visit:

https://samuelthomasfraser.com/
https://www.facebook.com/STFupperlip
https://twitter.com/STFupperlip
https://www.instagram.com/samuelthomasfraser/

A NOTE FROM THE AUTHOR

In the modern world of digital publishing, word-of-mouth and person-to-person buzz can make or break an indie title. If you enjoy this work, please consider leaving a review on Amazon or recommending it to your friends in person or on social media. Happy reading!

BOOK ONE:

IN THE BEGINNING

THEN

CHAPTER 1

RENDER UNTO CAESAR…

ANOTHER MATCH failed, and Don's cigarette remained stubbornly unlit.

He cursed, insinuating that the match had had improper carnal knowledge of a family member. He threw a hard look at the matchbook, trying to intimidate it into cooperating with him. He promised the matchbook that this really was his last cigarette, honestly, and wasn't a man's last cigarette more than enough reason to give him a light?

And it was going to be his last one, too. For real this time. He had sworn to Karen he would quit when the baby arrived, and he'd already cut down to only two or three smokes a week.

But. But, but, but. He had said "when the baby arrives" and not a split second before. And Karen had been in labour nearly eleven hours now.

Jesus. Eleven hours in the worst storm to come up the coast of BC in 15 years. Don had heard of natural births before, but this was fucking ridiculous.

They'd all told him it had to be this way, Karen included. Something about ley lines and chaotic energies and ancient traditions. Something about imbalance in the mystic equilibrium, which would alter the electric potential in the atmosphere and wreak havoc on the complex mechanical systems in a hospital.

In Don's opinion, the whole thing had a pretty pungent odour of bullshit.

He finally got his cigarette lit and took a walk around the beach. The island was a half-mile of rock and trees, with one log cabin stuck in the middle of a clearing on the nearby hill. It was what Don's father-in-law would have called 'a real strip-of-piss.' As lightning struck the next island over, Don told himself there wasn't anything to worry about. Really, there wasn't. That 200 pounds of rugby muscle wasn't just for looks: he knew how to handle himself in a fight. So did Karen, if it came to it.

Not to mention the retinue of freaks, said a voice in his head. Then, *Holy shit, there's a Word of the Day for you.*

"Lovely night for it, eh?"

Don turned and saw a man approaching him from the cabin. Enter Freak Number One, said the voice.

The man shouted at Don over the howl of the wind, and his long Inverness coat billowed behind him. "I said, 'lovely night for it, eh?'"

Don didn't answer as the man in the Inverness coat drew close to him. He was shorter than Don's six-three, and much thinner, with goofy oversized ears and a square chin, but there was something about him—some presence in his bright green eyes—that was naturally, effortlessly commanding.

One of the green eyes winked, and the man in the Inverness coat whispered, "Oh, to be in Canada now that autumn's here." He spoke with a soft English accent and a cheeky, joking note in his voice.

Don wasn't in much of a joking mood, and he looked straight past the Englishman to the log cabin. "How is everything in there? I mean… is she here yet?"

The Englishman shook his head. "Not quite yet, but I'd say she's very near, going by the state of things." He glanced at the sky as he said this, as if the 'things' in question would suddenly blow down from one of the dark clouds above.

Don turned back toward the water, and the Englishman closed his eyes like he was meditating. It was several minutes before the Englishman gripped Don's shoulder and whispered, "She's here." As the wind died away, Don heard an infant crying in the distance. He threw his cigarette into the waves and charged toward the cabin, excited and terrified in equal measures. He could hear the calm, measured footsteps of the Englishman jogging after him.

Inside the cabin, Karen Henderson was lying on a creaky twin bed in one corner, trying to soothe what looked like a very noisy pile of old dishrags. She was a small, round-faced woman, like a child's doll come to life. Not at all, then, like the two women flanking the bed, who could both have passed for angry villagers in a Universal monster movie.

The woman on the right was a tall, muscular Haitian with a lot of dark hair pulled back in a tight ponytail. Natalie Arnaud wore a bulky, dirty trench coat over an equally dirty tank top, khaki pants, and heavy steel-toed boots. The whole ensemble suggested that she'd been working nights in either a munitions factory or a slaughterhouse.

The woman on the left looked like an older version of Karen. Stout of frame and straight of back, 'Grandma' Meg McAllister had a glass of single malt scotch in her hand. It was not her first one of the night.

Don stood with his back to the door for a moment, staring at the squirming, noisy bundle in Karen's hands, until the Englishman gave him a nudge. "I think some introductions are in order, Donald."

Karen looked up and nodded, beckoning Don over to her. As he approached the bed, she glanced at the Englishman and said, "You too, Simon." The two men huddled around the bedside as Karen gave the child a gentle pat on the back and said, "Don… say hi to your daughter."

Grandma Meg put down her Scotch and gently placed the child in Don's arms. His whole body froze as the baby's weight settled against him, and he imagined that the slightest tremor would offend her. Only his mouth moved as he whispered, "She's gorgeous…"

This was, of course, a clever lie. She was a newborn baby, and all newborn babies look like flesh-shaped balloons filled with prune juice and raspberry jam, but as far as Don was willing to admit, the child was perfect.

"So, what do we call her?" Simon asked. "Only I feel like 'Small Human-in-Progress' is a tad wordy."

Karen smiled and shook her head. "We call her 'Abigail.'"

Grandma Meg nodded and took a sip of her scotch. "Aye," she said, in a broad Yorkshire accent, "Abigail Margaret 'enderson." Then she smirked and added, "My suggestion, of course."

Don nodded and rocked the child in his arms. "Abigail. Abby, for short." He leaned in close to his daughter and whispered, "Do you like that? Do you like 'Abby'?"

Abby made a gurgling noise of assent and reached for Don's nose with a fat, sausagey arm. As her eyes opened and she took a first look at the room around her, the party went quiet and just watched her, forgetting that there was a world beyond their log cabin.

So it came as a huge shock when somebody knocked on the door.

Knock-knock-knock. For a second, nobody moved. Then Natalie pushed aside her trench coat, letting her hand rest over the hilt of the long machete she had strapped to her leg.

Knock-knock-knock. Grandma Meg reached for the Webley revolver she'd holstered at her hip and thumbed the hammer nervously.

Knock-knock-knock. Simon closed his eyes and nodded once. "It's him."

The door crashed against the wall as a rush of freezing wind howled through the cabin. Don held Abby close to his chest and turned his back to the chill, while Natalie and Grandma Meg trained their weapons on the figure in the doorway.

The newcomer was not quite a man, nor was it quite a monster. It was human in shape, but it was cloaked in a set of white floor-length robes, with gold at the sleeves and collar, and a purple hood that hid its eyes.

The thing in the robes glided into the cabin, hands folded in front of it, heedless of the venomous looks it received. Behind it, the door slammed shut and locked itself. The thing whispered, *"The weather is… pleasant, is it not?"* Its voice was like the crunch of dead leaves underfoot, and the way the corners of its mouth twitched upward suggested that it was attempting irony.

Natalie stepped forward and touched the point of her blade to the creature's throat. "What the hell do you want, you son of a bitch?"

The robed figure raised its hands submissively. *"Such language,"* it wheezed, *"and in the presence of a child…"*

Natalie leaned in and pressed the blade harder. The robed figure winced as the tip of the blade bit into its neck, and a thin track of blood seeped into the collar of its robes. "I'm warning you, Deacon," she hissed.

The Deacon flicked one of his raised hands and the machete sank to the floor like a lead weight, taking Natalie with it. He moved his hand again, and the weapon leaped out of Natalie's grip and flew toward Grandma Meg. The Deacon made a fist and the machete screeched to a halt, its tip inches from Grandma Meg's heart.

"Do not test me, woman," the Deacon hissed at Natalie. *"I do not come here to quarrel with any of you. But, if I am met in the spirit of war, I will take steps to… defend myself!"* He opened his fist, and the machete jumped forward another inch. Grandma Meg retreated back against the wall.

Simon raised his hands. "All right! Everyone just take a deep breath. This is not a fight we wish to have." Then, pointedly, to Natalie, "Any of us."

With a curt nod to Simon, Natalie backed away from the Deacon and raised her hands. Behind her, Grandma Meg dropped the Webley and kicked it across the floor. The Deacon flicked his hand again, and the machete veered right, sinking into the far wall.

"Cooler heads prevail…" the Deacon whispered, glancing at Simon. *"And the wisdom of the ages shines bright."* He turned and glided toward Don, extending a hand. Abby whined and kicked as the Deacon's slender fingers brushed against her swaddling clothes. *"Please. I wish to consider my… investment."*

Don shook his head. He didn't realize it, but every muscle in his body was vibrating with fear and fury. "She's a baby…" he whispered. "She's just a baby…"

The Deacon's thin lips stretched into a grin. His teeth were like piano keys: shining white and perfectly straight. *"Soon,"* he vowed, *"she will be much, MUCH more."*

Before Don could respond, the Deacon tore Abby from her father's arms and rearranged her swaddling clothes, smiling the whole time. Don looked back at Karen, who was struggling to rise from the bed. But the labour had left her exhausted, and she sank back into the pillows.

The Deacon bowed his head over Abby and opened his mouth. Don and Karen both gagged as the Deacon pressed his tongue to Abby's pink flesh, right over her heart, then tracked it up her chest, her throat, all the way to the top of her head. Abby began to sob and Don's hand curled into a tight fist. But he dared not move. Not against the being that had saved his life.

When the Deacon was finished, he licked his lips and hissed, *"I can taste it on her already. I can feel the energy crackling and burning within her. She will have great power before long…"* The Deacon passed Abby back to her father, and he tried to calm her down. *"You see? I have no ill intentions toward you, Hendersons."* He bowed low in an exaggerated gesture of mock-respect. *"I will, of course, honour our arrangement, so long as you do me the same courtesy."* He straightened up again and pointed a thin, bony finger toward the wall behind Karen. *"Use your time wisely, for it is short."*

Scritch-scratch-scritch. Wood chips sprinkled onto the bedspread as an invisible knife carved a number into the wall, right above Karen's head. *"Render unto Caesar,"* the Deacon rasped, *"that which is Caesar's… and render unto God…"* He pointed at Abby and loosed a short, devious laugh. *"The things that are… God's…"*

Nobody heard him. They were too fixated on the number above Karen's head, which glowed bright red like a fireplace ember. In the howling storm outside, a bolt of lightning struck the shore opposite the tiny strip-of-piss island.

The following thunderclap made Abby cry again and snapped everyone back to reality. Don looked back and saw the Deacon had vanished. The door of the cabin was still locked tight, and the only sign that he had ever been there was the mark carved into the wall.

25.

CHAPTER 2

THE BIRTHDAY GIRL

"ABBY? IT'S time to go. Abby? I say, Abby?"

Abby Henderson felt a hand jostling her shoulder and looked up from her school planner. She'd been doodling in the margins again and hadn't heard the final bell. All the other desks in the classroom were empty, and the only person left was her English teacher, Mr. Lockhart. "What time is it?" she asked, setting down her pencil.

"Nearly quarter past three," Mr. Lockhart replied. "I rather think it's time you were getting home."

Abby craned her neck to look out the door of the classroom. The hallway was teeming with kids running in every direction, riding that Friday afternoon high. "Can I have five more minutes?"

Mr. Lockhart followed Abby's gaze out the door and saw three tall, athletic girls in green t-shirts, with yellow printing on their chests that said "FBSS VOLLEYBALL". A blonde, a brunette, and a redhead. Riley Carson, Jenna Jackson, and Lisa Sheehan. They were speaking in hushed tones, looking in the direction of Mr. Lockhart's room every now and again, and laughing behind their hands.

"Ah," he said, and marched toward the door. "I'm glad you asked me that, Abigail!" he announced, putting on a show for the girls outside. "You see, I think what Irving intended with

'The Legend of Sleepy Hollow' was—" He shut the door fully and turned back to Abby. "That lot giving you trouble again, are they?"

"'Again' suggests they stopped at one point," she muttered.

Ever since elementary school, Abby had had trouble with bullies. It was bad enough that she was too shy to ask a stranger for the time of day, but she wasn't what you would have called a "traditional beauty" either: she was thin as a rail no matter what she ate; her frizzy brown hair stuck out every which way like a startled ficus tree; and a row of shining braces in her mouth spanned a large gap between her front teeth. Nor were there many girls her age who took to Sinatra, Stephen King, and *The Twilight Zone* the same way she did. The kids in her neighbourhood even had a nickname for her: Abby Normal. As in, "That girl is very strange." "Strange? She's not strange, she's Abby Normal!"

But it seemed that all the heckling and the insults had gotten exponentially worse since Abby had started Grade 8 at Frederick Banting Secondary School. The trouble had begun early in September. Abby was in a Grade 8/9 split PE class with Riley and Lisa, and one of the first classes of the semester had been indoor volleyball. Missing two consecutive passes had been bad. Fumbling her first serve right into the net had been worse. But when Abby went for an overhead serve and smashed the ball right into Lisa's face? That was when she had irreversibly fucked up.

Abby was losing track of how many times she had tried to apologize in the last month, but every time she met Lisa's eye, the other girl would just sneer at her from behind a chipped front tooth and a bent nose.

"You mustn't be afraid of people like that, Abby," Mr. Lockhart said as he crossed to the desk beside her. "There will always be people in this world who don't take to you, wherever you go, and at some point, you just have to let them alone. Filter out their venom and live your life on your terms." He pulled out the orange plastic chair and lowered himself into it, a look of profound discomfort creasing up his face. "Blimey, these things are uncomfortable. I can see why so many of you little animals don't sit still."

Abby giggled behind her hand, and this got Mr. Lockhart giggling. He always knew how to make her smile.

Abby had known Mr. Lockhart for a few years before she came to Fred Banting. He was an old friend of Karen's and he often joined her for a cup of tea at the Henderson house on the weekend. He always had a silly grin on his face and a cunning look in his eye, like he was privy to some grand secret that he wasn't going to tell you, and his soft English accent made everything he said sound a lot cleverer than it probably was. Truth to tell, Abby adored Mr. Lockhart, and he excited her in a way her other teachers didn't. She rated a consistent C+ average in all her other classes, but she was one of the top three English students in her grade. When nobody else was paying attention, Mr. Lockhart would always smile at Abby and say, "Top of the class, Henderson."

The chatter outside the classroom died down and Mr. Lockhart went to the door for another peek. "Looks like they've moved on. Best make your escape while you can."

Abby got up and grabbed her bag. "You don't have to tell me twice."

As she left the room, Mr. Lockhart waved her goodbye and told her to give her parents his best. Abby confirmed that she would, then pulled her portable CD player from her backpack and slipped on her headphones. Nothing like a bit of Bob Dylan for that rainy walk home.

She passed two more classrooms and the first-floor girls' bathroom before she heard the footsteps behind her. This was joined by some stifled giggling, and then the world went dark as someone slapped their hands over her eyes.

"Guess who?" the someone laughed.

Abby smiled and grabbed the someone's wrists. "Hello, Kelly," she said as she turned around and locked eyes with the fair-haired, freckle-faced ninth-grader standing behind her.

Kelly Munro pouted. "How did you know?"

Abby laughed. "Who else around here has this many Band-Aids on their hands?" She turned Kelly's hands over in hers and inspected them. "Or this much dirt under their fingernails?"

Kelly snatched her hands away and rubbed them on her pants. "So I like to roughhouse a bit. Big whoop."

"I'm serious. Speaking as someone who just had her nose an inch away from your hands, you need to wash them suckers."

Kelly rolled her eyes, still smiling. "Fine, Mom. If it'll shut you up." She tugged Abby's headphones off her head and heard a few chords of Bob Dylan leak out. "Are you still listening to this garbage?"

Abby snatched her headphones back and stuck out her tongue. "Bob Dylan is not garbage. And 'Watchtower' is one of his best."

Kelly shook her head. "I've said it before, I'll say it again: the Hendrix cover blows this version out of the damn water."

Abby sighed dramatically. "You poor, naïve child. Must you continue to fight me on this?"

Kelly smiled and marched into the girls' room. "Pistols at dawn, butt-munch. And who are you calling 'child'?"

Abby followed her and said, "What are you doing here anyway? Don't you have soccer practice on Fridays?"

"Cancelled 'cause of the weather," Kelly grumbled. "It's pissing rain today." She soaped up her hands and looked at Abby's reflection in the mirror. "So, what's the story, Jaws? You decided what you want to do for your birthday? Thirteen! That's a big number."

Now Abby rolled her eyes. About two days after they'd first met, Kelly had decided that Abby's new name was "Jaws," because of the gap between Abby's large front teeth. It wasn't as funny as Kelly thought it was, but it beat the hell out of "Abby Normal.".

Abby put her CD player back in her bag and said, "I was actually thinking about a sleepover at my place. We could put sleeping bags out in the living room, roast marshmallows in the fireplace, tell ghost stories—"

"Sacrifice a rooster and summmon Ichthuantl'k'til, Dark God of the Everlasting Fire?" Kelly suggested. She shut off the water and shook her wet hands in Abby's face. "There. All clean."

Abby laughed and smacked Kelly's hands away. "You're kind of a bitch, you know that?"

"Okay, I'll shut up. So, who all were you thinking of inviting? Besides me and my awesome personality?"

Abby shrugged. "I don't know. Wanda. Lauren. Samantha. You know."

Kelly nodded. "The usual suspects, huh?"

Abby stifled a smile, slouched, and scrunched up her shoulders. She adopted her best sleepy-eyed hangdog look, like Benicio del Toro in the film, and slurred, "Gimme de fuggin keys, you cogsugger, whadafuck."

Kelly toppled against the sink, shrieking with laughter, which sent Abby into hysterics as well.

Then the bathroom door opened, and they both stopped laughing. In walked Lisa, Riley, and Jenna, who circled Abby and Kelly like sharks hungry for chum. Lisa, the Queen Bee of Fred Banting, crossed her arms and snapped, "What are you losers laughing at?"

Abby looked at the floor and went very quiet. "N-nothing," she mumbled.

"Nothing! Nuh-nuh-nuh-nothing!" Lisa crowed. "Guess all that metal in your face makes it pretty hard to talk right, doesn't it, Abby Normal?"

Kelly was about to step up and smack the grin right off Lisa's face, so Riley, who was a head taller than Kelly, grabbed her by the shoulders and held her back. Meanwhile, Jenna moved around to the sink and pumped the soap dispenser while Abby fumbled for a response.

"Actually, we heard you two from outside," Lisa continued. "The language in here! Ugh! You know what they used to do to kids who swore at school?" She spun Abby around to face Jenna. "They'd wash out their mouths!"

Jenna shoved her hand—and the inch-thick coating of soapy froth around it—right into Abby's face. As Abby gagged and coughed bubbles, Kelly broke away from Riley and ran at Lisa. "What the fuck is your problem, bitch?"

Lisa grabbed Kelly's wrists and held her off. "Back off, Munro! There's plenty of soap in here!" She planted her feet and shoved Kelly to the floor. With one hand, Abby helped Kelly up. With the other, she scrubbed the soap out of her own mouth. Meanwhile, Lisa and her coven vacated the bathroom, laughing.

"What a cow," Kelly muttered. Abby didn't respond, still spitting out soapy bubbles, and Kelly noticed that Abby was crying. "Hey, come on, Jaws—" Abby sniffled and ripped a paper towel out of the machine to wipe her eyes. "Come on, Abby. Lisa Sheehan's had her head up her ass since kindergarten."

Abby blew her nose into the paper towel. "I know. But why does it have to be me all the time? I've apologized up and down for the volleyball thing."

Kelly patted her on the shoulder. "I don't think it's that anymore. I think it's 'cause you're smart. And Lisa hates smart."

Abby sniffed and smiled. "Thanks, Kel. You're pretty smart too."

Kelly held up a gold charm bracelet. "Goddamn right I am."

Abby gasped. "Ohmygod! Is that—did you—"

Kelly spoke for her. "Is that Lisa's favourite bracelet? And did I swipe it off her wrist when she pushed me? Yes. Yes, I did." Without another word, she walked into the nearest stall and dropped the bracelet straight in the toilet.

"Oh. My. God. You are bad, Kelly Munro!"

"Especially when people mess with my friends," Kelly snarled. She flushed the toilet, shouting at Abby over the rush of water. "So, tell me again about this sleepover thing?"

*****

"Within minutes," Kelly whispered grimly, "half the student body had gathered outside her dorm room to see what the matter was." She paused and let her hand fall into the flashlight's beam, casting a ghastly shadow on the back wall.

It was the last Saturday of October, and Abby could not have asked for a better atmosphere for a spooky birthday/early Halloween sleepover. The rain was coming down in buckets from a coal-black sky, and the wind was throwing pine needles and dead leaves at every flat surface for ten blocks. The fire was crackling, the bag of marshmallows was half-empty, and the five girls had already polished off three rounds of s'mores. Wanda—supposedly the most "grown-up" of Kelly and Abby's friends—was currently building her fourth, despite Abby's warnings that she was going to fall into a sugar coma.

"The girl reached up," Kelly continued, "her hand trembling, and pointed." Here, she extended a hand and pointed just above her friend Lauren's head. Lauren shuddered and implored Kelly not to do that. "And there, on the wall above her roommate's body, was a message written in blood: 'Aren't you glad you didn't turn on the light?'"

Kelly dropped the flashlight and clapped her hands together. A terrified shriek rippled through the living room as one of the girls burrowed into her sleeping bag.

"Jeez, Kelly! Warn us before you do that!"

Kelly smiled. Of course Samantha would have been the one to break first.

"It's just a story, Sammy," she said as she picked up the flashlight.

Samantha crawled back out of her sleeping bag, her glasses akimbo and her red hair flying everywhere. "Yeah? Well, I think your 'story' made me pee a little bit."

"I'll take that as a compliment." Kelly thrust the flashlight toward Abby. "Come on, Jaws. Your turn. Let's see what Stephen King's biggest fan has to say for herself."

"Cawmf omf, Avvy!" That came from Wanda, whose mouth was full of s'more. Translation: *Come on, Abby!*

"It's your turn!" said Lauren.

Samantha, who had forgotten all about her previous scare, pumped her fist in the air and chanted, "Sto-ry! Sto-ry! Sto-ry!"

Abby stood and handed the flashlight back to Kelly. "Oh, you'll get your story," she vowed, "but not yet, 'cause I need to use the bathroom."

The others moaned and protested like candy had just been outlawed. Lauren was especially pouty: "You can go after your story!"

Abby shrugged, gave a quick apology, and climbed the stairs. As she went, she could hear Kelly whispering to the others: "I bet my story was too scary for her. That's why she has to go all of a sudden."

*****

In the years to come, Abby would often think back to this night, and she would curse herself for not seeing the warning signs.

The first thing she should have noticed, as she walked down the hall, was the night light right outside the bathroom. As she got near it, it buzzed and flickered wildly, creating a dizzying orange strobe effect. But Abby barely noticed; the house was old, and the wiring was less than reliable.

The second thing she should have noticed, as she closed the bathroom door, was the noise. A low, groaning whisper seemed to come from behind the walls. It was the same collection of sounds, repeated over and over: *Kha'al Azna'ghal ixxi. Kha'al Azna'ghal ixxi. Kha'al Azna'ghal ixxi.* Again, Abby ignored this. The pipes in the house made a lot of weird noises in the dead of night, and the wind was really howling outside. It was surely just a breeze blowing around the house that made it sound like whispering.

The third thing she should have noticed, as she sat down, was how cold it got. The toilet seat felt like it was made of ice, and Abby felt a shiver run up her entire body. Her teeth chattered and she had to tuck her hands under her arms for warmth. But still, she put this down to the house. Her parents had often complained of a distinct draught in this part of the house, and the heating was completely knackered.

As she flushed and went to wash her hands, Abby assured herself that the night of ghost stories, bad weather, and spooky TV was simply starting to play tricks on her. There was nothing lurking in the shadows waiting to grab her. Besides, she had other things on her mind: she knew a thousand ghost stories by heart, but she still had to pick one that would scare the hell out of her friends. *Bloody hook on the door handle?* Too obvious. *Caller inside the house?* Way overdone. *Killer... in the... back... car... seat...?*

Suddenly, the room tilted dangerously. Abby's legs went numb and she grabbed the vanity to keep herself from falling. With hands and a head that were suddenly made of lead, she turned off the water and pulled herself back up. She tried to yawn but closed her mouth as soon as she opened it. She wanted to throw up all of a sudden, and opening her mouth would surely break the seal.

Abby looked in the mirror to see if she could see what was wrong. But what she saw looking back at her was more wrong than anything she could have dreamed.

There was no Abby and no bathroom on the other side of the mirror. There was instead a large, decrepit hospital room with cracked tiles in pale white and snotty green. Rusty, leaking pipes snaked up drab concrete pillars to a ceiling fifty feet high. The walls were covered in rows upon rows of strange sigils and pictograms like Abby had never seen.

In the center of the room was an obsidian altar measuring twelve feet by seven. There were no tool marks on its smooth surfaces, and it looked as though nature itself had constructed it that way.

And then she heard the chanting. It was a low, guttural sound, a canid growl with a serpentine back beat. And it was the same odd collection of non-words that she had chalked up to the whispers of the wind not two minutes ago: *"Kha'al Azna'ghal ixxi. Kha'al Azna'ghal ixxi. Kha'al Azna'ghal ixxi."* The chanting seemed to come from everywhere at once, but the room was empty.

And then it wasn't. A horde of weird figures in black robes and blood-red hoods marched across the mirror, close enough that Abby thought she could reach out and touch them. Of course, when she tried, all she felt was the smooth glass. Yet still the figures marched, paying Abby no mind. It was as if the mirror had ceased to be a mirror, and had become a window into some dark, unknown dimension beyond time and space.

The image changed, and Abby jumped back. The hooded figures were standing in a V-formation, facing her. Thin, luminous bands of coloured light surrounded the figures at the front of the V, and when Abby concentrated on the lights, she could instantly tell what the hooded figures were thinking. They were watching her. They wanted her. She couldn't see their eyes, or much above their mouths, but one look at those auras and she could feel their eyes boring into her. They were still chanting that horrible chant in perfect unison, but lower this time. The words came in a hoarse, whispering chorus. *"Kha'al Azna'ghal ixxi. Kha'al Azna'ghal ixxi. Kha'al Azna'ghal ixxi."*

At the very point of the V, one figure was not chanting. His robes were not like the rest, either: rather than black, he wore brilliant white, with gold accents at the collar and sleeves, and a hood of deepest purple. Abby looked past the figure to his black-and-green aura and her eyes read it like a barcode. In the image centers of her brain, she saw a large serpent, the size of a city bus, with the snarling head of an alpha male lion and two gargantuan, veiny bat-like wings on its back. The aura whispered to Abby that this lion-snake creature was the white-robed figure, with all his coverings removed, and that he was in charge. And he was called the Deacon.

Abby didn't know where these people had come from or why they were so interested in her. She didn't know how she instinctively knew so much about them, things that she didn't want to know. She just wanted to get out of here. She backed up, flat against the shower door, and the Deacon started to speak.

Abby decided she'd liked the Deacon better when he was just staring at her. Every sound he made pierced the air like a gunshot, even though he barely spoke above a whisper. The words he spoke made no sense to Abby, but his followers obviously understood perfectly.

"Ko kxx grav ak ra sytqa lach, Kha'ell Ag'haz lekxxo tov godaj-xu. Ek rataz haec Godaj-pael, ek-eli karnu godaju izot ynhash allac cymhael li tazhael. Paka ko sidit karnu."

As the Deacon spoke, the hooded figures stared even more intently at Abby. Slowly, they began to chant again, but a different chant this time.

"Ka ag'haz dul kxx. Ka ag'haz dul kxx. Ka ag'haz dul kxx."

Abby knew she had to get away from here. More than anything she wanted to run, to scream for help, but her legs were paralyzed and her mouth refused to make any sound beyond a small, terrified squeak.

The Deacon raised his hand, and the chant grew louder, faster. *"Ka ag'haz dul kxx. Ka ag'haz dul kxx. Ka ag'haz dul kxx."*

The hooded figures were working themselves into a frenzy, though they remained stock-still. Their auras intensified, and Abby could see in their deepest hearts the monsters they really were. Hybrids of humanity and cetacean, baying hounds with too many eyes, goat-legged monstrosities with tentacles falling out of their mouths. Every one had a monster in its core, like the Deacon and his lion-snake, and the monsters were rabidly excited.

"Ka ag'haz dul kxx. Ka ag'haz dul kxx. Ka ag'haz dul kxx."

Abby's heart was pounding. The hooded figures followed the Deacon's example and raised their hands, trying to reach for her. The chanting was still getting louder and faster.

"KA AG'HAZ DUL KXX! KA AG'HAZ DUL KXX! KA AG'HAZ DUL KXX!"

And then the impossible happened. The glass separating Abby from this terrifying spectacle dissolved, and the Deacon glided forward like a phantom. His hand reached out of the mirror.

Abby started to cry. Her heart jackhammered against her breastbone and the sweat poured off her like a waterfall. A voice inside her head was screaming, *RUN! Open this door and RUN!* But she knew she couldn't. Her whole body was shaking, and she couldn't get it under control long enough to take two steps in any direction.

"KA AG'HAZ DUL KXX! KA AG'HAZ DUL KXX! KA AG'HAZ DUL KXX! KA AG'HAZ DUL KXX!"

The voice in her head continued: *If you can't run, then scream. Cry, yell, bang on the door, just get somebody's attention! Just do something, anything, that will help you GET! OUT! OF! HERE!*

And then the Deacon spoke again. But this time, Abby understood what he was saying. *"Abigail. Abigail... Henderson..."*

He knew her name. Dear God, he knew her name. How did he know her name?

Suddenly, Abby found her voice again. And she screamed.

*****

Her friends heard her from downstairs, and they all jumped to their feet as Abby came sprinting out of the bathroom, still screaming blue murder.

She so badly wanted to get away from the Deacon that she completely forgot about the stairs. When she reached the end of the second-floor hallway, she turned and took another step, but her foot dropped into empty space. As her whole body pitched forward, Abby realized her mistake two seconds too late.

Crash. Bang. Thud.
Smash. Boom. Smack.
Bump. Whack. Thwack.
Crash. Bang. Thud.
CRACK.

Abby's friends were speechless as they gathered at the bottom of the stairs, huddling around her limp, pale body. She was covered in scrapes and reddish bruises and one of her wrists was bent the wrong way around.

Terrified, Kelly bent down to check on her friend and then shouted upstairs: "MRS. HENDERSON!"

CHAPTER 3

SIGHT UNSEEN

THIS WAS not how Karen had been hoping her daughter's birthday would go. She and Don had worked tirelessly for a week to make sure this was the best night of Abby's life, and now they were sitting in the waiting room at Lions Gate Hospital at 3:00 in the morning, waiting for the doctor to complete his examination.

The scream had woken them both, but the crack had drawn them from their bed. When they had met Abby's friends at the bottom of the stairs, there was a brief moment when the sight of her crumpled body had put a very grim, very final thought into both her parents' heads. But then she began to stir, and everyone in the house let go a tightly-held breath.

With shaking hands, Don had dialled 911 from the landline in the kitchen, while Karen got her cell phone out and rang the other girls' houses one by one to arrange pickups. While they waited for the ambulance and the other parents, Don and Karen tried to establish a dialogue with Abby. They were worried about a concussion and wanted her alert and thinking, but beyond that, they were desperate to know what had so terrified her.

Because, in the deepest pits of their hearts, they were pretty sure they both knew the answer already.

*****

The first time Abby's powers kicked in, she was barely five years old. It was just after Grandma Meg had passed away, and Don and Karen had elected to leave Abby in the care of Nana and Grampa Henderson while they went to the funeral. As Abby herself would later explain to the first of her many therapists down the years, Mommy and Daddy tried to be quiet about it. They didn't tell Abby why they were going out, dressed up as fancy as they were. But Abby—always too curious for her own good—latched onto Mommy just before she was out the door, and she wouldn't let go until she had the truth.

So, Mommy took Abby aside into Nana and Grampa's living room and sat with her on the couch beneath the large grandfather clock. Mommy held Abby's hand and brushed Abby's hair away behind her ear in the way that Abby liked but pretended to hate. Then Mommy said, almost in a whisper, "Abby, someone in our family has... gone away. And they're not coming back."

Abby didn't understand. "Where did they go?"

"Well, I'm not entirely sure. Nobody's really sure where people go when they... go away like this. All we know is they can't come back from wherever it is they go."

"Don't they have buses in this place?"

Mommy laughed at that, and this made Abby laugh. She was glad to see Mommy smiling again, though she was starting to suspect that Mommy's sadness had to do with this person going away.

"Abby, do you remember Grandma Meg?" Mommy asked.

Abby thought for a second. She remembered last Thanksgiving, where she'd met an old lady with a funny English accent who kept doing silly made-up magic tricks like palm reading and such.

And when she put a face to the name, Abby smiled. "The magic lady!" she declared triumphantly. She was very pleased to have solved Mommy's riddle.

Mommy sniffed and blinked hard. "Yes. The magic lady. You see, Abby… this place, the one I was telling you about, maybe it does have buses; nobody really knows. But those buses only go one way. They can take people there, but they can't bring them back. It's just… how this place works. And Grandma Meg—the magic lady—she got on one of those buses last week, and now Daddy and I have to go say goodbye. And it's sad when you have to say goodbye to someone like that, because you know you're not going to see them again. Maybe you will many, many years from now, but it won't be here. It'll be in that place with the one-way buses."

Now, Abby was beginning to understand. "And you're sad because… you miss her. You miss the magic lady?"

Mommy finally broke down. "Yes, Abby, yes. I miss her."

Then Mommy hugged Abby right to her chest, said Abby was the most important thing in her world, left her with a Sesame Street video and a juice box, and walked to the bathroom to freshen up before she and Daddy left.

Abby watched quietly until the video started to glitch, and Big Bird and Snuffy disappeared under the snow on the screen. She got up and did what Daddy always did when the VCR went funny at home: she smacked it with her hand and called it a dirty ess-oh-bee.

The video stayed glitched, but Abby wasn't too fazed. That trick rarely worked for Daddy either. In the corner of the room, the grandfather clock began to chime its Westminster Chimes. Abby turned and smiled up at the clock. The ding-dong-ding-dong of Nana and Grampa's clock was one of her favourite sounds in the world.

But in the middle of the gongs that marked the hour, Abby heard another sound, like somebody whispering from inside the clock.

"Hello?" Abby whispered back. She crept toward the clock and reached out to touch it, but swiftly drew her hand away when it gave her a zap.

Abby heard someone behind her, chuckling sweetly. *Oh my word. You are beautiful, aren't you?*

Abby spun around and gasped. She was alone. But the voice was still there, in her head.

'Ow old are ye now, luv? the voice asked. It was a woman.

"I'm five years old!" Abby replied proudly. She didn't know why she'd answered so quickly. She didn't know who was talking to her, but she felt like she could trust them.

My, my, the voice said. *You're getting to be a big one, aren't you?*

"Who are you?" Abby asked. She climbed up onto the arm of the couch and tapped the clock's glass face. "Are you in the clock?"

No, I'm quite a bit further away than that now, Abby.

Abby gasped again. "You know my name?" she whispered.

There's lots of things I know, luv. I'm sort of magic that way.

Abby smiled. "Magic lady!"

The voice chuckled again. *That's me. Now, Abby, I don't 'ave much time, so you need to listen carefully.*

"Where are you? Are you on a bus? Are you going to that place Mommy was talking about?"

I suppose you could say that. But listen, now, because I'm going to 'ave to get off the bus soon, and then we won't be able to talk.

"Okay, magic lady."

Yer mum and dad are sad right now, Abby, and they're scared. But you need to tell them they don't need to be. They need to be brave now I'm gone. You need to tell 'em that, because I won't really be gone. The magic will still be with 'em, ye see?

"How?" Abby asked.

You, luv. The magic will be there in you.

Abby looked down and put one hand on her chest. "I'm… what do you mean I'm magic?"

'Ow do you think we're having this talk? This is a secret, special talk that only certain people can 'ear. People that are a bit mad, and a bit magic.

Abby smiled. She'd always wanted to be magic. Mad, she wasn't so sure about.

Now, this is the important bit, Abby. You need to remember the magic. You need to keep it safe and use it properly. I'm sorry to tell you that, because there will be times when it will be bloody difficult, if you'll pardon my French. There will be times when the magic will be 'ard on you, and it will seem mad, and not always in a good way, but no matter what 'appens, you need to keep it in your 'eart. Can you promise me that, Abigail? Can you promise me you'll remember the magic, and keep it in your 'eart?

Abby paused for a minute. Nobody ever called her "Abigail" unless they were talking about something very serious, or if they were punishing her. The magic lady didn't sound like she was punishing Abby, so Abby decided she must be very serious.

"I promise," Abby said.

The clock finished its hourly gong and Abby leaned over to look at the glass front, trying to see if she could see Grandma Meg. Then she heard a gasp behind her and felt two hands around her waist, pulling her down from the arm of the couch.

"Abby! What on earth are you doing up there? You could break your neck!"

"I'm sorry, Mommy. But the magic lady wanted to tell me something."

Mommy sat Abby down on the couch and paused. "W-what did you say?"

"Grandma Meg! She talked to me out of the clock!" Abby said.

Abby could feel Mommy's hands starting to shake as they came off Abby's waist. "And what did Grandma Meg have to say?" Mommy asked.

"She said you and Daddy shouldn't be scared. Because she might be gone, but the magic isn't! The magic's still in me!" Abby stood up on the couch and put her arms around Karen. "Isn't that cool, Mommy? I'm magic!"

Karen smiled weakly and hugged Abby again. "Yes, sweetie. That's very cool. Now, your father and I are leaving, so you just sit tight here, and we'll see you later this afternoon."

Abby sat back down and grinned. "Okay!"

*****

Minutes later, Karen had joined Don in the car and immediately broke down crying. There was a number scratched in the dashboard, right above the radio. A message from their deepest nightmares.

20.

And ever since then, the Deacon had checked in with them at least once a year, whenever Abby's power surged. He was clever enough to make sure they never saw him, but they always got a hint that he could see them.

Like when Abby was six, and she had told Daddy not to take his normal route to work, because she'd dreamed there was a bad accident on the Lions Gate Bridge. Initially, Don laughed the warning off as nothing, but Abby insisted that the Lions Gate was dangerous that morning, so Don took the Second Narrows Bridge instead just to humour her. He stopped laughing during the evening news, when he saw the story about a semi truck that had overturned on the Lions Gate that morning and killed four people. The number had been scratched onto the back of the remote control, and Don felt it before he saw it.

19.

Or like when she was ten, and the family dog had been hit by a car, except Abby swore blind that she saw him running around the front yard four days later like nothing was wrong. By that time, Abby had been old enough to understand that people and animals didn't just come back from the place with the one-way buses, and she spent the next week bombarding her parents with questions about ghosts. She never noticed the fresh scratches in the kitchen table.

15.

It was like he was taunting them at this point. The Hendersons were slowly going mad under the pressure, and the Deacon was just pointing and laughing at them.

He wasn't the only one. When Abby had seen her dead dog playing in the front yard, she had told some of the kids at her school, and they had heckled her mercilessly for it. Nobody was really sure who had come up with that nickname, but it had stuck like glue. Abby Normal.

From then on it was "Seen any ghosts lately, Abby Normal?" or "Hey, Abby Normal, tell my grandma I said 'Hi'!" Whenever Abby saw something impossible, she would reach out to someone for validation, for assurance that she was not crazy, and they would laugh at her. They would sit as far away from her as they could. They would chant on the bus, "Ab-by Nor-mal! Ab-by Nor-mal! Ab-by Nor-mal!"

The Hendersons had tried to keep their heads down. They had tried to shelter Abby from the Nocturn, the Elsewhere, all of it. They had tried to calm her down when a piece of unreality slipped past their defences and frightened her. They had tried, against Grandma Meg's wishes, to make Abby forget the magic. But that wasn't going to work anymore.

Abby had never had such a visceral reaction to an apparition. She was not going to forget this for a long time, and she was going to want answers when she woke up. Her friends and their parents would want to know what in the Hendersons' upstairs bathroom was so traumatic. The kids at school would hear the story, and they would be curious. And if Abby did tell anyone—if the truth was half as bad as Don and Karen feared—then that would be the final straw. Nobody would believe a word of it, and they would declare that Abby Normal was going completely insane.

After a brief eternity in the waiting room, a nurse finally came by to update the Hendersons about Abby's condition.

Her ulna was broken in two places and she had suffered a mild concussion, but based on the description of her fall, she was actually very lucky. She'd have to wear a cast for six weeks and would be discharged in the morning, after a proper night's sleep.

As they took the elevator up to see Abby, Don turned to his wife and asked her point-blank: "What did you tell the other girls' parents?"

Karen slumped back against the wall. "I told them the truth, Don. Abby saw something that frightened her, and in her haste to get downstairs, she tripped. Anyone could have done the same."

"I think we both have a pretty good idea what she saw," Don muttered.

"Don, don't—"

"You heard her screaming as well as I did. She was absolutely panicked."

Karen ran her hands through her hair, tearing out a few loose strands. "Can we just leave it for one night? Let's just thank our stars she's all right and not think about it for now."

"Karen, we can't kid ourselves like this. There's only one thing that could possibly have scared her that badly."

The elevator doors opened with a ding, and Karen sped toward Abby's room. Right now, she just needed to see her daughter, to hold her and not let go. Deacon? What Deacon? Never heard of him. Abby was the only thing that mattered.

"She knows she's different, Karen! She knows it's unusual, seeing what she sees."

Karen turned on her heels and glared at Don. "Don't you think I know that? I've seen what a tough time she has at school! I've seen how she keeps to herself! Of course she knows! But what do you want to do about it, huh? You know what will happen if we tell her!"

"We can't leave her completely in the dark, Karen! We need to give her some kind of clue, so she can be prepared, so she can defend herself! Can you imagine what'll happen if the clock runs out and she doesn't know? What happened tonight will look like a day at the beach!"

Karen put a finger to her lips. "Damn it, keep your voice down!"

From the shadows behind them, a third voice added, "Yes, Donald. Try not to wake your daughter."

Karen and Don stepped back as Simon Lockhart emerged from the darkness. His long Inverness coat trailed behind him, and one hand rested in the pocket of his velvet waistcoat, fiddling with the chain of a gold pocket watch.

Don turned on Simon and poked him in the chest. "And you, I don't know who the hell you think you are, thinking you can just waltz in and out of our lives whenever it strikes your fancy—"

Out the corner of her eye, Karen could see Abby stirring in her bed. "Donald, shush! For God's sake!"

"No, not 'shush,' Karen. He needs to hear this!"

"You'll wake Abby!"

Don followed Karen's gaze. He, too, saw Abby stirring, and this finally shut him up. Simon, for his part, never acknowledged Don's finger in his chest. He put a hand on Don's shoulder and whispered, "If you don't mind, Donald, I need to talk to Karen alone."

Don wasn't having it. He batted Simon's hand away and hissed, "Anything you say to her, you can say to me."

Simon's expression hardened and he squared his shoulders. He pressed one finger to Don's forehead, just between his eyes, and spoke in a flat, mechanical voice. "Donald, I need to speak to Karen. And I need to do it alone."

A confused Don blinked several times. Then his eyes glazed over, and he smiled. He didn't know why he was smiling, but he didn't feel like stopping. He was at complete peace, and he couldn't remember what he and Karen had been fighting about.

"Yes. Yes," he repeated with a nod. "You need to talk to Karen."

"Perhaps you should take a walk."

"Yes. I should take a walk."

"I only need five minutes."

"Of course. Five minutes."

Simon removed his finger and Don walked away in a befuddled daze.

Abby was sleeping peacefully once more, and Simon followed Karen into her room. They brought a couple chairs over to Abby's bed, and drew the curtain for privacy. While Simon contemplated the sleeping child, Karen turned to him and said, "You didn't need to do that."

Simon shook his head. "The Mind Lock doesn't do any harm. No more than a night of hard drinking at least. Which reminds me: black coffee, a teaspoon of Worcestershire sauce, and three egg whites. It'll help with the headache tomorrow."

Karen chuckled and put her arm around him. "You didn't have to come, Simon."

"Yes, I did. For her sake, I did." He looked at the snoring girl in the bed before them. "Karen, I sent Don away because he's too close to all this. Too emotional. But he is right. The best thing we can do, for Abigail's own good, is to tell her what she is. She's got no chance otherwise."

Karen closed her eyes and sighed, shaking her head as if to knock Simon's words right out of her ears.

"Look, I'm doing what I can to help her at school," Simon continued, "but Mr. Lockhart only has so much access. I can't be seen playing favourites with my students, and especially not a thirteen-year-old girl. If just one person got the wrong impression and raised a fuss, that could well be it for me. The best way to protect your daughter is to teach her to protect herself. And to teach her what she needs protection from."

Karen coughed twice and rubbed a hand across her eyes, trying to stifle a sob.

"You know what Abigail saw tonight," said Simon. "I know it. Don knows it. She needs to know it."

"How?" The cold tears stung on Karen's cheeks. "How do we tell her? You know what happens if we break the Pledge!"

Simon tented his fingers under his nose and raised his eyes to the ceiling. "I've been giving that some thought, actually. There may be a way to teach her without technically violating the Pledge."

Karen wiped her eyes with her hands. "How?" she sniffed.

Simon froze in his seat, his eyes locked on one of the ceiling tiles. Then he put a finger to his lips and looked at Karen, then back at the ceiling. Not here, said his eyes. Not now.

Karen looked where Simon was looking. She doubled over in her chair, weeping, as Simon continued to stare at the ceiling. At the Deacon's mark scratched into the stained plaster. It wouldn't be wise to make plans now. Not so long as he was watching.

12.

CHAPTER 4

THINGS FALL APART

IT WAS over a week before Abby returned to school. On one hand, Karen and Don insisted that she needed some time off to recover from the accident, and on the other, Abby was terrified of how her classmates would react when the story got out. If she hadn't been a sideshow attraction before, well…

At least Abby's friends had the tact to keep their questions to themselves. But for the rest of the school, it was: "Did you hear what happened to ol' Abby Normal?" "They say Abby Normal's going crazy again." "I bet she had a vision of herself in ten years." "Yeah, she's going to be standing on a street corner wearing a tinfoil hat."

The mockery never ceased, and by mid-November, Abby was spending every free moment she had in either the girls' bathroom or the school library: hiding from the world behind a wall of Bob Dylan and Frank Sinatra and trying her hardest not to exist.

She told herself it was better this way. Let the other kids spread their rumours. They had some pretty wild theories about what she'd seen, but nothing they came up with held a candle to the Deacon and his hooded horde. If Abby told anyone the truth, their reaction would be a thousand times worse than it already was.

And then the nightmares started. Every night, Abby was transported to that hospital room, where the hooded figures would cackle as they stripped her down and clapped her in iron chains. They would lie her down on the obsidian altar, and the Deacon would make her drink something vile that burned her insides, and she would see horrible things. Dark clouds with human faces stretching out of them would dance in the sky, and the faces' mouths would move noiselessly, wailing in agony and pleading for death. The hooded figures would split open like banana peels, and the monsters inside them would crawl out of the offal and chase people through the streets, flossing with their tendons and gnawing on their bones. And she would see herself, standing over it all, her eyes red like fire, laughing as the world burned beneath her. But then she would look again, and it wouldn't be her standing over everything, it would be—

And then, just before she finally saw the monster she was turning into, she would wake up screaming. Her parents would come running and tell her everything was okay, but she would know they were lying. They didn't know about the Deacon. They couldn't understand him! How dare they presume to tell her what was okay?

Then she would sit in the shower and cry because she was so scared and she had nobody to talk to and she couldn't even go pee in her own house without having a panic attack. Every night, Abby would sit there and let the water run over her, and she would hear the bullies laughing at her in her head. She would scream and beat her fists against the wall to drown out that horrible nickname: Abby Normal. Abby Normal. Abby Normal.

But she couldn't—she wouldn't—say any of this to the people closest to her. They couldn't possibly understand, and the whole story would probably get her locked up in a mental institution. Because they couldn't break down the wall Abby had built around herself, the exhausted Hendersons left the job to the professionals. For the next few months, Abby bounced around from one therapist to the next, but none of them could do more than slap a Band-Aid on the problem and call it a day.

Ultimately, time was the only thing that helped. By the middle of spring, the Mirror Story was growing stale in the minds of Abby's classmates. Everyone had heard three competing versions by now, and with no new Abby Normal freak outs to report, the gossip eventually died of overexposure. Much of the teasing died with it, and Abby slowly came back out of her shell.

When the soccer season began, Kelly encouraged Abby to try out for the school team. Abby's soccer experience was limited to backyard games with family, but she was a lightning-fast runner, and her natural speed won her a position as a midfielder. It was about this time, too, that the teachers at Frederick Banting started thinking about exams, and the students' homework load more than doubled. Pretty soon, Abby just didn't have the time to think about the Deacon, and when she didn't think about him, the nightmares became less frequent. They didn't stop altogether, but by the time summer break arrived, Abby sometimes didn't dream of the Deacon for six or eight weeks at a time.

For a time, Abby's future looked brighter than ever. With the Deacon no longer haunting her, she once again felt safe outside her shell and her circle of friends expanded. All of her grades improved as she grew more comfortable with flaunting her smarts. Even her therapist was surprised by the improvement, and he assured Abby's parents that she no longer needed his help.

Don wasn't convinced. Abby had had periods of mental stability like this in the past, but they had never lasted. Every time her well-being rose to a peak, there was always a nearby valley that it could plummet into, and each one was more difficult to climb out of than the last. Something always came along to send Abby back into crisis mode, and Don advised

Abby that she should continue working with Dr. Blum in case there was another incident.

But Abby refused. She had been sent to shrink after shrink for nearly a year, and she was sick of it. She had finally found peace, and she wanted it to last. She wanted to be mentally sound, and having a shrink meant she was still not quite there. It meant that she still needed a shrink. So, it was au revoir to Dr. Blum. After all, if she didn't have a shrink, then she obviously didn't need one. Therefore, she was mentally sound. QED.

And still, Don knew that it wasn't nearly so simple. For fourteen years, the Hendersons had been standing on a cliff, slowly creeping closer and closer to oblivion. Eventually, something was going to come along that would push them down into the void where they couldn't be helped.

That something came on her fourteenth birthday, and the trouble started, as it always did, with another crazy Abby Normal dream. But what the Hendersons never expected was that Don would be the first person to fall off the cliff.

*****

Abby knew she was dreaming the moment she sat up. A few seconds ago, she'd been in bed, and now she was lying on a grassy hillside. The moon was full in the sky above her and the stars twinkled brightly. Abby drew her knees to her chest and looked up at the sky. It was an absolutely beautiful night, and so quiet, too. Such a refreshing change from her usual dreams. Abby smiled at the unbroken stillness of it and closed her eyes.

Then she heard a scream and multiple gunshots, followed by a laugh so high and cruel it made Abby's blood run cold.

Abby stood and followed the noise. Far away, at the top of the hill, was a large brick building in a state of considerable disrepair. Two figures moved about by the front steps of the building, and even from the distance she was watching, Abby was struck by how familiar they seemed.

Abby crouched low and crept through the high grass, trying to get a better view. As she got closer, she could hear the two figures speaking.

"Please... please..." the first one gasped. It was a woman. She was on the ground, clutching a wound at her side. "It isn't fair..."

The other figure hissed and laughed. "Fair? It was hubris that brought you here... That led you to think you could defeat us... You were warned, but you did not listen. This is exactly as 'fair' as it should be!"

Abby ducked behind a fallen log only a few metres from the two figures and peeked out over the top. What she saw nearly made her faint.

The woman on the ground was none other than her mother, looking younger than Abby had ever seen her. She was dragging herself across the grass, leaving a dark red trail behind her. A shotgun lay near her, but its barrel had been bent almost to a right angle.

Karen's aura was cracked and flickered like a faulty light bulb. Black spots danced in a band of sickly yellow and blue — the colours of fear and grief, pockmarked by intense pain. A thin, gossamer thread of white wrapped around it all like a helix. Abby focused on that thread, and she saw herself in it. Her thoughts, her desires, all her yesterdays and all the tomorrows she might still have. This white thread was the very start of Abby Henderson.

The vision of her mother, then, must have been from the earliest stages of pregnancy.

Abby noticed another figure, a man, lying still across from Karen. Blood streaked his face like war paint and soaked his shirt. He had no aura around him, and Abby was certain he was dead.

The third figure was majestic in his white robes, and the lion-snake inside his aura gyrated in a grotesque victory dance. Abby went very still and held her breath. Fortunately, the Deacon hadn't seen her yet, but she was very determined to make sure it stayed that way.

Abby watched in silent horror as the Deacon gloated over her mother's wounded frame. Slowly, Karen crawled over to the man lying still in the field and sat down beside him. Pulling his head up to her chest, she cried softly for a moment.

Abby gasped. Underneath all the blood, she recognized the dead man as her father.

"Please," Karen sobbed as she held Don close to her. "Please, you have to help him. I'll do anything."

"Anything?" the Deacon asked, intrigued.

"Anything!" Karen cried.

"I want... the child..."

Karen looked up at the Deacon. "W-what?"

"We must have the child..."

Karen shook her head. "No! No, you can't! Not that!"

"But you must... I can give you what you want, and I shall take what I desire."

The Deacon knelt and drew back his hood. A white string of light appeared above him and wrapped around his aura, similar to Karen's. For a moment, the lion-snake inside the Deacon's soul retreated, and a man—a proper human man— stepped forward. Abby focused on the man, trying to get a read on him. She'd never seen the remotest spark of human spirit inside any of the Deacon's followers before; what made the big boss so special?

The Deacon shifted on his haunches, and the white thread in his aura blurred. Now when she looked, Abby couldn't separate the white string of humanity from the black-and-green rainbow of the lion-snake. She couldn't read the man, because she was receiving too much interference from the monster. But the monster, too, was fuzzier than before, obscured by specks of the man.

Her head started to hurt and she gave up on trying to read the Deacon. Instead she focused on his conversation with

Karen. Abby surmised that she herself was the "child" they were talking about, and the Deacon had just extorted Karen into selling her to him.

Karen sobbed freely for several minutes as the horror of what she was doing set in. Finally, she took a deep breath and whispered, "Yes..."

Crying, Abby sprang to her feet and shouted, "NO!"

But neither Karen nor the Deacon heeded Abby's presence. The Deacon simply laughed his high, harsh laugh as he took Karen's hand in his.

Then there was a blinding flash of red light and Abby woke up.

*****

She nearly fell out of bed as she turned on the reading light. She wiped the sweat from her brow and took five long, deep breaths, trying unsuccessfully to will her heart to beat slower. A couple breaths later, she heard her parents' footsteps in the hall, and she wondered if she'd had it wrong all this time.

Karen rapped her knuckles on the wall as she opened the door. "Abby? Sweetie? Did you have a bad dream?"

Abby looked away from her mother and shook her head. "I... I don't want to talk about it..."

Don joined Karen at the door. "Abby... we're not going to make you talk if you don't want to. We just want you to know we're here for you."

Those last four words stung most of all. Were they truly there for her? Abby wanted what she had seen to just be a dream, but all her better judgement screamed that it was real.

Don and Karen watched their daughter stewing in complete silence for a moment before resigning themselves to the fact that she was not going to talk. "Well," Karen sighed, "we're going to go back to bed now. But we're just down the hall if you need us."

Karen took Don's hand in hers and they turned to walk back to the master bedroom. But then Abby whispered, "Wait..."

They stopped and turned. Slowly, timidly, Abby slinked out of her bedroom, staring at the floor, and said, "I... I saw you."

Karen knelt down and put a hand on Abby's shoulder. "What do you mean, 'you saw us'?"

"In my dream," Abby whispered. "I saw you and Dad both. You were... you were hurt..." she sniffed, trying not to cry. "And there was... a man..."

"What man?" Karen asked.

Abby shook her head. "I... I don't know his name. He just called himself... the Deacon."

Karen stifled a gasp. Her voice trembled as she asked, "What did the Deacon do?"

This was more than Abby had ever told her parents before. She had to watch their reactions, had to find out for certain what they knew or didn't know. What were they not saying about the Deacon?

Karen repeated her earlier question. "Abby... what did the Deacon do?"

A tear rolled down Abby's cheek as she relayed what she'd seen. "Dad was... he was hurt. Badly. And the Deacon was... he said he could help... But he wanted you to give him something... In exchange..."

"What did the Deacon want?" Karen asked.

Abby slumped against the wall and slid down to the floor as she began to cry. "He wan—he wanted... m-me!" she sobbed. "He wanted you to give me to him."

Karen sat on the floor and squeezed Abby tightly. She held Abby's head to her bosom, brushed her hair behind her ear and whispered, "Oh, Abby. Oh, god, that must have been awful. But it was only a dream, and nothing like that would ever happen in this house."

Abby wiped her nose on the sleeve of her pyjamas and looked at her mother. "You— you sure?"

Karen kissed Abby on the forehead. "I promise you, Abigail. That nasty Deacon can't hurt you here. And if he tried, he would regret it. I would never let somebody take you away like that."

Abby reciprocated her mother's hug and cried into her nightgown. "Thank you," she whispered. "Thank you."

Karen helped Abby to her feet and kissed her again. "Now, try and get some sleep. You have school tomorrow."

Abby nodded and smiled. "Y-yeah," she sniffed. "It was just a stupid dream."

"Of course it was. Now go to bed and we'll just try to forget all about this Deacon business."

Reassured, Abby crawled back into bed. "Night, Mom," she said. "Night, Dad."

Karen and Don each gave her a warm "Night, Abby" as Don shut the door.

*****

Abby's parents listened at the door for a moment. When he was satisfied that Abby was asleep once more, Don grabbed Karen's hand and marched her downstairs.

In the living room, he backed his wife up to the couch and hissed, "What. The. Hell. Was that?"

Karen was taken aback. "Don, what's gotten into you?"

Don just shook his head. "No, don't do that, Karen. Don't play innocent with me. You just lied through your teeth right to our daughter's face!"

"I never did!" Karen spat back.

"You told her the Deacon could never hurt her!"

"I said he could never hurt her here! Check the tapes, Don: every word I said was the honest truth!"

"Whatever, call it sin of omission then! You're still not being honest with her!"

"Well, what should I have said? 'Yes, Abby, it's all true! Your father and I nearly got ourselves killed fourteen years ago and we had to sell your soul to dig our way out of it'?"

"We need to tell her *something*!"

"We've had this discussion, Donald! He has us by the throat!"

"Every time... every time something like this happens, we have the same fucking argument!"

"Because you keep bringing it up every time something like this happens!"

Don scoffed. "Oh, so this is on me, is it? Let me tell you something, Karen: I never asked to be brought back. Hell, I didn't ask to be dragged into this in the first place! All these secrets, all these lies, they're on you!"

"So what are you going to do, huh? March upstairs and tell her everything?"

"I don't see what choice I have! First thing tomorrow, I'm going to sit down with Abby and I am going to tell her the whole story. From Dasriel right down to fucking Grandma Meg! I will skip work if I have to! I will pull her out of school! If it takes all day, I am going to tell my daughter exactly what she needs to know!"

Karen grabbed Don's hand. "No, Don, please..."

Don broke away. "I am not having this discussion right now." Then he walked to the closet and got out his winter jacket.

"Where are you going now?" Karen asked.

"I am going for a walk," Don snapped as he put on his jacket and his shoes. "I don't know where and I don't know for how long. I'm just... going for a walk."

Then Don marched out the front door without looking back.

CHAPTER 5

LELAND

HE DIDN'T keep track of the time. Every day, for nearly fifteen years, Don had thought about that night when his wife had signed away their daughter's life. By all rights he should have died that night. Or more accurately, he should have stayed dead.

The McAllisters had a long history with the Deacon. The first time he attacked the family had been nearly a century ago, back in Britain. They had immigrated to Canada to get away from him, and multiple generations of the family—Karen included—had been raised as warriors, ready to fight back when he made a move against them. When Don had met Karen, he had quickly learned that the constant threat of the Deacon was a non-negotiable part of the deal.

There was a very real danger to living life as a weapon. The McAllisters were always picking fights with some truly nasty enemies, and to lose often meant death.

But winning was even worse. When you won a fight against a bloodthirsty monster that was twice your size and had four times as many teeth, you tended to get cocky. You started to feel like nothing could ever harm you, which made it all the more painful when something did.

Karen had been cocky once. So had Don. Before Abby was born, they had tracked down the Deacon and mounted an assault against him. But they'd seriously overestimated their own abilities, and the Deacon had flattened them. He'd nearly killed Karen, and he had killed Don. But then he had offered a way out. He had told Karen he could undo everything he had done to them, and guarantee them a supplemental period of peace and quiet, provided he had free access to Abby after a certain amount of time. He had big plans for her, but he needed her to be vulnerable. Karen, young, headstrong, and in way over her head, had taken the deal in a moment of absolute desperation, and that was it. Calling on a power that even he shuddered to comprehend, the Deacon had healed them and sent them on their way, for the low, low price of their daughter's soul. The worst part was he never let them forget it. Every number scratched onto the wall was another reminder of this curse and another victory lap for him.

Now, Don was sick of it. He could no longer stand idle while his baby girl went to pieces because of this monster. He had to tell her the truth while there was still time. He'd watched her for fourteen years; now Simon and Natalie could take up his quarrel for the next eleven. They could train her to fight the good fight. Don was sorry he wouldn't see any of it, but that was just the way it had to be.

Don stopped walking and looked up at the starry sky. It was a far cry from the weather on that strip-of-piss island so many years ago. Closing his eyes, he took a deep breath and hoped that somebody upstairs was listening. "She will know. So help me God, my daughter will know what's coming for her."

The thing that answered Don's oath was not God. It was about as far from God as it could get. It stood in the shadows, listening to Don for a moment. Then it cleared its throat.

Don turned at the noise. The street light above him flickered and buzzed, and a figure moved in the dark across the street.

A man in a grey suit stepped out of the shadows. Or rather, the shadows seemed to recede from around him. He sauntered toward Don, his steps punctuated by the *tap-tap-tap* of the brass-headed walking stick in his left hand. A shock of white hair rose from his high forehead, and he ran slender fingers through it as he purred, "Lovely night for a walk, isn't it?" His voice was like somebody strumming an acoustic guitar: a soft, measured baritone with a twang of the American South. In another life, this man had been known as Dr. John Leland. Perhaps a part of him still was. But on most days, he was the Deacon.

"You heard that?" Don grumbled.

"Every word," Leland confirmed as he stepped in front of Don. He pushed a pair of half-moon spectacles up his birdlike nose and winked. His bright eyes twinkled in the dark and a smile crept onto his face. It was times like these when Don noticed that Leland bore an uncanny resemblance to William Hartnell, Abby's favourite Doctor Who actor.

Don threw a glance across the street. "Where are your flying monkeys, then?"

Leland shook his head and chuckled. "We're not standing on ceremony tonight, Donald. No robes, no 'flying monkeys,' no pretence. Just me. I've been feeling a bit cooped up lately. I wanted some fresh air. Is that really such a crime?"

"I'm going to tell her everything. First thing tomorrow."

Leland pursed his lips and shook his head. "That's not how this works, Donald. You know what'll happen if you tell her."

"Right. A bolt of lightning will come right out of the blue to strike me dead." Don shook his head and sighed. "You know what, Deacon, maybe that'd be best. My daughter has spent her entire life living in misery because of you, and she needs to know the truth. I don't care what happens to me if it means Abby has a fighting chance when your precious Alignment comes."

Leland considered this, drumming his fingers on the head of his walking stick. He gave a small nod and then took a step back.

Don advanced toward him, but Leland pressed the base of his stick into Don's chest. Don looked curiously from Leland to the stick and back, but Leland still said nothing. He smiled, winked again, and thrust his stick forward.

Don's feet left the ground and he flew backward. Leland grew smaller and smaller in his vision, and Don's chest felt like someone had cracked it open with a sledge hammer. He slammed into the next traffic light half a block down, and something in his back snapped. He fell uselessly to the ground with a thud, and saw spots dancing before his eyes.

Tap-tap-tap. He could hear Leland approaching, but his eyes and his brain had lost communication and he couldn't see a thing. He wrapped his hands around the lamppost and tried to pull himself up, but his legs gave way as soon as he put any weight on them.

"Donald, Donald, Donald," Leland said with a sigh. "You do me a tremendous disservice. If I left you to the Pledge, that'd be it! A flash of light, a tightness in your chest, and you'd be gone. It wouldn't last…"

Don blinked and shook his head. His vison cleared as Leland crouched before him, his eyes flinty and sharp, like the head of a spear.

"No… no, this is the kind of score one must settle personally." Leland gently stroked Don's cheek. From the corner of his eye, Don imagined that Leland's fingertips were turning black, that his nails were growing thicker and longer, morphing into deadly claws.

He stopped imagining when Leland brought up both his hands, curled them into fists, and then plunged his thumbs deep into Don's eye sockets.

Don shrieked madly as Leland worked his terrible claws around inside Don's head, severing nerves, rending muscle and vein, and peeling the sclera like an orange. He heard the pop as Leland pulled the two fleshy orbs from where they sat in Don's head, and the squelch as Leland crushed them under his walking stick. He felt blood trickling down his cheeks like tears, and Leland began to sing.

"'It has served our fathers
It has served our fathers
It has served our fathers
And it's good enough for me…'"

Then it was over. Don was still standing with Leland's walking stick poking him in the chest. Leland's fingernails were still just fingernails—meticulously trimmed and cleaned, with nothing of claws about them. Don waved a hand in front of his face to confirm that, yes, both his eyes were still in their sockets.

"Now, I want to be very clear on this point, Donald," Leland said. "I brought you back into this world, and I can throw you out again just as soon as look at you. But if you break the Pledge, it will not be nearly so simple as that. You are kidding yourself if you think your daughter is the only one around here with psychic prowess, and that little vision quest I just sent you on is not one-tenth of one-tenth of the metaphysical whammy I have planned for you should you attempt to go behind my back on this matter. If you tell Abigail anything, understand that you will be raising the full ire of Hell itself. I will send you into the undiscovered country screaming and writhing, driven mad by a pain worse than any pain anyone on this tiresome blue rock has ever felt at any point in all of recorded history."

Don backed away. His tongue darted around inside his mouth, trying to work up some saliva, but all the moisture seemed to have transferred to his forehead and his palms. His bladder quivered and his bowels felt like water. And Leland was just warming up.

"Of course, you know I wouldn't stop there. The Pledge only protects you and your family from my… 'flying monkeys,' as you so quaintly put it. There are still six billion other stupid apes on this planet that I would gladly rip to pieces if it meant getting you to toe the line. And I'd start with that little tramp from Abigail's soccer team. *Kelly.*" Leland spat the name out like it was something foul and revolting. Then he smiled. He smiled the warmest, most earnest smile a man could smile and he patted Don on the cheek. Don flinched, terrified that Leland was going to sprout claws again.

"I want you to cogitate on this, Donald," Leland cooed. "As long as your daughter draws breath, I hold all the cards. And you would be doing everyone a kindness if you just turned around and walked away."

As Don walked away, Leland tapped his walking stick twice on the ground and whispered something in a strange, alien tongue. Don turned to look behind him, but Leland had already disappeared. Don's hand started to sting, and he looked down to see two long cuts in his palm.

11.

*****

On the walk back home, Don kept thinking about what Leland had said.

As long as your daughter draws breath, I hold all the cards.

It was true, too. The Pledge would stand for another eleven years, and Leland would be watching them like a hawk every day. There wasn't a good goddamned thing Don or Karen could do to protect Abby from that. That was eleven more years of helplessness and guilt for them. Eleven more years of deception, resentment, and argument.

No way they were going to make it that long. If Don and Karen's marriage didn't implode under the strain, then Abby would figure out the truth somehow. She was too damn curious for her own good, and hadn't she come close tonight? Whatever vision she'd had had shown her all she needed to know. Someday, she would put two and two together, and Don didn't think she would ever forgive her parents then.

And what next? What did they have to look forward to when the last grain of sand fell from the hourglass, and the Deacon came to collect? If everything went his way, there would be chaos in the streets. Forty years of darkness, wailing and gnashing of teeth, rivers of blood, horses turning and eating each other, and all that jazz. But if it didn't, if the ritual failed, then the Deacon would not take it well. He would probably still raise the full ire of Hell, and the Hendersons would have their own personal forty years of darkness to contend with.

As long as your daughter draws breath…

The stairs creaked underneath him, and Don paused for a moment. He didn't want to wake Karen or Abby. He knew how he could save them all, but he wanted them asleep. If he did it while they slept, they wouldn't hurt. They wouldn't be scared if they never expected it.

As he made the slow ascent to Abby's room, Don felt the weight of the gun in his hand. Karen had hidden it well, no doubt to keep Abby safe. But she still needed that one keepsake for herself, didn't she? That one physical record of her old life.

Don bounced Grandma Meg's Webley in his hand, and he thought how poetic an ending it was. The old woman had started this whole thing, and now she would finish it. She would take all the Deacon's cards from him and toss them in the fire. Don knew that for all the Deacon's bluster, he was lost without Abby. He had planned a long game which revolved entirely around her, and if she were removed from the equation, the whole thing would collapse. And it wasn't like the Deacon could resurrect people any day of the week: he'd had to borrow a lot of power from some big-time cosmic forces just to bring Don back the first time around. Doing it again would put him hugely in debt to things you didn't want to be in debt to, and Don doubted the Deacon would take that risk.

Don opened the door to Abby's bedroom and carefully loaded the first of three rounds into the gun. Abby, then Karen, and finally him. He would pull the wool over the Deacon's eyes and take them all where the Deacon would never find them.

Don stood over his daughter's bed and brushed her hair out of the way. He laid the muzzle of the gun against her skull, just behind her left ear, and closed his eyes.

"It's okay, Abby. It's going to be okay."

One of Abby's eyelids fluttered, and through a fog of heavy sleep she mumbled, "Dad?"

Don nodded. "I'm here, sweetie. Just go back to sleep."

It might have been the delirious tone of Don's voice, or the unfamiliar feel of the metal resting on her head, but something in Abby's brain started shrieking at the rest of her to wake up. She rose with a jerk and turned on her light, throwing off Don's aim.

"Go back to sleep, Abby. Just please go back to sleep."

Abby drew her covers up to her chin and asked in a small voice, "Dad. What are you doing?"

Don raised the pistol to chest level and shushed her. "Just go back to sleep, baby. I promise, I know what I'm doing."

Abby pressed herself against the back wall so hard that she started to wonder if she could melt through it. "Get out of here, Dad. Please, get out. Y-y-you're scaring me."

"I don't want you to be scared, Abby. That's why you have to go to sleep."

"MOOOM!" Abby shrieked. "MOM, HELP!" She threw her pillow at him and jumped out of bed, screaming at him to "get out, get out!"

Don backed Abby into a corner and gripped the revolver with both hands, mumbling, "Go to sleep. Please go to sleep, Abby. Go to sleep, just go to sleep." As his shoulders wracked with heavy sobs, his voice grew louder and quivered with desperation. "Go to sleep, Abby! Please! Please go to sleep!"

Don's arm spasmed, and the gun went off. Abby shrieked and dropped to the floor as the shot went over her head. Her dad was shouting at her: "Go to sleep! Please, go to sleep, Abby! Please, please!"

He was being kind to her. Why didn't she understand that? He was trying to save her from a horrible fate. He knew how bad it looked, of course he did! It wasn't like he was a lunatic. He could save her if she would just calm down for a minute. And she would calm down if she would just—

"Go to sleep, Abby." Don fired again, into the baseboard this time. Goddamn, his daughter was fast. She had rolled right out of the line of fire at literally the last second. If Don hadn't been so frustrated that he'd wasted two of his shots, he would be bursting with pride at his daughter's quick reflexes. He lined up his last shot—*have to make this count*, he thought— and massaged the trigger with his index finger.

And then someone was behind him, grabbing his wrist. With a jerk, Karen brought her husband's arm around behind his back and twisted it until he dropped the gun. She kicked it toward the doorway, far away from Don's reach. Then she stuck her leg out and swept it through his, finally bringing him down.

Don hit the floor with a *thump* and lay still for a moment. Then he sat up, crying like an infant, and pulled Karen into a tight embrace. He wept openly, and Karen wept too when she realized what he'd been reduced to. She laid his head on her shoulder and nodded quietly while he kept mumbling to himself. "Go to sleep. Go to sleep, Abby. Go to sleep…"

"Abby," Karen said softly, "I want you to go and call an ambulance."

*****

"And how's your father doing now?" Mr. Lockhart asked.

Abby just lay her head down on the desk and said nothing in response.

It had been nine days since her dad had been taken to the hospital, and Abby didn't think he was ever going to get out. The way her mom had explained it, Don had had a massive psychotic break and entered a quasi-catatonic state. All the doctors could get out of him was, "Go to sleep. Please, go to sleep, Abby," and there was talk of moving him to a care facility if he remained nonresponsive.

Karen had barely been home since the incident. Every hour she wasn't at work, she spent at the hospital, trying to elicit some response from Don. But this was fine by Abby, who was now more suspicious of her parents than ever. How extraordinary a coincidence would it be if she had a nightmare about the Deacon, and then her dad just decided to try and kill her a few hours later? It must have been guilt, and a parental instinct gone horribly awry. Don hadn't wanted her to be scared, after all…

Mr. Lockhart had been standing on his desk and throwing paper airplanes across the room when Abby had knocked on the door, but he'd quickly put those away and tried desperately to make it look like he was doing some real work when he welcomed her in.

He'd already heard about what happened from Karen, but he still listened intently as Abby gave her version of that night. Then he looked to the ceiling for a minute in deep thought.

"I just don't understand, Mr. Lockhart! Why would my dad do something like this?" Abby asked.

Enough was enough, thought Simon Lockhart. This poor girl had been suffering all her life, and nobody was doing a thing to help her. Since Abby had broken her arm last year, Simon had tried on eight separate occasions to open a dialogue with Karen, to seriously discuss training Abby in the mystic arts. And on eight occasions, Karen had blown him off. "We'll talk about this later," she would say. "Abby's under a lot of pressure. It's not a good time for her right now."

It was never a good bloody time. Simon was convinced it was never going to be a good time. As long as Karen Henderson had the final say, Abby would be trapped in this hole her parents had dug her.

Well, sod that for a game of soldiers. Simon had given Karen plenty of rope over the years, and now she'd gone and hanged herself with it. Like the man said, if you wanted something done right…

Simon tugged at the lapels of his waistcoat and put on his Stern Teacher Voice. It was Mr. Lockhart who cleared his throat and said, "Abigail."

Abby looked up, and he fixed his eyes on her. "I can't tell you why your father did this. I suspect he's the only one who could. But I can tell you this: your father was terribly scared. He was scared of his past, and he was scared of your future. He was ashamed of his mistakes, and he was ashamed of the lies he and your mother have told you."

"What do you mean?" Abby asked.

"Your parents have a secret, Abby. They have a secret they have been keeping from you your entire life. In the wrong hands, it is an absolutely dreadful and horrible secret, but in the right ones, it is a positively wonderful secret. It all depends on how you use it."

Abby blinked. "M-me?"

A solemn tilt of the head. "Yes, Abby. *You* are the secret."

"What are you talking about?"

Mr. Lockhart walked over to a large wooden cabinet at the back of the room and pulled a battered brass key from his pocket.

Normally, students had free range of Mr. Lockhart's classroom, but this cabinet was an exception. It was always locked, and students were under strict orders not to touch it, or Mr. Lockhart would give them an automatic failing grade. Every time he repeated this warning, it was without the slightest hint of mirth or irony, and so nobody ever challenged him on the issue.

The cabinet rumbled as Mr. Lockhart stuck the key into the lock. He ran his hand along its side and whispered gently to it. "All right there, old thing?" The rumbling stopped, and Mr. Lockhart opened the cabinet.

Abby rose from her desk to see what was inside, but Mr. Lockhart repositioned himself to block her view. She craned her neck high and bobbed low to get a peek, but he moved with her every time as he continued to rummage. Abby got the message and sat down.

A moment later, Mr. Lockhart pulled away from the cabinet with a large bundle in his hands and carried it over to Abby's desk. Behind him, the cabinet swung shut and locked itself.

The bundle was wrapped in a thick black cloth and tied off with a shiny silver string. Laying the whole thing on the table, Mr. Lockhart gave the string a tug, and the cloth unfolded.

Inside was a majestic, antique book, nearly as big as the desk itself. Its cover was bright red with a sapphire blue trim made up of small, intricate animal designs. A large gemstone was inset at each corner, and smaller gems placed equidistantly around the perimeter broke up the animal designs. There was a golden circle in the middle of it all, stamped with a strange rune. The title of the book ran above the circle, in a flowing Insular script: *Historia minor hominum callidōrum*. To the layman: *The Lesser History of the Cunning Men*.

Abby's mother had once shown her some pictures of the Lindisfarne Gospels, a gorgeous illuminated manuscript from the early eighth century. Abby had thought at the time that it was the most incredible book she'd ever seen, but the Historia minor was so resplendent that it made the Lindisfarne Gospels look like a children's colouring book.

Abby looked at Mr. Lockhart, her eyes wide with awe, and asked in a small voice, "What's... what is this?"

"Abby," Mr. Lockhart said with a smile, "we have *a lot* to discuss."

All along the watchtower, princes kept the view
While all the women came and went, barefoot
servants, too

Outside in the distance a wildcat did growl
Two riders were approaching, the wind began to
howl
*

"*All Along the Watchtower*"
Bob Dylan

BOOK TWO:

HERE THERE BE MONSTERS

NOW

CHAPTER 6

HAPPY HOUR

ABBY HENDERSON'S last therapist had once told her to find the positive in any negative situation.

The negative: MacReady's Social House was stupidly, crazy busy, and Abby could barely hear herself think over the din of the other patrons' dinnertime conversations.

The positive: All the chatter did drown out her friends' terrible singing.

No, scratch that. To call the noise 'singing' would be to grossly devalue the musical arts. At best, Kelly and the others were engaged in a round of rhythmic shouting. And Abby wasn't too sure about the rhythm part.

MacReady's Social House was a two-floor, warehouse-sized restaurant on Robson Street, one of the hottest consumer districts in the city of Vancouver. The first floor was set up for casual dining, while the upper level was dedicated to the bar, lounge, and kitchen. It was upstairs where Abby found herself on the auspicious occasion of her 25th birthday: crammed into a large U-shaped booth with five of her favourite people in the world, looking out MacReady's ceiling-high front window at the Vancouver nightlife, and trying not to die of shame as her friends screamed a drunken, tuneless rendition of "Happy Birthday" at her.

Kelly and Wanda were at the far ends of the booth, with Lauren and Samantha on their insides. Abby was stuck in the middle, the Woman of the Hour. And beside her, almost shoulder-to-shoulder, in fact, was the mastermind behind this party.

Leanne Waller was a short, round woman with a blonde bob cut and thick black-framed bifocals, in the fine tradition of Buddy Holly or Velma Dinkley. She was also Abby's roommate and steady girlfriend of three years. As one of five children, birthdays had always been a big deal to Leanne, though she was aware that Abby had her reasons for disliking hers. It had taken some coaxing, and two weeks of social media tag to get everyone's schedules aligned, but Leanne had finally convinced Abby that 25 was a perfect reason to go nuts.

As the girls all took a moment to admire their terrible singing, Abby peeked at Leanne out of the corner of her eye and caught Leanne peeking back. Smiling, Leanne nudged Abby with her shoulder and asked, "Having fun?"

Abby sighed. "Why must you torture me like this?"

Leanne gave Abby a gentle smack on the arm. "Oh, cut it out. You are having fun! I can see it in your eyes!"

Abby stared hard at the still-smiling Leanne for a moment, daring her to see it in her eyes. But eventually, she gave up the grumpy charade and broke into a wide grin. Giving Leanne a quick kiss on the cheek, Abby admitted. "Okay, you got me: tonight has been pretty rad so far. But I could do without the—"

Kelly stood and raised her glass. "'FOOOOOOOORRR...'" she began.

"'She's a jolly good fellow!'" the ladies sang. "'For she's a jolly good fellow!'"

Abby dropped her head onto Leanne's shoulder and groaned. "Kill me now."

"'For she's a jolly good fell-ooooooow—'"

"'Which nobody can de-nyyyyyyyy!'" finished the big man in the red suspenders and polka-dot bowtie. He was approaching the booth with a fresh bottle of wine, and as he held the last note, Abby's face went extremely red.

"Not you too!" she groaned.

Adam Sakurai was the manager at MacReady's: a man as trendy as the restaurant he ran. The son of Japanese immigrants, Adam combined the physique of a stereotypical sumo wrestler with the full beard and hairy arms of a West Coast lumberjack. He was also Abby's boss.

As Adam uncorked the bottle with a flourish and topped up everyone's glasses, Abby looked at Leanne and wondered aloud, "Why did I let you make a reservation here?"

Adam smiled. "Because you couldn't bear to part from my sparkling company for a single second. Not even on your day off."

Abby rolled her eyes but accepted a refill anyway. "Yeah, that's it. Couldn't be the staff discount or the fact that everywhere else was booked up."

Adam set the bottle down and winked. "Hey, gift horses and mouths and all that. I've got to check up on the kitchen staff, but I'll probably swing by later on to humiliate my favourite hostess some more."

Abby raised her glass. "I'd be disappointed if you didn't, Adam."

As he turned and marched away, Lauren kept her eyes on Adam's backside. She licked her lips hungrily and leaned over to Abby. "You've been holding out on me, Henderson! Why didn't you ever say your boss was so cute?"

Abby laughed and shook her head. "Don't even bother, Lauren. Man's as gay as the day is long."

"Good thing, too," said Leanne. "If any straight guy ever winked at you like that, he'd have me to deal with."

"Planning to defend my honour, Lee?"

Leanne nodded. "If I had to, yes." Abby started laughing and Leanne asked, "What's so funny?"

Through intermittent giggles, Abby answered, "Lee, I once saw you jump about a foot in the air when you found a crane fly in the shower! I think you'd die of fright if you actually had to duel someone."

Leanne frowned. "Hmph. Now I kind of wish someone would look at you funny, just so I could show you how wrong you are."

Abby gave Leanne a soft kick under the table. "How much have you had to drink already?"

Leanne smiled and stuck her tongue out at Abby. "Enough to make you look attractive."

"Oof. In that case, you must be *hammered*."

*****

Abby and Leanne had met quite by accident. Abby was still a student then: studying English at Simon Fraser University as her mother had done. The day she met Leanne, Abby had sat a particularly rough midterm for her 18th century Romantics class, and then grabbed a bus back down to her crappy apartment in the city.

Unfortunately, traffic was at a standstill along Hastings Street, the main east/west thoroughfare in Vancouver. It would have been faster to walk where she was going, so, at the next stop, Abby got off the bus and did exactly that.

Doubly unfortunately, it started to rain two blocks later. Abby didn't have an umbrella or a hood for her jacket, so she ducked into the next store she saw.

The shelter she had chosen was a two-storey building with dusty windows, a ratty purple awning, and a sign hanging above the door that read "THE OLDE CURIOSITY SHOPPE". It was a used bookstore that Abby had passed by several times before, but this was the first time she had gone inside.

The Shoppe was a labyrinth of high book shelves, arranged in every configuration that would fit into the space. The product that wasn't shelved was arranged in precarious stacks around the store or leaning against the dusty windows. A handmade sign near the staircase said "MORE BOOKS

UPSTAIRS", and there were even books propped up against the wall on the individual steps.

Abby started browsing to kill time until the rain eased up. She was in the Horror section, thumbing through the 'K' authors, when she picked up a paperback of *The Girl Who Loved Tom Gordon*. That was always her favourite. Her own much-loved copy had met a rather ignominious end some months before when she dropped it in the bath, and she hadn't yet had a chance to replace it. This copy was in excellent condition—it looked almost new, in fact—but Abby could find no price tag on it.

There came a voice behind her. "Can I help you?"

Abby turned around. The first thing she noticed about the bespectacled blonde in front of her was the way she smiled. It was the kindest, gentlest smile Abby had ever seen, and when Abby followed it up to the deep blue eyes behind the bifocals, it felt like she was looking at the face of God. This was no mere customer service smile, either. It was the kind of smile that Shakespeare would have written a sonnet about. It was the kind of smile you took home on the weekend to meet your parents. Forget that Mona Lisa chick; this was the kind of smile da Vinci *should* have been painting.

Abby wanted to say something like that to the woman in the glasses. She wanted to run her hands through that blonde bob cut and kiss those smiling lips. But all she managed was, "Um."

The blonde paused and blinked awkwardly, then resumed smiling. "So, can I help you find something, or are you just browsing?"

A voice in Abby's head went off: *She's talking to you, you idiot! Say something!* Shaking herself out of her trance, she replied hastily, "Yes, sorry, help! That... that would be good."

"Okay. What do you need help with?"

Thankfully, Abby found that her mouth had re-established its connection with her brain. "I was wondering if you could tell me how much this book was."

The blonde laughed and smacked her forehead. "That's where I put that! God, I am such a basket case sometimes."

"Huh?"

"Sorry, it's just I've been catching up on some reading during my breaks and right now I'm on a bit of a Stephen King binge. I brought that in with me three days ago, and I must have left it on the shelf by accident! Classic Leanne." A pause. "I'm Leanne, in case you were wondering. See?" She moved closer to Abby and pointed to the title page, where the words "PROPERTY OF LEANNE W" were written in ballpoint pen.

"Oh," Abby said, a little disappointed, "I guess I should give that back to you then."

She handed the book back to Leanne, blushing a little. The voice in her head remarked, *Smooth move, Henderson. Real frigging smooth.*

Seeing Abby's disappointed look, Leanne tucked the book under her arm and said, "We might have a copy or two in the back, if you want me to check."

Abby smiled and nodded. Any excuse to stay in here a little longer, where she could avoid the rain and re-evaluate her terribly awkward pickup strategy, was okay by her. "That'd be great, thanks."

"Won't be two minutes," Leanne replied, as she turned and jogged toward a door marked "EMPLOYEES ONLY".

By Abby's count, it was exactly two minutes before Leanne returned, empty-handed and with a little less bounce in her step.

"No joy in Mudville, I'm afraid. We sold our only remaining copy last Friday."

"Oh. Shoot."

"I know, I'm sorry."

A croaking, elderly voice came from upstairs: "Leanne, are you down there? I need you to come up here and help me with something."

Leanne shouted back up, "I'll be there in a minute, Mrs. Clifford! I'm just helping a customer down here!"

The elderly voice replied tartly, "Now, if you don't mind!"

For the first time since Abby had entered the Shoppe, Leanne's smile strained. "All right! I'm coming!" She shrugged apologetically to Abby and ascended the stairs. "Sorry, my boss. But if there's anything else you need, just let me know!"

And then Abby said something profoundly, tremendously stupid. As Leanne and her beautiful smile walked away, Abby called after her, "How about your phone number?"

*****

Lauren was the first to speak after Abby and Leanne concluded their verbal sparring match: "It's so great having all of us in the same room again. I seriously can't remember the last time I've had this much fun!"

Wanda smiled. "I know! It has been way too long since we did something like this!"

Kelly stifled a Heineken's-scented burp and slurred, "I'll tell you one thing: this is definitely turning out better than your thirteenth birthday, right, Jaws?"

Lauren gasped. "Oh my God, you're right, Kel! 'Cause that was the night she freaked out and fell down the stairs! Man, that was scary."

Leanne looked around the table, perplexed. She knew everything there was to know about Abby, and she definitely hadn't heard this story before.

"Sorry, what happened when Abby was thirteen?"

Lauren was agape. "Whoawhoawhoa, you mean she never told you?! Okay, so what happened was we had a sleepover for her birthday, and we're sitting in her living room, just hanging out, telling scary stories at fuck knows when in the morning—"

Abby closed her eyes and winced. For once—for once—she would like it if her birthday wasn't spoiled by the Deacon. She scratched the table top with her fingernails and mumbled, "Lauren, could we please not talk about this?"

"Hang on, hang on, I'm telling Lee what happened. So, we're just screwing around in her living room, like whatever, and then Abby says she has to go to the bathroom, so she goes up that big set of stairs they got—what am I talking about? You've been to her parents' house; you know what it's like…"

Abby's hand shook, and she curled it into a tight fist. She wasn't going to freak out. Not tonight. Not to-bloody-night.

"So, she goes upstairs for a pee, right? And then we hear this huge scream, like something out of a horror movie…"

By now, everyone could see the pressure building behind Abby's strained expression. Everyone except Lauren, who never took notice of much. Samantha leaned past Wanda and gave Lauren a hard nudge. "Actually, Lauren, maybe we shouldn't—"

"Shush, shush, I'm nearly done. So then, there's this scream, and Abby comes shooting out of the bathroom like she's seen a ghost or something. She's screaming at the top of her lungs, and she runs to the stairs, but then she trips, and just does a header straight to the bottom. Boom! I swear to God I've never seen a human wrist bend that way."

Wanda shouted, "Lauren, for God's sake, knock it off!"

But the damage was done. Abby's breathing came fast and shallow and she started chewing one thumbnail so her mouth would have something to do besides scream. She dared not open her eyes. If she did, the Deacon would be there, reaching out of the mirror.

"Kha'al Azna'ghal ixxi. Kha'al Azna'ghal ixxi. Kha'al Azna'ghal ixxi."

Abby got up suddenly and wormed her way out of the booth. A few tears had already squeezed past her eyelids, and she wanted to escape before the dam burst. This was supposed to be a fun occasion, goddammit. As she hurried out of MacReady's, the only excuse she offered was a half-hearted "I need some air."

*****

Bracing herself against the cold, Leanne stepped out of MacReady's and looked around. She found Abby standing under a streetlight near the corner, eyes wet and wide as dinner plates, arms crossed defensively over her chest.

Leanne slowly approached and asked, "Are you okay?"

"I'm fine," Abby lied. She wiped her eyes with one hand.

"You sure? Because I feel like we might have opened a wound that should stay closed."

Abby turned away from the light pole and opened her arms, welcoming Leanne into them. "I'm sorry, Lee. It's not Lauren's or yours or anyone else's fault. It's just… you know the nightmares I told you about? Way back when?"

"Yeah?"

"That was when they started. That bathroom was where I first saw… him."

Leanne gasped. "The… *the Deacon*?" she whispered.

Abby nodded.

Apart from her parents, Leanne was the only person in the world whom Abby had ever talked to about her abilities. She hadn't planned it that way, of course, but after the first night she and Leanne had slept together, there hadn't been much choice.

Abby had woken screaming after her first nightmare in nearly a year, thrashing around in a panic and nearly kicking Leanne out of the bed. It had taken a hard slap in the face from Leanne to calm her down, and then everything had just poured out. Abby had hardly paused for breath as she told Leanne about the day of Grandma Meg's funeral, about how she sometimes knew things would happen before they happened, her nightmares about the Deacon, and her suspicion that he'd had a hand in driving her dad insane.

Abby had expected Leanne to laugh, or call her crazy, or walk out, but Leanne hadn't done any of that. Instead, she had taken Abby's hand, told her to shut up, and kissed her like Abby had never been kissed before. Then she had whispered, "I believe you. You're probably not used to hearing that, but it's true. I believe you now, and I will believe you if anything like this ever happens again. Foreverways."

Abby had blinked at her, confused, and rubbed the tears out of her eyes with one hand. "What's 'foreverways'?"

"Something my brothers used to say when we were kids. It means I've got your back, 100%. I will be there for you, Abby Normal."

Leanne hadn't said the nickname with malice or mockery, but with trust and love. Remembering that night now, Abby realized it would be an insult to that trust not to tell Leanne everything.

"Okay. It happened like this..."

When the story was over, Leanne just pressed herself tighter against Abby and whispered, "I can't believe you never told me this."

Abby tilted Leanne's face up and kissed her, then slowly pulled away, smiling broadly. "Thanks for understanding, Lee. It really means a lot to me."

Leanne nodded and started to pull Abby back toward the restaurant. "We should get back. The others are probably wondering where we've gotten to."

"I don't know," Abby said, "maybe we should just call it a night."

Leanne stamped her foot. "Absolutely not! I worked my butt off getting the girls to come out. The least you could do is show a little appreciation."

Abby smiled. "For your efforts or for your butt?"

"Either one works," Leanne replied coyly.

Abby put her arm around Leanne as they walked back into the club. Slowly, her hand crept down Leanne's back and past her belt...

Leanne let out a small yelp and smacked Abby's hand away just as the door closed. "Maybe not that much appreciation," she whispered.

*****

As the two had talked under the street light, neither one had thought to look up at the building across the street. If they had, they might have noticed a tall black woman in a very old trench coat standing on the roof, with a machete strapped to her leg. They might also have noticed that she was holding a pair of binoculars, which were pointed straight at Abby.

"I can't believe that's her." Natalie Arnaud murmured. "*Mon Dieu*, but she grew up fast."

"Or we were moving slowly," Simon Lockhart replied as he stepped up beside her. He took the binoculars and caught a glimpse of Abby just as she was attempting to cop a feel on Leanne. He chuckled. "Abigail Henderson, all grown up."

Abby had changed a great deal from the squishy, crying lump she'd been when Simon and Natalie had first seen her: her hair was cut short and dyed a bright fire-engine red; her chest, back, and arms were a stunning canvas of tattoos; and her ears were extensively pierced. Only the gap between her front teeth remained the same.

Neither Simon or Natalie, however, had aged a day. They never did. Death and decrepitude were abhorrent concepts to them, and they'd both sworn off aging a long time ago.

Natalie snatched her binoculars back—Simon had grabbed them while they were still dangling around her neck—and clicked her tongue behind her teeth. "Time's up. And she has no idea what's coming."

"Oh no, she knows exactly what's coming. She just doesn't realize it yet." Simon paused and then grinned. "Come on, let's see if we can find seats inside! I think I heard them playing 'Live and Let Die'!" He rubbed his hands together eagerly and jogged toward the fire escape.

Natalie rolled her eyes. "You and your bloody Wings obsession."

"Oh, not this again," he groaned.

She shrugged. "I'm just saying, this partnership can never truly work until you accept that McCartney hit his peak when he was with the Beatles."

"You know, Natalie, it really wouldn't hurt for you to broaden your mind, culturally speaking."

Natalie spluttered, "*Me* broaden *my* mind?! This coming from the man who hurled my Zeppelin LPs out the window and called them 'abominable rubbish'?"

"I just knew you would throw that back in my face one of these days!"

*****

While Leanne was leading Abby back up the stairs, and while Simon and Natalie were being told there'd be a 20-minute wait, Karen Henderson was loading her gran's old Webley and staring anxiously at the clock above the fireplace, where Abby and her friends had once roasted marshmallows.

Abby had been born at 9:28pm on October 27, 1994. The clock above the mantel was ticking 8:45 just now. That left just about three-quarters of an hour until the Pledge officially expired, and the Deacon came to collect. Three-quarters of an hour for Karen to get in her car, get across the Lions Gate Bridge, find her daughter, and try to repair 25 years of fuckups in one fell swoop.

"K-K-Karen?" whispered a thready, tired voice.

Karen stood as her husband—40 pounds lighter than he'd been at his peak—wheeled himself into the room.

"You should be in bed, Donald," she admonished.

For four years after he'd tried to shoot his only child, Don Henderson had lived in a psychiatric facility out near the University of British Columbia. For most of that time, he'd been little better than a vegetable. But then, around the time

Abby turned 18, he began to show more signs of life. He became more vocal, more responsive, and could even navigate around his room in a wheelchair by himself if so asked.

The facility was shut down around this same time, deemed unsustainable amid a bloated provincial budget and a badly out-of-date infrastructure. Karen made the difficult decision to move Don back home, where he would occupy a ground-floor bedroom that was once Karen's study, while she took over Abby's old bedroom upstairs.

The first year under this new arrangement had been rough. But when Karen turned 50, she had taken a step back from her lecturing duties at SFU. Suddenly, she had more time to spend at home, and she and Don got to know each other all over again. Because he no longer possessed the verbal capacity of his youth, there was no fighting. No arguments over Abby's future. What there were, were many long, silent stretches when Don would just look at his wife or his daughter, think back to the threats the Deacon had made to them all, and thank God that at least he (Don) was still here with them. As a wise man once said, it could've been worse. It could've been raining.

Now, Don Henderson rolled himself into the living room and looked at his wife. His pyjamas hung off his slack, atrophied frame and his hair, once black and bristly like a shoe-shining brush, shone pure white. A fuzzy blue blanket fell around his drooping shoulders. "C-couldn't. C-c-couldn't sleep," he stuttered. "A-A-Abby."

After all these years, Don and Karen had developed their own language. He couldn't get much more than three or four words out at a time, but she always knew what he wanted to say.

"I know. I'm worried about her too." Karen snapped the Webley's breech shut and put the gun in the leather shoulder holster she was wearing.

"G-going?" Don asked.

"One of us has to. You were right, Donald. All these years, you were right. And I was wrong. I've failed as a mother. I've been sitting on my hands for so long while the Deacon's been gloating and driving our daughter insane. I haven't kept her safe by hiding the truth. I've only made things worse."

Don blinked and nodded once. There was a spark in his wife's eyes tonight. It was a spark he hadn't seen there since before Abby was born. God, he'd forgotten how beautiful that spark was.

"It ends tonight," Karen continued. "In less than an hour, the Pledge will expire. Then the Deacon won't have any more hold over Abby than he has over the tides. I'm going to find our girl, and I'm going to take her straight to the Letterbox. I'm going to tell her everything and then I'm going to let Simon and Natalie whip her into shape."

She adjusted her holster and then strode toward the front door of the house. Don reached up and took her hand as she passed him by. "Karen," he said. "If… I-i-if…"

Karen kneeled and kissed her husband. Kissed him like she was a newlywed again. "If something happens, if I don't come back, I want you to keep going. Just keep going, Donald. Keep healing, keep living as well as you can live. I don't think the Deacon will come after you. I think he's… *proud* of what he did to you, in some way. You're his masterpiece, and he'd be loath to destroy you. But you can show him up. Be more than what he made you. Be more than what he made us. Leave the heroics to Simon and Natalie; that's what they're good at. You just move forward."

Don nodded. "F-f-find Abby. S-s-save her."

"I will. I love you, Don."

Don trembled in his wheelchair. The words were there, in his head, but it was tricky getting his mouth to line up with his brain these days. "L-love. I. Love. Y-y-you. Karen."

Don kissed Karen's hand one last time and then she walked out the door to go save their daughter.

As the door closed, Don felt a chill behind him. He shivered and wrapped himself tightly in his blanket, turning in his wheelchair to look at the banister at the bottom of the stairs. The same banister that Abby had smacked her head against when she fell so many years ago.

The Deacon's mark had appeared on the banister sometime that morning. Karen hadn't said a word about it, but she knew as well as Don did. Of course she knew.

The moonlight shone on the scratch marks in the white wood, and Don remembered the feeling of the Deacon's claws inside his head.

0.

CHAPTER 7

THE SHADOW-WALKER

"I MEAN it, Abby, I really do. I—I'm really sorry for what I said."

Abby nodded and gave Lauren's hand a reassuring squeeze. "It's okay, Lauren. I know you didn't mean it."

Lauren shook her head. "No! No, I should have thought! I know how tough this time of year is for you, what with your dad and all, and… God, I'm so stupid! I shouldn't have said anything."

"Hey, Lauren, look at me. We're good. Honestly."

Lauren smiled and expelled a sigh of relief. After pulling her foot out of her mouth, she had poured multiple shots down it in rapid succession and was now overflowing with emotion. She did her best to reach across the table and give Abby a hug but couldn't manage much more than a pat on the shoulder without knocking over several drinks.

Samantha swirled her straw in her second Diet Coke and asked, "Speaking of which, what's the whole… deal there? I mean, if I'm not getting too personal, how is your dad?"

Abby's friends all looked at her. To one extent or another, all of them knew that Don had suffered a kind of nervous breakdown several years ago, though Abby had edited the revolver out of the story in the retelling.

Abby gulped down a third of her drink in one go. "My dad is… he comes and goes." She shrugged and tapped a finger on the glass. "He's a little more… there than he was the last couple of years. For one thing, he actually acknowledges you when you're in the room with him. He smiles, he waves, and he never did that after… after his episode. But, I mean, he still doesn't say a lot, and he's not much for walking or anything like that. It's… I don't know, he does what he can, I guess."

"I think it's really sweet that you and your mom still take care of him," Wanda said earnestly. "I don't know if I'd be able to face something like that, and certainly not for eleven years."

"Well, he's my dad, you know? Warts and all, he's still family."

Warts, revolver, deal with the Devil and all, whispered that little voice in her head.

Leanne drummed her hands on the table. "Anybody want another?" she asked, looking right at Abby.

Abby was relieved at the change of subject and smiled when Leanne gave her a knowing wink. "Yeah, Lee, I think I could use another."

Wanda and Kelly echoed the sentiment, while Lauren and Samantha contented themselves with soft drinks. Leanne flagged down their server, and a few minutes later the girls were busying themselves with their next round.

As she accepted her drink, Abby looked around at her friends and smiled. Lauren's little faux pas had been forgotten, and the night was back on track. If they could just sit for a little while and finish their drinks, Abby would have finally survived one birthday without anything going spectacularly wrong. With a silent prayer in her heart for things to end on a high note, she raised her glass and said, "I really want to thank you guys all for coming out. I've never had things as easy as some other people, and I know it makes me a bit of a mess sometimes, but it really helps having friends like you to back me up. You guys are always there for me, and I hope you always will be." She wrapped her other arm around Leanne and kissed her on the cheek. "Especially you, Lee."

"I'll drink to that!" Lauren announced. Five more glasses rose to meet Abby's, and cheers were exchanged all around.

Wanda's face flushed as she set her glass down and announced, "Woo! This might be my cut-off point! I think I'm getting a bit woozy."

Leanne coughed as a few drops of her wine went down the wrong way and nodded. "I know what you mean. My head is spinning!"

Kelly gave Leanne a nudge and smirked. "Hey, what did you put in these drinks, Lee? You trying to roofie us or something?"

Leanne opened her mouth in an exaggerated gasp and clutched a little golden cross that hung around her neck. "A good Christian girl like me? Never! It was probably one of you godless heathens!" She waved an accusatory finger at the others, but quickly dissolved into uncontrollable giggles.

Samantha took a sip of her Diet Coke and gagged. She slapped a hand over her mouth as something unpleasant danced around on her tongue, and then latched itself to the back of her throat as she swallowed. It was cold and slimy and sharp, like the carapace of some ugly, swamp-dwelling insect.

"Hey, are you okay, Sam?" Kelly asked.

Samantha mutely shook her head and grabbed a napkin off the table. She coughed into it several times, trying to bring up the bug that had jumped inside her, but it wouldn't budge. Lauren slapped her on the back, but it was no help. Samantha retched as the thing reached down with a slimy tendril and clutched her esophagus, pulling itself downward toward her stomach. She heaved and spasmed as her body tried to eject the bug, but it held on for dear life. The other girls cleared a path for her, and she bolted for the ladies' room.

She didn't make it that far. Ten feet from the table, Samantha's legs gave out, and she stumbled into a busboy clearing a nearby table. The pair went down with a crash of dinnerware, and gasps of shock and confusion went up throughout the lounge. Abby and Lauren both rushed from the table to check on their friend, and two servers formed a perimeter around the spot where Samantha lay unconscious.

"What's wrong with her?" Lauren shrieked. "What's wrong?"

One of the servers declared her first-aid credentials and bent down to check on Samantha. She was breathing and her pulse was steady, but she was completely unresponsive.

"Should we call an ambulance?" Abby asked.

The server didn't say anything and kept trying to revive Samantha. Nothing more happened, and eventually she said, "Okay, who has their phone on them?"

A half-dozen cell phones came out of a half-dozen pockets and were thrust toward the concerned server. As she took one, a shriek broke the air, and a glass smashed.

Abby and Lauren looked back. Wanda was out of her seat, frantically shaking an unconscious Leanne. She and Kelly had slumped over each other as they passed out almost simultaneously, and Kelly had knocked her drink to the floor when she went.

"Oh Jesus…" Lauren said. "Abby, what the hell's going on?"

The server reached out and grabbed Lauren's hand. "Ma'am, listen to me, it's going to be okay. We all just need to stay ca—"

She fell flat on her face before she could finish that statement. Lauren followed a moment later, and then Wanda collapsed. Abby's pulse sped up as the others in the restaurant fell like dominoes around her. At the edge of the lounge area, to the left of the stairs, one could see down to the first floor. It was the same scene there, as one by one, staff and patrons alike closed their eyes and collapsed to the ground like puppets with their strings cut. Glasses smashed as they fell from hands, chairs and stools slammed as people took them down with them, and tables creaked as bodies thumped down on top of them.

As the last bodies fell, the restaurant's state-of-the-art sound system squealed and crackled, killing the funky pop anthem that was being piped throughout the restaurant. There was a moment of silence, and then a slow four-part harmony began to play. The sound was distant and hollow, like a recording played on a very old gramophone, but it filled the room entirely.

It was good for our mothers
It was good for our mothers
It was good for our mothers
And it's good enough for me...

Soon, Abby was the only person standing in MacReady's Social House. Her heart slammed against her ribcage and her breath came in rapid, shallow gasps. She ran back to the booth and crawled underneath the table just as the chanting began.

"Kha'al Azna'ghal ixxi. Kha'al Azna'ghal ixxi. Kha'al Azna'ghal ixxi."

"Not now," Abby pleaded. "Please, please, not now!"

The temperature plummeted, and the drink that Kelly had spilled hardened into a patch of ice before Abby's very eyes. She peeked out from under the table and stared at a small dark spot on the floor, near Lauren and Samantha. The dark spot bobbed and rippled and crept over the unconscious forms of her friends. Curls of inky blackness rose up from its surface and the black spot grew in time with the chant, bubbling like lava as it rose up toward the ceiling. The blackness cohered into a central mass with two arms, legs, and a head. A layer of skin developed over the smoke, filling in the details of lips, nails, and hair, while black robes threaded themselves together from nothingness to cloak the figure's naked form.

A few seconds later, Abby was staring at one of the Deacon's hooded followers. Its body rippled and shimmered under a thin film of the black smoke, and waves of the same stuff dripped from the bottom of its robes down to the ground, keeping it suspended in midair. Even the creature's aura was made of shadows, and when Abby tried to read it, her brain responded with a 404 error.

Abby and the creature simply stared at each other for a moment, each daring the other to break the silence. It became clear to Abby that the creature would not make the first move, so she cleared her throat and asked, "Wh-who are you? D-did… he send you? The Deacon?"

The hooded creature jerked its head in what might have been a nod. With a rough, toothy voice like the growl of a mastiff, it replied, *"I am The Kin of the Hound; I am The Speaker with Many Tongues; I am Varr'rak, which is called The Shadow-walker. I am an envoy of the Eldest One."*

"The Eldest… you mean the Deacon? Is that your name for him?"

"I do obey the Deacon's will," the thing called Varr'rak confirmed. *"I come to you tonight, Abigail Henderson, with a message from him. The peace between you and he ends this night. The debt must be paid, that the Eldest One might walk among us again. You must come with me now, to prepare for the Enlightening."*

Abby's whole body jerked involuntarily. Her vision went white for a brief second, like there'd been an explosion in her brain, and she heard the chime of an old clock in her head. When the explosion went off a second time, Abby sniffed and gasped, "Remember!" She wasn't aware of it yet, but a thin stream of blood was leaking out of her nose and down her chin.

Whatever Varr'rak was expecting, this wasn't it. He cocked his head to one side and snarled, *"Remember what?"*

The word 'Enlightening' was buzzing in Abby's head like a nervous bee. It was important somehow, and as it jumped around in her head it poked and prodded at every hard surface. Her brain exploded again and the chimes of the clock—the Westminster Chimes she'd once loved so dearly—got louder.

"*Remember WHAT?!*" Varr'rak demanded.

Abby closed her eyes and grimaced. The Chimes were so loud they hurt, and all she could smell was her own nosebleed. Through gritted teeth, she forced out two words. "The magic!"

Varr'rak growled and thrust his hand toward Abby. "*I have no time for this. For 25 years now, we have honoured the Pledge, Abigail Henderson. It is time for you to do the same!*"

Abby shook her head and wiped her nose with her hand. Her nosebleed was clearing, but the Chimes were still there. Sort of in the back of her ear now, like tinnitus. "I'm not going with you," she stated. "I'm not going anywhere the Deacon asks me to go!" She wrapped both arms around the leg of the table. If this thing wanted to take her to the Deacon, it would have to drag her out of here.

Varr'rak kept his hand extended, but Abby could see the other one at his side, curling into a fist. "*You will come, or you will pay a heavy price. The Deacon has shown you mercy before this day. Do not spurn his kindness.*"

"I'm not going with you!" Abby screamed. "I'm not going anywhere."

Varr'rak lowered his hand. "*Very well, Abigail Henderson. If you refuse to make the right choice, the right choice shall be made for you.*"

Varr'rak extended his arms and lifted his head. Ropes of inky darkness branched out from his outstretched fingers like the limbs of a dead tree and he unleased an unspeakable, monstrous howl. It sounded like the call of a giant wolf, mashed together with the caw of a crow the size of a minivan.

Abby slammed her hands over her ears as the howling continued, and the black branches of Varr'rak's fingers speared the lights above her head. Thick, syrupy blackness filled the room, and Abby lost all sense of direction. She let go of the table and groped around on the floor, trying to avoid the falling glass. She needed to find her phone, which was somewhere in her purse.

A chill crept across the back of Abby's neck, and the chants of *"Kha'al Azna'ghal ixxi"* grew louder as she located her bag and rummaged through it blindly. She found her phone just as a hand wrapped around her ankle and yanked her sharply backward. As she skidded the length of the floor on her belly, bumping and scraping past the unconscious diners and waitstaff, Abby fumbled with her phone and tried to find the flashlight application.

Flipping over onto her back, Abby turned on the flashlight and directed it to her ankle. It was not a hand that held her, but a tentacle of the smoky blackness that had emerged from Varr'rak's robes. When the light shone on it for a few seconds, the darkness stuttered, and cracks of white crept over the surface. Abby traced the flashlight beam up the length of the tentacle that held her, to where Varr'rak hovered in the centre of the room.

The beam shone in the creature's face, and he hesitated for a brief moment. He raised his free hand in front of his hood and hissed in pain, and Abby's journey along the floor halted. Specks of blackness tore away from him like paint peeling off an old fence, and a spider web of white cracks broke over his features.

Light! Light! screamed the voice in Abby's head. Whatever Varr'rak was, he did not respond well to the light. She redirected the beam of her flashlight to the shadow holding her ankle and thrust her phone closer to it. The shadow stuttered at a greatly increased rate, and more of the darkness peeled away. Then Varr'rak cried out and the shadow let go of her.

Holding her flashlight in front of her, Abby turned and bolted toward the stairs. Behind her, Varr'rak conjured a thin spike of darkness in his hand and threw it into Abby's shoulder.

Abby screamed as the spike pierced her skin and exploded like a firecracker. Her arm went numb and icy cold, and she dropped her phone. It slid across the linoleum floor and right through the gap at the bottom of the railing, smashing on the ground far below.

As Abby fell, two shadowy ropes caught her around the throat and the waist and started to squeeze.

"Now, Abigail Henderson, you see what you stand against. Surrender yourself this night, and our quarrel need not escalate."

And then a human-shaped freight train smashed through the kitchen doors and flattened the Shadow-walker. The black ropes dissolved as he hissed and tried to fight his attacker off, but she scooped him over her shoulder and carried him across the full length of the room. The two careened straight through the perimeter railing to a spectacular crash landing on one of the tables below.

With tremendous effort, Abby managed to sit up, and scooched herself over to the railing. She watched in awe as the madwoman in the trench coat lifted Varr'rak above her head and threw him down onto the next table over with a furious roar. The table snapped in two as Varr'rak landed, but he dissolved into black mist and fled halfway across the restaurant before the madwoman could finish him off.

*****

Natalie turned as Varr'rak re-solidified. He streaked toward her in a flying tackle and tore up a strip of carpet as he dragged her along the floor. Natalie kicked him off like a bucking bronco, and Varr'rak retreated again. Shadowy, razor-sharp tentacles burst from his robes, and Natalie bobbed and weaved across the restaurant as Varr'rak tried to fillet her.

Natalie fought her way to the hostess stand, using her machete to cut away the tentacles when they got near. She picked up the heavy computer monitor that tracked bookings and seating and started ripping out cables by the fistful to detach it from the rest of the equipment. Then she threw the whole thing at Varr'rak's head.

It was a direct hit. As Varr'rak fell to the ground, Abby pumped her good arm in the air and cried out, "WOOO! Fuck him up!"

As Varr'rak recovered from the shock of some 20 pounds of electronics hitting him in the face, he looked up to the second floor and unleashed another earth-shaking howl. He pointed a hand at Abby and a thick plume of shadows raced toward her.

*****

"Oh shit." Realizing her mistake, Abby dropped her arm and pulled herself backward along the floor. The shadows shaped themselves into a large, clawed hand, and the fingers flexed and pawed the air eagerly as Abby scooted along on her butt.

"Eagan heofena!" A beam of white light sliced two of the fingers clean off the shadow-hand at the second knuckle, and Varr'rak screamed in agony. The hand stopped dead and the light burned a hole right through its palm as Varr'rak kept screaming.

Abby looked up to find the source of the light—for it was coming from behind her—and nearly fainted dead away. "Mr. Lockhart?!"

He stood at Abby's shoulder, both arms stretched out in front of him. The light came from his hands and the air around him crackled with energy. He saw Abby staring and smiled at her. "Hello, Abby! Happy birthday!"

The shadow-hand dissolved completely with a final howl from Varr'rak, and Mr. Lockhart lifted Abby to her feet. "Right then, we need to get you out of here. Are you hurt?" He lifted Abby's numb right arm and flicked a finger against the inside of her elbow. "Hmm… looks like a minor Numbing Curse… probably the same that's done for the rest of this lot, but a smaller dose. Should wear off by morning, at worst!"

Mr. Lockhart smiled, booped Abby on the nose, and pushed her toward the kitchen.

"I don't understand this!" she protested as Mr. Lockhart marched her through the kitchen doors. "What the hell are you doing here? What debt was that thing talking about?"

"Yes, yes, yes, yes, time for all that later. Right now, it's time to run."

A tremendous cacophony rose from below as Varr'rak crashed into a large collection of plates and dishes. He howled again, and Natalie howled back.

"Probably best to run fast," Mr. Lockhart admitted.

They ran. Abby hopped over the unconscious kitchen staff and kicked open the fire door. She could feel the impact of the madwoman's battle with Varr'rak coming up through her feet.

She started down the fire escape. With a cry of *"HEEEENDEEEERSOOOOOOON!"*, Varr'rak the Shadow-walker came flying up the stairs, through the kitchen, and straight at Abby. He tackled her like the star quarterback and took her straight over the fire escape, down 40 feet to the ground.

Abby braced herself for the wet, sticky impact she was about to make, but Varr'rak lurched to a halt two feet off the ground, and she and he floated gently to the ground.

Varr'rak held Abby by the front of her blouse and snarled, *"You're lucky we need you alive. If it were up to me, I'd snap you in half right here."*

Abby looked around. Mr. Lockhart had been knocked flat when Varr'rak raced past him, and he was plainly out for the count. The madwoman in the trench coat was still inside, and there was no way she'd make it out here before Varr'rak did whatever he needed to do.

And then: "Not tonight, you bastard!"

Varr'rak and Abby both looked up. A female figure stood at the mouth of the alley, holding a revolver. The muzzle flashed twice, and Varr'rak stumbled. White light burst from two holes in his torso, and he screeched as the shadows around the wounds blistered and cracked.

"You?" he howled, clamping a hand over one of his wounds. *"What are you doing?!"* He was shouting over Abby's head now, apparently oblivious to her continued presence.

"I'm owning up to my mistakes," the gun-toting silhouette replied as she stepped forward.

"We had a deal, McAllister!" Varr'rak screamed.

Karen Henderson reached down the back of her pants and pulled out a second gun. It was a lot stubbier than the revolver in her dominant hand, with a wider barrel and a bright red coat of paint. She levelled it at the Shadow-walker and ground her teeth together. "Your clock must be slow, Varr'rak. The deal expired ten minutes ago."

Abby covered her eyes as Karen fired the flare gun. The shot hit Varr'rak dead centre and he doubled over like he'd been punched in the gut.

"Oh, you absolute cu — "

The flare, and Varr'rak, exploded. A fountain of inky, foul-smelling black sludge sprayed the walls of the alley and tatters of Varr'rak's robes fluttered to the ground, while the light from the flare stripped away the cloying shadows. As Abby shielded her eyes, Karen grabbed her wrist and hauled her to her feet. "Come on! That won't keep him down for long!"

"It won't?" Abby yelped.

Karen holstered the revolver and stuck the empty flare gun down the back of her pants. She dragged Abby to the street and answered, "Trust me, Varr'rak is a tough son of a bitch!"

Karen's car was on the curb outside MacReady's, its engine still running. Karen threw Abby into the passenger's seat and got behind the wheel. "Buckle up, Abby."

"No, no, no, hang on!" Abby spluttered. "We're not just skating over that Varr'rak comment! Are you telling me — "

Karen glared at her daughter, and the look in her eyes could have shattered glass. "Abigail Margaret Henderson, I am your mother. When I tell you to buckle your seatbelt, you buckle your seatbelt."

Abby gulped and nodded. "Yes'm."

CHAPTER 8

THE HARD WAY

KAREN ROCKETED through three red lights before the feeling began to return to Abby's right hand. As Abby flexed her fingers, she planted her other hand on the dashboard to steady herself while her mom drove like she had a death wish.

"I don't believe this. I don't believe this! You did know! All these years I thought I was going crazy, but you knew everything, didn't you? About the Deacon, those hooded guys, all of it!"

"Abby, I'm trying to concentrate." Karen's eyes were locked on the road ahead, and she was squeezing the steering wheel so hard it was creaking.

"That wasn't just a dream!" Abby exclaimed. "The night Dad snapped on me, after I had that nightmare about the Deacon: that wasn't a dream! That all happened, didn't it?"

"Abby, I'm not afraid to admit that I screwed up. I made a lot of stupid mistakes when I was young, and my family got hurt because of them. That's on me, and I am sorry for it. But can we please not do this right now?" Karen jerked the wheel hard to the left, and the Mazda swerved around a stopped bus.

"Why did you tell me I was dreaming?! You said you wouldn't let the Deacon hurt me! How could you lie to me like that?!"

"Jesus Christ, Abby! I didn't have a choice! You don't know the Deacon like I do! You don't have the first clue what he would have done to us!"

Abby sniffed and felt her mascara running. She hadn't even realized she was crying. "I don't have the first clue, Mom?! No, *you* don't have the first clue! You have no fucking idea what kind of shit I had to put up with at school! What kind of shit I put myself through because I thought I was insane! There were times—Jesus, there were times when I honestly wished I'd let Dad pull the trigger on me that night!"

"You don't mean that."

"Yes, I fucking do! Do you know why I have these chains tattooed on my wrists, Mom? It's not just because I like *BioShock*! Look!" Abby thrust her left hand out underneath her mother's nose, and Karen slammed the brakes.

For the first time in her life, Karen could see the little horizontal scars on her daughter's wrist, hiding beneath Andrew Ryan's Great Chain. Then she herself felt like crying.

"I did that for the first time," Abby sobbed, "about two weeks after I moved out on my own. I didn't stop until I met Leanne."

Karen reached out to brush Abby's hair behind her ear, but Abby bitterly swatted away her mother's hand.

Karen blinked back a tear. "I'm sorry, Abby. All of this is my fault, and you have every right in the world to be angry with me. But I promise, I'm going to fix this. Starting now." She pointed to the glove compartment. "Look in there. You'll see a purple crystal in there with a string attached to it. I need you to give that to me."

Not sure what else to say, Abby wiped her eyes and opened the glove compartment. The said crystal was tucked behind the car's owner's manual. Abby held the crystal out for Karen, who told her to tap it against the dashboard.

Abby did, and the crystal began to glow and hum. Karen took it from Abby and spoke to it. "Simon. Natalie. One of you, talk to me!"

A deep female voice with a Haitian accent filled the car, and Abby knew it could only belong to the woman in the trench coat. "That was fast work, Karen. Didn't think you still had it in you."

The start of a smile twitched on Karen's face. "Slaying demons is like riding a bike. Not something you ever forget."

"Amen, sister. Listen, Karen, I'm sorry we let the Following get this close. Simon and I should have—"

"It's okay, Natalie. You did everything you could. I've got Abby right here and she's fine. Well, as fine as can be, considering."

Abby looked at the crystal, bewildered. It sounded like the other woman was sitting right behind her. And beside her. And in her head.

"Okay," said Natalie. "Okay, where are you now?"

"Granville Street near Nelson."

"Okay, I'm pretty close," Natalie said. "Karen, I'm thinking some directions at you. Meet me there and I'll escort you to the Letterbox."

"What about Simon?"

"He's still at MacReady's. Varr'rak dosed everyone with one hell of a sedative, and Simon's trying to bring them around. He tells me a few of them are already awake, but they don't remember passing out."

"Okay, we'll meet you. But be ready for a fight. Varr'rak won't be sitting around licking his wounds for much longer."

"Roger that."

The crystal stopped glowing and Karen dropped it in her lap. Abby shook her head. "Jesus Christ. Can we gear down the big rig here? Mom, did I just hear you say 'demons'?"

Karen nodded. "That's what they are. The Deacon and his helpers. They're demon cultists who can enter human bodies. They have some scary name in their own language, but I've always called them by the English translation: The Following."

Abby was starting to get a headache. "'Always'? How long have you known about this shit, Mom? How do you know that lunatic in the trench coat? And why was Mr. Lockhart at Mac's?"

Karen smiled to herself. "Now that is a long story if there ever was one."

"Mom, I'm dead serious. You said you wanted to fix your mistakes. Well, that starts with telling me what the fuck is going on right now."

"Abby, I promise you: there is a logical explanation behind all of this." Karen paused, then doubled back. "Well, that's a half truth. There is an explanation, but it hasn't been on speaking terms with logic for a long time." Out of the corner of her eye, Karen caught Abby's stare. It was the same glass-shattering look she herself had used not ten minutes ago. "I am going to fix this, Abigail. You are going to learn everything you need to know before this night is out. But before I can tell you anything, we need to get somewhere safe. Somewhere they can't find you."

"Why?" Abby demanded. "What's special about me?"

KER-RUUUNCH! The Mazda bucked as a black wrecking ball landed on the hood. The windshield disintegrated, the front axle snapped, and the bumper dislodged and clattered onto the road.

"Oh shit," Abby whispered. The wrecking ball unfurled and reshaped itself into Varr'rak the Shadow-walker. As Karen reached for her gun, Varr'rak looped a shadowy tentacle around her forearm, forcing it back against the seat.

"Do you have ANY idea how much that hurt?" Varr'rak seethed.

Karen blinked and sucked in a deep breath. Abby could hear the nervous tremble in her mother's airways as Karen said, "Abby. Run."

Abby unbuckled her seatbelt and threw the door open just as Varr'rak launched another shadow-tentacle at her. She tucked herself into a ball and rolled onto the pavement.

Not long after she'd learned to walk, Abby Henderson had learned to run. She always loved the chill she got from the wind biting against her cheeks and zipping through her hair; hearing her heart thump in her ears as she pushed herself forward; that split second of weightlessness when she launched herself from the ground with one of her freakishly long legs. On the weekend and during the summer, Abby enjoyed a regular run through the park or down by the Seawall.

But this wasn't summer, and she wasn't down by the Seawall. Abby's heart had been pounding in her head since way back at the club and her knees were knocking so bad they couldn't launch her. Yet for the first time in her life, she had real cause for running. This wasn't a Saturday afternoon jog in Stanley Park. This was The Hunt: one of the oldest known reasons to run. So despite her weak knees and her nervous heart, Abby bent low, took a deep breath, and really opened 'er up.

Abby took off like a bullet fired from a rifle, and Varr'rak the Shadow-walker howled his terrible howl. He jumped from the crumpled hood of the Mazda and raced after his prey, carried forward on a cushion of shadows. His robes fluttered behind him and he gnashed his teeth like a mad dog.

Abby hopped onto the sidewalk as a car horn blared in the distance. *Thump thump thump thump.* Was that noise coming from her heart or her feet? She didn't have a clue.

There was another howl behind her, and Abby turned her head. Varr'rak was close enough now that she could see the white froth bubbling at the corners of his mouth. It gave a whole horrible new meaning to the term 'spitting mad.' As he flew, Varr'rak pointed his hands at the ground beneath him. Shadows rolled off his arms and pooled on the ground, then sped across the pavement.

The black cloud streaked right past Abby's feet, and her eyes followed it. It stopped six feet ahead of her and swirled like a tornado, and then morphed into another Varr'rak, complete with glaze of shadows. Abby couldn't stop in time, and she crashed right into The Second Varr'rak. The Second Varr'rak stood his ground, and Abby bounced off him onto the hard pavement.

She looked over her shoulder and saw The Prime Varr'rak land softly behind her. She looked back at the Second Varr'rak, who smiled down at her and laughed.

"That's just not fair," she whimpered.

*****

As Varr'rak the Shadow-walker launched himself off the hood of her car, Karen Henderson yanked her gun from its holster. She aimed at the fleeting black shape, but her wrist was shaking too much to get a clear shot. Besides, Abby was right on the other side of Varr'rak. Dammit. It wasn't worth the risk.

There were more flares in the trunk of the car, but he'd be expecting them now. No way she could fool him twice like that. It was time to get creative…

Karen threw the Webley onto the passenger's seat and gripped the steering wheel. With her free hand, she turned the keys over in the ignition and…

Nothing. The engine coughed pitiably a few times and died.

Somewhere down the street, Abby gave a little whine. Karen looked up in time to see her daughter fall back, surrounded on two sides by Varr'rak the Shadow-walker.

"Come on, you son of a…" Karen turned the key again and the engine grumbled a little louder this time. Then the engine died again. She bashed the dashboard with her fist and swore a blue streak. She turned the engine over one last time and the car roared to life. She gripped the steering wheel tight with both hands and slammed the gas pedal to the floor.

*****

Abby made a little whining noise in the back of her throat as The Prime Varr'rak walked around her and stood beside his twin. The Second Varr'rak dissolved, and his shadows flowed back into The Prime Varr'rak. A thick black tentacle wrapped itself around her throat, and Varr'rak squeezed hard. Then, he simply revolved 180° where he was, so the tentacle was coming out the small of his back. He whispered a chant in a language Abby didn't recognize and twirled his hands in the air in an intricate pattern. At the climax of this routine, he clapped his hands together hard and then thrust them out to his sides. There was a sound like a falling tree as the very fabric of time and space tore itself apart, and then a large hole appeared in front of Varr'rak. It opened onto a winding tunnel devoid of light, and Abby imagined the Deacon on the other side, standing in that creepy hospital room. Waiting for her.

"Enough games. It's time to keep your appointment, Abigail Henderson."

VROOOOMM! Varr'rak turned back, and the one working headlight on Karen's Mazda blasted him in the face. The car was making some very unhealthy grinding and creaking noises as it sped toward Varr'rak and Abby, but Karen pushed it as far as she could nonetheless.

A shocked Varr'rak looked at Abby, then at the car, then at Abby. Abby could see the wheels turning in his head. The Deacon needed Abby alive, and Varr'rak had Abby here and now: signed, sealed, and ready to deliver. But Karen's car was aimed straight at Varr'rak, and Abby was in the danger zone. Wouldn't do much good if she was a sticky paste on the hood when Varr'rak delivered her.

Varr'rak screamed angrily and threw Abby aside, well out of the Mazda's path. A second later, Karen Henderson drove into him at nearly 50km/hour. Now Varr'rak was the sticky paste on the hood as Karen drove straight into the dark tunnel and out of sight.

The hole in reality started to close, and Abby pulled herself up off the pavement. She stumbled forward, still hearing the whine of her mother's car and the Westminster Chimes in her head. "Mom!" she hollered. "MOM! Come back! Please!"

But the hole in reality closed up with a pop, and Abby was alone in the street. She dropped to her knees, breathless, and she had a horrible feeling that she was never going to see her mother again.

*****

Four-and-a-half seconds after Varr'rak the Shadow-walker opened a hole in time and space, and more than a hundred kilometres away, the Deacon stood on a grassy hillside with four of his black-robed minions flanking him. All five of them were grinning ear-to-ear and chanting reverently as they peered into the black tunnel.

"Kha'al Azna'ghal ixxi. Kha'al Azna'ghal ixxi. Kha'al Azna'ghal ixxi."

They stopped chanting when the headlight of Karen's Mazda appeared in the darkness and the engine roared in their general direction.

"Move!" the Deacon commanded. *"All of you, move!"*

The five hooded figures scattered as the Mazda shrieked past them out of the tunnel, straight into a patiently waiting Douglas fir. As the car crumpled, Varr'rak dissolved into a black mist and floated toward the Deacon. He solidified again at the Deacon's right hand, swayed for a moment, and then dropped to one knee.

"Are you injured, O Shadow-walker?" the Deacon asked.

Varr'rak snarled and grabbed the Deacon's robes for support. His head lolled from side to side and his shoulders sagged. *"No, my lord. No."* He looked up, saw his hand on the Deacon's robes, and pulled away, stammering nervously. *"I am sorry, my lord! I am sorry! I did not mean to — I lost my head for a second!"* He pulled himself up and bowed. *"Forgive me, O Deacon."*

The Deacon took a step back. His voice came out cold and reproachful. *"Perhaps… you should rest, O Varr'rak."*

Varr'rak shook his head. *"No. No, I will recover shortly. It would take more than a hatchback to unsteady the hand of the Eldest One."*

"Wisely spoken, O Varr'rak. Yet you return here without my prize…"

Varr'rak's shoulders slumped and he looked at the car. *"Ask her about that."*

One of the Deacon's acolytes glided over to the car and yanked open the driver's door. It was barely hanging on by a thread, and it came free from its hinges as it swung open.

The steering column had been ejected from its moorings, thrust up into Karen's chest. She was hunched over it with her eyes half-closed and her hair falling in tangles around her face. There was a deep cut above her left eye, which she'd squinted shut to keep the blood out of it. Her nose was badly broken and she had several lacerations on her cheeks, where the few remaining pieces of the windshield had flown into her face.

"Bring her to me," the Deacon barked. His acolytes swarmed the car and dragged Karen roughly out of her seat. Her left shoulder was dislocated, and three fingers on her right hand were bent the wrong way. Nevertheless, the acolytes threw her to the ground at the Deacon's feet and made a circle around her, daring her to move against them.

"Karen Henderson," hissed the Deacon. *"You were… unwise to interfere."*

Karen set her right arm flat on the ground and slowly pushed herself up to her knees, groaning the whole way up. She smiled at the Deacon with smashed, bloodstained teeth. She tried to laugh, though every movement of her chest felt like someone was punching her in the heart. "You sent your best man… You sent the Teacher's Pet after my daughter, and it wasn't enough. I'd be rolling on the floor if it didn't hurt so much."

"We made your daughter a peaceable appeal," the Deacon answered, *"yet she spat in our faces. YOU spat in our faces. Despite your debt."* He knelt before Karen and placed a hand on her dislocated shoulder. *"There must be... reparations."*

Karen yowled in pain as the Deacon tightened his grip on her. She glared at him furiously and spat blood on the ground. "Go ahead and kill me. But they will stop you. Simon and Natalie will stop you."

The Deacon's mouth twitched and a hint of emotion crept into his words for the first time. A hint of anger. *"They will NOT."* The last word rolled past his lips like thunder. If he wasn't whispering, he could almost have been shouting.

Karen smiled—she was getting to him. "They've done it before."

"Before? That was... an anomaly."

Karen shook her head. "They've stopped you before and they'll stop you again. And with Abby on their side, they'll be twice as powerful. Those three together will burn your little cult to the ground."

The Deacon's mouth twitched again, and he laughed in Karen's face. His minions began laughing too, and Karen's defiant façade dropped. *"Perhaps you speak truly. Perhaps we shall fail. Perhaps we shall be forced to find another, come the next Alignment."* The Deacon grabbed a handful of Karen's hair and pulled her so close that she could feel his breath on her face. *"But, if this happens, I shall take comfort in killing your champions, your daughter, and everyone she loves..."* His thin mouth twitched underneath the hood and slowly twisted into a snide, hungry smile. *"That. Is. A promise."*

Karen watched as the Deacon's fingertips hardened, and his nails stretched into shining black claws. There was a dark flash, and she coughed twice. Blood dribbled onto the ground, and Karen could hear her own breath wheezing out through the hole in her neck.

The Deacon's index finger had punctured her neck to the second knuckle, just in front of her left carotid artery. He dragged it slowly to the other side, opening her throat like a zipper. Karen's vision went dark as her warm blood spattered onto the grass, melting the frost that always formed in the Deacon's wake.

The Deacon stood and slowly, decadently sucked Karen's blood off his claw. Then he turned to his followers and said, *"Go. We have many preparations to make. But I would speak with you privately, O Varr'rak."*

The four acolytes in their black robes bowed low, and then, in perfect unison, they turned and marched up the hill, leaving Varr'rak and the Deacon standing over the corpse of Karen Henderson.

"Kha'al Azna'ghal ixxi. Kha'al Azna'ghal ixxi. Kha'al Azna'ghal ixxi."

When the acolytes had departed, Varr'rak bowed his head again. *"My lord,"* he said quickly, *"you need not speak. I know my failure tonight was great. I am ashamed to return to you without the girl. I only beg that you can — "*

The Deacon raised a hand, and Varr'rak fell silent. *"Speak not to me of failure, O Varr'rak. It was I who did not foresee Karen Henderson's interference. I thought I had broken her spirit many years ago. Clearly, I underestimated her…"* The Deacon looked at the corpse and thought for a moment, then returned to Varr'rak. *"We cannot let this interrupt our timetable, yet we must consider the possibility of further interference."*

Varr'rak cocked his head to one side. *"My lord?"*

The Deacon smiled. He slowly drew back his hood, and Dr. John Leland spoke. "You are a credit to us all, O Shadow-walker. But your strength is in your aggression, your sheer brute force. It is tantamount to performing surgery with a sledgehammer. But right now, we don't need a sledgehammer. It is clear to me that our foes will oppose us in ways we did not previously consider, so we must be smart. We will step back for the moment to re-evaluate our strategy. And when next we strike, we shall be prepared for any contingency."

A low growl rumbled in Varr'rak's throat. *"Very well, my lord. We will, as you say, step back."*

"Excellent. And who knows? If worst comes to worst, there may yet be use for a sledgehammer."

Varr'rak smiled.

CHAPTER 9

HANGOVER

THE GRAVEL path crunched under Abby's feet as she ran for the large wrought-iron gate. A howl split the air behind her and the air crackled with electricity, like the few seconds before a lightning strike. She felt a building pressure behind her eyes and her ears rang. Varr'rak howled again, and her nose started bleeding.

The gate was situated beneath a large stone arch with a letter 'A' carved into it. On each side of the arch, a large statue with black wings and a hood stood guard. The gate swung open with a creak, and Abby heard another howl. She turned back to see the cloudy form of Varr'rak the Shadow-walker flying toward her.

She put on one last burst of speed and jumped through the gate just before it slammed shut. Varr'rak solidified and the gate groaned as he slammed into it. He reached through the bars with one hand that groped and clawed at the air, but Abby backed out of his reach.

She sniffed as the blood dribbled freely from her nose down into her mouth. The pressure in her head squeezed her brain, and she dropped to her knees with gritted teeth.

Ba-boom! An explosion went off in her head, and she heard the Westminster Chimes again. From some dark hiding place in the back of Abby's brain, there came a sudden tidal wave of thoughts and memories. She remembered sitting on the floor of Mr. Lockhart's room, stuck in some kind of trance while he read aloud from a large book. She heard a voice whispering a lot of words in her ear. *Following... Azna'ghal... Enlightening... Gospel... Vanguard...* She thought she knew what these words meant, but she couldn't place them right now. The pressure in her head was too great.

The Chimes suddenly stopped. A female voice with a heavy Yorkshire accent said, "Don't be scared, Abby." Abby opened her eyes and wiped her nose with the back of one hand. "Meg? Grandma Meg?"

"Listen to me, Abby, you 'ave to wake up. You can't remember the magic all at once. There's not enough room in your mind," said Grandma Meg.

"Wake up?" Abby gasped. "What are you talking about?"

"You're 'aving a dream right now. But you're not ready for this kind of dream. Everything you know, everything 'e taught ye, it's all comin' back. But it's comin' back too fast. You 'ave to wake up and slow down, or you'll go mad."

"Taught me? Who taught me? What the hell are you talking about?"

Ba-boom, ba-boom.

Two more explosions in her brain, and the dam in Abby's memory centres burst. The wave of names rushed through her mind again: *Following, Azna'ghal, Enlightening, Gospel. Vanguard. Following, Azna'ghal, Enlightening, Gospel. Vanguard. Following —*

BA-BOOOOOM.

Abby shrieked in pain and clutched her head in both hands. Her teeth rattled in her mouth and a red river poured out of both nostrils. She started to hyperventilate.

"Meg..." she pleaded. "Meg, help... it hurts!" *Ba-boom.* "It hurts so bad!"

"I know, Abby," Meg said. "And I'm sorry, but there's nowt I can do for that right now. I'm too far away, see. You need to wake up, and you need to find that mad git Lockhart and get 'im to put ye right."

"Lockhart?!" Abby gasped. "Why did you say Lockhart? Gran, what the hell is he? What's happening to me?"

"Everything," said Meg. "Everything that's meant to 'appen, and everything that was bound to 'appen. I'm sorry I can't say more now, but it would take too long, and if you don't wake up, you'll lose yer mind."

Ba-boom! Abby's brain exploded again. She closed her eyes and screamed as she felt a sensation like a red-hot nail stabbing into her head. She stuffed her fingers in her ears to block out the clanging of those bloody Westminster Chimes. Her lips and chin were growing sticky as her nosebleed started to dry and her whole head shook like a boiling kettle.

Then the Chimes stopped. The pressure in her head disappeared, and Abby felt a hand on her shoulder. She took her fingers out of her ears and opened her eyes again. Mr. Lockhart was kneeling before her, smiling. Slowly, his hand still on her shoulder, he leaned in close and whispered, *"Heorcne."*

*****

Abby awoke in her own bed, in her pyjamas. The clothes she'd been wearing at MacReady's were in a pile on the floor. Dull, autumnal daylight was creeping through a gap in the curtains. Abby crawled out of bed and took slow, heavy steps toward the apartment's tiny bathroom. Her memories of the previous night—after Varr'rak had disappeared with her mother—slowly came back over the next few minutes.

She remembered hearing a car horn beep behind her a few moments after the portal closed. She'd been kneeling in the street, crying. When the horn beeped at her again, she had crawled over to the side of the road and sat on the curb, sobbing into her scraped and bloody knees. She'd remained there for a few moments until a police officer approached.

He'd looked at her with kind eyes and asked her if she needed help. Through her tears, Abby had eventually managed to give the officer her name and address. He'd offered to take her home in his cruiser. She'd told him to call Leanne instead. She'd given him Leanne's number. Then she'd just sat and watched the traffic pass her by. She remembered seeing an ancient Ford Thunderbird drive past at one point. She'd thought at the time that the Thunderbird's driver—a black woman with a long ponytail—had met her eye and given her a sorrowful look, but the car had passed by before Abby could really process the image.

After that, things got fuzzy. Leanne and Kelly arrived in a cab about fifteen minutes later—by then, the cop was sitting on the curb with Abby, trying to engage her in conversation as a way of keeping her calm. Then there was the cab ride back to Abby and Leanne's apartment, during which time Abby said barely a word. She'd sat at the table and cried for a time, and then Kelly had looked out the window and said a police car was parking outside the building. Someone knocked on the apartment door a few minutes later, Leanne had invited two police officers in, and they'd spoken very softly to Abby. She didn't hear a word they'd said, but the gist of it was obvious: they'd found the wrecked Mazda, with Karen Henderson dead behind the wheel.

There'd been no consoling Abby after that. She'd cried herself hoarse for most of the next hour, and when she glimpsed a flash of reflected light off the bathroom mirror and started screaming, Leanne had insisted she get some rest. The last thing Abby heard before she shut the bedroom door was Kelly, who said there was no way she was leaving Abby's side at such an awful time.

Abby came to a stop just before she reached the bathroom. She heard voices outside the apartment door and a key jingling in the lock. Kelly and Leanne came inside a second later, their arms laden with groceries. When they saw Abby standing there like the world had just ended, they dropped the bags on the table and gathered around for a hug.

"Abby, I can't… I'm so sorry about your mom… If you need anything," Kelly paused and gave Abby a squeeze, "I'll do it. I'm not going anywhere. If you need to cry or talk or watch *Mystery Science Theater* or absolutely anything, I am here."

Abby squeezed back and let go. "Thanks, Kel." She stifled a yawn and said, "What time is it?"

"It's almost noon. We tried to wake you, but you were out like a light."

"We went to go see your dad this morning," said Leanne as she gave Abby a squeeze.

"How is he?"

Leanne sighed. "Not well. He didn't seem to see us half the time. He was screaming his head off, throwing things. He kept calling your name and telling you to 'go to sleep.' He took a swing at Kelly at one point."

"A good swing too," Kelly admitted. "I didn't know he could move like that."

"I had to phone the number your mom keeps on the fridge," said Leanne, "and one of the nurses from the home-care service came and talked him down." She suddenly took off her glasses and wiped tears out of her eyes. "I just said 'keeps,' didn't I? God, Abby, I can't believe… I mean, I always thought your mom…"

Abby sniffed and closed her eyes. "Yeah. I always figured she'd be here forever. It was going to be her and the cockroaches, running around after the nuclear apocalypse." She pulled away and ran a hand through her hair. "Goddammit. I should have been there. I should be there now. I have to call him, let him know I'm okay."

"I think the nurse was trying to get him down for a nap when we left when we left," Leanne said. "You won't reach him right now."

Kelly laid a hand on Abby's arm. "Take care of yourself first, girl. Get some food in you. Have some tea. Have a shower. Then call your dad."

Leanne pointed at the grocery bags. "I got some eggs, ham, green onions… why don't you freshen up and I'll make you an omelette or something?"

Abby kissed her and smiled weakly. "Damn. You really know what buttons to push, don't you?"

Leanne nodded. "I really do."

By the time Abby had freshened up and eaten, it was approaching one in the afternoon. As soon as she put her dishes in the sink to soak, she borrowed Leanne's cell phone and dialled Don and Karen's home number. "God, I hope he's okay. A guy as fragile as my dad, the stress of this whole thing could kill him."

"I don't know if 'fragile' is the word I would use," said Kelly. "I mentioned he took a swing at me, yeah?"

Abby held up one finger to shush her. "It's ringing." The fingers of her free hand drummed nervously on the kitchen counter and she muttered to herself, "Come on, Dad, pick up, pick up…"

The phone went to voicemail, but the ringing didn't stop. The apartment tilted at a 45° angle, and Abby fell against the wall. *Ba-boom, ba-boom, ba-boom.* Her brain exploded in time with the beat of her heart, and she screamed as an invisible hand drove long, sharp fingernails into the side of her head.

"Abby! Oh my God, Abby!" That was Leanne, who had one arm around Abby's shoulder and a hand on her forehead. "Abby, are you okay?"

Abby blinked and stared straight past Leanne, dropping the phone. Blood trailed from her nose and ears, and a thin trickle leaked out the socket of one red, bloodshot eye. In a deep, guttural voice, she growled, "Do you think you are winning this fight? I have you here, do I not?"

Ba-boom! Abby snapped to her feet and clutched her head in both hands. In a mock English accent, she said, "Oh, to be in Canada now that autumn's here."

Ba-boom! She doubled over, screaming again. "No, no!" she shrieked in her own voice. "We're past that!" *Ba-boom.* She straightened up again and looked at Kelly. With a cheeky wink, she said, "I'll see you in the funny papers, kid."

Kelly ran around behind Abby and locked her arms around Abby's chest. Abby struggled and writhed in her grip like a fish on a hook, screaming and spitting and ranting madly.

"What the hell's wrong with her?" Kelly demanded. "Abby, what's gotten into you?!"

Leanne stepped forward and grabbed Abby's hand. "Abby, Abby! For God's sake! It's us! Please, just calm down!"

Abby looked Leanne dead in the eyes and flashed her teeth angrily. In an exaggerated Southern accent, she hissed, "Clean yourself up, Abigail. You have a big day ahead of you." Then she raised one leg and kicked Leanne square in the stomach.

"Jesus Christ!" shrieked Kelly. Leanne toppled to the floor, coughing and gasping for breath.

BAAA-BOOOOOM! Abby wrenched herself free of Kelly's grip and collapsed on all fours, gasping and retching. She wanted to throw up, and her limbs shook as they tried to support her weight.

"Abby…" Leanne croaked with a weak cough. "Abby, what the hell was that?"

Abby looked up at her partner, who was sitting hunched over with one hand over her stomach, trying to catch her breath. She was crying.

Abby stood slowly and backed away from both Leanne and Kelly. "Oh God, Lee. What—what did I do? Jesus, I am so, so sorry! I don't know what came over me!"

Leanne scooted backward toward the bedroom door. She didn't say a word, but the terror in her eyes was real.

Kelly shook her head. "What the fuck was that, Jaws? It was like you weren't… you anymore. Like something had you possessed!"

"I—I don't know," Abby stuttered. "I don't—I don't—I don't—I don't—"

Leanne, having found her breath, straightened up. "Abby, what's happening to you?"

"I DON'T KNOW!" Abby screamed, and she started crying again. "I don't know what's going on, Lee! My mom's dead, my dad's insane, and I just… I just… I just…" Suddenly, her mind went blank. A dull fog descended over her memory, and Abby forgot why she'd been crying. She sniffed, and was surprised to find that her nose was bleeding. She slowly lifted a hand to her face and wiped away the blood, staring at the red smear on her fingers with a puzzled expression.

She looked at Leanne and Kelly, blinked twice, and declared, "I need to find Mr. Lockhart."

Then she collapsed to the floor, unconscious.

CHAPTER 10

TEACHER'S PET

FOURTEEN-YEAR-OLD Abby Henderson sat cross-legged on the floor of Mr. Lockhart's classroom, her eyes closed and her breathing heavy. She had fallen into a deep sleep—most of her, anyway. There was a small part of her brain that was more awake than ever.

When Abby opened her eyes, she could see herself sitting on the floor several feet away. She leaned down and poked at her still body, but nothing happened. The hands that did the poking were blurry and fuzzy, like images projected onto a screen through a dirty lens.

After Mr. Lockhart had taken that old book out of the cabinet, he had cleared a space on the floor and told her to sit. Then he pulled out his pocket watch and waved it in front of her face until she felt very sleepy, and at the last moment he had touched a finger to her forehead and whispered one word to her in a dead language.

"Heorcne."

With that word ringing like a bell in her head, Abby's conscious mind had shut down, and her unconscious had jumped out of her body. Now, it was walking around the classroom, halfway between real life and a dream. As Mr. Lockhart started to read from the book, Abby's unconscious sat down beside her body and listened.

"Every culture, every religion in this world since ancient times, has had an idea of evil," Mr. Lockhart said. "In Ancient Egypt there was Apep, the serpent who sought with each passing day to devour the sun god Ra. Islamic teachings speak of Iblis, who refused to bow down to Adam. And Christianity, of course, has Satan. All of these stories come to us from one source. His followers call him The Eldest One, but his true name is Azna'ghal. He is the King of Demons."

Abby blinked and whispered, "Demons?" To her surprise, her corporeal body repeated the word.

Mr. Lockhart nodded and turned the page. "Many centuries ago," he explained, "before the Age of Christ, this world was a crossroads. A beacon for spirits and all manner of magical creatures who co-existed with early man. Some of these spirits were of the race that we now call demons. Man and demon lived in relative peace for a time, but eventually the demons got greedy, and their leader, Azna'ghal, set out to conquer the mortal realm. Many species were driven close to extinction in the ensuing war, and many more were wiped out entirely. Eventually, the demons were banished from this earth, but at a terrible cost."

Abby whispered into her body's ear, "What does this have to do with me?" Her body repeated the question in a slow, sluggish voice.

Mr. Lockhart turned to another page in the book. "In this same Age of Magic, as man and demon lived amongst each other, there eventually came into being a race of half-breeds. Children born of human mothers and demon fathers. These half-breeds, in time, came to be known as the Gospels. For their ability to speak the *gōd spell*—the good news—you see. The Gospels were great prophets and psychics: their mix of human and demon blood gave them the unique ability to see beyond the barrier that separates our physical world from the Elsewhere, the world of the spirits. By communing with the spirits, the Gospels unlocked the secrets of telepathy, psychometry, astral projection, telekinesis, spirit channelling, and even the ability to see the future."

Abby swallowed. "Am… am I…?"

Mr. Lockhart nodded. "Well done. You, Abigail Margaret Henderson, are a Gospel."

That one word, "Gospel", scurried into Abby's ear all the way up to her brain, and it started to build itself a nest. All she could hear was that one word, repeated *ad infinitum. Gospel. Gospel. She was a Gospel. No, she was THE Gospel. There had been many before, but they were nearly gone now. The Gospel was her. She. She was. Was she? The Gospel. Who? It was her. Yes. Always her. Gospel…*

Mr. Lockhart turned the *Historia minor*'s broad pages and said, "This is why the Deacon is so interested in you."

The voice in Abby's head went quiet. She looked at the book and saw a sketch of a large ceremonial chamber, with about two dozen Following acolytes gathered around a black stone altar. The Deacon himself stood at the centre of the demonic horde, holding a large wooden chalice over his head. Several of the Following were holding down a young girl. She couldn't have been much more than sixteen, and she was naked from head to toe. Abby could just barely make out some strange tattoos running up and down her torso. No, scratch that. Not tattoos. Carvings. Somebody had gone to great pains to etch some very eerie markings into the poor girl's skin.

Mr. Lockhart stared grimly at the sketch and said, "Ancient wisdom speaks of a ritual called the Enlightening: an arcane rite with the power to collapse Azna'ghal's astral prison and allow him to walk the earth once again. The Enlightening requires a human sacrifice, but not any human will do…"

Abby's body gulped audibly. Her soul whispered, "They need a Gospel…"

"Exactly," said Mr. Lockhart. "Demons like Azna'ghal and the Deacon can only survive on Earth for extended periods if they possess human bodies. But Azna'ghal's power is so great that any purely mortal body he inhabited would burn up in a matter of hours. The only vessel that could safely contain him is a Gospel in the prime of life. It has been the Deacon's goal for most of a century now to conduct a successful Enlightening and free his master from confinement. But Gospels are few and far between, so when the Deacon finds one, he won't give her up easily."

****

For the second time that day, Abby awoke with a splitting headache and the taste of blood in her mouth. After she had passed out, Leanne and Kelly had evidently carried her back to bed. She was still dressed, and she was lying on top of the rumpled, messy bedsheets. She must have been out for a few hours at least, because the light coming through the curtains was the dull orange of twilight, and she felt hungry again. She needed to use the bathroom too, but she didn't feel up to the task of facing Kelly and Leanne right now.

She could hear them outside the door, talking in low voices so as not to wake her. Abby slid off the bed and crept to the door as silently as she could. She put her ear to it just below the handle and listened.

"I'm really worried," Leanne was saying. "I've never seen her like that before."

"Yeah. That was just… scary," said Kelly. "You hear those… voices she was doing? Where the hell did that come from?"

"I don't know. I really don't."

"What about you? Are you okay, Lee? She gave you a pretty good boot back there."

"I'm… I don't know," Leanne said in a shaky voice. "I know that's not Abby. I know it." She paused. "But… what if it could be? She's… struggled with her mental health before. What if what happened to her mom is just too much for her to handle? I mean, I could see she was having a rough night even before she disappeared from MacReady's."

"Do you think that has something to do with it? You know as well as I do, the place was a mess when we left, and Abby was already gone. Do you think she saw something?"

There was a long, heavy silence before Leanne replied, "Something like what?"

"I don't know. Something that scared her off. Lee, she left her purse behind when she booked it. Her phone looked like somebody threw it down the stairs. I'd bet my apartment that something happened at MacReady's, and that's why she was freaking out. It wouldn't be the first time."

Another silence, and Abby could tell they were both thinking of the mirror incident. Leanne's next words were very carefully chosen. "You're right. It wouldn't." Then, she quickly changed the subject before Kelly could press it any further. "What did she mean she had to 'find Mr. Lockhart'? She wasn't talking about her old teacher, was she?"

"I don't know," Kelly said. "I know she liked Mr. Lockhart a lot, and I think he helped her out with some extracurricular stuff for a couple years, but he left Fred Banting years ago. Same time she did, I think. I heard he went back to England." A chair groaned as one of them got up and started walking around the apartment. The next time Kelly spoke, she was much nearer the bedroom door, and Abby held her breath so Kelly wouldn't know she was listening. "I don't know what to say, Lee. This whole thing is way above my pay grade. How long did you say it's been since she saw her therapist?"

"Nearly eight months."

"It might be as simple as that. It might be time for her to get some real help and get her head on straight."

"You might be right, but she'd never go for it. When she was seeing Dr. Bell, all she did was complain about 'Band-Aid solutions.' It would be like pulling teeth convincing her to go back."

Kelly sighed deeply. "Well… maybe it's time somebody else made the choice."

"Are you saying she needs to be committed?" Leanne asked.

"This might be the psych major in me talking, but let's look at the facts. Abby's had anxiety since we were kids, and none of the treatment she's had has worked for her. She doesn't ever talk about it, but I know she had problems with self-harm before she met you. There's a family history of mental health issues, and the last time she walked into this room, she had a violent psychotic episode right in front of us."

"Maybe you're right," Leanne said. "We need to think about what's best for her." There was a pause before she said, "You know, I… I said a prayer for her last night. First time in nearly two years I've actually gotten on my knees and prayed, and then this happens. It almost feels like a sign…"

"Maybe it is," said Kelly. "What's the line? 'More things in heaven and earth'?"

Abby pulled away from the door. She'd heard enough. Forcing back tears, she laid down on her side of the bed and stared at the wall. She knew she wasn't crazy. She knew it! But she'd always had Leanne on her side. If she couldn't even count on that anymore…

If you don't even deserve that anymore… said a nasty little voice in her head. Abby buried her face in the pillow. She had crossed a line today. She knew she had. She'd tried to fight the attack when it came on, but there it was. It didn't matter that it was unintentional, Abby had physically assaulted the person she loved the most. Who was to say it wouldn't happen again? If she crossed another line or, God forbid, if she started telling Leanne to 'go to sleep'… The thought of an institution started to look halfway decent when Abby weighed it against the possibility of really hurting someone she loved. And modern mental institutions weren't like the ones in the movies, were they? The overcrowding and abuse you read about in places like Bedlam or Riverview Hospital or Applegate Asylum didn't happen anymore. Besides which, Abby knew for a fact that her dad's room when he had been in a facility had been larger than her first studio apartment.

Abby reached over to the bedside table and picked up a framed photo that stood next to her reading light. It showed her, her parents, and Mr. Lockhart in the theatre at Frederick Banting Secondary School. Karen, Don, and Mr. Lockhart were all dressed nicely, while Abby wore a hideous pink Tudor-style dress that was too long in the sleeve and not wide enough at the hips. Despite this, she had the biggest smile of any of them.

The picture had been taken when Abby was in Grade 11, on the opening night of the school play: *Much Ado About Nothing*. Abby had played Beatrice. She rolled onto her back and held the picture at arm's length, staring at it and trying to convince herself that yes, it was true, there had been a time in her life when she'd been that happy.

Mr. Lockhart had given Abby the picture himself on the last day of her Grade 12 year, about a week before he left the school for good. If she closed her eyes, she could almost picture his classroom as it had been then: chairs stacked against the back wall; piles of old papers, used thumbtacks, spent staples, and faded posters cluttering up the desks; large cardboard boxes stacked around Mr. Lockhart's own desk, containing books and other supplies; and a dusty outline on the floor showing where the big wooden cabinet had been. She remembered how the man himself had been unsticking a *Jonathan Strange & Mr. Norrell* poster from the large whiteboard at the front of the room, and how he'd bounded over to greet her when she knocked on the door. The poster had been left hanging by two pieces of masking tape at its bottom corners.

*****

"Abigail!" he exclaimed with a smile. "Come in! Come in! What can I do for you?"

Abby shuffled into the room and stopped short. She cleared her throat and murmured, "I, uh, I heard a rumour that you were leaving at the end of the year and I guess I just had to... I dunno, see it for myself."

Mr. Lockhart nodded and looked around the room. "Yes, well, it's time for me to move on, I think. That's the problem with me: I always have to keep moving and try new things. I've been seven years at this school and I am absolutely gasping for a change of scenery!"

Abby laughed. "I know the feeling. So, where are you gonna go?"

"I'm not sure," Mr. Lockhart admitted. "Though I would like to go back to England for a time. It seems like I haven't been there in a hundred years."

Abby just laughed some more.

"What's funny?" Mr. Lockhart asked.

"I don't know... just... I'm just thinking about you. I mean, I've known you for seven years, but... you don't look like you've aged a day in all that time."

"Good genes, I suppose," Mr. Lockhart said with a shrug.

"Well, I... I guess I just wanted to say thanks for... I don't know, everything. You've been such a good friend to me these past few years," Abby said.

Mr. Lockhart blushed and looked away.

"What's up?" Abby asked.

Mr. Lockhart shook his head. "I feel like I should... give you a hug or something, but I'm concerned that might be the sort of thing the school district normally gets angry letters about."

Abby laughed and grabbed Mr. Lockhart in a powerful hug. A single tear rolled down her cheek as she sniffed, "God, I'm going to miss you!"

"There, there," Mr. Lockhart whispered as he gave her a gentle pat on the back. "I'm sure we'll see each other again one day."

They pulled away from each other and Mr. Lockhart reached into his pocket. "I want you to have something. To remember me by." Then he pressed the photograph into her hands.

"Oh my God," she groaned, stifling a laugh. "That stupid dress is going to haunt my nightmares."

"It certainly did make an impression. You know, I was rather proud to see you on that stage, young Henderson. You made for quite the sharp-tongued Beatrice. And that Colin McRae was rather a dashing Benedick," he added slyly.

Abby's face went pink. "I don't know if dashing is really my type these days," she mumbled.

Mr. Lockhart seemed to miss the implication. "Anyway, you've had quite a rough go of it these last few years, and I wanted to leave you with a reminder of the good times. If ever you should find yourself adrift, lost in a world that seems inescapably mad, I want you to look at that photo and remember: your friends are always with you. Even if you can't see them."

"Thank you," Abby said, as she put the picture in her back pocket. "Thank you for everything, Mr. Lockhart."

He shook his head. "Simon. You're not my student anymore, Abigail. You don't have to be so formal." He stuck out his hand and said, "Call me Simon."

Abby shook his hand and wiped back another tear. "Thank you for everything, Simon."

"Now go on and live your life. Your friends are probably waiting for you."

Abby nodded and turned toward the door, looking back briefly for a last wave goodbye. As she left, she could hear Mr. Lockhart talking to himself. "Top of the class, Henderson..."

*****

As the memory faded, Abby rubbed her eyes and looked at the photo-facsimile of Mr. Lockhart. "I wish I could talk to you," she told him. "I want to ask you so much. Why were you at MacReady's? Why does Meg want me to find you?"

Suddenly, the tiny photo-facsimile of Mr. Lockhart started moving. Abby sat bolt upright and breathed in through clenched teeth. In the picture, Mr. Lockhart removed himself from the trio of Hendersons, who remained statue-still. He looked at Abby—the real Abby, who held the photo in her frozen hand—and jerked a thumb over his shoulder. He cupped a hand to his mouth and mouthed the word *Behind.* He repeated the thumbing gesture and mouthed *Behind* again.

Abby looked behind her and saw a blank wall. She looked at the photo again. Mr. Lockhart was shaking his head. He held one hand up in the air, palm out, and turned it so that Abby was looking at his knuckles. He did this twice more and mouthed *Behind* again.

"Behind *you!*" Abby exclaimed. "Why didn't you say so?" She placed the frame on the bed, glass-side down, and opened the back with shaking hands. Blue sparks crackled on the white photo backing, moving to write a message in Mr. Lockhart's handwriting. It took Abby a moment to work out what the message said, as Mr. Lockhart's handwriting had always been appalling.

What the message said was: *You've opened the door. Now's the time to step through that door and see what lies beyond. Come to this address and you will find the answers you seek. Tell no one.* The address was written below and circled.

Abby doubled over, laughing to herself. "Oh my God. You sneaky, sneaky bastard! You knew, didn't you? All this time, you knew! Just like Meg said, this was all bound to happen, and you wanted to make sure it did!" She kissed the photo and whispered, "You. Are. *Good!*"

The door opened and Kelly poked her head in. Abby quickly hid the photo beneath a fold in the bedsheets. She tried to make her voice sound natural as she said, "Hey."

"Hey." Kelly looked around the room curiously. "Were you talking to someone just now?"

Abby shrugged. "Just woke up, really. I might have been yapping in my sleep."

Kelly nodded, but her voice sounded disbelieving. "That might have been it. How are you feeling?"

Abby exhaled. "Better, now. I'm feeling a lot better."

That, at least, was the naked truth.

CHAPTER 11

THE ANOINTED GATE

ABBY WOKE bright and early the next morning, before Leanne had gotten up for work. She walked into the living room and stopped herself before she tripped on the large purple yoga mat laid out in the middle of the floor. Kelly was on the mat, her back arched in a downward dog pose. When she heard the door open, Kelly looked up and gave Abby a nod. "Hi, Jaws. How are you feeling today?"

Abby inched around the yoga mat toward the couch where Kelly had been sleeping these last two nights. Kelly's blanket and pillow had been folded haphazardly and tucked against one arm of the couch. Abby sat down at the other end and stared up at the ceiling. "I feel like I wish people would stop asking me that," she muttered.

"Sorry?" Kelly said. She had moved from downward dog to the child's pose, and was now speaking directly into the yoga mat.

"I'm… I don't know how I'm doing," Abby said, shaking her head. "Tired."

"Rough sleep?" Kelly asked.

"That's one way of putting it." In fact, Abby hadn't slept much at all the previous night. Her thoughts had been consumed by Mr. Lockhart's moving photograph. When she went to bed, Abby had imagined herself going to the address he'd given her. Mr. Lockhart's old wooden cabinet had been there, and when Abby had tried to open it, she'd heard the Westminster Chimes clanging all around her, so loud that they made her nose bleed again. Then she had opened the cabinet, and Varr'rak the Shadow-walker had jumped out and seized her by the throat with one of his tentacles. He had laughed as he strangled her, and then she'd woken up. She'd spent the rest of the night staring at the dark ceiling.

"Well, I filled the kettle when I got up," said Kelly. She was looking at Abby from between her own thighs, the top of her head resting against the yoga mat. "You can have a cup of tea and wake up." Abby walked over to the kitchenette and poured herself a cup of tea. Kelly took up a warrior pose and asked, "So how come you're up so early?"

Abby thought of the picture, which she'd stuffed under her pillow just before she went to bed. It hadn't moved at all in the evening, but the message on the back was still there. Abby had checked a couple times just to make sure. As she had lain awake in bed, she'd decided that it had to be today. She had to find Mr. Lockhart and ask him every burning question that had been swimming in her mind since Varr'rak had attacked her. "Well, I figure I wasted half of yesterday in bed, so I need to make up for it today."

"You also had a serious panic attack yesterday and the night before that," Kelly pointed out. "Are you sure you're ready to go out and carpe the diem so soon? There's no shame in taking some time to do nothing and recharge your batteries, especially now."

Abby smiled a little. "I appreciate the concern, Kel. But I'm okay, really. Besides, it's not like I'm going to run off and climb Mt. Everest today. I'm going to have a shower, eat a decent breakfast, and then I'm going to go for a good long walk to clear my head."

Kelly raised an eyebrow. "A walk? In this weather?" Raindrops drummed on the window outside, and the sound carried from one end of the apartment to the other.

Abby looked her friend in the eye, nodded, and lied through her teeth. "Yeah, a walk. I thought I'd go down to English Bay for a while. That was…" She cleared her throat and looked at the mug of tea in her hands. "That was Mom's favourite spot."

"Oh," Kelly said. "Yeah, I get you. I can come with you, if you want."

Abby shook her head. "That's okay. I think I'd like some privacy."

"Whatever you need." Kelly got off her yoga mat and walked over to Abby. She stretched her arms out and asked, "Hug time?"

Abby put down her mug and blinked away tears. "Sure. Hug time."

*****

An hour later, Abby set out for the address Mr. Lockhart had given her. Leanne had got up and had breakfast by that time, and Abby hugged and kissed her goodbye before Leanne set off for work. However, Abby noted with some concern that Leanne didn't look her in the eye once all morning. The hug was also looser than Abby was used to, like Leanne was subtly trying to keep her distance, and it seemed like she was in a rush to get out of the apartment ASAP.

Before Abby left, she borrowed Kelly's phone on the pretext of sending a message to her dad, and conducted a Google Maps search for the address Mr. Lockhart had given her. It was a corner lot at the intersection of Clark Drive and East 6th, hardly a stone's throw from the East Van Cross monument. Abby committed the route to memory, gave Kelly her phone back, nipped into the bedroom and snuck the picture into her purse just in case, and then set out to catch the nearest SkyTrain.

When she finally reached her destination, Abby wondered for a moment if there'd been some mistake. Had Mr. Lockhart written down the wrong address? Or (more likely, given his shockingly bad penmanship) had she simply read it wrong? Either way, something was amiss, because there was nothing on the corner lot. There was an abandoned post office one door down, but that had probably been shut down some time in the late '70s, from the look of it. There was a pawn shop across the street with plywood covering its front window, but the corner lot was an empty patch of brown grass adorned with discarded grocery bags and cigarette butts. Abby reached into her purse and pulled out the picture. She double-checked the address on the back and confirmed that she had read it right.

Abby shook her head. This wasn't a mistake. It couldn't be. There was more to the puzzle that she just wasn't seeing, some kind of trick or clue. If Mr. Lockhart could throw light from his hands and make a photo move, what was stopping him from hiding an entire building if he really wanted to? She paced the empty lot for a few moments, carefully examining the grass beneath her. When she couldn't find anything there, she ran her hand along the wall of the post office.

The answer was well-hidden. If she hadn't been looking for it, Abby probably would have missed it completely. It was a small iron circle, no bigger than a signet ring, set into the wall about halfway down and masked by old graffiti. Carved on the circle was a strange rune that Abby thought she recognized, though the details escaped her now.

Below that circle was another circle of identical size, with a slot in it that looked like it would fit a key. But where was the key? Abby searched the lot for a few more minutes trying to find it, but she came up empty. Leaning back against the wall, she looked at the picture and said, "I don't understand you. I'm here now. Where am I supposed to go?"

In the picture, Mr. Lockhart held up both hands. He tugged at one sleeve and then the other to show he had nothing hidden up them, then made a fist with one hand and shook it in the air. He snapped his fingers and opened his fist with a flourish.

The picture got heavier. Abby turned it over and saw a little brass key taped to the back, right over the address. She peeled the key off the back of the photo and slid it into the keyhole. The key turned with a click, and Abby heard the chug of heavy machine parts coming to life on the other side of the wall. She backed away as a lot of whirring and clanking joined the continuous chug-chug-chug. Whatever was on the other side, it was way too big for this dusty old post office.

As the noises grew louder, the entire lot folded like construction paper. The ground Abby stood on became parallel with the wall, and the two surfaces moved toward each other, determined to become one. A steam whistle joined the industrial cacophony and Abby shut her eyes, worried that the wall of the post office would squish her when it met the grass. She felt the brief sensation of a warm bucket of molasses pouring over her head, and then everything just stopped. The invisible machines went silent, and the ground beneath her felt solid and stationary once more. Everything was dark when she opened her eyes.

"H-hello?" she called out. "Is anybody there? Mr. Lockhart?"

"For heaven's sake, Abby, I've told you once already! Call me Simon!"

Four wall-mounted torches ignited spontaneously, bathing the room in light and making Abby jump.

She stood at the end of a large octagonal room with great marble pillars at each corner, rising up to a high domed ceiling. On the stone walls there hung several grand tapestries, glittering so beautifully that they must have been woven with gold. A plush, purple rug covered the floor, with several tatty armchairs, scratched-up side tables, and a threadbare couch atop it, while a large wooden cabinet rested against one wall.

When she saw that cabinet, Abby almost felt like crying. Her last memory of it was its absence when he and she had parted ways. But it was here now. Breathless, Abby crept across the room toward the cabinet and held up a hand. She had to touch it, had to feel that it—that he was really there.

"I might not be your teacher anymore, but there are still rules," said a voice behind her.

Abby stopped dead and turned as a small shiver ran across her back.

Mr. Lockhart—Simon—was standing in the middle of the room, arms folded behind him, his face half admonishing and half giddy. Beside him was his machete-wielding partner.

Simon took a step forward and raised an eyebrow. "Abigail Henderson..." he said in a dramatic tone.

"Y-yeah?" Abby replied, a little unsure.

Suddenly, Simon sprinted forward and grabbed Abby in a bone-crushing hug, grinning from ear-to-ear. "It's about *bloody* time you showed up!"

Simon pulled away and looked proudly at Abby for a second. She blinked a couple times, dumbstruck. Everything she had wanted to say and all the questions she needed to ask suddenly flew out of her mind like air let out of a balloon. Her brain couldn't process the sensory information she was receiving, so she gave up and did the only thing that seemed natural.

She fainted.

"But I don't want to go among mad people," Alice remarked.
"Oh, you can't help that," said the Cat: "we're all mad here.
I'm mad. You're mad."
"How do you know I'm mad?" said Alice.
"You must be," said the Cat, "or you wouldn't have come here."
*
Alice's Adventures in Wonderland
Lewis Carroll

BOOK THREE:

THE GOSPEL TRUTH

CHAPTER 12

THE LETTERBOX

ABBY WOKE up stretched out on the threadbare couch, with an itchy wool blanket draped over her. She felt like she'd been asleep for years, but the chime of an old grandfather clock on the far side of the room told her it had only been about an hour.

Abby threw off the blanket and sat up, running her hands through her hair. Time and space had folded around her and transported her from an abandoned post office in East Van to a medieval dungeon that was furnished like an Edwardian drawing room. That cinched it: Abby Normal was going crazy. They'd shut her up in an asylum somewhere and she was bouncing off the walls of a rubber room, ranting about demons and magic and psychic visions. It was the only explanation.

"First, no, you're not crazy. And second, this place is called the Letterbox."

Abby looked up. To her left, Mr. Lockhart and his lovely assistant with the machete were standing under the arch of a stone doorway. A stone doorway which Abby knew for certain had not been there when she looked earlier.

"Mr. Lockhart," she said with a weak smile. "I, uh, I got your message."

"For the last time," he fussed, "call me Simon!" He strode into the room and sat down beside her. "And it occurs to me that you've not been formally introduced to my associate here," he added. "Abby Henderson, Natalie Arnaud. Star of stage, screen, and rescuing you from a fate worse than death."

Abby froze. This was the first time she'd really had a good, up-close-and-personal-type look at Natalie in the light of day, and the full picture was more intimidating than she'd realized.

Abby was tall for a woman, at 5'8" and change in bare feet, but Natalie Arnaud was some seven or eight inches higher than that. She had the musculature of an Amazon, but her skin was bizarrely sallow and seemed almost too tight in places, like they had tried to stretch it over her frame but found they didn't have quite enough. Her fingernails were cracked and yellow and, it occurred to Abby, her grey, sunken-in eyes had not blinked once since Abby had been watching her. The full effect was creepy and uncanny, like Grace Jones mixed with Frankenstein's Monster.

Abby didn't dare to say any of this out loud. She cleared her throat, tried for a smile and a nod, and squeaked, "Pleasure."

"Sorry I couldn't come back for you on your birthday," Natalie grunted. "I saw that cop with you and I didn't need that kind of attention."

"Yes, we've had some, er, trouble with local law enforcement before," Simon added. "We generally like to be quite a long way away when they start asking questions."

"S'okay," Abby mumbled, still staring at Natalie. Natalie stared right back as if she'd seen this kind of reaction before and was just waiting for it to be over. Abby quickly looked away and took in the room around her. "So… the Letterbox, huh?" she said, trying to diffuse any awkwardness.

Simon grinned and giggled like a child. "Get it? Because it used to be a post office and now it's our secret headquarters and—oh well, never mind, I thought it was funny."

Abby laughed, a little bemused. "Your secret headquarters is inside a forty-year-old post office?"

"Oh, it is so much more than that!" Simon beamed. "We've a library, a gymnasium, a laboratory, and a sauna! Among other amenities."

Abby looked sceptically at him.

Simon frowned. "You don't believe me, do you?"

Abby smiled. "Understatement of the year."

Simon jumped to his feet. "All right, clever clogs! I'll prove it!" He patted the wall with his hand and shouted to the ceiling, "Library, dear, quick as you like!"

A heavy wooden door under another stone arch appeared right where Simon's hand was. Abby didn't even see the wall shift or morph or anything; one second, Simon was leaning on cold stone, and the next second, it was bird's eye maple. Shaking her head in disbelief, Abby got up from the couch and scurried over to the door, groping and pawing at it for an excessive length of time to make sure it was really there.

The door swung open helpfully, like the Letterbox was showing off. *Oh, the door's real, all right, Abby imagined it saying, and wait till you see where it leads.*

The door opened onto a spectacular library lined with forty-foot-high shelves, upon which there were more books than even the Olde Curiosity Shoppe could contain. The floor was covered with a lush, red velvet carpet and there was a large mural on the domed ceiling of a group of people in rich green and gold robes standing in a field. They looked so lifelike Abby almost thought they were moving.

As she stepped into the library, she asked, "How the hell can you fit all of this in an old post office?"

"Well, it's not *technically* a post office, strictly speaking," Simon replied as he joined her in the library.

Abby turned to him with a raised eyebrow. "Then what is it, strictly speaking?"

"When you turned the key on the outer wall, did you notice how everything sort of folded? Like the very fabric of space-time was retracting in on itself?"

"You know, now that you mention it, that did kinda stick out," Abby deadpanned.

"Yes, quite so. Well, you see, Abby, that fold in reality was created by a device known as an Anointed Gate."

"A what?"

"It's a very complex piece of magical technology which can latch onto two locations in space at the same instant in time, and temporarily reshape the matter around those two locations in order to draw them together into itself, so that the two locations exist, for the briefest of moments, at very nearly the same coordinates. With an Anointed Gate, it is possible to travel instantaneously from one end of the universe to the other."

Abby looked to Natalie for help. "Am I supposed to have understood that?"

Natalie shrugged. "Best just to smile and nod politely when he gets like this."

Simon patted Abby on the shoulder. "Look, all you need to know is that that keyhole activated a portal which took you from East Van into the Letterbox."

Abby turned back to Simon. "Okay, well, you still haven't answered how this all fits into a post office."

"Ah, yes, that's the brilliant part. The Anointed Gate out there is not just a portal between two points on Earth; it's a portal between two dimensions. All these rooms, these walls that make up the Letterbox, they are a pocket dimension. A tiny alternate universe tucked away inside the regular universe. And this pocket universe does not have the same dimensions as the world outside, so we can fit a hell of a lot more into the Letterbox than we could into that old post office. The Anointed Gate you stepped through has one anchor in the bosom of our own *terra firma*, and the other wrapped around this little custom-built parallel reality."

Abby blinked. "Uhhhh…"

"Smile and nod," Natalie reminded her.

Simon led Abby out of the library and shut the door, which quickly turned back into a stone wall. She sat down on the couch, while Simon took the chair opposite and Natalie hung back in the corner. "Mr. Lockha—*Simon*," she corrected herself, "what's really going on here? Why am I so important to the Deacon?"

"You already know the answer to that, Abby. You just don't realize it."

"Sorry?"

Simon sat back and folded his arms. "Tell me, Abby, what do you know of the Enlightening?"

In her head, Abby heard the *click* of a key turning in a lock, and suddenly the answer was right there in her mind, like it had always been there and was always supposed to have been there. Another *click*, and it escaped onto her tongue and then past her lips. Without thinking, she answered, "The Enlightening is an arcane ritual wherein the Following will sacrifice a Gospel in the prime of her years to Azna'ghal, thus opening a door between this world and the next. The blood of 23 demons must be drawn and collected in a vessel made of pure oak. The Deacon offers his own blood as first tribute, in order to show his loyalty, with the vessel passing to each subsequent acolyte in order of how many lives they have taken in Azna'ghal's service. Once the blood of the loyal has been collected, the Deacon will force the sacrifice to imbibe and induce in her a trancelike state called a Bridge. The Bridge opens the mind and allows the Gospel to transcend this world and cross over into the Elsewhere, where she may communicate freely with any spiritual entity she wishes and even offer up her own body as a temporary vessel, so the spirit can enter our world for a limited time. Normally, the Gospel is supposed to be able to control the Bridge, but they say that when a Gospel ingests the blood of a demon, that demon gains the ability to take that control away from her. By taking away her control of the Bridge, a demon like the Deacon could force the Gospel to open her mind to a malevolent entity like Azna'ghal, and he could gain total and permanent control over her body, thus freeing himself from his prison in Hell, and allowing him to wage a new war on the gods."

Simon nodded. "But there's a catch, isn't there? What about the Alignment, Abby?"

Abby snapped to attention again and blurted out, "The old histories tell us that the Enlightening can only be performed under very specific astral conditions, when the magic binding Azna'ghal to the netherworld is weakest. These conditions are known as the Alignment, and their occurrence in the universe is highly unpredictable. The last known Alignment occurred for nine days in the spring of 1914, its epicentre being in a village in the western part of Yorkshire, in the north of England."

As the shock of that much exposition wore off, Abby blinked and slapped a hand over her mouth, like she had just uttered a terrible profanity in the presence of the Queen. She looked at Simon and asked, "Where the *hell* did all of that come from?"

Simon shared a knowing look with Natalie and said, "That was you, Abby. You're remembering."

"What am I remembering?"

"Everything you need for the coming battle."

Abby remembered what Varr'rak had said, about her and the Deacon: *The peace between you and he ends this night.* "That's how this has to end, isn't it? That's how this was always going to end. Me and the Deacon, in the arena, one on one."

"I'm afraid so," Simon answered. "The Deacon's been after you since you were born, Abby. A long time ago, Natalie and I vowed to safeguard you in case anything happened to your parents, and to give you the tools that you needed to defend yourself. We have been watching you from the shadows for many years."

Abby nodded. "You knew Varr'rak would show up at MacReady's."

"Well in advance of his arrival, I'm afraid. But we couldn't warn you ahead of 9:28pm, per the terms of a contract to which we were all bound."

"That was my mom's deal, yeah? The one she made with the Deacon?"

"Broadly speaking," Simon answered. "The Deacon's terms were literally peace and quiet: a cessation of open hostilities between us and the Following from the time the deal was struck until the moment you turned 25, at which point you would be given over to him as an offering. But you had to be kept in the dark about it all, lest you try and prepare yourself in any way to fight them off when the time came."

"Jesus… how could she agree to that?"

"I'm sure only she could tell you. It is one of the great regrets of my life that Natalie and I weren't there that night. If we had been, your mother and the Deacon would never have made that deal."

Natalie piped up. "Obviously she felt some buyer's remorse at the end. For better or worse."

A thought suddenly struck Abby, and she gratefully latched onto the chance to change the subject. "Hold on. If I was supposed to be kept in the dark, why do I know so much as I know? How can I remember about the Following and the Enlightening and all of it if there's nothing to remember? Why do I keep feeling like there's a part of my brain that I never realized was there the whole time? Why do I keep getting these damn headaches and nosebleeds?"

Simon stood and cleared his throat. "Ah, yes. I am sorry about that, but I'm afraid it was unavoidable."

Another nail pierced Abby's grey matter, followed by another explosion. She swooned as her inner eye took her back to Frederick Banting Secondary, where she saw herself sitting on the floor of the classroom, listening as Simon read from the *Historia minor*.

"In the earliest days of recorded history, the earth was dominated by three races," he said. "First were the humans, the mortal children of the lesser gods, made in their image to cultivate and protect Middangeard, the natural world. Then there were the demons, spirits from the Elsewhere who entered Middangeard and were made flesh by the gods. Lastly came the Vanguard, the keepers of True Magic. The Vanguard were not spirits like the demons, but at the same time they were something more than simple flesh-and-blood primates. They were a powerful race of spellcasters and magicians, possibly more powerful than any mortal force that has existed in this world before or since their time. Terribly brilliant, fantastically long-lived, and brewers of some of the finest mead you will ever taste. The Vanguard acted as mediators between the demons and the humans, who loved nothing more than to wage war on each other and would use whatever primitive conjurations were at their disposal to trick and bedevil their opponents at every turn.

"There was peace for a time, but eventually the demons raised an army under Azna'ghal, said to be the first demon who came into being, and waged war on the other races. This Last Great War of the Ancients raged for 1500 years across every dimension and plane of existence. After centuries of unspeakable bloodshed, the Enlightened Council of the Vanguard—the most powerful and holy beings in Middangeard—summoned all the strength they had and banished Azna'ghal and his armies to Niðerdæl—the lowest realm of the Elsewhere, which we today call Hell. Unfortunately, the energy required to accomplish the banishment spell drained the Vanguard of their life force completely, and they died out shortly thereafter. The entire race was wiped out as a result of that terrible war and the secrets of the ancient magicks were thought lost forever. Or... very nearly, at any rate."

Abby watched as Simon smiled sadly to himself. Then the scene disappeared in a blinding flash and she was returned to the Letterbox. Simon was looking at her like she was a scientific experiment on display.

"I... I remember now!" Abby stammered. "Jesus, yes, I remember! I mean, how could I forget?! You taught me... everything! The Deacon, the Enlightening, the Gospels... you were teaching me all those years, and I never even knew it!"

Simon broke into a mad grin and spun on his heels. "Top of the class, Henderson! Top! Of! The! Class! You see?" He turned to Natalie. "You see, Natalie?! I told you it would work and it bloody well *worked*!" He jumped onto the couch and hollered, "Simon Phineas Lockhart, you are a genius!"

Natalie raised her hands and tried to talk him down. "Okay, okay, Simon, easy! Yes, it worked, and yes, you're a genius, but... let's try to take it down a notch!"

Simon hopped off the couch and flicked a hand through his hair. "Sorry, sorry, yes, it's just I love it when I'm brilliant."

"I don't get it," Abby said. "What's brilliant? Why couldn't I remember?"

With a cunning grin, Simon paced around the couch, speaking with his hands. "The Deacon had your parents over a barrel. They couldn't tell you anything about your powers or about the Enlightening or else they'd be violating their contract with him, in which case the consequences would have been very bad indeed, but I tricked him, you see! I discovered a loophole! It wasn't breaking any rules if you forgot the information you learned as soon as you learned it, so I told everything to your subconscious mind. Every Wednesday lunch, from the week after you turned fourteen until you graduated, I put you in a magical trance called a Mind Lock, and I snuck bits and pieces of the truth in the back door, until you had everything you needed to know. And every time I woke you from the trance, I instructed you to forget the lesson until the contract expired, and you could learn without consequence. Thus, I ensured you would have everything you needed when you needed it, while honouring the letter of the contract! And now... here we are," he said with a flourish.

Abby was quiet for a minute. When she was young, Mr. Lockhart had always felt like a big practical joke that the universe was playing on her. Nobody as ridiculous and spectacular as he was could really exist in her shitty life without some strings attached. But he did. He was who he was without any asterisks or conditions or bet-hedging. It felt like cheating, to think that Abby Normal—the girl who got kicked around by life at every turn—could have someone like Simon Lockhart to turn to. But there he was. There he still was, unflinchingly unchanged.

When the silence continued on past the 90-second mark, Simon started to look a bit awkward. He cocked his head to one side and narrowed his eyes, like he was trying to read Abby. In a puzzled voice he asked, "What's... what are you smiling at?"

Abby leaped to her feet and wrapped her arms around Simon. "Oh *God*, I missed you!" she exclaimed with a grin.

Simon felt he had no choice but to grin back and return the hug. "Top of the class, Henderson."

Even Natalie cracked a smile.

*****

Abby spent the next few hours by herself, meditating in a chamber deep within the Letterbox. Simon explained that the headaches and nosebleeds were a side-effect of all her knowledge trying to force its way from her subconscious into her conscious mind. Meditation would help her relax and safely draw the information out of hiding at her own discretion.

By mid-afternoon, she had re-learned everything Simon had taught her way back when. He let her take a half-hour for lunch, and then he escorted her to the gymnasium, where Natalie was waiting to administer Abby's physical exam while he conducted the oral. In practice, this meant that he would lob questions at her from across the room while Natalie goaded Abby into trying to attack her and then knocked her to the padded floor in a series of increasingly rough and painful holds, blocks, and throws.

"What," Simon shouted, as Abby hit the floor with a thud, "is an aura?"

Abby grunted and rose from the mat. "An aura is a projection of the mystical energy that surrounds and passes through all creatures born of Earth and the Elsewhere, and someone's aura will vary in strength according to their magical ability!" She jumped back as Natalie threw a punch at her head. "Every living creature radiates an aura, and it is possible to read an aura and understand the creature's innermost spirit!" She dodged another punch, and threw a jab at Natalie's midsection, which Natalie blocked easily. "It takes rigorous training before a Gospel can read auras consistently, but when they can, it's the purest method there is of reading others' minds!" Natalie came in with a roundhouse kick, but Abby caught it in mid-air and held Natalie's leg aloft. Natalie smiled, shifted her weight, and fell onto her back. Abby yelped and fell with her, and the next thing she knew, Natalie's legs were wrapped around Abby's neck. "Again," Natalie commanded.

Abby was getting stiffer and sorer as Simon kept bombarding her with questions and Natalie sparred with her. From a tight headlock, she tried to explain that the "Last Great War of the Ancients" was a misnomer, because there had been so many smaller conflicts between humans and demons since the beginning of time that magical scholars could not agree on whether these battles constituted one war, or several, or whether the entire history of combat between good and evil could be summed up as a single never-ending cold war.

As she dodged a flying kick aimed at her head, Abby explained that it was considered a sacrilege for the Following to remove their robes without verbal permission from the

Deacon, like if they needed to go undercover. Ducking under Natalie's leg so she could scurry around behind her, Abby enumerated the demons' weaknesses.

"You have to destroy the heart or the brain!" She aimed a kick at the small of Natalie's back. "But the weapon has to pass through a flame kindled by a religious authority before it can do fatal damage!" Natalie turned and swept the kick aside. "Ugh, dammit! That's called cleansing in holy fire!" Abby adjusted her stance and jabbed at Natalie's head a few times. "They're compelled by holy writ to truthfully answer any question asked in the name of God!" Abby threw out her left hand to fake Natalie out, and then rammed her right fist into Natalie's face.

"Oof!" Natalie stumbled back and her hands flew up to her nose. Abby seized the opportunity and kicked Natalie in the stomach.

"And," Abby panted, as Natalie dropped to her knees, "and they can't stand the touch of religious totems, or the sound of people praying. It's agony to them."

"As long as..." Simon prompted her. Abby was now walking over to Natalie to offer her a hand.

"As long as the person holding the totem or saying the prayer really believes in that power," Abby replied. "If an atheist tries to hold a demon off with a cross, say, it won't do jack sh—"

As Abby reached for Natalie, Natalie grabbed both her wrists and spun around. Abby went flat onto her back and Natalie climbed on top of her. She was smiling, and seemed more than a little amused that Abby had managed to hit her. "Not bad," she said with a nod. "Again."

*****

It was almost twilight before Abby left the Letterbox, stiff and sore all over. Some of the hits Natalie had given her while they were sparring were starting to turn into obvious bruises, and Simon instructed her to drink from a small green glass bottle he was carrying with him before she left. "If you go home looking like that," he said, "you may have to answer some difficult questions. Best to avoid that while you can."

There was a homemade label on the bottle, written in Simon's infamous hand. The label read:

GRANNY LOCKHART'S HOME-STYLE BONNESANTE POTION

Provides relief from cuts, bruises, broken bones, minor amputations

Not for use if you:

Are currently pregnant or breastfeeding

Have a heart condition

Are a zombie, ghoul, vampire or any manner of undead

WARNING: Not for use on critical wounds. Always seek the aid of a credible physician/wise woman/hoodoo priest for permanent restoration of health.

Abby looked sceptically at the bottle for a moment. Simon gave her a reassuring nod, and she drank it with some trepidation. As soon as she passed the empty bottle back to Simon, her body started to tingle as it repaired itself from the inside. She felt re-energized and alert, and the pain disappeared completely. She looked at her right arm, where there was a particularly noticeable red patch on the inside of her elbow. Before her very eyes, the discolouration faded away until it looked like she'd never been hit at all.

"There is one more thing," he added, and he passed Abby a small package wrapped in brown paper. Abby ripped it open and found a large black-and-purple crystal inside, like the one her mother had had in her car.

"This is a Vokarion crystal," Simon explained as he reached into his shirt and pulled out an identical-looking crystal that was hanging around his neck. "It's a telepathic amplifier. Vokarion crystals tune into a person's brainwaves and establish relays between each other so we can stay in constant communication. Much more reliable than a mobile phone, especially for people like us."

"What do you mean, people like us?" Abby asked.

"I'm sure you've noticed by now, there's not a single electronic or digital device in the Letterbox," said Simon. "That's because powerful magic greatly interferes with the normal flow of electricity in modern machines. When the two mix, electronics tend to malfunction in very unusual ways, or stop working entirely. Even low-level magic like your own may cause electrical systems to degrade faster than normal."

Abby nodded. "I do have to change the lightbulbs in my apartment pretty often. I always thought that was just shitty wiring."

"Fortunately, there's not a single electrical component in a Vokarion crystal, so it's not subject to the same issues. I've got one, Natalie's got one, and so long as you've got one, we'll be able to talk to one another, day or night. The brilliant thing is you don't even have to talk. Just think what you want to say and the crystal will pick it up all the same. Go on, try it out."

Abby closed her eyes and concentrated. *Testing... testing... one, two, three...*

Simon's crystal glowed as her words reverberated around the room. "Testing... testing... one, two, three..."

Abby opened her eyes. *Whoa, trippy...* she thought.

"Whoa, trippy..." the crystal repeated. Everything the crystal said had an echo to it, which made the words sound very spooky and ethereal.

Abby giggled and closed her eyes again, concentrating hard on what she wanted to say next.

Simon's crystal glowed brightly as Abby's voice boomed, "I! AM! OZ! THE GREAT AND POWERFUL!"

Simon rolled his eyes and tucked the crystal back into his shirt. "Thank you, Abigail. I think we've established that it works."

Abby opened her eyes and grinned cheekily, front-tooth gap on full display. "Sorry. It's kinda fun." Then her voice echoed from the crystal again: "Simon, you must go to the Dagobah system and learn the ways of the Force from Yoda."

Simon shook his head. "The Vokarion crystal is not a toy. It is an elegant magic, for a more civilized age." At this, he gave Abby a sly wink, and they both started laughing.

It was a long way from the Letterbox back to the apartment, so Natalie offered to give Abby a ride in her car—a very tired-looking blue 1959 Ford Thunderbird with a missing tail light, a large scratch in the driver's door, and a rear bumper that looked like it was being held on by a copious amount of duct tape and fervent prayer. Abby gratefully took the offered ride, though she was unsure if the car would even make it in one go.

Miraculously, it did. When they got to within a few blocks of Abby's building, Abby told Natalie to let her out and she'd be able to find her way home from there. She didn't want to show up in front of the building in a car that was more than twice her age, driven by a mysterious corpselike woman with a large machete strapped to her leg. What would the neighbours say?

After Natalie drove off, Abby popped into a jewellery store across the street from her building. The small, elderly Chinese woman behind the counter looked up at Abby through thick glasses, smiled at her, and asked in heavily accented English, "Can I help you?"

Abby nodded and said, "Yeah, I think you can." A devilish smile crept across her lips. "What can you show me in a nice cross?"

CHAPTER 13

MEET THE NEW BOSS...

GENERALLY, LYDIA Clifford liked a quiet house. Her hearing had started to go when she was in her early 50s, and the hearing aids she now wore sometimes worked a little too well. If a car backfired or a motorcycle raced by the Olde Curiosity Shoppe, she'd feel the noise right down in her bones.

She'd always been sensitive to noise. That was half the reason why she and Duncan had never had children. Children were only good for two things: making noise and making a mess.

And yet, she now had a dog which performed the same functions admirably.

The dog had been Duncan's idea: a big, salt-and-pepper husky named Samson, who had a bark that could wake the dead and breath that could stop a charging bull. In his waning years, Duncan Clifford had devoted himself entirely to Samson. He'd fed him the best leftovers from the table and walked him twice daily at 8:00am and 8:00pm. But Duncan had been gone for some years now, and it was down to Lydia to handle Samson's feeding, walking, etc.

Despite her thoughts on noise and messes, Lydia too had learned to love Samson in her own way. Maybe it was because caring for him kept some shade of Duncan alive. When she arrived home each night, Lydia would turn down her hearing aid, letting Samson bark himself silly when she came in the door. Then, after dinner for one and a glass of wine from the box, she'd take him for a long walk. Some nights they'd be out for an hour or more.

Arriving home this night, Lydia Clifford was struck by the uncharacteristic silence of her little house on Gilmore Avenue. Samson should have started a barking fit the moment she stepped out of her car. He should have been scratching at the front door before she had her keys out of the purse. But he didn't. If she pressed her ear to the door, Lydia couldn't even hear his claws clicking over the hardwood floor.

She felt an uncomfortable tightness in her gut and jingled her keys in the lock. "Samson? Samson?" She whistled and jingled, but Samson still didn't answer. Lydia wondered if she'd locked the back door that morning. But Samson wouldn't have wandered far, surely? He was a notorious homebody.

She threw open the door and the cold hit her like a slap in the face. Lydia gasped as she stepped in the house and dropped her keys in the bowl by the door. She held her bony hands together and blew on them, clenching her jaw so her teeth wouldn't chatter. She wrapped her scarf tighter and called once more: "Samson?"

A single, contented *woof* answered her from the den, and Lydia exhaled. Stupid, really, to be so paranoid. He'd probably just been sleeping when she came in. Lydia fiddled with the thermostat controls and re-adjusted her hearing aid to normal levels. She stopped again. There was music coming from the living room: a low, male harmony, like a church hymn.

Makes me love everybody
Makes me love everybody
Makes me love everybody
It's good enough for me...

Below that, Lydia could hear Samson's tail thumping as it wagged on the floor. And somehow, she didn't think he was wagging for her.

"Hello?" she called as she stepped into the living room. "Who's in here?"

From the armchair in the corner, there came a languid sigh. "There's just something about a dog, isn't there?"

Lydia gasped and stared at the tall, white-haired stranger sitting in her favourite easy chair. The man, who was dressed in a strange floor-length robe, was giving Samson a friendly scratch under the chin and asking him who was a good boy.

"Simple animals, really," the man said in a cool, alluring Southern drawl. "All the brains of a toddler, but give them a tennis ball or a hambone, and they're yours for life. I lose track of all the lives I've lived at this point, all the faces I've worn, but I've known a few dogs over those many lives. Them, you can't ever forget."

Lydia stepped forward and called Samson to her. "What do you want, sir? I don't have any money!"

The man smiled and let Samson go. "Honestly, do I look like a man who needs money?"

"All right then, I demand to know who you are!"

The white-haired man looked up and adjusted his half-moon spectacles. "That would take a very long time to explain, Lydia."

Lydia froze and swallowed. "Have we met?"

"Not formally," said the man. "Though Abigail may have mentioned me. The Deacon? The bogeyman in her mirror?"

"Abi — do you mean that Henderson girl?"

The Deacon nodded. "So you do know her."

"She's been to my store, yes, but I don't see what's so important about that!"

The Deacon looked Lydia in the eyes, and the room suddenly grew even colder. His thin, lipless smile looked like a knife wound in this light, and he hissed curtly, "If you will stop interrupting me for two seconds, maybe I can explain."

Lydia said nothing. The Deacon nodded his thanks and stood. "I'll make this short," he promised. "You see, I've made some plans in which Abigail Henderson plays a vital role. Unfortunately, convincing her to play the role as scripted has been, shall we say, challenging. The direct approach has failed, so now I have to exploit her pressure points."

"Kha'al Azna'ghal ixxi. Kha'al Azna'ghal ixxi. Kha'al Azna'ghal ixxi."

Lydia screamed. Two tall figures in shapeless black robes leapt from the shadows, then grabbed her arms and yanked them behind her back.

"Wh-what are you doing?!" Lydia pleaded. "What is this?!"

The Deacon raised his right hand. His index finger turned black and the nail grew and thickened into a long, sinister talon. "Relax, Lydia. The procedure only takes a minute."

"P-procedure? What are you going to do? Why me? If this is about Abigail, I promise you, I hardly know her!"

"I'm aware of that. But Leanne Waller is your employee. You see, Lydia, I've studied Abigail Henderson for many years now. She's become a bit of a hobby of mine. And if I've learned one lesson in all those years, it is this: if you want to attract Abigail Henderson's attention, you must first attract Leanne Waller's attention."

The Deacon raked his claws across Lydia's throat. Blood poured down the front of her blouse and onto her pants. It spattered onto the floor, and steam rose from the puddle as it met the cold air. Samson sat patiently at her side, his head cocked curiously at the odd spectacle.

Lydia collapsed to her knees as the world went dark. The last thing she saw was the Deacon, his free hand outstretched toward the growing pool of blood, reciting a chant in some profane dead language.

*****

Thick black smoke rose from beneath the blood. The Deacon flicked his wrist toward Mrs. Clifford, and the smoke shot straight up her nose and into her slack mouth, filling her body from head to toe.

The Deacon raised his hood and hissed, *"How do you feel now?"*

Lydia Clifford's hand went to her throat. The wound had closed perfectly, like it was never there. If Lydia Clifford were still alive, she probably would have been grateful.

But Lydia Clifford was dead. It was the demon now living in her body who spoke: *"I am ready to serve, O Deacon. To see the will of the Eldest One done is my only wish."*

"Good. Then rise, Sel'uk the Inquisitor. Rise, and embrace our covenant."

As Sel'uk stood, one of the robed acolytes looked at Samson and said, *"What of this creature?"*

The Deacon looked at Samson. The dog sat patiently at the Deacon's feet, his tail brushing the floor curiously. He'd evidently decided by now that the Deacon was someone he could trust to give him scratchies.

The Deacon smiled and pressed his black claw into the palm of his other hand, opening a narrow cut. He closed the same hand into a fist and let it bleed for a moment.

The blood of a demon is a toxic substance to most creatures in Middangeard. When a demon possesses a living soul, their dark magic corrupts every cell of their host body like a virus. Blood cells are among the first to be afflicted, and if the blood of a demon-possessed creature is transferred to another living being, it can corrupt the body and mind of that being in similar ways to a full-tilt possession, without causing them to lose control to a demon consciousness.

This was what the Deacon was counting on when he opened his hand and kneeled before Samson. He extended his palm, inviting Samson to lick it, and the dog obliviously complied. As Samson lapped up the Deacon's blood like it were water, the leader of the Following preached to the faithful. *"And he took the cup, saying, 'Drink ye all of it, for it is my blood of the covenant.'"*

The Deacon stood, and the acolytes prayed. Samson started to cough and hack. His shoulders shook, and his back twisted into a high arch. Thick, foul-smelling drool dripped from his lips, and when next he opened his mouth, he vomited a spray of black slime onto the floor, tinged with red flecks of blood.

Samson dropped to the ground and rolled onto his back, yelping in pain and fear as the Deacon's blood took him. His black sick smeared into the fur on his forelegs, and as he rolled and convulsed, tufts of his coat fell into the carpet. The Deacon smiled as Samson's claws stretched and hardened, reshaping themselves to resemble his own. His coat grew out, shaggy like a lion's mane, but the flesh beneath rushed after it as the dog's bones and muscles engorged and lengthened. The hair on Samson's back sloughed off like seeds from a dandelion and green scales erupted from beneath his skin, spattering Mrs. Clifford's carpet with more blood as they cut him from within.

Samson howled once more, and as he did, the call got deeper and more jagged. Angrier. The dog lay still on the floor for a moment, adjusting to his new body. Then the Deacon whistled. *"Here, boy."*

Samson gave his head a shake and stood up. His eyes blazed with a green glow as he looked up at the Deacon. His muscles were stiff and alert, as if awaiting orders.

"Go," said the Deacon, and he pointed at Sel'uk. *"Go with your mistress."*

Sel'uk raised an eyebrow, slightly bemused by the Deacon's logic.

The Deacon saw his acolyte's curious look, and his shoulders twitched in what might have been a chuckle. *"You are a fearsome combatant, O Inquisitor. But even you should never underestimate the value of a hunting dog."*

CHAPTER 14

THE VISITORS

"DO YOU truly believe she is ready, Brother Dearest?"

A gloved hand hovered over Abby's snoring face and came to rest on her exposed shoulder.

"I think she will surprise you, Sister Dearest. I have watched this child, and I rather get the sense that she is made of stronger stuff than you give her credit for."

"Have you watched her, or will you watch her?"

"Both and neither. I promise you, she is, was, and will be ready."

It was two in the morning, the day after Abby had discovered the Letterbox. A man and a woman stood over the bed, watching as Abby did her best impression of a ferret trapped in the drive shaft of an eighteen-wheeler. One of Abby's hands was tucked under the pillow, clutching a small silver cross necklace she'd purchased from the jewellery store on the way home. Leanne was fast asleep on the other side of the bed, completely oblivious to what was going on around her. (God bless the man who invented ear plugs.)

The woman—whose hand was vibrating with every snore—lifted it off Abby's shoulder and gently stroked her on the cheek. "If she wishes to move forward, she must be."

Abby stopped snoring and blinked her eyes open. "Snuh—whuh—zuh—whuz goin on?"

The man smiled and bowed his head respectfully. "Ah, I was hoping you would join us, dear."

Abby flipped on the light and sat up, thrusting the cross out in front of her and glaring menacingly at the two strangers. They were both very tall, dressed in Victorian-looking formal wear, and smiling kindly, as if they had encountered Abby during a pleasant stroll through the park, rather than sneaking into her bedroom at two in the morning when she was dreaming rather inappropriate dreams about Jennifer Lawrence. The man wore a pair of pince-nez spectacles on the end of his nose, and the woman was holding a parasol above her head. When either of them spoke, it was with the kind of clipped, sophisticated voice that English newsreaders had. The kind of voice that sounded rehearsed, and which you knew in the back of your mind no actual person spoke with naturally.

The woman very calmly plucked the cross out of Abby's hand and placed it on the bed. She tutted and said, "Please don't insult us with this frivolous idolatry. We are quite above such concepts, I assure you."

Abby shook her head and rubbed her eyes. "I'm dreaming," she assured herself. "This is just another crazy, screwed-up Abby Normal dream..."

The man shrugged. "Perhaps it is, but why should that change anything? How can something be any less real simply because it is the product of fantasy?"

"For example," the woman added, "to the untrained outsider, a monster reaching out of a mirror to attack a frightened young girl would surely seem like the product of fantasy, yet here we are."

"What do you know about that?" Abby asked. "Who the hell are you two anyway?"

The man bowed. "We are who we say we are."

The woman nodded. "And nothing more."

Facing the woman, the man took her by the hand and said, "We are two halves of a third."

"Part of a set of four, which is five," replied the woman as she put her hand on the man's shoulder.

"You will meet our remainder in time," finished the man as he wrapped his other hand around the woman's waist.

Abby stared in bemusement as the two did a box step around the room. That hadn't actually answered anything. Trying a different tack, she asked, "What do you know about the Deacon?"

"We know only what we see," said the woman.

"We will see what we have seen," added the man.

"And we have seen what we will see," said the woman, as the pair concluded their dance.

"What we see now," the man said in an ominous whisper, "is a half-truth."

"Which you perceive as a whole reality," the woman said in an equally ominous whisper.

Each put a hand on the other's shoulder, and they spoke to Abby in unison. "You see the Deacon as a singular entity: one mind and one body."

"You should," said the man in the woman's voice, "instead see the sum, greater than the constituent parts."

"When the parts will not mesh, the sum is vulnerable," said the woman in the man's voice.

"Listen now to what we tell you: it happened before, and the eyeless face saw it all."

"Something is missing. Someone is not whole."

"He looks like your friend, but sometimes she sleeps."

"When what we have said is true, we hope only that you will place some trust in us."

The light flickered for a second, casting the room into darkness. When it came back on, the mysterious duo was gone.

And then Abby woke up.

CHAPTER 15

CURIOUSER AND CURIOUSER

JESUS, DAD, no wonder they put you in a padded room.

Abby put down her toothbrush and spat into the sink. She'd been sweating bullets ever since she'd returned from the Letterbox yesterday, trying to keep a straight face while her mind raced with thoughts of the Enlightening, the Following, and the War of the Ancients. Trying to pretend that life was still normal. She hadn't been at it for 24 hours and she felt ready to crack. But keeping up the masquerade for 25 *years*? It was a miracle her dad hadn't snapped years earlier.

Abby reached for the mouthwash. She had to tell Leanne. If she didn't, if Leanne found out the hard way when the Following kicked down the front door one night, Abby would never forgive herself. But what would Leanne even say? Leanne had always taken her Christian faith seriously, but there was still a big difference between the theological abstract of Heaven and Hell, and a literal war between the two.

Abby spat a blue spray into the sink and stared into the mirror. "Leanne, I have something… impossible to tell you. It's probably going to sound crazy, but it's important. And it needs to be said before anything—"

She cut herself off. The face in the bathroom mirror looked very unimpressed.

"Jesus, do you realize how stupid you sound?" Abby's own reflection retorted. "That's never going to work."

Abby shook her head. Dammit, this wasn't going to be easy.

"The Deacon is real. The Devil is real. Hell is real. The Deacon works for the Devil and he wants me for a ritual that will—"

"Try again," Mirror-Abby grumbled.

"Hey, you know what? At least I'm pitching!" Abby snapped at herself. "You're just being all… judgy."

"Oh, you want a pitch? How's this? Hey, Leanne! Guess who has two thumbs and could kick-start the apocalypse! This gal!"

"Gee, thanks for the help."

There came an urgent knock at the bathroom door, and Abby turned away from her reflection. Unhelpful bitch.

"Abby? Are you nearly done in there?" Leanne asked from the other side.

Abby thumped her head against the wall and sighed. "What's the worst-case scenario here? She calls you crazy and walks out the door? At least she'll be safe that way…"

Another knock. "Abby? Are you talking to someone in there?"

"Sorry, I'm just… yapping to myself…"

"Well, could you do it out here? I'm in a hurry."

Abby opened the door. Leanne was already dressed, munching on a crust of toast and clutching a thermos. Kelly had her yoga mat laid out on the other side of the couch, and gave Abby a wave from her bridge pose as Abby cleared the way for Leanne.

"Thanks," Leanne said, polishing off her toast and wiping the peanut butter from her lips. "I'm already behind."

"What's the rush?"

"New consignment of books at the Shoppe. Mrs. Clifford wants me down there ASAP so we can catalogue them." She was brushing her teeth as she said this, so Abby only caught about half the words.

"I won't keep you then," Abby said. "But listen, Lee: there's something we have to talk about. It's, uh… it's pretty big."

Through a mouthful of toothpaste, Leanne said, "Tell me after work. Consignment days are always crazy, but Mrs. C. sometimes lets me off the hook early if the Shoppe's not too busy. Soon as I get home, I'm all yours."

She spat, rinsed, and ran for the door, but Abby grabbed her arm.

"Wait a second, wait a second, Lee: before you go, I just want to check that we're cool. After what happened the other day. We are cool, right?"

"Sure, we are." Leanne went for the door again, but Abby still held her.

"I mean it. You know that wasn't me, right? Whatever happened to me, I couldn't control it. I'd never want to hurt you, I promise."

Leanne stopped. "I know. But I'd be lying if I said it didn't freak me out. I think it still does, and there's a tiny piece of me that isn't convinced it can't happen again."

"Be honest, Lee: do I frighten you?"

Leanne shook her head. "Not you, Abby. Never you. But lately, these visions of yours… these dreams… that… fit you had … that all scares the bejeezus out of me." She wrapped her arms around Abby. "It's almost like… you haven't been you this week. This is some new part of Abby Normal I've never seen before, and I'm not sure I know how to respond to her."

Abby hugged back. "But you're still there, right? Like you said you'd be? Foreverways?"

Leanne straightened up and met Abby's eyes. She studied her partner for a moment, and then she smiled and nodded. "Foreverways."

"Thank you."

Leanne finally left for real. Before she closed the door, she said, "By the way, Adam called before you woke up. He said he had to talk with you. Today, if possible."

"Did he say why?"

"He just said to meet him at MacReady's when you had the chance."

"Isn't Mac's closed for repairs?" Abby said.

Leanne just shrugged and left.

*****

Mac's was indeed closed for repairs. When Abby arrived at the restaurant later that morning, she found half the lower level sealed off. Hammers, saws, and drills pounded behind temporary plywood walls, and a few hard-hatted construction workers with armloads of lumber and equipment were the only living souls Abby saw on the way up to the manager's office.

The staff-only section of MacReady's was generally undamaged. Abby found Adam in his office behind the kitchen—though to call it an office was perhaps overly generous. Abby had always thought of it as a broom closet with ideas above its station. There was just enough room for a computer desk, a phone, a filing cabinet, and a couple of chairs. And that was when the room was empty.

"I've been told you wanted to see me?" Abby said as she entered.

Adam looked at her like she'd just told him his mother was dying. "Thanks for coming in, Abby. Please, have a seat."

Abby sat, her shoulders tense and her back stiff. "What's this about?"

"Relax, Abby. You're not in trouble or anything. I just wanted to ask you some questions."

"What about?"

"I'm not sure if you're aware, but the night you were here for your birthday is the same night the restaurant got smashed up. I've been looking over the security feed from that night, in case the vandal or vandals showed up on film."

Abby gulped. In the heat of the moment that night, she'd completely forgotten about the restaurant's extensive network of cameras. "Did, um, did the cameras see anything?"

"No, that's the strange part. Around 9:30 that night, all the cameras just switched off. They came back online half an hour later, but half of them weren't working right. I had to go into the computer and reboot the entire system to get them running properly."

"Huh. Weird."

"That was what I said. And I thought this was pretty weird too." Abby gulped again as Adam turned the monitor so she could see it. He hit a button on his keyboard and the security footage played. It showed a wide shot of the second-floor lounge. In the bottom third of the screen, Abby saw a tiny Samantha hastily rise from her seat and stumble across the floor before ultimately knocking over a busboy.

Abby shuddered as the scene played out again. Bodies falling, dinnerware smashing, people panicking. There was no audio in the security feed, but Abby remembered all the noise perfectly, and the soundtrack played in her mind in perfect sync with the video.

Adam paused the video. The last of the patrons had fallen, and one figure stood alone among the chaos. "The feed goes dead two seconds later," he said. "But that right there…" He tapped the frozen image on the screen. "That's you, isn't it? Everyone here drops like a bag of sand, except you."

Abby opened her mouth, searching for words that weren't there.

"Don't worry, I'm not accusing you of causing any of this damage. Don't take this the wrong way, Abby, but you don't have the strength to do half of what was done to this place. But I wonder if you might have seen or heard anything after the cameras went down."

"Well, I… I mean, uh… look, Adam, no matter what I tell you, you're not going to believe it…"

"I won't know that until you tell me something."

"Okay, um…"

The brilliant excuse Abby was trying to concoct died before it started. Suddenly, her ears rang and she swooned toward the desk. She inhaled sharply as her nose began bleeding into her mouth, and when she closed her eyes, she saw the Olde Curiosity Shoppe. A strong, icy gale was blowing, rattling the wooden sign and the tatty awning. The door opened suddenly, and Abby saw Leanne shivering behind the counter. The radio on the counter crackled to life, and Abby heard the same creepy hymn that had played when Varr'rak attacked.

It was good for the prophet Daniel…
It was good for the prophet Daniel…
It was good for the prophet Daniel…
And it's good enough for me…

Abby snapped back to life with a gasp. "Leanne!"

Adam blinked. "Leanne? Abby, what's your partner got to do with this?"

Abby snatched the telephone off the desk and dialled the Shoppe's number from memory.

"Abby! Abby, what are you doing?"

"Sorry, Adam, I—I have to make a call!"

"What on earth are you talking about?"

Abby ducked out of the office with the phone to her ear, holding her breath while it rang.

Leanne answered after a minute. "Olde Curiosity Shoppe Used and Antique Books, how may I—"

Before Leanne could finish, Abby blurted out, "LEANNE?!"

"A-Abby? Is that you?" Leanne asked, a little surprised.

"Yeah, it's me! Listen, Lee, I know this is going to sound crazy, but you have to get out of there!"

"What? Why?"

"I think something bad is about to go down at the Shoppe! You have to go now!"

"Abby, what on Earth are you talking about?"

"It's really tough to explain over the phone, but... look, would you believe me if I said I had a vision?"

"A vision?"

"Yes! Of you, of the Shoppe, of... something *really, really* bad! You have to trust me on this!"

"Well, what was it that was so bad?"

"It would take too long to explain now! Please, just trust me that something isn't right!"

"Abby, Abby, slow down!" Leanne commanded. "Look, I can't just up and leave, but I'll talk to Mrs. Clifford and try to make up an excuse. Would that make you feel better?"

Abby breathed a sigh of relief. "Yes! Thank you! Just so long as you can get out of there!"

"Okay, I'll see what I can do. Right now, I have to get back to work. Mrs. C. is already giving me one of her looks."

Leanne hung up. Abby dropped the phone and reached down her shirt. She pulled out the Vokarion crystal Simon had given her and thought hard.

Hello? Hello, Simon? Are you there?

She heard a voice in her head. *Abigail? Is that you?* It was Natalie.

Natalie, hi! Is Simon there?

No, he's out running an errand right now. Is everything all right?

I had a vision. I think the Following are going to go after my partner.

Dammit. I thought they might pull something like this. Where are you?

MacReady's.

Okay, stay there. Remember, you're the endgame. If they're targeting your loved ones, it's to draw you out. I'll come pick you up.

Do it! Drop everything and get in the car NOW!

Okay, I'll be there soon as I can!

That was the last Abby heard. She hid the crystal under her shirt again as Adam stepped out of the office. "Abby!"

Abby handed the phone back to him and smiled. "Sorry! I had to make an emergency call."

"Abby, are you feeling okay? Do you want some water or something?"

"That might help, yeah. Is the kitchen sink still running?"

"No, no, no. You stay here and rest. I'll get it."

"You're the boss."

Abby took her seat in the office again, trying to stop herself from shaking.

*****

Leanne hung up the phone and walked into Mrs. Clifford's office on the second floor of the Shoppe. The old woman was flipping through a stack of consigned books, checking each volume for damage. On the floor, around the corner of the desk, Leanne could see Samson's tail swishing back and forth. It wasn't uncommon for Mrs. Clifford to bring the big dog with her to the Shoppe and let him hang around the office.

Mrs. Clifford didn't look up, and her voice came out like a rusty hinge. "Who was that on the phone?"

"Abby."

Now Mrs. Clifford looked up, with a face like she'd just eaten the sourest lemon in Creation. "Hasn't that girl gotten herself into enough trouble lately? What did she want?"

Leanne had never been much of a liar, but this performance could have played at Cannes. "There's been an accident at home. It sounded bad. I-I need to go check on her, see if she's okay."

"Now?"

"Right now. Please, ma'am, I think something awful has happened."

Mrs. Clifford, unfortunately, was not on the jury at Cannes. "Absolutely not! I need someone to cover the front and I'm far too busy to do it myself."

Going for broke, Leanne turned on the waterworks. She snivelled pathetically and forced herself to cry. "Please, Mrs. Clifford. I heard sirens in the background! I think something's really wrong!"

Mrs. Clifford shook her head. "I'm sorry, Leanne, but I can't spare you. You can keep your cell phone on if you like. If it's very serious, you can leave on your lunch hour. Not a minute before. Now go mind the front of the store. I think I hear the door."

Leanne gave Mrs. Clifford a weak "Thank you" and walked back downstairs. At the bottom, she straightened up and muttered under her breath, "Cranky old witch." There was another word she was thinking of, that rhymed with 'witch' and started with a 'b,' but of course she would never say something like that out loud.

The door slammed behind her and Leanne jumped. Bad case of the nerves today.

Leanne liked to think she was supportive of Abby. She always listened and tried to understand when Abby got freaked out, but some deep-seated part of her had always wondered how much of what Abby saw was actually there. As far as Leanne could tell, none of Abby's visions had ever taken that final step toward reality. Even when the Deacon had come at her from the mirror: Leanne noticed that, in the retelling, Abby had specified that the Deacon never actually touched her. Leanne had always been able to take the stories in her stride because, as far as she could ever tell, they were just stories. Shadow puppets on a wall and flickers in the corner of the eye.

But the last week had been different. Something had done some serious damage to MacReady's. Then there was that fit Abby had had in the apartment the day after her birthday. Kelly had used the word "possessed" then, and it fit perfectly.

The flicker in the corner of the eye wasn't just a flicker anymore, and Leanne feared that something much more sinister was at work.

Leanne had been raised in a devoutly Catholic household. Though she had walked away from the capital 'c' Church after she came out, she still held a firm belief in the sacrifice of Jesus Christ. But it was only logical that if that force of good existed in the world, there had to be an opposing force of evil. Leanne was as sure that there was a Devil as she was that the sun rose in the east. If the flickers in the corner of Abby's eye were real, if the Deacon was out there somewhere, then he was surely an agent of Satan. Things like the visions that Abby described simply could not exist in the face of Leanne's God unless they had the power of Hell at their backs.

Leanne shivered as she took her place at the front counter. Little crystals of frost were starting to creep up the window panes at the front of the store. Above her, the lights flickered, and she cowered away from the shadows on the wall. She wrapped one hand around the little cross around her neck and squeezed it tightly for comfort.

*****

When Leanne had left her alone, Sel'uk the Inquisitor set down her book and paced slowly across the office, feeling the floorboards creak beneath Lydia Clifford's feet. The Thing That Had Been Samson gave a grunt and a low growl as it stood, then it padded over to her side.

Sel'uk the Inquisitor looked out the office door and observed the half-dozen customers on the floor below. One of the customers, sensing her, looked up and gave her a quick, imperceptible nod. Sel'uk nodded back at the undercover acolyte and Samson's tail wagged low.

The six acolytes on the floor were all blessed to go without their robes, as was Sel'uk herself. The Deacon had impressed upon them an honour they could not forsake or fail to uphold.

Sel'uk knew that the Deacon had positioned more acolytes nearby, and she promised herself there would not be a repeat of the… what was the word the humans used? Clusterfuck. There would not be a repeat of the clusterfuck at MacReady's.

Sel'uk reached behind her back and drew a thin, curved dagger from the leather sheathe hanging at her waist.

"Kha'al Azna'ghal ixxi. Kha'al Azna'ghal ixxi. Kha'al Azna'ghal ixxi."

CHAPTER 16

INQUISITION

ADAM GAVE Abby a reassuring smile as she finished her water. "How do you feel now?"

Abby put the glass down and exhaled. Well, she was still scared as hell, waiting on tenterhooks for Natalie to show up, and adding water on top of her rattled nerves just made her want to go to the bathroom.

She smiled back and said, "Fine."

"Good to hear. Now, I think you were going to tell me something about this video?"

"Was I?"

"Yes. Something I wasn't going to believe, apparently."

"Oh. Okay. Um, I... Well..." She got up from her chair. "Actually, sorry, Adam, do you know if the bathrooms up here are still working? I'm just feeling kind of out of it today, could probably use a minute to just get my head on right."

"Abby, why won't you talk to me? Is there something wrong?"

As Abby opened her mouth to speak, blood streamed out of her nose and her brain exploded again. The ringing in her ears was so loud that she couldn't hear herself screaming when she fell out of her chair and started tearing her hair out.

Adam moved around beside her and shook her violently. "Abby?! Oh my God, Abby?!"

Abby gritted her teeth as more images rushed through her mind, crashing against the walls of her brain. She saw Mrs. Clifford, creeping toward Leanne with a nasty look on her face. She saw bookshelves toppling all over the Shoppe and she saw a pair of broken black-framed glasses lying abandoned in a pool of blood.

Abby started to hyperventilate as the images continued to march in front of her eyes. She could hear Adam frantically asking what was wrong, and she gasped, "LEANNE!"

"Leanne, what about Leanne?"

"Leanne... trouble... danger... have to... get help!" Abby hissed through clenched teeth.

"Help! Right!" Adam picked up the phone and dialled "9" and "1".

"NO!" Abby cried. "Need... help... need... Natalie..."

At that moment, a shadow fell across Abby's face as Natalie filled the doorway, her face tight with determination and her machete strapped to her thigh. She looked at Adam and shouted, "Get back!" as she pulled Abby to her feet.

"What's going on? Who the hell are you?" Adam spluttered.

"I'm someone who can help a lot more than you can!" Natalie said. She turned and marched Abby out of the office.

"She has to go to a hospital!" Adam shouted as he ran after them.

Natalie turned on him and glowered. "Seriously, you sure you want to do this?"

Adam was over six feet tall, but he was quite soft and doughy. The woman in front of him clearly was not. Adam wisely decided that this was not someone he wanted to fight with, and he backed off. Natalie nodded at him and said, "Good call."

The Thunderbird was right outside MacReady's with its engine still running. As Natalie hurried her to the car, Abby asked, "How'd you know where I was?"

"You kidding? I heard the screaming half a block away. Where to now?"

They buckled their seatbelts and Natalie reversed out of the alley.

"The Olde Curiosity Shoppe!" Abby said. "I'll give you directions!"

*****

Leanne shivered again and crossed her arms. She rubbed her hands up and down her forearms and gave an apologetic smile to the customer she was servicing. "Winter's coming, huh?" she said as she punched a few buttons on the register.

The customer said nothing, but cocked her head to one side and gave Leanne a vague shrug. The light above them buzzed and flickered. Leanne tried to ignore it and said, "And how will you be paying today?" She did her best to keep her voice level and friendly, but she couldn't stop thinking about how Abby had screamed at her.

The little FM radio on the counter hissed and Leanne jumped back a step. As she reached out to touch the dial, it crackled and hissed again. This really scared her, because the batteries had died two days ago.

And then the static faded, and a song began to play.

It was good for the prophet Daniel...
It was good for the prophet Daniel...
It was good for the prophet Daniel...
And it's good enough for me...

As the customer reached into her purse for her wallet, Leanne cranked the knob on the radio and turned the volume to zero. But as soon as she took her hand off the receiver, it started again, louder than before.

Leanne picked up the radio and stuffed it under the counter, behind her purse, her jacket, and her water bottle. The sound only seemed to get louder, and the hairs twitched on the back of her neck.

The customer slid a few crumpled bills along the counter toward Leanne. One of them was a $2 bill with a robin on its face. Leanne blinked in surprise. The $2 bill hadn't been in circulation for 20 years…

Leanne slid the $2 back to the customer and shook her head. "Sorry, I don't think I can accept this."

The customer grabbed Leanne's wrist and squeezed. Leanne jumped, but the woman's grip was strong. Leanne couldn't move her hand at all. Couldn't even lift it off the counter.

"What is this?" she demanded. "What are you doing?"

The woman didn't say anything. She just reached over the counter, grabbed Leanne's other wrist, and then pulled her over the counter and threw her to the floor near the stairs.

Leanne coughed and blinked in shock. She was heavy for her size—she'd never denied it—but the customer had just thrown her around as easily as a pile of dirty laundry. She adjusted her glasses, which hung askew from one ear, and tried to sit up.

"I told you I needed you here, Leanne."

Leanne gulped as Sel'uk the Inquisitor and The Thing That Had Been Samson descended the stairs together. All the customers in the Shoppe dropped what they were doing and turned to look at Leanne, whispering a low chant of *"Kha'al Azna'ghal ixxi."*

Leanne pulled herself backward on her elbows. That chant was just as Abby had always described it, and Leanne suddenly understood on an intimate, primal level exactly how her partner must have felt as a girl, looking into that bathroom mirror.

"Y-you're with him!" Leanne stammered. "The Deacon sent you, didn't he?"

Sel'uk the Inquisitor smiled. *"Ooh,"* she cooed, *"pretty AND smart. I like this one already."* She looked at one of the acolytes and snapped, *"Take her."*

The acolyte grabbed Leanne by the front of her shirt. She squeezed the acolyte's wrist with both hands and screamed, "Stay back! For the love of God, stay away from me!"

Something bizarre happened then. The acolyte shrieked and pulled its hand away. The skin on its palm was burning red, and the little gold cross around Leanne's neck seemed to be glowing.

One of the other acolytes lunged at Leanne, but she unclasped the chain and held the cross at arm's length. As the acolyte reached for her, she pressed the little cross against the back of the creature's hand. Smoke rose from the point of contact. The acolyte screamed and drew away, clutching an angry cross-shaped burn.

Leanne looked at her little necklace in amazement. It was true, then. The Deacon's forces were creatures of Hell. They must be, if they reacted so badly to His Name.

As Sel'uk raised the curved dagger, Leanne closed her eyes and hugged the cross to her chest. She began to pray as loudly as she could. "Deliver me, O Lord, from the evil man: rescue me from the unjust man…"

The cross glowed brightly in her hands and she felt a warmth pass through her, as if she were sitting in a hot bath and nursing a mug of hot chocolate. The acolytes covered their ears and wailed in pain and horror. All except for Samson. Though his mind had been corrupted, his soul was still his own. It did not have the taint of Hell on it that made the demons so averse to faith. Sel'uk noticed this after a moment, pointed at the dog, and told him to, *"Shut her up!"*

The Thing That Had Been Samson bared his teeth and hunched his shoulders, ready to tear Leanne's throat out. She opened her eyes and screamed as he leaped at her. She jumped to her feet and ran toward the tall bookshelves that dominated the floor, shoving the cross into her pocket. With her prayer cut short, the demons recovered their senses. If they could not hear the Word of God, they would not be hurt by the Word of God.

Samson pursued Leanne, barking furiously and spraying the walls and the floor with black spittle. Near the first row of shelves, there was a wheeled trolley loaded with books. Leanne grabbed the trolley with both hands and heaved it at the creature, knocking him to the floor and sending books flying everywhere.

In the few seconds that bought her, Leanne bobbed and weaved through the shelves, scattering books on the floor behind her. But Sel'uk just raised her free hand and jerked two fingers toward the ceiling. With a low groan, the shelf nearest the demon slowly floated off the floor like an inflating balloon, disgorging its contents onto the floor.

The six undercover acolytes lifted their hands in similar fashion, and more shelves heaved and groaned and rose into the air. Heavy tomes fell all around Leanne, and she curled into a ball to protect herself, earning multiple nasty whacks on her arms, her shoulders, her back, and her butt.

When the dust had cleared, the bookshelves were all lying comfortably on the ceiling, and Leanne was completely exposed. The demons moved their arms in unison, and four of the heavy shelving units slammed down around her, penning her in. Sel'uk thrust her arms out in front of her, and the makeshift cage shot across the Shoppe before crashing into the back wall, taking Leanne with it.

"For your own sake," Sel'uk grumbled, *"I suggest you not make this any more difficult than it has to be."* She approached the cage, and Samson stood by her side glaring at Leanne.

Leanne tried to push one of the shelves out of her way, but it was far too heavy even without fifty pounds of books weighing it down. Through a gap in the shelf, she looked at Sel'uk and asked, "Why are you doing this? What do you want with me?"

"With you?" Sel'uk laughed. *"Idiot child, it is Abigail Henderson we want!"*

The front door exploded out of its frame and flattened one of the undercover acolytes as Natalie reversed her

Thunderbird halfway into the Shoppe. She looked at Abby with a smirk. "I mean, you can't ask for a better entrance line."

Abby was gripping the dashboard with both hands and feeling extremely sick. "Can't quip right now," she gasped. "Too busy not throwing up."

As the demons picked their jaws up off the floor, Natalie jumped out of her seat and hurdled over the back of the car to the Shoppe floor. She pointed at Abby, who nodded and pushed a button on the car's dashboard. The Thunderbird's trunk popped open, and a long pump-action shotgun jumped from the trunk into Natalie's hand. As soon as she caught it, she fired at the acolyte who'd been hit by the door. Leanne screamed and covered her ears as the top half of the demon's head exploded.

Natalie pumped the shotgun and smiled. "Fun thing about the age of gunpowder," she said, looking at Sel'uk's dagger, "modern guns take really well to the holy-firing treatment." She pointed the gun at Sel'uk's head. "Now drop the knife."

Abby climbed out of the car and came to stand beside Natalie. She was gulping down water from a plastic water bottle and holding one hand over her stomach. "I am never getting a ride with you again," she stammered.

Sel'uk stared at Abby incredulously. *"You actually came here yourself? You are even stupider than you look!"*

Natalie grinned. "Is that what you think?" She looked at Abby and shouted, "NOW!"

Abby threw the water bottle high into the air. Natalie shot it to pieces and a fine spray of water splashed on the demons. They screamed as their bare skin crackled and popped into burning red blisters wherever the water touched them, and they shrank away from the Thunderbird. Amid the confusion, Natalie blew the heads off two more acolytes.

"Holy water," she announced. "Courtesy of Rev. Mathieu Aucoin at Holy Rosary Cathedral. And there's more where that came from."

Abby's hands tightened into fists, and she squared her shoulders in what she hoped was an intimidating display. Seeing the demons brought low like this suddenly made her feel a lot braver. "If you hurt her," she said, nodding toward Leanne, "we'll burn every one of you assholes like Christmas dinner."

"You're bluffing," Sel'uk growled.

"You want to put money on that?" Abby snapped.

Sel'uk snarled and flicked her wrist again. Two more shelves slammed to the floor and onto the hood of the Thunderbird, blocking the front window and the rest of the doorway. *"A counter-offer: there are three of us and one very angry dog, and there are two of you. If you surrender to me now, Henderson, I will not spill your mate's intestines on the floor."*

Abby sighed. "I really wish you hadn't said that." She reached into the trunk, pulled out another plastic bottle, and threw it right at Sel'uk. Natalie fired again, and this time all the water hit Sel'uk in the face.

Sel'uk fell to her knees, shrieking and clawing at her eyes. The lenses of her glasses had shattered and smoke leaked out from beneath her eyelids. Abby took off in a run toward the back of the Shoppe and Leanne's wooden prison. One of the prostrate acolytes grabbed her by the ankle, and got a savage kick in the face for its trouble.

Samson jumped at Abby and brought her to the ground with his front paws on her chest. She caught his jaws with her hands and tried to push him off as he barked and snapped at her.

Natalie pulled a small knife out of her boot and threw it to Abby. In a blind panic, Abby rammed the blade into Samson's foreleg and shoved the dog on top of the acolyte that had tried to take her down. The acolyte snarled and reached for her as she got up, but she pulled the knife out of Samson and stabbed the demon in the eye.

Bright orange flames gushed out of the wound and Abby jumped back with a yelp. Fire spread over the rest of the demon's body, and Samson rolled off with a howl of pain. In seconds, the demon was a pile of ash and the flames arced up before plunging down into the floor. When the flames had disappeared, Abby grabbed the little knife, tucked it down the back of her pants, and kept running before Samson got his second wind.

Natalie reloaded her gun from an internal pocket of her trench coat and weaved around behind the final acolyte. She blew the back of its head open and it, too, burst into flames. Sel'uk hollered, *"Samson! Kill!"* and the dog charged at Natalie. She trained her gun on him, but he skittered to one side as she fired and the shot pinged off the floor.

Natalie fired again, but Samson jumped right over the bullet, pointing all his teeth and claws at her. His jaws clamped down on her right forearm and she howled in pain before falling back into the Thunderbird's back seat.

As Abby passed, Sel'uk swung the dagger at her. The demon missed by a country mile, and for a second Abby looked right in Sel'uk's eyes. They were red and watery, with milky white pupils. The skin around Sel'uk's eye sockets was badly scarred, and she seemed to be staring right past Abby. Sel'uk looked around wildly as Abby ran toward Leanne's cage, but she made no attempt to pursue.

She's blind, whispered a voice in Abby's head. She started laughing as she leaped over a pile of books from the trolley, and this thought doubled her courage.

Sel'uk got to her feet and jumped fifteen feet into the air. She landed on the second-floor railing like a great bird of prey, stuck two fingers in Mrs. Clifford's mouth, and whistled.

Abby stumbled and fell to her knees. She felt hot iron nails in her brain, and in her mind's eye, she saw fifteen Following acolytes flying—swear to God, flying—over the rooftops toward the Shoppe. Their auras were like wildfire, shining red and angry, and Abby saw the beasts inside the human bodies—scaly, horned, and cloven-hoofed—whooping and hollering like mandrills fighting over a mate.

"What is that?" Leanne asked. "Abby, what was that noise?"

Abby picked herself up and lurched over to the cage of bookshelves. She wiped the blood from her nose and tried to make a gap in the shelves wide enough for Leanne. "These clowns are just the advance guard! There's a whole platoon of these ugly bastards heading right for us!"

From the back seat of the car, Natalie suddenly howled and stood up, holding the thrashing, kicking Samson above her head. Abby jinked to one side and Natalie threw Samson into the bookshelf facing Leanne. As the big dog rolled on the floor in a daze, Abby grabbed the side of the shelf and told Leanne to do the same. Together, they pushed the shelf over, and it landed on Samson with a nasty *crunch.*

Abby helped Leanne over the upturned shelf. Leanne's eyes were shining behind her glasses, and she looked through the gaps at the dog. He was unconscious but breathing weakly. "Poor Samson," she whispered.

"Trust me," Abby said. "That thing is not Samson anymore."

"Then what is it?" Leanne snapped, blinking away tears. "Abby, what the hell is going on?"

The bookshelf blocking the front door exploded into a hail of wood chips. An acolyte raced into the Shoppe and tackled Natalie mid-air, driving her across the Shoppe and pinning her to the back wall.

Abby grabbed the Shoppe's heavy cash register and lifted with all her might. It must have weighed 50 pounds, but she worked up enough momentum to smash it across the acolyte's head. When the demon fell, Natalie gave Abby a thumb's-up and hacked open its skull with her machete.

Leanne shrieked as the demon ignited. Abby set the register back down and gasped, "Short version: I'm psychic, they're demons. They want me for a ritual that'll unleash this big bad super demon, and that shit's not gonna fly!"

The front window smashed as a Following acolyte punched straight through it, groping blindly between the shelves, and three more acolytes touched down in front of the Thunderbird.

"Can we fight through them?" Abby asked.

"Not forever," Natalie admitted. She gave a short, sharp whistle and the Thunderbird rumbled as the engine turned over. A newly-polished AK-47 jumped out of the trunk into her hands, and she dropped two acolytes without breaking her train of thought. "Good thing is, we don't need forever. Just enough time for you to get the hell out of here." She fired another burst that nearly ripped the third acolyte in half.

"What about you?" Abby asked. Three more acolytes were storming toward the Shoppe even now.

"I can handle myself!" Natalie shouted. "Just go! Remember, you're the endgame!" She screamed with rage as she fired the gun again.

"Come on!" Leanne said. "The fire escape! Upstairs! We can slip out the back!"

Abby looked up. One blind demon that way versus a whole squad out front? Wasn't much of a competition. They bolted up the stairs and the sound of gunfire stopped. Abby looked back and saw a fresh magazine jump out of the trunk into Natalie's hand. She had a feeling that Simon had placed some enchantments on the car for situations just like this.

Sel'uk's head perked up at the sound of Abby and Leanne's footsteps. As the two reached the top, Sel'uk jumped down from the stairs and swung her dagger wildly. She got lucky, and Abby went down screaming with one hand clamped over a shallow gash in her side.

Leanne stopped two stairs from the top. "Ohmygod! Abby!" she cried.

Sel'uk looked in Leanne's general direction and stuck out her hand. Invisible force lashed out and smacked Leanne in the chest, sending her tumbling back to the bottom of the stairs. Abby screamed, "Lee!" and reached out to catch her partner. She missed.

Sel'uk looked at Abby and smiled. *"Found you."*

Without thinking, Abby headbutted Sel'uk in the stomach. The demon doubled over, and Abby pulled Natalie's boot knife out of her waistband. She weaved behind Sel'uk and stabbed the demon in the back. As Sel'uk reached behind her to pull out the knife, Abby grabbed Mrs. Clifford's thin wrists and twisted her arms into the small of her back. Then she slammed the old woman's face down onto the railing.

Mrs. Clifford's nose broke and Abby hurled Sel'uk over the railing down to the first floor. She booked it into the Biographies section as Sel'uk reached out and grabbed the lip of the floor with her free hand. The second floor of the Shoppe was reserved for nonfiction and reference materials, so Abby was on the lookout for any heavy textbooks or large atlases that might take the wind out of Sel'uk's sails.

Sel'uk panted and puffed as she hauled herself back up over the railing and staggered toward the shelves. She twirled the dagger in her hand and called out, *"You cannot run forever, Gospel! You have a duty to the Eldest One!"*

Abby knew exactly what Sel'uk was doing. The demon was trying to get her making noise so she would give herself away. But that gave Abby the advantage, didn't it? She could lead Sel'uk wherever she pleased as long as she made the right amount of noise at the right time. She wormed her way into the Canadian History section and called back, "Is that what you think? You really think I have to live up to some great destiny no one bothered to tell me about?"

"If you don't like the arrangement, talk to your parents! Oh. Oh, I forgot…"

Abby bit her tongue and listened to the demon's breathing. Sel'uk was getting closer. Abby crept along the shelf and shoved a few books to the floor on the other side. She watched as Sel'uk started walking in that direction, and then she doubled back the other way.

"I'll give you points for tenacity," Abby said. She paused for a moment to let Natalie's gunfire carry across the Shoppe. "You assholes just don't quit, do you? No matter how badly you get beaten! I don't know whether to call it stubbornness or masochism at this point!"

"The Eldest One's will is great," purred Sel'uk. *"His might is superior."*

From Canadian History, Abby weaved into World History. She was walking in a crouch to keep her footsteps quiet and pushing books through the shelf every so often. "You know," she mused, "that actually makes me wonder. "If Azna'ghal is so all-powerful, if he really is the terrifying elder god you all make him out to be, then how come I'm three steps ahead of you guys?"

Sel'uk scoffed. *"Do you think you are winning this fight? I have you here, do I not?"*

Abby doubled back around a shelf. Sel'uk was three aisles down and moving parallel to her. "Oh, you absolutely do, and I'm not saying otherwise. But think about it for a second: my girlfriend has worked here for as long as I've known her, and we've been together three years. How many times do you think I've stopped in to say 'hi' on my day off? How many books do you think I've bought here?"

"What is your point?" Sel'uk asked suspiciously.

"My point, jackass, is that I've spent ages walking through these shelves. I have learned a lot about how the Shoppe is constructed." She paused where she stood and gripped the shelf tight with both hands. "And if there's one thing I've learned in all that time, it's that World History is a frigging death trap." She gritted her teeth and pushed the shelf toward Sel'uk. It groaned noisily and fell into the next one over, which fell into the next one after it. Abby ran back toward the stairs as the shelves toppled like dominoes and several tonnes of wood and paper collapsed on the screaming Sel'uk.

Abby covered her ears as the whole building shook with the impact. Natalie and Leanne looked up at her in wide-eyed shock and the demons finally broke through the line. Natalie got three rounds off before the gun was empty again. She whistled at the car, but no spare magazine jumped out at her.

"Dammit!" Natalie threw down the gun and bolted up the stairs, hauling Leanne to her feet along the way. "So, tell us where this fire escape is again?"

"This way!" Leanne said. Abby took her hand as they scrambled over the fallen shelves toward the fire escape.

Varr'rak the Shadow-walker howled his unmistakeable howl and the ceiling lights exploded in a shower of hot glass. The metal fire door bent inward as something slammed into it on the other side. Then a shadowy tentacle punched right through it and lashed at the girls. Natalie fell to the ground screaming as the razor-sharp point of the tentacle sliced across her face, from the corner of her mouth all the way up to her hairline.

Abby pulled Natalie to her feet, and Varr'rak's tentacle split into four points that sunk into the door like a grappling hook. He howled again and ripped the fire door clean out of its frame. Leanne grabbed Abby's hand and pulled her and Natalie toward the office, yelling, "Not that way! Not that way!"

They scrambled into the office and Leanne locked the door behind her. Natalie heaved Mrs. Clifford's desk onto its side and shoved it against the window. Varr'rak howled again and Leanne pulled the little cross out of her pocket. She began to recite her psalm once more, and raised her voice to a shout when she reached, "Keep me, O Lord, from the hands of the wicked!" Her cross began to glow white again and Varr'rak stopped dead. "Preserve me from the violent man!"

Natalie pulled out her Vokarion crystal and said, "Simon, I don't know where the hell you are right now, but we could really use your help!"

The crystal glowed as Simon's voice reverberated around the office. "Just think the address at me! I'll be there in two shakes!"

Natalie closed her eyes for a moment and concentrated. Then Simon said, "Righto! I've got it now!"

Suddenly, Abby heard an electric hum behind her. A ring of blue-and-green sparks formed at the back of the office and the air pressure in the room shifted, making her ears pop. There was a flash of light and suddenly Simon was sitting on the floor, eyes bugged out of his head like a startled deer. The noise shocked Leanne out of her prayer, and the light from her cross faded. Varr'rak took a tentative first step toward the office and Simon pulled the girls toward him. "Sorry to drop in so suddenly! Didn't miss anything exciting, did I?"

"I'll fill you in," Natalie said. "Just get us the hell out of here."

"Right!" Simon jumped to his feet, extended his hands in front of him, and shouted, *"Duru onhlīde on lyfte!"* There was another flash of light as a circular portal opened in front of them, just like the one Varr'rak had made on Abby's birthday, except this one was ringed with blue-green sparks.

Simon, Natalie, Abby, and Leanne all threw themselves into the portal. It closed with a flash and a bang, two seconds before Varr'rak burst into the office.

CHAPTER 17

DEAD WOMAN WALKING

TWO SECONDS later and half a city away, there was another flash and a bang, and Abby and her friends stumbled into a concrete stairwell with pale blue walls, kicking up a cloud of dust beneath them as they landed.

Leanne coughed and stuffed her cross back into her pocket. "Okay, one more time: Abby, *what the hell* is going on here?"

Simon smacked himself on the forehead. "Oh for... where are my manners?" He shook Leanne's hand vigorously and announced, "Simon Lockhart! Demonologist, scholar, and gentleman sorcerer extraordinaire! At your humble service!"

He bowed. Natalie hid a smirk behind her hand. "You left out 'egomaniac' and 'undiagnosable lunatic.'"

"Thank you, Natalie!"

Abby put an arm around her partner. "Leanne, Simon and Natalie. Simon and Natalie, Leanne. Those hooded creeps are called the Following, they tried to kidnap me back at MacReady's, and these two stopped them."

Leanne nodded. "Roger that."

Simon started hurrying down the stairs and gestured for the others to follow him. "We'd do well to keep moving. Teleportation magic is rather messy. Leaves a large energy signature. The kind of signature an organized group like the Following can track with their eyes shut."

"He's right," said Natalie. "They could be behind us already. We need to get out of here now."

"Speaking of: where is here?" Abby asked as they turned down a small landing toward a door with a large white '19' painted on it.

"Couldn't tell you," Simon admitted. "My aim with the teleport isn't what it used to be. I can confidently say we're still in the city, though!"

"At least that narrows it down," said Abby.

Suddenly, dark smoke began to bubble on the landing below them. A shadow-covered hand rose from the floor and Varr'rak the Shadow-walker growled, *"Henderson…"*

Natalie moved to the front of the group and drew her machete, but the shadowy hand lashed out and caught her by the throat before she could make her move. Then a dark tentacle rose from the floor and speared her through the heart.

Blood poured out of Natalie's mouth and her eyes went blank and glassy. Varr'rak emerged from the dark and ensnared her in his black tentacles, then threw her down the dark shaft in the middle of the stairwell. Abby and Leanne cried out as Natalie disappeared into the darkness, but Simon shouted at them to keep moving and pushed them back up the stairs. He turned toward Varr'rak, raised his hands, and yelled, *"Eagan heofena!"*

Light erupted from Simon's palms. Varr'rak evaporated in a black cloud and flew around the beam before he re-materialized in front of Abby and Leanne. But then Abby looked back and saw, to her horror, The Second Varr'rak materialize behind Simon. The Second Varr'rak grabbed Simon by both shoulders and spun him around so they were face to face.

"Fool me once," growled The Second Varr'rak, *"shame on you…"* Then he opened his mouth and exhaled thick black smoke in Simon's face. It streamed up his nostrils and into his mouth like it was on a mission, and Simon started to shake and convulse in the Second Varr'rak's arms.

Abby screamed and tried to reach Simon as The Prime Varr'rak wrapped a tentacle around her waist. "Get away from him!" she hollered.

But The Second Varr'rak just let go of Simon and hissed, *"Fool me twice…"*

Simon looked up at Abby and Leanne with eyes as black as pitch and smiled wickedly. He was possessed. He nodded at the Second Varr'rak and said, "Shame on me."

The Prime Varr'rak marched Abby and Leanne back down the stairs, holding his tentacles taut in front of him. The Second Varr'rak and the possessed Simon stepped into the corridor of the 19th floor first, and The Prime Varr'rak followed with his prisoners in tow.

Evidently, the building was in the middle of a massive reno job. All the offices along the corridor were devoid of people, with only scattered construction equipment suggesting recent human activity. Some of the walls were unpainted plywood, and more than a few ceiling panels were missing. Loose wires hung down all over the place, capped off with electrical tape or plastic cone connectors. The Two Varr'raks brought Abby and Leanne into an abandoned corner office with floor-to-ceiling windows, and The Prime Varr'rak threw them to the floor.

Abby coughed and blinked sawdust out of her eyes. "Okay, now you're just playing dirty!" she snapped at The Prime Varr'rak. "You can't be in two places at once! That's totally not cool!"

The Prime Varr'rak smiled like he'd never heard such a perfect straight line in his life. *"You're so right,"* he hissed, *"I can't be in two places at once."* He spread his arms and howled, and three more clones of himself burst out of his robes. One of them bound Leanne's hands behind her back and wrapped a shadowy tentacle around her mouth so she couldn't throw the Word of God at them. Another grabbed Abby's arm and twisted it as far as it would go in the socket, and then a little further, until the pain left her immobile.

"I can be in six," The Prime Varr'rak declared. He kneeled in front of Abby and yanked her face up to his. *"Now LISTEN to me, you infuriating little bitch! The last time we met, you got lucky. That will not happen again. You are going to come with me now, or your friends are going to die. It's really that simple."*

The Fourth Varr'rak twisted Abby's arm even further, until it was right on the verge of dislocating. She screamed and The Prime Varr'rak hissed, *"Make your choice now."*

Abby was silent. The Prime Varr'rak sighed deeply and straightened up. *"You really don't get it, do you? After all you have seen, all we have taken from you, you still do not understand how wide the Eldest One's reach is. You do not understand the extent of his power."*

The Prime Varr'rak pulled back his hood and the shadows surrounding his face peeled away. Abby and Leanne both went white.

Kelly Munro shook her long blonde hair out and smiled viciously at Abby, her eyes glowing yellow like two dazzling lanterns. "I always thought you were the smart one. Jaws."

"No," Abby whispered. "No, no, no, no, no, no, no, no, not her… not you, Kel, not you…" When she looked her friend in the eye, it was the final push she needed to break through the shadows. She saw clearly now into Varr'rak's aura, and what she saw was a barren, bleak hellscape covered in thick black clouds. Kelly Munro — naked, emaciated, and bleeding — sat huddled on a high stone pillar, sobbing into her knees. Six large wolf-like creatures paced around the rock in hungry anticipation, licking their lips and howling Varr'rak's signature howl. Then the vision faded, and Abby's ears rang as the words of the mysterious Victorian twins echoed in her head. *He looks like your friend, but sometimes she sleeps.*

The Prime Varr'rak threw Kelly's head back and laughed. *"Oh, now I've got your attention, eh? The big secret's finally out! You have no idea how badly I've been wanting to play this card, Henderson! All that sanctimonious heart-to-heart bullshit was driving me nuts!"* He gestured at Kelly's face and snapped,

"The Deacon wanted to save this for a last resort! The nuclear option! But screw him, right? He doesn't know what a fucking nightmare it is to live with you, Jaws."

"Give her back!" Abby screamed. "Give me back my friend, you fucker! I'll fucking kill you myself, you bastard!" She twisted and jerked on the floor in a fit of mad rage. The pain in her shoulder made her eyes water, and she knew that The Fourth Varr'rak was half a second away from dislocating her arm.

Let him, said a furious little voice in her head. Abby remembered the healing potion that Simon had used on her the first day at the Letterbox. She decided that any physical pain the Following inflicted on her would not hurt half as badly as the knowledge that she'd lost Simon, Natalie, and Kelly to these things so soon after she lost her mother.

Abby bit her tongue to stop herself from screaming, and rolled to one side. She heard a loud pop and felt the bone come loose from its socket. The Fourth Varr'rak's grip loosened in surprise, and Abby flipped onto her back and kicked him right in the stomach.

The Fourth Varr'rak doubled over, winded. Abby got up and sprinted toward a row of workbenches surrounded by yellow construction lights. As the Fourth Varr'rak evaporated and flew toward her, Abby picked up one of the lights from the floor, switched it on, and spun around.

The cloudy Fourth Varr'rak screamed as the light hit him dead-on and his shadows scattered in all directions. Abby turned the construction light toward the other solid clones and they started screaming as well. Varr'raks Two through Five exploded into black clouds and fled to the dark corners of the room. Abby could see their shadows creeping toward her, so she set down the light she was holding and ran around the workbenches turning on all the other lights. As each one came on, the shadows around her screeched and re-positioned themselves. Abby was careful to keep herself in the light at all times so the Shadow-walkers couldn't reach her.

Abby shouted over the shriek of the demons: "Leanne! Do the thing!"

Leanne was on her feet and sprinting away from the possessed Simon, who was hurling blasts of ice and winter wind at her. She looked at Abby and started searching her pockets. "Right! Right! The thing!" She pulled her cross out of her pocket and screamed a prayer over the cacophony. The possessed Simon dropped to his knees and clapped his hands over his ears. As Leanne's cross glowed brightly in the swirling darkness, she called out, "Sorry about this!" and slammed the cross against Simon's forehead.

Simon arched his back as Varr'rak screamed from within him and the black smoke poured out of his nose and mouth. The smoke raced away from him as fast as possible and he shook his head slowly. When he opened his eyes, they were back to their normal green. "Blimey, I'm going to have a headache for weeks after that."

Leanne helped Simon to his feet. As the cloud of shadows raced toward them, Simon raised his hands to the ceiling and roared, *"Eagan heofena!"* At the same instant, Leanne raised the cross above her head and shouted a prayer. The shadows instantly turned tail and fled back toward the Prime Varr'rak. He howled as the entirety of his essence poured back into the one body, and then he sank into the floor.

Two seconds later, there was an explosion of shadows beneath Simon and Leanne's feet. They both went flying as Varr'rak rose from the spot where they had stood, his tentacles flailing in every direction. One of them caught Simon around the middle and threw him to the ground with enough force to knock him out cold. Another looped around Leanne's ankles and dragged her across the office. Abby reached for one of the work lights and Varr'rak screamed, *"Not one more step, Henderson!"*

Abby's heart stopped. Leanne was hanging upside down about five feet in the air, with Varr'rak's tentacle wound around her body from ankles to elbows. He was pressing her hard against the office's large window, which creaked and groaned under the strain.

"Give me a reason," hissed Varr'rak. *"Give me one fucking reason and I will throw her."* He slammed Leanne against the window and it rattled in its frame. *"Nineteen floors down. That won't be a pretty picture."*

Abby took half a step forward and Varr'rak rattled the window again. *"I mean it! Not one step, or I smash her like an egg!"*

Abby stopped moving and raised her good hand. "Please. You don't want to do this."

Varr'rak pressed Leanne hard against the glass. A small crack appeared behind her head. *"Oh, believe me: I really do."*

"No, you don't," Abby insisted. "Not you, Kelly. Never you. I know you, and I know you wouldn't do something like this."

"Kelly can't hear you anymore," Varr'rak said.

"Yes, she can! I know she can! Kelly, if you're in there anywhere, I know you can hear me. You don't want to do this! You don't *have* to do this! This thing has a hold on you now, but you can fight it! Fight it, Kel! Please! *Please.*"

Kelly's eyes blinked. For a split second, the yellow light in them faded. "Abby?" she whispered. "Abby, I—"

Kelly's head jerked to one side and the yellow glow returned. She exhaled black smoke, and Varr'rak the Shadowwalker laughed. *"No, I don't think so. It's not that easy. Would Kelly ever do something like this?"*

The window shattered. Leanne screamed. Varr'rak let go.

"NO!" Abby cried. "Lee!"

Time seemed to slow to a crawl. As Leanne disappeared out the window and her screams faded away, Abby's brain raced at a million miles a second. She remembered her mother, at the wheel of the Mazda, driving straight toward her when Varr'rak had her in his clutches. She remembered him letting her go when Karen put her in the line of fire.

As much as Varr'rak and the rest of the Following surely hated the idea, Abby's own safety was paramount, and letting her come to serious harm was absolutely out of the question. And that put the ball squarely in her court. Abby broke into a sprint, breezed straight past Varr'rak, and hurled herself out of the shattered window after Leanne.

The rush of wind as she fell stung her face and brought tears to her eyes. She blinked them away and saw Leanne's arms and legs flailing wildly. Abby straightened her legs and used her good arm to hold her bad arm firmly against her side. Her shoulder burned in agony, but she bit her tongue and angled her body into something resembling a vertical dive.

She couldn't hear anything over the sound of the wind. She saw Leanne open her eyes and mouth something like, "Are you insane?!" Abby was pretty sure she answered in the affirmative, but the details were fuzzy.

Nine floors down, Abby caught up with Leanne and grabbed her tight around the waist with her good hand. Leanne wrapped her arms around Abby's shoulders and hollered, "What the hell are you doing?!"

"Trust me!" Abby screamed. "I have a plan!"

"How is this a plan?!"

A demonic howl cut through the wind and a black cloud spilled out of the window on the 19th floor. As the cloud streaked toward them, Abby buried her face in Leanne's shoulder and whispered, "Don't let go."

The cloud enveloped them completely and they jerked sharply toward the building. Leanne screamed and wrapped her legs around Abby's hips as Varr'rak crashed through the window on the seventh floor. He evaporated, and the girls rolled across the cold linoleum until they hit a concrete pillar. They disentangled from each other and lay on the floor for a moment to catch their breath.

"How are you doing?" Abby asked hoarsely.

"Well, I'm torn," Leanne panted. "I'm not sure if I should throw up or pee my pants."

"Oh good. I thought that was just me."

Varr'rak howled, and Leanne and Abby both sat up. As the cloud of black shadows raced toward them, Leanne stood, took a deep breath, and moved in front of Abby. Varr'rak began to solidify, and Leanne pulled out her cross and did the thing.

"O God the Lord, the strength of my salvation!" she screamed. "Thou hast covered my head in the day of battle!"

The cross burst into blazing white light. Varr'rak screamed and tried to change course, but Leanne reached out and grabbed his wrist. Immediately, he dropped to the ground and became fully solid. "Grant not, O Lord, the desires of the wicked! Further not his wicked device!" She shoved the cross right into Varr'rak's coat of shadows and pressed it against Kelly's chest. The Shadow-walker screeched as his shadows began to crack and white light streamed from beneath them. "Let burning coals fall upon them! Let them be cast into the fire; into deep pits, that they rise not up again!" With one final scream, Varr'rak evaporated into a black cloud and streaked out of the window in pure terror. Leanne fell to her knees as he escaped and looked at her empty hands. "He… he took my cross…"

"At least he'll be occupied for a while," said Abby.

CRACK! A sudden wind raised the hairs on the back of Abby's neck, and she turned to look behind her. A large, black portal, like the one Varr'rak had made the other night, stood open at the far end of the room. One bony, elderly hand reached out of the portal, and then Sel'uk the Inquisitor emerged. Samson was two steps behind her, his teeth bared in a snarl and his shoulders hunched. Leanne turned and gave a small whine as the portal closed.

The falling shelves had broken most of Mrs. Clifford's fragile bones. Her shoulders weren't level; her right arm was bent at the elbow almost 90° behind her; her legs had buckled inward so her knees were almost flush with one another; and three vertebrae had broken the skin and now protruded out the side of her neck, so that her head lolled against her ribcage. But as she limped closer and closer to Abby and Leanne, the wounds healed. Her limbs snapped back to where they should be with a series of gut-wrenching cracks, and the gashes and cuts closed up without a trace of scarring.

"Do you know what it means?" Sel'uk asked. *"'Kha'al Azna'ghal ixxi'?"* She raised a hand and pointed at Abby and Leanne. *"Azna'ghal rises."*

Samson charged. Abby took Leanne's hand and they ran to the far end of the room, where the construction crew had left most of their equipment. There was a ceiling-high scaffolding rig with sheets of translucent plastic draped over it to wall off one section of this floor. Many of the ceiling tiles on the other side of the scaffolding had been removed, and loose wires hung down all over. Two hand-painted signs on this side of the scaffolding marked that side as a hard hat area and an electrical hazard.

As Samson's massive paws hammered on the floor behind them, Abby told Leanne to take a deep breath. "Suck in your tummy now."

Before Leanne could ask for a clarification, Abby sprinted through a gap in the scaffolding to the other side. Leanne took a breath, tried to make herself as thin as she could, and wormed her way through with a little help from Abby.

Samson slammed into the scaffolding at a full sprint and the whole rig rattled where it stood. One of the plastic sheets burst as Samson stuck his head through it and barked, trying to force himself through.

"Yeah, that'll hold you!" Abby jeered at the dog.

Samson pulled his head out of the hole and backed up. Then he charged at the scaffolding a second time. It shook as he struck it, and then he did the same thing again.

Leanne pulled Abby away from the scaffolding as Samson hit it for the fourth time. They'd run about twenty feet when there was a deafening crash of metal and wood behind them. The whole floor shook and Abby, despite herself, risked a look back as Samson stepped lightly through the gaps in the rig, a section of which now lay on its side.

As the dog charged again, Leanne grabbed a fistful of low-hanging wires and started unscrewing the plastic connectors on the end that made them safe. She yelled at Abby to do the same, and Abby, with her one functioning arm, complied as best she could. She took the wires in hand one by one and attempted to unscrew the connectors with her teeth. A little voice in her head whispered that this was probably an exceptionally good way to get herself electrocuted, but she was too focused on the dog to really care.

As Samson pounced, Leanne took a fistful of the wires Abby had exposed and added them to her own bundle. She pulled on them until they were taut, and waited until Samson was within arm's length. Then, she rammed the exposed wires right into Samson's open mouth. The dog's eyes went wide and he started doing a twitchy, spastic dance on the spot as a lethal electrical current passed through his body.

At least, it should have been lethal. At the last moment, as Leanne let go of the wires, she gave the dog a hard kick in the chest that knocked him back several feet. He lay on the floor for a moment, dazed, and then he got up and scurried away over the fallen scaffolding with a frightened whine. "Damn," Leanne panted, slightly impressed, "that thing is *resilient.*"

The air cracked and the wind howled behind them as Sel'uk stepped through another dark portal. She smiled and boasted, *"He gets it from his master."* Then she reached a hand toward Abby.

Abby felt like an invisible rope had suddenly tightened around her waist. Sel'uk made a fist, and the telekinetic force pulled Abby right toward the portal. She tumbled headfirst through the darkness for a brief second, and then emerged in the concrete stairwell again.

As she pushed herself up to her knees, Abby blinked and let her eyes adjust to the dark. There was a large 'P2' painted on the door some ten feet ahead of her, and the floor was wet and sticky.

Abby looked around and stifled a gasping sob. Natalie lay face-up on the stairs, her head bent to one side and her neck obviously broken. Blood had soaked out from the hole in her chest and the back of her head, which had been smashed in when she landed on the stairs.

Sel'uk stepped through the portal behind Abby, and it closed with another CRACK. Abby fell on her butt, exhausted, and pulled herself toward the P2 door. Sel'uk advanced slowly, looking at her with blind, milky eyes and laughing. *"You can't run from me, Gospel. I smell your fear."*

And then Abby remembered her silver cross necklace. She hadn't even thought about it when she put it on that morning, and she'd completely forgotten it between visions of Leanne and fighting for her life, but there it was under her shirt, next to her Vokarion crystal.

Abby pulled the cross out of her shirt and thrust it out in front of her. "The power of Christ compels you!" she shouted. "The p-power of Christ com-compels you! THE POWER OF CHRIST COMPELS YOU!"

Sel'uk kept advancing and laughed as Abby repeated the oath. *"Not the same as when she does it, is it? You speak the words, Abigail Henderson, but they mean nothing to you! Not as they do to Leanne! You have never believed in, never loved, never suffered for the powers you invoke! Without faith, your idols are mere trinkets! Your words, just noise!"*

Abby pushed herself backward with only her legs. Her shoulder was killing her, and she was taking bets on whether it would be the pain or the fear that made her pass out. "Okay!" she admitted. "Okay, maybe I'm not the most religious person in the world! Sure, I didn't go to church when I was a kid, and we never said grace before dinner, but let me tell you something about faith! This last week, I have seen some really, really messed-up shit! I have seen a kind of ugliness and evil in this world that I never dreamed could have existed! But I have also seen true good!"

Sel'uk paused as a white spark flew off the cross. Abby felt a warm spot deep in her chest, and she remembered one of Simon's old lessons. He had told her once that the primordial energies which saturated the world—what magical scholars called the True Magic—were fuelled and shaped by people's emotions. Faith was one facet of this: the ability to humble oneself and admit that there were some truths that one could not know, some forces one would never understand, and to trust that these forces would work toward the good of one's fellows. But it was really only one small part. Joy, grief, anger, and hope could all manipulate magic in equal measure, and so could love. Love was just as powerful as faith, and in some cases more so. Like faith, love had to be built on trust and a belief that things would work out even if one could not always see every piece of the puzzle. Indeed, to love another person often was the greatest act of faith there was. Christ was supposed to have died for His love of humanity, and He had been rewarded with faith. As she reflected on this, Abby started to think about who she loved, and who loved her.

"That woman right there, she risked everything to keep me safe from your kind! She died protecting me, and I didn't know her name until this week! She was good! And Leanne? The woman you were going to use to get to me? She's as good as good can get! She has never let me down once in the last three years! She is *always* there for me, no matter how crazy fucked-up my life gets!"

Sel'uk cringed and hissed at Abby. White light engulfed the cross, and the warm spot in Abby's chest grew. The more she focused on love, the more she felt its energy around her. She stood and took a step toward Sel'uk, smiling as the demon shied away from her. "I'm not much for God," Abby declared, "but sometimes I look at Leanne and I think, 'Yeah. There has to be something out there!' No chaotic, uncaring universe could just randomly throw together enough particles to accidentally create someone like her! Something has to be up there planning for the existence of people that good and that loving, just to bring some of the joy back to this shit-storm of a planet! And there must be some kind of divine judgement in place to lay a holy, Sodom-and-Gomorrah smackdown on monsters like *you* who try to fuck with that goodness!"

Sel'uk screeched in terror and retreated. *"How are you doing this?!"* she demanded. *"What is this magic?!"*

"This is the wrath of God!" Abby shouted. "This is what happens to things like you when you try to hurt the PEOPLE! I! LOVE!"

Sel'uk screamed and sobbed. *"No! Please!"*

Abby bared her teeth. "Now, I'm going to say this one more goddamn time: the power of Christ FUCKING COMPELS YOU, BITCH!"

Abby pressed the cross to Sel'uk's forehead, and it burned the demon like a hot poker.

Sel'uk collapsed on the floor, wailing, and covered her blistered, smoking forehead with her hands. As the demon sobbed, Abby limped up the stairs, stepped over Natalie's body, and picked up the machete. Then she walked back down to Sel'uk and sliced the demon's head off.

As the dead demon burned up, Mrs. Clifford's glasses landed in a puddle of Natalie's blood, exactly as Abby had seen in her vision. Then the door to the parking garage opened and Leanne poked her head out. "Abby?"

Abby dropped the machete and ran to Leanne. She gave her partner a one-armed hug and kissed her so hard that Leanne stumbled back against the wall. "I'm so glad you're okay."

Leanne laid her head against Abby's chest. "I heard what you said. All of it."

"Good. 'Cause I meant all of it. I don't think I could go on if I didn't have you beside me."

"Good thing I'm not going anywhere, then."

"Yes, I should bloody say so." Simon stepped out of one of his blue-and green portals and gave Leanne a nod of approval. "I haven't seen faith that strong for many a year, now."

Abby kissed Simon on the cheek and hugged him. "I'm glad you're you again. When Varr'rak got in you, I just… I mean, it was bad enough that Kelly…" She broke off and cleared her throat. Her eyes stung and there was a lump in her chest that hadn't been there before.

Simon nodded. "I know. We can count our losses later. Right now, we have to get out of here and get you patched up."

Leanne looked over at Natalie. "Speaking of losses," she said, her voice cracking, "what should we—"

Simon walked toward Natalie in complete silence, his unblinking eyes fixed on her empty ones, and Abby put her good hand on his shoulder. "Simon, I'm so sorry. I know you and she were close."

Simon lazily brushed Abby's hand away. "Hmm? Yes, well… can't be helped, I suppose. Can't at all be helped." He stuck his hands in his pockets and puffed out a breath.

Natalie suddenly blinked and looked directly at Simon. She lifted her head off the stairs and Leanne screamed and grabbed Abby for support.

"What's—oh, goddammit. How long was I out?" Natalie groaned.

"Long enough," Simon replied casually. He pulled her to her feet and she rubbed a sore spot on the back of her head. She looked at the bloodstains all over her clothes and sighed with the weary expression of someone who has just spilled coffee on a brand-new shirt.

"I have absolutely had it with this day," she grumbled.

Abby's jaw hit the floor. She blinked and pinched herself until she was absolutely sure she wasn't going loopy from the pain in her shoulder. Natalie's clothes were torn up where Varr'rak had stabbed her, but there wasn't a single mark anywhere on her body. Her neck was unbroken, and there was no dent in the back of her head from when she hit the stairs.

"Whuh—how—but—you—dead—how—"

Natalie rolled her eyes and picked up her machete. "Do we have to do this now?"

"You were impaled!" Abby shouted. "Varr'rak threw you down the stairs! How are you standing—why—what the hell are you?"

Natalie smirked. "Well, I'm not dead, that's for sure."

CHAPTER 18

WELCOME TO THE NOCTURN

"SO," LEANNE said, "demons."

"Correct," replied Simon. He closed the *Historia minor* and replaced it on its lectern in the Letterbox's grand library. "I understand if this is difficult to accept."

Leanne shook her head. "That's the weird part. I think I *do* accept it. It's the only thing that really explains everything. Demons that can possess people and… and burst into flames when they die…"

"Actually, I was going to ask about that part," said Abby. "What was up with the whole spontaneous combustion thing?"

"A demon can't survive on Earth without a host body," said Natalie. "Not for long, anyway. If the host body is destroyed, the demonic spirit is usually sucked back to Hell pretty quickly, and the energy from that release often burns up the body."

"And… and this is what you two do every day?" Leanne demanded. "Kill demons and do magic and live in a secret pocket dimension inside an old post office?"

Simon smiled. "Well, when you put it that way, it sounds perfectly absurd."

Leanne reached across the table and squeezed Abby's hands. As soon as they had reached the Letterbox, Simon had given Abby a draught of his Bonnesante Potion. Her arm had clicked back into its socket without any fuss, and all the cuts and bruises she had received over the course of the day had faded into bad memories.

"When you said you had a big important thing to tell me," Leanne stammered, "I never even imagined… I mean, this is… this… what even happens now? There's no way we can go back to our apartment with those… Following things running around! For God's sake, Kelly was there! She… she has a key…" She made the sign of the cross and whispered, "Mother of God, I shared a bathroom with a *demon*."

"Until this is over, you'll stay here," Simon said. "The Letterbox has enough space for all of us. We can provide most of the creature comforts of life, and there are ways to procure what we don't already have. The protective charms around the Anointed Gate ensure that nothing gets in here if I don't want it to. As for Miss Munro, I'll admit that I don't know how long she's been Varr'rak's host. That was… not a twist I expected. But I swear, if there is any possibility of saving her, I will do my best to make it happen." He looked Abby in the eye and added, "Don't forget, she was one of my students too."

"And none of this is permanent," said Natalie. "The Enlightening only works during the Alignment, and the Alignment never lasts more than a couple weeks. If we can keep Abby out of the Following's hands until it's passed, then that's it. The Deacon's whole plan is screwed."

Leanne laughed nervously. "Yeah, and then what happens? You guys said it yourselves: The Deacon's been planning this for 25 years! If we just try to wait him out, there's no way he'll take it lying down! He'll keep throwing everything he has at us!"

"And we'll throw it right back," Abby said. "We'll fight and we'll keep on fighting as long as we have to. We'll beat this thing, Lee."

"You mean like your mom fought?"

Abby looked away.

"I'm sorry, Abby, I—I didn't mean that! I don't know what I'm saying! It's just… this whole thing is completely Looney Tunes."

Abby shook her head. "It's okay. You're just scared. So am I."

Leanne nodded. "Yeah. I'm freaked out, is all. I need time to adjust to all this. Simon, you mentioned creature comforts. Are hot baths and green tea something you can provide?"

"It could be arranged," Simon said with a wink. "Natalie, be a dear and show Ms. Waller to the powder room, please. I think she needs some alone time."

Natalie led Leanne out of the library. As the door closed, Abby turned on Simon and said, "So, are we just going to ignore it?"

Simon blinked. "Ignore what?"

"I don't know, how about the elephant in the room that has *a tentacle sticking through its heart*! Damn it, Simon, I thought we were done with all the secrets and lies! I thought nobody was going to keep me in the dark anymore!"

"Ah." Simon sat back and tented his fingers. "You're afraid I've been withholding information."

Abby's nostrils flared. "'Withholding information'? Is that what you call it? Natalie *died* two hours ago. We all saw it. Varr'rak impaled her, and ten minutes later she's up and walking around like it's a fucking mosquito bite! So, I'm only going to ask once, and you better tell me straight up. What the hell is she? And what the hell are you? Because I don't think the answer is 'human.'"

Simon exhaled. "Well, you're half right about Natalie. She was human at one point."

"Was?"

"It was quite some years ago now. I was in the colony of Saint-Domingue, tracking a necromancer who'd been causing trouble in the area. This necromancer knew I was after him, so he created a powerful weapon to use against me. He raised the corpse of a recently-deceased resident of the island and imbued it with unnatural strength and speed."

"A zombie…"

"Exactly. Zombies are the ultimate assassins. They require no food, no rest, they never age or decay, and they can heal from any mortal wound. They exist only to serve their masters, and they will not stop until they have carried out their orders. But this creature was not like that. Something had gone wrong during the conjuring process, and the corpse still had a shred of humanity in it. A tiny piece of its original soul. I spoke to that soul. I appealed to the better instincts the creature wasn't supposed to have, convinced it the necromancer was in the wrong, and took it for an apprentice."

"And that zombie was Natalie."

"Not quite. That was the reanimated corpse of a woman called Natalie. But it took me years of hard work and education to transform that corpse into our Natalie. The Natalie who never has, never will think twice about taking a bullet for her friends."

"You should have told me."

"Maybe yes, maybe no. Think about how you and Leanne reacted back there. If I'd revealed that particular truth to you when you were a child, you would have run screaming from my classroom, Mind Lock be damned."

Abby conceded the point. "And what about you, Simon Lockhart? You haven't aged a day since I've known you, and you told me you met Natalie in the colony of Saint-Domingue. But Saint-Domingue hasn't existed since the 1800s."

Simon waggled his eyebrows mysteriously. "What's your theory, young Henderson? Use the lessons I taught you. Show your work."

"You don't use magic like the Following do. You're more… verbal and hand-wavey than they are. So, you're not a demon. I saw you eating an apple the other day, so you're not undead. But you've been alive for more than 200 years…" She paused, thinking. "What was it you told me about the Vanguard? They died out during the War of the Ancients… 'or very nearly, at any rate.'"

Simon nodded. "Top of the class, Henderson." He smiled, and his eyes were suddenly filled with pain and incalculable age. In his aura, the grief was so strong that Abby felt it like a stab in the heart. "In the Old Times, the Enlightened Council was made up of thirteen members. Thirteen votes cast on whether or not to make the ultimate sacrifice to stop Azna'ghal. Six were in favour, six opposed. I was the tiebreaker. I fought at the Battle of the Five Gates, when the armies of Niðerdæl launched their final offensive on Middangeard, and I saw my friends, my family, my lover, I saw them all fall to prevent the greatest force of evil this universe has ever known from seizing total control. I don't know why I was fated to live, but I did.

"And I press on, alone. To this day I fight to uphold the laws the Vanguard swore by, even though nobody remembers those laws ever existed. The Enlightening spits in the face of everything I believe, and I will do everything I must to make sure it never happens. The Following tried it once before, and Natalie and I stopped it then, but we knew the Deacon would find another Gospel. So, we tried to find her first."

Simon took Abby's hand and gave her a father's smile.

"I have been watching you for so very long, Abigail Henderson. I have seen you grow from a very strange, very wonderful little girl into an intelligent and beautiful young woman with a hell of a lot riding on this. I'm proud of the progress you've made in this short time, and I know you've got many more remarkable things up your sleeve. I intend to see that you accomplish them."

*****

The next two days passed largely without incident. The most excitement Abby had was when she stubbed her toe on a large grimoire Simon had carelessly left on the library floor. It was during dinner on the second night that Simon announced he had good news for them all.

"Thus far," he began, "the Following have had us permanently on the defensive. We don't know when they're going to strike or where they're striking from. We need to take the fight to them, on their home territory."

Natalie looked up from her seat in the corner of the room. She'd spent the last fifteen minutes cleaning and sharpening her machete while the others ate. "Problem is, we don't have a clue where their home territory is. Karen and Don got close the night they made their pact with the Deacon, but he wiped the location from their minds when he fixed them up."

Simon smiled. "You're almost right, Natalie. We *didn't* have a clue. Until today." He reached into his pocket and retrieved a small scroll of parchment. "I had a communiqué this morning from one of my Nocturn contacts. He says he can tell us where the Following are hiding."

"Sorry, 'Nocturn'?" Leanne asked.

"It's not just demons and zombies and insane wizards running around out there," Natalie said. "There's about a couple hundred breeds of magical creatures just on this continent alone. They maintain their own society called the Nocturn, with their own government and laws and everything, on the back of human society but hidden from it at the same time. And most Knocks, as they call themselves, have their own horror stories about the War of the Ancients. They don't want Azna'ghal to take over any more than we do."

"Yeah, but the Deacon is seriously dangerous. Why would anyone want to risk squealing on him?"

Simon said, "Some Knocks are very brave, others are very foolish, and still others know that information like that is worth a hell of a lot of money to some people."

Abby could see where this was going. "Some people being us."

"Precisely."

Natalie shot a suspicious look at Simon. "Wait a minute, Simon. We're not talking about Whittaker, are we?" He nodded, and she groaned. "Goddammit, Simon, you know we can't trust that little worm!"

"Who's Whittaker?" Abby asked.

Simon turned to Abby. "Whittaker is… well, there's no easy way to say it. He's a crook. A fence, a card shark, a confidence man, and a swindler of the highest order. He's an imp who runs a nightclub called Avalon in the Downtown Eastside. All of Whittaker's illegal business—and believe me when I say that is *a lot*—he conducts out of Avalon. Of course, this all gives Whittaker a… unique perspective on the Metro region. From Avalon, he has an eye on pretty much the entire city, so if we want answers…"

"No better place to start," Abby said.

Natalie nodded at Simon's parchment. "What does the little creep say?"

Simon gave it another glance. "He wants to meet at Avalon tomorrow night, 8:30 sharp. He says he can tell us exactly where the Deacon is." He read a little further and made a discomfited noise in the back of his throat. "Ah."

Natalie narrowed her eyes. "What is 'ah,' Simon?"

Simon cleared his throat. "He insists that we all go to see him. He says he won't deal unless Abby's there."

"Dammit," Natalie growled.

Abby blinked and looked around the table. "Is that a problem?"

"Avalon is not normally the kind of place one brings humans to," Simon said. "You see, most Knocks are rather distrustful of the human race, and of Gospels doubly so. They consider it unnatural, humans talking to spirits and whatnot. There's a lot of unpleasant characters hanging around Avalon, and many of them would think nothing of flaying you alive where you stood."

"Then why does he want to see me so badly?"

Simon shrugged. "A show of good faith? Information only you can decipher? Could be any one of a hundred reasons, knowing him."

"What if we just don't go?" Leanne said. "Any of us? There has to be some other way to find what we need."

Simon shook his head. "If we don't go at all, we're just inviting more trouble for ourselves. Imps are of the Fair Folk, and the Fair Folk exist by an incredibly strict code of barter and trade: 'equal pay for equal favours,' as they like to put it. I didn't approach Whittaker for information; he heard about our Following trouble through one of his contacts, and he approached me. By Fair Folk law, he has made us an offer in good faith, and it would be fair payment for us to open a dialogue with him. But if we refuse his service sight unseen, things could get very ugly. There are creatures in the faerie lands that are much nastier than the Following, and Whittaker would be within his legal right to throw them all at us if we don't talk to him."

Abby drummed her hand on the table. "I mean… if that's what it takes, that's what it takes. We don't know jack shit at this point, and if the Following can get to someone like Kelly, their reach is pretty much endless. If this Whittaker guy thinks he can help us, I'm willing to hear him out. Whatever the price."

Simon nodded. "Very well. After dinner, I'll send Whittaker a message with our answer."

*****

Contrary to popular belief, Vancouver's Downtown Eastside is not really "Canada's poorest postal code", but it does look the part. The neighbourhood has the highest rates of crime, poverty, drug addiction, and prostitution in the city, and only the very brave or very foolish walk its streets after dark. As Abby and her friends passed the tent city in Oppenheimer Park, she couldn't decide which one she was.

Abby had seen some strange and disturbing things in the DTES before, and that was without the benefit of her Gospel senses. Now, as she examined the dark corners and stinking alleyways for Following activity, her second sight made everything look much spookier.

An elderly First Nations woman shuffled past on a walker, and Abby caught sight of a leering, red-eyed homunculus clinging to her back. It flashed Abby a nasty grin, and she remembered seeing its picture in a grimoire from the Letterbox library. In a doorway across the street, a pale bald man with long fangs sucked on the arm of a strung-out prostitute. Up ahead, a man with horns and furry goat legs ducked into a shabby SRO. Simon had told her that the DTES was where most of Vancouver's Knock community hid out, but Abby hadn't expected such a sensory overload. Everywhere she looked, magical energy swirled and rippled in the air, and she had to close her eyes before she fainted.

It was starting to rain, and Abby was anxious to get inside. When Simon stopped abruptly and announced that they had arrived, she sighed in relief. But then she stopped to think about it and said, "What? Really? Here?"

They were huddled at the corner of Cordova Street and Gore Avenue. To their right, a cluster of homeless people in tattered sleeping bags rested on the concrete steps of St. James' Anglican Church. Across the street was the Firehall Arts Centre. There was no sign of a magical nightclub.

"You sure this is the place, Simon?" Leanne asked.

"What were you expecting? A neon sign reading 'All hope abandon'? The whole point of the Nocturn is that it's *hidden*." Without explaining further, he turned and jogged up the front steps of St. James,' approaching a lumpy duvet with a floral print on it.

As the ladies watched, Simon cleared his throat and nudged the lumpy duvet with his toe. "Zolem," he cooed. "Wakey, wakey!"

The lumps shifted and a hand emerged from under the duvet. A gruff voice with a thick Slavic accent grumbled, "Goway. Mmsleeping."

Simon kneeled and shook the duvet. "Up and at 'em, Zolem. We've an appointment with Whittaker."

The duvet flipped over and the largest lump emerged from beneath it. He was short, wide, and hunched over, with tanned, leathery skin that disappeared into a thick black beard. Abby had read enough Tolkien to recognize a dwarf when she saw one.

When the dwarf stood and looked at Simon, he smiled and shook Simon's hand with vigour. "Ætheriċ Wulfrecgson. You a sight for sore eyes." He drew the syllables out individually, dividing each one into its own triumphant word: *Ath-e-rich Wulf-redge-son.*

"Keeping your nose clean, Zolem?" Simon asked. "Staying out of trouble?"

Zolem's smile dropped. He shook his head. "This is bad days, Ætheriċ. Lots people scared. Zolem sees things. Black robes. White robes. Many robes, all chanting. Even up Avalon: chanting! Is Following hard at work, eh?"

"I'm afraid so. That's why we're here." He jerked a thumb back toward Abby and the others.

Zolem looked past Simon—not easy, considering Simon was taller by a foot-and-a-half—and shuddered. "*Karam vazhi!* Whittaker said something about a new Gospel, but Zolem didn't believe. Zolem still don't believe."

Abby stepped forward and offered her hand. "Zolem, is it? I'm Abby. Abby Henderson. Ætheriċ is right: we need to see Whittaker."

Zolem shook Abby's hand reluctantly. "Abby. Pretty name for pretty girl. Pretty girl who shouldn't be mixing with Following. Should be going parties, making jokes with other pretty girls."

"I totally agree," Abby said. "And Whittaker says he's got information that can help us beat the Following."

"You let us into Avalon, Zolem, and this pretty girl can go back to her parties and her jokes," said Simon.

Zolem scratched in his beard for a moment, then nodded. "If Whittaker says he has, Whittaker probably has. Okay, you go up." He reached under his lumpy duvet and pulled out a round pink stone the size of a grapefruit. "Party of four?"

Abby nodded.

Zolem nodded back. "Party of four to Avalon." Then he tapped the stone four times on the concrete step. With each tap, the stone chimed like a bell.

On the last tap, thunder rumbled above and a tinny female voice said, "Ground floor. Now boarding for Avalon."

Abby turned. An antique-looking elevator car, complete with glass windows and gilt scissor gate, stood in the middle of the street, awaiting her and her friends.

With a flourish of his long coat, Simon gestured to the elevator and said, "You heard the lady. All aboard."

Abby, Natalie, and Leanne followed Simon into the elevator. The gate shut automatically behind them, and Zolem tapped his pink stone on the steps once more.

Thunder cracked again, and the elevator ascended.

CHAPTER 19

CASTLE ON A CLOUD

A FEW hundred feet above Vancouver, the elevator punched through a dark rain cloud and came to a stop. Abby leaned against Leanne and yawned, trying to equalize the pressure in her ears. The ascent had been rapid and dizzying, and she wasn't confident of her ability to walk under her own power.

Simon was the first out of the elevator. He jumped onto the cloud's grey surface with both feet and bounced slightly as he landed. "Right, come on, then. No time to lose."

As the rest of them stepped out of the elevator, Leanne looked over the side of the cloud. She could see the edge of the Gastown neighbourhood and the Waterfront transit station below, with a clear view across Burrard Inlet to the North Shore Mountains. She whistled. "Jeez, Simon. When you said Whittaker had eyes on the whole city, I didn't think you meant literally!"

"Don't let the scenery fool you, Leanne," Simon advised. "Avalon's not the kind of place to let your guard down."

They made their way across the cloud's surface to a long, low building all in white marble, with a glass dome roof and lots of blue and green trim. The high double front doors were a thick hardwood with iron bands across them, and the painted sign above said AVALON in shining gold letters. To the left of the door at about eye level, there was a brass plate with an inscription:

HOUSE RULES:
Two-drink minimum.
No credit.
No IOUs.
No freeloaders.
No exceptions!

Simon thumped on the door with his fist and waited as a small hatch in the door slid back. A pair of big yellow eyes stared out from the hatch and a rumbling voice said, "Password?"

Simon looked into the yellow eyes and replied, "*Malleus Maleficarum.*" After a moment, the doors opened, and the four walked into Avalon.

The layout of the place looked like someone had been told about human bars in the vaguest detail, and had filled in the blanks by flipping to random pages in a D&D manual and underlining words with their eyes shut. The club's floor was the same carved marble as the building's exterior, as was the long bar that took up one wall. The shelves behind the bar went right up to the ceiling and were so jam-packed with bottles of unusually-coloured liquids that they looked like a stained-glass window in some Gothic cathedral. Rows upon rows of oil lamps hung from the ceiling. All the lamps had blown-glass coverings with elegant and complex designs etched into them.

The circular tables were all made of weather-beaten old wood. Each one stuck up from the floor on one central leg, and these legs all had five spokes sticking out from them to which the circular seats were attached, so that from above, each table had the appearance of a five-pointed star.

There was a large stage in the centre of the club, where a four-piece band was just finishing a set. They appeared to be playing a mix of wind and string instruments from the Late Middle Ages. Large go-go cages hung from the ceiling—two at either end of the stage—and in each cage an inhumanly beautiful woman was dancing in time to the music. Each of the women was nude, except for a wreath of bulrushes in her hair and a white silk loincloth.

"Naiads," Simon said, noticing how Abby stared at the dancers. "River nymphs. Beautiful, but viciously jealous."

Toward the back of the club there were more painted signs directing patrons to the washrooms and the manager's office. This end of the club was set up for recreation: there was a dart board on one wall, a pool table, and an antique Wurlitzer jukebox with cracked tubes and a dusty front panel. The club's more human-looking patrons—the werewolves, the practicing witches and wizards, and the vampires, to name a few—were huddled in this section. There appeared to be an unofficial policy of segregation in Avalon, as the clearly nonhuman patrons—among them short, flame-haired leprechauns, broad-shouldered centaurs, and grey-faced ghouls—made sure to keep their distance from the part-humans.

Abby's Gospel senses were going into overdrive. A cluster of magical auras danced in front of her eyes and addled her senses. All the psychic information being thrown her way was too much to handle and it made her feel lightheaded.

Leanne held Abby's hand. "Hey. Just look at me. You're okay."

Abby concentrated on Leanne's aura until her sixth sense calmed down. Then she smiled and nodded at her partner. "Yeah, I am."

The door closed with a slam and Abby grabbed Leanne tight. The yellow-eyed bouncer stomped around in front of the group and crossed his arms with a snarl. He was seven feet tall, with scaly dark red skin, two horns jutting out from his brow, and the muscles of an Olympic weightlifter. Abby remembered seeing an illustration in one of Simon's books of a very similar creature, identified there as an ogre. Not true fae, like the imps, but a distant offshoot native to Earth.

The bouncer glared at Simon and said, "What do you want, Ætheriċ?"

"And a fine 'hello' to yourself, Oz." Simon pulled the slip of parchment from his coat pocket and held it high for Oz to examine. "I have an appointment with Whittaker. He should be expecting me."

Oz looked at the note and nodded. "Yeah… he mentioned you might be by. But I thought he was kidding about the… skin-apes." He sniffed deep in the back of his throat and spat a gob of mucus at Abby's feet.

Simon's face flushed. "'Human beings' is the term you're looking for, Oz, and I'll thank you to keep a civil tongue in your head."

Oz sneered. "I'll think about it. I'll tell Whittaker you're here. But you stay here, and you stay put." He glared at Abby and Leanne. "We don't want the… filth making off with the good silver, do we?"

Simon looked like his head might explode, but he quietly swallowed his anger and said, "Of course. We don't wish to overstep our bounds."

Oz smiled. "Good." Then he turned and stomped toward the back of the club, down a long, dark corridor past the old Wurlitzer. Without needing to be told, the Knocks in the club gave him a wide berth as he passed.

When Oz had left, Simon found a clear table for them with a direct line of sight to the entrance. As they sat, Leanne leaned in and whispered, "So, tell me about the Fair Folk. Because I get the sense that Mother Goose left some parts out."

"It's kind of hard to explain," Natalie admitted. "See, the problem is nobody really knows a hell of a lot about the Fair Folk. They don't come from this dimension, and they're not made of the same stuff we're made out of. They're split into two kingdoms: Oak and Holly, which are sometimes called Summer and Winter, or the Seelie and the Unseelie. They can teleport anywhere at will, they can create illusions that feel real to the touch—that's where the whole thing about leprechaun gold comes from—and they love to play tricks on people, but that's really it. I can tell you one thing I know from personal experience, though: if one of the Fair Folk ever tries to start a conversation with you, they either want to sell you something or take something from you."

Leanne thought about this for a moment and smiled. "Hmm... devious creatures that are impossible to understand and always have an ulterior motive for talking to you."

Abby nodded and grinned. "Man, Tinder must be swarming with faeries."

The ladies laughed, while Simon just looked incredibly perplexed. "I don't get it," he said. "What's the joke?"

That just made the three laugh even harder. Simon, still looking confused, got to his feet. "Riiiight… I'll just get the drinks in, shall I?"

Abby got up too. "Want some help?"

They stuck close to one another as they cut through the crowd toward the bar. Abby heard a crackle of static electricity, and then a mournful squeal as the old Wurlitzer tried to play a tune. A gaunt man with dark sunglasses, a greasy ponytail, and a leather jacket gave the old jukebox a kick, and then the first chords of "La vie en rose" flitted across the club. As they reached the bar, Abby turned to Simon and asked what the deal was with the old jukebox.

"One of Whittaker's eccentricities," Simon said with a shrug. "He's been in the hospitality business for close to a century, and he's brought that old thing with him to every place he's managed since it was new. Gods know why, really. It barely works anymore, with all the magic flying around. But try telling him that."

"Seems a little out-of-place for a crowd who hate humans so much."

"Well, Whittaker's not really like that. Compared to a lot of Knocks, his views are practically enlightened. It's his customers you have to watch out for."

At that moment, the gaunt man in the leather jacket slinked over to the bar and inserted himself between Simon and Abby. He smiled at them, revealing a set of stained gold dentures sat where his top incisors and canines should have been. "Ætheriċ Wulfrecgson. We don' see you much around lately." His words came out in a slurred, Quebecois-accented jumble, and Abby suspected he was on something stronger than booze. "You been 'iding yourself, *mon frère.*"

Simon pursed his lips. "Marseille. I'm surprised they let you back in here after what happened last time."

Marseille laughed. "That was jus' jokes, *mon frère.* Guys being guys, you know? You know what it's like, Ætheriċ, bein' a guy." He put one hand on the bar and walked it on two fingers toward Simon's arm. "Only some of us wonder sometimes, if you do know 'ow to be a guy." Marseille's fingers nudged Simon's elbow, and Simon jerked his arm away. "You don' fight," Marseille whispered. "You don' fuck. What kinda guy don' fuck?"

Abby shifted uncomfortably on her bar stool. Without looking at her, Marseille clamped his other hand down on her shoulder and squeezed. "Tell me you're a guy, Ætheriċ. Tell me you're fucking the little Gospel. Cuz if you ain,' I sure will."

Marseilles leered at Abby and opened his mouth. The dentures fell out as a set of elongated canines and serrated incisors grew out of his gums.

"Okay, break it up!" The vampire's head jerked back suddenly, and there was Oz the ogre, with his hand wrapped in Marseille's ponytail.

Oz slammed Marseille face-first into the bar and then threw him to the ground. He let go of the vampire's hair and kicked him right between his splayed legs.

Abby and Simon sat frozen. A small, slim figure in a pinstripe suit stepped past Oz, looking at Marseille and clicking his tongue in disappointment. "Marseille, buddy…

House Rule Four: no freeloaders. You wanna drink in my place, you pay just like everyone else."

Marseille the vampire rolled onto his back, his eyes watering as he cupped his obliterated groin with both hands. "*Tabarnak*, Whittaker!" he squeaked. "I was just 'aving a bit of fun!"

Abby looked at the character in the suit. If she was honest, she had expected more of the fabled imp. He was just shy of five feet tall, with bright yellow skin, pointed ears, and a slick black Elvis Presley pompadour. He looked less like the heart of organized crime in Vancouver and more like a used-car salesman.

His most distinguishing feature, however, was his aura. Which is to say, he was distinguished by the fact that he didn't have one.

The Fair Folk weren't native either to Earth or the Elsewhere. Their domain—the "Otherlands," as they called it—was far beyond the place where even the spirits came from, and magic interacted with their bodies differently than it did with just about everything else in the universe. One side effect of this was that pure-blooded faeries didn't project auras. Nobody could say why this was, but it was.

As Simon had warned Abby on the way over, this made the Fair Folk a danger even to the Gospels. Because if you couldn't look in someone's aura and decide whether they were a straight shooter, how were you to know if they were jerking you around?

Whittaker picked up Marseille's dentures and dunked them in a dirty glass on the bar, swirling them in the stale backwash at the bottom. Then he took them out, shook them dry, and kneeled over Marseille. As he popped the dentures into Marseille's mouth, Whittaker smiled and whispered, "Listen to me very carefully, Marseille. Ætheriċ and his friends are here as my guests. You mess with them, and you're messing with me. Got it?"

Marseille gave a small gurgle of agreement and nodded frantically. Whittaker let go of him and stood. "Now go. Get the hell out of my sight."

Marseille crawled away on his knees and elbows, trembling like a half-drowned cat. Whittaker looked at Abby and flashed her the same smarmy grin. "Sorry about that. We get all sorts in here. You doing okay, chickadee?" He clapped her on the shoulder with the same hand he'd used to defile Marseille's dentures.

Abby flinched, unsure how to respond. Or how to stop her own hands from shaking. "I, uh… I-I'll be fine. In a minute."

Whittaker nodded. "I get you. Always rough meeting a vamp the first time. Ain't no twinkling pretty boys, that's for sure. You say the word, and I'll tell Oz to give that creep the bum's rush right off the edge of this cloud."

"T-thanks."

"I look after my customers, chickadee." He looked at Simon and gave him a soft punch on the arm. "Don't just sit there like a log, Ætheriċ! You gonna introduce us or what?"

Simon still looked rather off-balance himself, but he cleared his throat and made the introductions. "R.G. Whittaker, Abby Henderson. Abby, Whittaker."

Whittaker extended his hand. "Henderson, eh? I thought you looked familiar. You got your dad's eyes, chickadee. Nose is definitely your mom's."

They shook. Abby was still feeling queasy when Whittaker clapped her and Simon on the shoulder again and asked, "So, what are you folks drinking?"

*****

They had their drinks, per House Rule One. The booze at Avalon was pretty strong stuff, and by the time she finished her second, Abby had managed to stop thinking about the thoroughly rapey vampire in the leather jacket, though she wasn't keen to run into him again.

Oz and another monstrous ogre, who went by Vince, escorted the four down the back corridor, to an unmarked soundproof door beyond the manager's office. Whittaker himself led the group, talking as he walked. "I'm telling you, Ætheriċ, when you see what I've got, you will not be sorry you made the trip. I've been waiting to see the look on your face, but the looks on your humans' faces? That'll be gold. I bet you ten bucks Glasses over there is going to make a puddle on the floor."

Vince—an azure-skinned beast with a single lump of horn in the middle of his forehead—produced a large brass key and unlocked the soundproof door. It was heavy enough that even he struggled to open it, though he was pushing with both hands.

The room on the other side was large and boxy. Flaming torches lined the walls, and this served both to light up the room like Canada Day fireworks and make it unbearably hot. There was a large chandelier in the middle of the ceiling, with dozens of lights illuminating three large brass circles set into the floor. In each corner of the room, a fin de siècle phonograph sat on an end table, playing a recording of the Lord's Prayer in English, German, French, and Latin, respectively.

There was a black-robed figure inside the smallest brass circle. His manacled hands were suspended above him by chains attached to the ceiling, and his feet were similarly anchored to the floor. A third ogre, with emerald green skin and short black horns across his entire brow, stood outside the circle, behind the chained Following acolyte. The ogre had a length of knotted rope in his hands, and as Whittaker and the others entered, the ogre gave them a nod and whipped the rope across the acolyte's back. A dull *thump* and a pained howl echoed around the room as Vince shut the door again.

Simon put a hand to his forehead and let his mouth hang open. "*Metodes miht,*" he swore.

Whittaker drew a pack of cigarettes from his jacket and lit one. "Good, isn't it? Found him about two days back. Apparently, him and the goon squad were tearing up some old bookstore near Cassiar, and someone stuck this on him." Whittaker reached into his pocket and pulled out Leanne's golden cross necklace. "Or should I say 'her.'"

Abby looked from the acolyte to the cross and back again. As the green ogre lashed the acolyte again, she took a step forward. "Kelly?" she whispered.

Varr'rak the Shadow-walker looked up. His coat of shadows had almost completely burned away in the torchlight, and his hood fell away so he could look at Abby through the tear-filled eyes of Kelly Munro. The bruises on Kelly's face were livid and vibrant in the light of the chandelier.

"KELLY!" Abby ran toward her friend, but as soon as her toes hit the first brass circle, there was a flash of light that knocked her flat. She got up and pounded on the force field, producing more green sparks that blocked her way.

Abby looked at Whittaker. "Let her go. Goddammit, let her go right now!"

Whittaker raised his hands defensively. "Whoa, whoa, whoa, slow your roll, chickadee. There's a certain system we need to honour here."

The green-skinned ogre lashed Varr'rak with the rope again, getting a scream in response. "For God's sake, stop!" Abby yelled as she hammered on the invisible wall. "That's my friend!"

Whittaker raised his eyebrows and smiled. "Really?" He stuck two fingers in his mouth and whistled to the rope-wielding ogre. "Yo, Treat! Take five! Come over here a sec!"

The ogre called Treat dropped the rope and stomped over to Whittaker. As he walked over each brass circle, sparks of green energy rippled on his head and shoulders. Apparently, leaving the circle was no problem. It was entering that was the trick.

Whittaker puffed on his cigarette and rocked on the balls of his feet. "So, chickadee… you and the Shadow-walker… you go back, huh?"

"Her name's Kelly. Kelly Munro."

"Kelly Munro…" repeated the imp. "Nice ring to it."

"This isn't a joke, Whittaker. I've seen through Varr'rak's aura. His host is still alive and aware of everything you're doing. You are torturing a human being."

"Well, ain't that a kick in the pants?" said Whittaker.

"Whittaker…" whispered Simon, "how on earth did you manage this?"

The imp smiled. "Zolem found her on the steps of the church downstairs. That cross was tangled up in her robes and her… goop, I guess you'd say. Must be some faith going through that thing, 'cause the magic was still going full blast, burning the hell out of her, if you'll pardon my pun. Our friend the Shadow-walker was half-dead, crazy with pain…" Here he paused and puffed on his cigarette again. "But I figured not enough pain. See, I've been letting the boys blow off some steam the last two days with our shadowy friend here. Faeries and ogres, we have longer memories than most. We lost some good people during the war, so I call this an eye for an eye. But here's the interesting bit: no matter what we've done over the last two days, no matter how many times we've stabbed him, shot him, burnt him, Varr'rak's barely said two words to us. Plenty of screaming and chanting, sure, but he hasn't been much for conversation. Except for two words. The same two words, over and over: 'Henderson. Henderson. Get… Henderson.'

"So, then I start thinking. See, I'm hearing rumours that there's a new Gospel in town, who's fallen in with a couple of local troublemakers and gotten herself in some hot H_2O with the Following. And I have to wonder, what would those folks be willing to give up for a captive Following acolyte, to do with as they please? And not just any Following acolyte, but the Deacon's right hand!" He smiled at Abby. "What would they be willing to give up, indeed?"

Abby crossed her arms and shot the imp a suspicious look. "What do you want?"

Whittaker considered the question seriously for a moment before saying, "Well, that's the real trick of it, isn't it? See, I came into this thinking I was just selling you the lease on a valuable hostage. A source of information. And in that case, it would have been a fair trade for me to ask for some information back. But now you tell me you're friends with Varr'rak's host. There's a sentimental attachment there. That's something we gotta factor into the equation. Getting something of sentimental value is gonna cost you something of sentimental value."

"Like what?"

Whittaker smiled. "You ever do much… writing in your life, Miss Henderson?"

"Writing?" Abby asked suspiciously.

"Writing. See, you strike me as the sensitive type. Sensitive and smart. I look at you, I think, 'There's a kid with a big heart and a big brain.' And that's a pairing I don't see too often in Middangeard. What I want, is for you to write me something right from that big heart and that big brain. A poem, a riddle, a song, I ain't particular. But it's got to come from inside, and it's got to be your own words. Handwritten and signed with your Jane Hancock."

Simon stepped forward, his hands curling into tight fists. "Whittaker, if you're asking what I think you're asking, it is *quite* out of the question!"

Abby said, "I don't get it. What's he asking?"

Simon turned to her. "Among the Fair Folk, words have remarkable power. The most powerful words are the true names of things. The faeries possess old magic, and they know ways of using words that can cut to a person's very soul and bind a person to them for life. Writing from the heart and signing it will give Whittaker knowledge of your inner self and your true name, and he could use that knowledge to place you under any one of a hundred enchantments. Or he could sell that information on to someone else with a… less merciful disposition."

Abby looked from Simon over to Whittaker. "Is that right?"

Whittaker shrugged, but didn't deny it. "This is business, chickadee. You want to ride the Ferris wheel, you got to buy a ticket."

Abby shook her head. "Sorry, Whittaker. My mom already sold my soul once. I'm not making the same mistake."

Whittaker shrugged. "That's no skin off my nose. But if that's really how you feel, then Blondie is staying with us." He snapped his fingers and the volume increased on the phonographs. Abby and the others had to stuff their fingers in their ears to block out the noise, and Kelly started screaming and shaking in her chains. "She's putting up one hell of a fuss, but don't let that fool ya!" hollered the imp. "I think she's really starting to like it here!"

"Okay, okay, stop it!" Abby yelled. Whittaker snapped his fingers again and the volume went back down. "Please, just don't hurt her."

"Hey, soon as you pony up, I can let her out of those chains. Because believe you me, she's not getting out by herself. Those things are cold iron treated with dragonfire. Hardest substance on my world. Makes a Congolese diamond look like wet toilet paper."

"I'm not selling my soul. But I'm not leaving without her either. There must be something else you want."

"It's that or it's nothing," said Whittaker. "See, one of two things is going to happen, chickadee. Either you're going to sit your perky little caboose down and do some creative writing for me, or my boys are going to politely escort you out the front door while I play some records for the Shadow-walker. Okay?"

"And what do you think will happen then?" Abby fired back. "You keep Varr'rak here much longer and the Deacon is going to notice. You said it yourself: Varr'rak is the Deacon's right hand, so you can bet the Following will be out here in numbers to get him back. They'll eat you alive without thinking about it."

Whittaker burst out laughing. "What do I look like, an amateur? Kid, I've been running scams and keeping ahead of the law since King Tut was getting his royal diapers changed! This whole place is enchanted so it's unfindable! If you haven't been here before, or you're not led here by someone who has, your eyes are gonna glaze over when you're six blocks away, and you're gonna walk right past St. James without a second look! Worst comes to worst, I can hit a switch in my office and have this whole cloud floating over the Sea of Japan in five hours! The Deacon can send out however big a search party he wants. He won't find this place in a hundred years!"

"And if the Deacon catches up with me? Are you really going to tell me you're comfortable sitting back and letting everything burn just because you couldn't make a compromise?"

"I'm comfortable if you are, kid. You wouldn't be out here if you didn't want to put a stop to this whole thing. Only idiots and the truly desperate ever deal with a guy like me, and you don't seem like an idiot. I can see it in your eyes. The guilt would just chew you up if you left your friend behind, and you are way too scared to face what comes after the Enlightening."

"And you're not? You've got a pretty good thing going here, Whittaker. How long do you think that will last if Azna'ghal comes to power?"

"Don't know, but the thing is I've got options. If this dimension goes tits-up, I can cut my losses and open a door to my own world. Demons can't get in without the go-ahead from one of the kings, so I can get refugee status for my boys and I can rebuild my business pretty quick. There's a lot of rich folks in the Otherlands who just want to have a good time." He checked his watch and blew smoke in the air. "Now look, I got a business to run here, chickadee, so if you're not ready to deal, then I'm going to need you to get the fuck out of my club. My time ain't cheap, you know?"

Abby squeezed past Vince and Oz and got right in Whittaker's face. "Okay, Whittaker. You want my voice? Then pull the smug out of your ears and pay close fucking attention. Now, I don't know what the normal operating procedure is in Faerie World or whatever, but I do know that you are not taking this nearly seriously enough. Two people have died this week because they had a connection to me. Varr'rak smashed my workplace to shit, and I don't know if I'll be able to make rent this month. And it's not like this is a new thing. The Deacon has been hanging over my head since before I was born. He drove my father insane, and he traumatized me before I got my first period. And in the end, I don't mean anything to him. I'm just a vessel for him to pour an ancient god of evil into so he can have his End of Days Party. I am a piece of meat to him and look how he's treated me! Can you begin to imagine what will happen to the poor saps out there if things go his way? He will brutalize them. Because he does not give the slightest goddamn about any single person, creature, or spirit in Middangeard. This isn't a crooked real estate deal or a backroom craps game. This isn't business. This is my life, and I'm not walking out of here empty-handed."

Whittaker laughed again and blew smoke in her face. "See? That's the kind of shit I'm talking about! That was one hell of a speech, kid, and if you can give me something like that on paper, the blonde is yours."

Abby clenched her teeth and racked her brains. She couldn't leave her friend at the mercy of this arrogant little shit, but she couldn't give him the keys to the kingdom either. What was the phrase Simon had used the other day? *Over a barrel.*

In the centre of the room, Kelly gave a weak moan. Her chains creaked as her head rolled onto her shoulders and she croaked, "Abby?"

Abby walked to the brass circle and tapped on the invisible wall to get Kelly's attention. She pressed her nose right up to the barrier and attempted to smile. "Kelly? Is it you? Or is it… the other guy?"

"It's me…" Kelly hung her head and wept. "Please, Abby! Please, don't leave me here! It… it hurts so bad! I feel him in me, and I can't—I can't breathe!"

Her head jerked around and her eyes started to glow yellow. Varr'rak the Shadow-walker laughed and growled, *"Go ahead, Henderson. Leave us hanging! I can take the beating! Her, on the other hand… oh, I think she's ready to crack…"*

Their eyes met, and Abby felt herself peering into Kelly and Varr'rak's combined aura once again. Five of the wolf-like beasts sat around the stone pillar, waiting for dinner to come to them. Kelly lay half-dead at the top of the pillar. She was tossing and turning like she was having a fit, and she'd fall soon enough if she were left to her own devices.

Abby dropped her shoulders and sighed. "If I say 'yes,' Whittaker, do you promise me you'll let her go?"

"Equal pay for equal favours," Whittaker said. "You'll get your friend and no more questions asked."

"Abby, be rational about this!" Simon implored. "You don't know what kind of target you're painting on your back here! When you're dealing with the Fair Folk, nothing is worth that kind of sacrifice!"

Abby turned to him, her eyes blazing with anger. "Kelly is! Simon, when I was little, you were my friend. You were someone I could turn to for help. But you weren't a kid. Kelly always stood up to the bullies. She could always cheer me up, in ways Mr. Lockhart never could. I couldn't call myself her friend if I left her here. If I left her at *his* mercy."

"Are you sure Kelly is still in there?" Natalie asked. "It could be a trick. The Following don't normally leave their hosts alive very long."

"Trust me, Natalie, I saw. She's alive in there. She was hurt, and there were these five wolf… things pacing around her, looking at her like she was dinner."

"Six," Leanne said.

"No, five! I counted!"

"No, Abby, Abby, calm down! Remember the other day? What did Varr'rak say then? He couldn't be in two places…"

Abby blinked. It felt like her heart had just dropped right out of her ass. *Something is missing*, the twins had said. *Someone is not whole.* "He can… be… in… six…"

The whole room shook. Varr'rak laughed and the flaming torches all snuffed it. The phonographs wound down and the room suddenly went freezing cold. Varr'rak rattled his chains and screamed with laughter. As the room shook again, he said, *"Cavalry's here, kids."*

CHAPTER 20

BALLROOM BLITZ

ABBY was the first to run back into the main section of the club, but the others were close behind. As she skidded to a halt on the dance floor, the graffitied Wurlitzer blurted out a verse of "Old-Time Religion".

It's good when I'm in trouble
It's good when I'm in trouble
It's good when I'm in trouble
And it's good enough for me...

The front door lay in two pieces atop the splintered remains of a table. Varr'rak the Shadow-walker—the Sixth Varr'rak, split off from his main body—stood in the entranceway, with a coterie of ten black-robed Following behind him.

"I tried the doorbell," Varr'rak said. He threw Zolem the dwarf's severed head onto the floor, where it landed with a squelch and sprayed blood onto the shining marble. *"It wasn't working."*

The club erupted in screams and cries for help as the patrons tried to escape, scrambling over each other for whatever alternate exit they could find or crawling under their tables and putting their hands over their eyes. Only a brave, stupid few dared to fend off the attackers.

The first of this latter group was Marseille the vampire. He sprinted toward Varr'rak, swearing at him in drunken French, and took out his dentures. As his fangs came in, Marseille leaped and sank his teeth into Varr'rak's neck. Varr'rak stumbled and snarled. Marseille lifted his head and spat out a mouthful of black goop. Then Varr'rak peeled Marseille off him by the back of his leather jacket and smashed a shadowy fist right into Marseille's face.

With Varr'rak's full strength behind it, the punch caved Marseille's head in like an overripe pumpkin. The vampire's face was gone when he fell to the ground, and Varr'rak stood there shaking bits of skull and brain off his hand. *"Trash,"* he growled.

Varr'rak marched through the club straight toward Abby, with the acolytes swarming in behind him. Varr'rak's shadowy tentacles speared every light above his head and the other acolytes tore through the Avalon patrons with tooth, claw, and dagger. Bodies tumbled to the floor and the Following sent more heads rolling than just Zolem's, painting the club with blood of every colour.

Suddenly, Oz broke ranks and rushed toward the Following. Without breaking stride, Varr'rak looped a shadowy tentacle around the ogre's thick neck and threw him into the pool table, breaking it in two. Then he snapped his tentacle like a bullwhip and crushed Oz's first three vertebrae. Varr'rak tossed the ogre's corpse aside and screamed, *"I am not fucking around tonight, Henderson! You and that Munro cow are both coming with me!"*

Abby reached behind her and felt Leanne's hand slide into hers. She pulled out her silver cross and knew that Leanne was thinking the same thing.

In a synchronized step, Abby and Leanne marched forward, holding their little icons high above their heads. They prayed together—Leanne reciting the Our Father, and Abby chanting "The power of Christ compels you" on a tireless loop—and their crosses shone white like cruciform lanterns. Abby and Leanne both felt it as the protective energy encircled them, enveloping them in a cheery warmth. The

Following's advance slowed, and Varr'rak looked a lot less confident.

Natalie drew a flat-bladed knife from one of her boots and threw it over Leanne's shoulder, dropping one acolyte. Abby and Leanne ran into the middle of the club, still praying, to give their friends room to move. In the interval, Natalie pulled another knife from her other boot and hurled it into a demon's eye.

Less than a dozen Knocks remained alive in the club, excluding Whittaker's crew. As the second acolyte burned, those remaining found their second wind and met the Following head-on.

Half the demons kept their eyes on Abby, but the other half got dragged into the mounting bar brawl. The acolytes were assaulted by bottles, glasses, furniture, and pool cues, and they returned the favour with razor-sharp steel. Even though they were outnumbered, the fight didn't last long. Nobody had thought to give Avalon's furnishings the holy fire treatment, and the acolytes shrugged off the attacks and slaughtered their attackers like cattle in a pen.

Treat the ogre emerged from the back of the club, brandishing a 12-gauge shotgun. He sprinted onto the stage and fired twice. The first shot blew an acolyte's stomach right out of it, while the second took off another acolyte's ear and reduced half its face to bloody coleslaw. The acolytes were still on their feet, and it fell to Natalie to put them down with her machete.

Two acolytes flew at Treat as he reloaded. One swept his legs out from under him and the other grabbed the gun out of his hands. As the second creature floated out of reach, the first held Treat down and jerked his head toward the ceiling. The second demon fired, and Treat's head exploded in a dark green spray.

Leanne shrieked and dropped her cross. Varr'rak came at Abby again as the prayer was disrupted.

Whittaker, standing behind her, spat out his cigarette and gulped. "Oh, fuck this!" He turned and bolted down the hall, in the direction of his private office.

As Varr'rak swooped in, Simon raised his hands above his head. A shower of blue sparks danced at his fingertips and he shouted, "Everyone get down!" Then he pointed a hand at the bar and bellowed, *"Hafenaþ on byreas!"*

The shelves behind the bar shook and shuddered like in an earthquake, and then disgorged their contents into the air around Simon. Heavy liquor bottles, mugs, and glasses of every size jumped into the thin air, mercilessly taunting gravity. Simon closed his hands into fists and swung them in a wide arc, shouting, *"Ðracu glæsene!"* The storm of glass projectiles surged toward Varr'rak and knocked him to the floor. When the Shadow-walker was down, Simon kept twirling his hands, sending the glass storm hurtling around the club like a tornado. The acolytes hissed as the glass pelted them from all sides, bloodying them, bruising them, and shredding their robes. As soon as one bottle or glass broke, its shards would jump from the floor back into the storm cloud and continue their flight. The longer Simon kept up the spell, the deadlier it got, as more and more pieces of sharp glass punctured the Following from every direction.

With the Following at bay, Abby chased after Whittaker. She caught up with him just outside the men's room and shoved him against the wall. "Just a minute, you little creep! We're not done!"

The imp looked at her like she was crazy. "Are you for real? Those things have slaughtered half my patrons! My insurance premiums are going to go through the fucking roof! You can stay here and get killed if you want but count me right the fuck out!"

"Oh, so now you're scared of the Following! Five minutes ago, you couldn't give a damn!"

"Five minutes ago, they hadn't ripped my doorman's head off!" He tried to wriggle free, but Abby tightened her grip.

"I meant what I said, asshole! I'm not leaving without Kelly!"

"Jumping screaming Jesus, you're a piece of work!" Somewhere on the dance floor, a go-go cage crashed to the floor with a terrible noise, and a naiad began to scream as one of the demons ate her alive. Whittaker looked from the noise to Abby and began to rummage in his suit pockets. "Okay, okay! Here!" He pulled out a small gold key and held it up. "This'll get her out of those chains! But you're going to owe me one for this!"

"Are you still trying to negotiate?" Abby spluttered.

"This is how it works for faeries! I don't make the rules! It's dishonour on both of us if we don't trade, and if the royal court suspect dishonour, they'll come down like a tonne of bricks! Trust me, you don't want to piss them off!"

"Fine, I'll owe you one!" At this point, Abby was ready to say anything to shut Whittaker up and get Kelly out of the back room.

"You promise?" Whittaker stuck out his free hand.

"I promise!" They shook, and Abby felt a force like a magnet pulsating inside her chest, drawing her soul and the imp's together. When she pulled off, there was a small red welt on the back of her hand shaped like an oak leaf. It was itching like crazy, and it seemed to radiate powerful magical energy in bursts that made her dizzy.

Whittaker pressed the key into her hand and patted her on the shoulder. "Pleasure doing business with you, kid. I'll see you in the funny papers." He snapped his fingers. There was a loud crack as the air shifted in the corridor, and suddenly he was gone.

"Goddammit!" Abby snarled as she ran back down the hall. In the club, the Following were still pinned down by Simon's glass storm, and the survivors of the attack were huddled around the old Wurlitzer jukebox, which continued to sing the praises of that old-time religion.

"Where's Whittaker?" Simon grunted. His forehead was shiny with sweat and he looked exhausted from maintaining the spell.

"He split," Abby said.

With a howl, Varr'rak evaporated and raced toward the group, solidifying again just in time to cold-cock Simon and knock him into the jukebox.

As Simon's spell broke and all the glass tinkled and shattered on the floor, Varr'rak roared, *"Enough!"* He floated up to the ceiling in the centre of the room and beckoned for the other acolytes to join him. *"You people have stretched my patience to its limit. And I am done. I am absolutely. Fucking. DONE! I am taking the Henderson bitch with me. I am going to get the rest of me out of those fucking chains in the back. And not one of you is going to stop me."* With that, he evaporated again.

The Following acolytes laughed and floated up to the ceiling. From their robes, each one extracted a small bottle, no larger than his palm, made of blue blown glass. Simon, his face white as paper, screamed, "EVERYBODY MOVE! NOW!" One of the acolytes hurled its bottle to the floor below, and Vince the ogre got to his feet and bolted for the exit.

The bottle went *FWACKOOM* as it shattered on the floor, and the whole club shook. A massive tongue of bright orange flame punched up through the floor from somewhere below, melting a hole in the tile through which the city skyline was visible. The demons flew out of the way as the fire grew, waiting with unrestrained glee.

Vince tripped over a Knock's corpse as the flames rose, and he thrashed on the floor like a fish out of water as he landed. Attracted by the movement, the flame looped itself around his leg, and he started screaming.

Nobody could do anything but watch as the fire crept over Vince's whole frame. He screamed even louder and rolled on the floor, but to no avail. The fire engulfed the ogre like a body glove, and he died slowly and terribly.

"What the hell is that?" Leanne wailed.

Abby recognized the shape of the blue bottle from one of her long-ago lessons and she automatically replied, "It's a Hellstroke! Concentrated Hellfire packed into an incendiary charge, enchanted with limited sentience so it can hunt down and destroy living souls!"

Ducking to avoid the smoke that rose from Vince's corpse, Simon coughed and gasped, "Top of the class, Henderson!"

Natalie reached out to grab Abby's hand as Abby crawled back toward the jukebox. "I thought Hellstrokes were illegal!"

"What do you want to bet the Deacon decided the law didn't apply to him?" Abby replied.

Leanne looked up at the Following, who were clearly enjoying giving their prey a moment to cower. The Hellstrokes had been enchanted to ignore Abby's Gospel energy, but everyone else was fair game. All the demons had to do was torch the club and wait it out. Abby's friends would be dead, and she would be hopelessly, hilariously outnumbered.

Soon, the moment of relish passed. Leanne cleared her throat nervously. "Uh, guys?"

The four looked up at the same time. The Following were staring down at them, winding up their throwing arms.

Just before Whittaker's soundproof back room, Abby had seen a sign pointing to the emergency exit. Pinching her nose to keep out the smoke, she jumped to her feet and legged it. "RUUUUN!"

The others didn't need to be told twice. As the first Hellstroke came whistling through the air, they all sucked in a breath and sprinted as one toward the emergency exit. Glass shattered behind them, and the fire expanded across every hard surface in the club, barbecuing dead Knocks and igniting spilled alcohol.

The flames raced along the ground at the group's heels, chasing them all the way down the back hallway. As the red glow of the "EXIT" sign became visible, hope swelled in Abby's chest. "We're gonna make it! We're gonna make it!"

And then a small blue bottle whizzed over her head and shattered against the doorframe. The blast it released knocked them all to the ground, and a massive gout of bright orange flames shot up from the floor to the ceiling. "God*dammit!*" Abby screamed.

Leanne looked around her. Surely there had to be a fire extinguisher around here, right?

Natalie guessed what she was thinking and shook her head. "No dice. No force on Earth can extinguish a Hellstroke. And no force on Earth—not even a demon—can survive one when it gets hold of them."

Abby snapped her fingers. "Wait a sec! I remember, I read once: Hellstrokes are like bloodhounds! You feed the fire something with your target's essence on it, and it'll hunt that target to the end of the earth! This is all just one big fire now, so we feed it something—a lock of hair, a piece of clothing, whatever—and it'll drop everything to go after that person! Then we just walk out of here!"

"Sure, great," Leanne coughed, "only, who's dumb enough to do that? Who's the target?"

Abby smiled. She ran into the soundproof room where Kelly was still trapped. As soon as her toes hit the magic circle this time, the green wall of energy shimmered and fell away. There was a matching green glow coming from her pocket where she'd put Whittaker's key, and she supposed it opened more than just the chains.

"Abby…" mumbled Kelly. "Abby, what the hell's going on? Why's it so hot?"

Abby grabbed the sleeve of Varr'rak's robes. "The other guy went to sleep, did he?"

"Guess he figured the other, *other* guy could handle this." Her head lolled to one side, and Abby lightly smacked her cheek.

"Hey, hey, stay with me, Kelly. I'm getting you out of here, I promise. But first…" She tore a long strip from Varr'rak's robes and scrunched it up in her hand. "I need to borrow this."

Running back into the corridor, Abby held the strip of robe above the fire. "Here goes nothing!" Then she opened her hand. The torn material burned in an instant, and the fire recoiled away from the emergency exit. It thought for a moment, trying to pick up the new target's trail. Then the flames gathered themselves together and raced out the front door in a thick fireball.

*****

Varr'rak—the one-sixth of him that wasn't chained up in Avalon's back room—stood on the edge of Avalon's cloud cover, facing the club and waiting for the fire to die down. Even at this distance, the light it emitted made him uncomfortable.

He shook out his robes. Phew, was it getting hotter? The light seemed to be growing, too…

Oh shit, thought one-sixth of Varr'rak the Shadow-walker. He didn't even have time to scream before the fireball hit him in the face.

*****

In the back room of Avalon, the rest of Varr'rak howled in extreme pain. Abby smiled. "That's going to hurt in the morning."

Outside, the flames hung at the edge of the cloud for a moment. They were confused. They had burned the target, the one called the Shadow-walker, yet there was still a trace of him in the air. In the very back of the club, inside a human female.

The fire was outraged. It had been tricked. It had never been tricked like that before. The flames bunched up into another fireball and stormed back into Avalon the way they had come.

"Uh, now what?" Leanne said. "Abby, now what?!"

"Gotta tell you, Lee, I didn't think this far ahead."

Simon took off his coat and marched forward to meet the oncoming fireball. "Everyone, stay well back. I'm about to try something very foolish." He rolled up his sleeves and stretched as the fire came.

The first flames rolled through the door and Marseille the vampire was quickly reduced to a blackened skeleton. Simon pointed both hands at Avalon's glass ceiling and hollered, "*Berst hrōf!*"

The ceiling splintered into thousands of tiny glass shards, each one no bigger than a dime. Still, the Following hid in the corners of the club and cringed in fear. They'd learned their lesson the first time.

Simon pointed both hands at the fireball and roared, "*Bryneweall!*"

The flames slammed against an invisible wall and stopped dead, six inches from Simon's nose. The hairs rose on the back of Abby's neck, and she felt that the whole club was buzzing with electricity. Electricity that seemed, oddly enough, to radiate from Simon's body.

A low wind picked up inside the club, blowing debris around his feet in a wide arc. The wind got faster second by second, and Abby grabbed Simon's coat before it was blown into the firewall.

A miniature cyclone appeared at Simon's feet and lifted him off the ground. He rose to the level of the shattered ceiling and the Hellstroke inferno obediently followed him. As the wind kicked up to hurricane levels, the fire began to twirl around his hands and he looked up to the stars. His eyes glowed with opaque blue electricity.

In a powerful, booming voice that made Abby jump, Simon proclaimed: "By the Anointed Gate, I am summoned! By the Seal of the Vanguard, I am empowered! By the Final

Proclamation of Ambrosius, I am ennobled!" His opaque blue eyes fixed on the Following congregation, all of whom shrieked in pure terror. "By the souls of the Enlightened Council, and in the name of those faces most noble and divine, the body of the High Celestial, I say unto ye, servants of the Eldest One: depart unto the Pit whence you came!"

Simon clapped his hands together, his fingertips pointed at the Following. The blazing Hellstrokes shot forth, bouncing off the walls of the club and burning the demons to a crisp. As the acolytes were incinerated, Simon pointed one hand skyward, and the excess flames shot into the upper atmosphere and disappeared.

And that was it. The club had been roasted beyond repair; red puddles of molten glass littered the floor; all the furniture and most of the patrons were ash and charcoal. But the Following and the Hellstrokes were gone, and Simon was floating back to ground level on his little cyclone. He was hunched over, his breathing tired and heavy. When he landed, he stumbled over to the bar and plopped against it. "Bloody hell, I need a drink."

Abby and the others gathered around him as he pointed at a smashed bottle on the floor. The bottle's many shards reassembled like a jigsaw and it filled with liquid from nowhere. Simon took a hearty swig from the bottle. He was pale and sweating, and his pupils were very dilated. Another spell like that and he would probably collapse.

"What happened?" Leanne said. "I thought you couldn't extinguish a Hellstroke."

Simon shook his head. "Didn't extinguish. Redirected. Hellstrokes will go away on their own if they eat up enough living souls. So, I fed them the Following, didn't I?" He dropped his head onto the bar and moaned like a dying moose. "Got a bloody awful headache, too. For my sins." He pointed to the back hallway. "Should probably get Kelly and get the hell out of here. There'll be more of them soon."

While Simon finished his drink, Abby went and got Kelly. As soon as the chains were off her, Kelly collapsed into Abby's arms and started crying.

"Oh Jesus, Abby. I'm so, so sorry. The things he… we… I saw it all…"

"It's okay, Kel. I'm here now. I'm not going to let him hurt you anymore."

"Don't let him take me again, Jaws. I don't want… I can't… I… can't…"

Then the last of Kelly's strength failed her and she fainted to the floor. Abby held her as she went down.

We have met the enemy and they are ours...
*

Commodore Oliver Hazard Perry
September 10, 1813

BOOK FOUR:

THE ENLIGHTENING

CHAPTER 21

THE BRIDGE

IT SEEMED that every time Abby blinked, the Letterbox revealed another secret to her. When she and her friends returned from Avalon, a section of carpeting in the front room melted away to reveal a stone staircase that spiralled far below street level. Casting a light ahead of him, Simon led the others down the stairs and along a serpentine corridor that branched off in several directions. At the end of this corridor was a pair of ten-foot-tall double doors. A small window covered in iron bars was set into each door at eye level, revealing a dreary scene beyond.

The dungeon on the other side of the doors was nearly a perfect circle, approximately forty feet in diameter, furnished only by a cot which was firmly bolted to the floor, a small writing desk, and a rough-looking three-legged stool, all lit by four wall-mounted torches. There was a chamber pot beneath the cot, and thick leather restraints laid over the mattress at chest level and again at knee level. The walls and floor of the room were covered in Nordic runes, as well as mysterious glyphs and sigils from a dozen untranslatable, extinct languages. The symbols bled magical energy, and Abby got the sense that even Simon didn't fully grasp some of the power they conveyed.

This dungeon was where Kelly—who up till then had been slung over Natalie's shoulder, unconscious—would reside for the time being.

During the car ride back from Avalon, Abby had had another look in her unconscious friend's aura and saw the whole story of how Kelly had joined with Varr'rak: a woman in a desperate situation, pleading for a way out; a tall figure in white robes approaching her with an offer; a protracted period of hesitation, before an ultimate acceptance of the deal.

Abby had watched as something forced its way into Kelly's body, then cloaked her in a black robe and marched her out into the night. Varr'rak's essence had forced Kelly's mind and spirit into a deep, dark corner where it hoped no one would ever find her and had controlled her every move for two years since then. She'd been forced to watch as he killed and maimed scores in the name of Azna'ghal. A helpless prisoner in her own body, screaming and screaming but never being heard.

They had to save her, somehow. Abby was determined they *would* save her. But they had to be careful about it; it was only a matter of time until the remaining five-sixths of Varr'rak awoke, and when he did, he was going to be *royally* pissed off. Hence the dungeon.

Natalie strapped Kelly down to the cot as tight as she possibly could, while Simon took Abby's and Leanne's cross necklaces and suspended them at strategic points above the cot with a levitation spell. Abby moved forward and urged Natalie to ease up on the restraints, but Simon held up his hand and told her to stay put.

"I'm quite serious about this, Abby. Stay exactly where you are. Until Varr'rak wakes up, we have to treat him like an unexploded bomb. We don't know when he'll go off and we don't know how big the explosion could be. The crosses will keep him in one place, and the enchantments in the runes will neutralize his powers, but he won't be pleased about it."

As if on cue, Kelly's eyes snapped open and she howled at the top of her lungs, like a panther caught in a trap. Leanne covered her ears and shrank back against the wall, while Simon and Natalie backed away from the cot like it had caught fire. Kelly struggled against the restraints and thrashed around, chanting, *"Kha'al Azna'ghal ixxi! Kha'al Azna'ghal ixxi! Kha'al Azna'ghal ixxi!"*

The shadows danced around Kelly, and a thin black haze formed over her hands. Against her better judgement, Abby took a step forward. She gulped, "K-Kelly?"

Kelly snapped her head around to look at Abby, eyes wide and unblinking. She spoke in Varr'rak's voice with fanatic zeal, in the Following's own language. *"Ka Elk'eht e-er kxx! Ke kela Kha'al okexx tok! Lash'e tov koda serak am lakash ter'ik sira dal ixxam!"*

Abby grabbed Kelly by the shoulders and leaned over her, their faces mere inches apart. "Kelly, listen to me! This isn't you! I know you're in there! Just talk to me!"

But Kelly had retreated back inside herself, and Varr'rak was in power again. As the shadows clouded over Kelly's face, Varr'rak bellowed, *"Ka Godaj-pael akrit kxx! Kha'al Azna'ghal kela dul ag'rava! Ka ag'rava sira guthet Mid-earn!"*

Abby shook Kelly with both hands, screaming, "Snap out of it, Kelly! Snap OUT of it!"

Kelly snapped her head forward and smashed her skull into Abby's. Abby winced and stumbled back, holding a hand over her nose as it started to bleed. "OW! Jesus fucking fuck!"

Simon pulled a tissue out of his pocket and offered it to Abby. "Kelly or not, this is still the same being that threw Leanne out a window."

Abby took the tissue and held it to her bleeding nose. With a grimace, she replied, "Nobody likes a smart-ass."

*****

The four locked Kelly in the cell and left her to her tantrum, hoping that she would tire herself out with all the screaming and thrashing around. Mostly she chanted and wailed in that guttural demonic tongue, but occasionally her human voice broke through to hurl English obscenities at her captors.

While the others watched the doors, Abby tried her best to stem her brand-new nosebleed. It was incredible, she thought, that this beast had been walking around in her best friend's skin for two years. How had she not seen it? The physiological changes in the demons' host bodies were blatantly obvious, as were the effects their magical energy had on the surrounding environment. But in those cases, the human souls that must have originally occupied those bodies had been practically nonexistent. There might have been a few shreds of the host spirit left—Abby theorized the demons had to hold onto a sliver of their human hosts in order to access the hosts' knowledge and memories—but nothing that could ever constitute a full human being. Nothing that was truly alive.

But Kelly was alive. There was enough of her spirit left inside that, if he needed to, Varr'rak could retreat into her core and let Kelly live as Kelly, with no perceptible changes, until such time as he needed to strike.

Trying to ignore the noise from the cell, Abby turned to Simon and said, "We have to do something. Varr'rak will tear her apart before long."

Simon nodded grimly. "I know, Abby, but it's just not that simple. We might be able to exorcise the demon, but that's not always a viable solution. The longer a demon resides in a single host, the deeper its roots spread into that host. If we try and pull Varr'rak out of Kelly, he might take part of her with him, in which case she could spend her remaining days as a vegetable. Alternatively, some part of Varr'rak's essence could be sunk so deep into her soul that even if she reclaimed her body, she may retain or redevelop some form of demonic power…"

"…So we'd be right back to square one."

Simon shook his head and laid a tender hand on Abby's shoulder. "I'm sorry, Abigail. I wish I could give you a rosier prediction, but exorcism is a nasty business and far from an exact science."

Abby gave him a hesitant look. "But... what if I went into Kelly's mind and tried to bring her back into the light?"

"Bridge with her, you mean?"

"Yeah. We know Kelly's still somewhere in her body, so what if I went into a Bridge and tried to enter her mind? Or Varr'rak's mind, or whatever. I might be able to find her."

Simon thought about this. "You know, in theory... that might actually work! Yes, if there is enough Kelly for you to see it in her combined aura, it logically follows that part of her will be floating around somewhere in the Elsewhere." He smiled and giggled. "I should say that more often: 'Somewhere in the Elsewhere.'"

Abby snapped her fingers. "Focus."

"Right, sorry! If you can project your spirit into the Elsewhere and find Kelly, it might be possible to pull her back to Earth."

"And if we can do that, we can save her, right?"

"If the High Celestial be merciful."

Leanne spun around. "Whoa, whoa, whoa, back up, Simon! I thought you said Bridging was dangerous!"

"If you're not in control of it, then yes, it's extremely dangerous. But if you have a coach with 350 years of clerical training behind him, then it should be a cake walk."

Abby put a reassuring hand on Leanne's shoulder and looked her in the eye. "I have to do this, Lee. For Kelly."

Leanne nodded. "Okay. For Kelly."

Simon clapped his hands. "Everybody, Vokarion crystals at the ready! I'll go make some preparations! Won't be a tick!" Then he turned and ran up the stone staircase.

He returned ten minutes later, with a teapot in one hand and a cracked mug in the other. The teapot was steaming, and the mug had "WORLD'S GREATEST SORCERER" written on the side. The four sat in a half-circle outside the dungeon doors, and Simon poured from the teapot into the mug. Then he handed the mug to Abby.

"Drink this," he said, "and the Bridge will begin. Your mind will be elevated to another plane of existence, and you will be able to connect with Kelly."

Abby looked suspiciously at the mug and its contents. The liquid was a deep green and smelled like incense mixed with burning tires. The thick steam rising off it made her feel woozy, and she was reminded of the first and only time she'd tried marijuana, back in university. The first sip of the liquid was hot, salty, and savoury. As she swallowed, Abby could feel a blossom of warmth growing in her chest. She drank the rest of the concoction and felt a soothing drowsiness, as if she were sitting with a good book in front of a fire on a rainy day. Her limbs suddenly weighed a hundred pounds each, but her head felt light as a feather. She wanted to lie down right here and sleep for days, but then her brain clicked into overdrive. She could hear the beating of her friends' hearts and feel the flow of energy through their auras. Every cell in her body crackled with electricity, and every nerve tingled. Abby felt like she could answer every question ever asked.

*****

When she opened her eyes, Abby knew she was not in the Letterbox anymore. She stood in a long white corridor with a high curved ceiling above her, an apparently infinite row of doors along each wall, and a long red carpet beneath her feet. Ivory pillars rose at regular intervals between the doors, supporting the ceiling on gleaming golden arches. The pillars, arches, and doors were all decorated with carved illustrations depicting the very history of the universe, from its beginning until the present moment. The golden door handles had similar illustrations and were speckled with small jewels, and the whole picture made Abby think of something from the

Old English epics her mother had studied for a living. Perhaps 'the Elsewhere' was just a fancy name for Heorot, the great mead hall from *Beowulf*.

Bright light shone from underneath each of the doors, and through them Abby could hear the sounds of the universe. The carpet flickered and shimmered beneath her, and when she bent down to get a closer look, she discovered she could almost see through it. She could just make out herself and the others, huddled in the Letterbox and looking like ants.

Abby stood and reached for one of the Anglo-Saxon doors. It creaked as it opened, and Abby saw herself standing in her apartment, looking down at someone and talking. The conversation was muffled and Abby only caught a few snippets.

"—nest, Lee: do I frighten you?"

"Not—ately—isions of yours…"

"—ill there—said—be?"

Abby realized she was listening to the conversation she and Leanne had had the morning of the Shoppe battle, but from Leanne's perspective. She was looking into Leanne's recent memories. She closed the door and turned away. God, that was a surreal feeling.

"Abby? Abby, can you hear me?" The voice sounded distant and ethereal, and it echoed around the White Hallway. "Abby?" it repeated. "Can you tell us what you're seeing?"

She looked up and called into the empty Hallway. "Simon? Is that you?"

"I'm here, Abby."

"What about Leanne? Natalie? Are you guys there?"

"We're here, too Abby," Leanne replied.

"You are doing fine, Abigail," Natalie answered.

"I can almost see you guys. When I look down, I mean. You're so far away…"

"Yes, very good," Simon said. "That means the Bridge is working. Now, tell me, what exactly are you seeing?"

"It's weird. I'm in a kind of hallway. There's all these doors, but they open onto, like, memories and thoughts or something."

"Yes. Your mind is reaching out into our minds because we're nearest. Is there any sign of Kelly anywhere?"

"No, I don't see her."

"Very well, then we'll have to take you to her."

Abby gulped. "You mean... take me into the cell? With Varr'rak?"

"It's the only way. We'll have to leave you alone with her or else the Bridge will become too muddled. There'd be too many voices shouting at you from all sides and you'd never find her. But we'll keep our crystals active so we can be there if you need us."

"All right, take me to her."

*****

Back in the Letterbox, Abby was still cross-legged on the floor. Her eyes were open, but she was blind to her surroundings. Leanne took her hand and stood. Abby rose as Leanne did, an unconscious movement driven by instinct. "Who's there? It feels like somebody's touching me…"

Leanne squeezed Abby's hand. "It's me, Abby. I'm right here with you."

In the dungeon, Kelly was asleep on the cot, breathing softly. Simon was quite happy to leave her that way. "Varr'rak must've worn himself out fighting his restraints. He's gone dormant again."

Led by Leanne, Abby entered the dungeon and groped at the side of the cot. "Are we here?"

"We're here," Leanne answered, and she laid Abby down beside the cot.

When Abby was on the floor, Simon knelt beside her and said, "Now tell me, Abby, what do you see?"

"It's the same hallway. Same number of doors. I can hear voices behind a few, but... no, it's still just you three."

"You don't see anything that might be Kelly?"

"No."

Simon stood. "Right, then we'll have to leave you alone now."

"So... what do I do when you're gone?" Abby asked hesitantly.

"Concentrate," said Simon, "and the answer will come to you. Remember, Abby, everything you need to know has been with you for the last eleven years. You just have to let it come back."

Abby paused for a minute, concentrating. There was... there was a speech... an invocation she needed to say to gain entry into Varr'rak's mind. Just in the back of her head... Then *click* went her brain, and she remembered.

"I've got it! I know what I have to do!"

Simon closed his eyes and nodded. "Excellent. Send the thought to me to demonstrate your grasp of it."

Abby concentrated and thought about what she had to do. Simon's crystal glowed and he heard her voice in his head as the information was relayed to him.

Simon opened his eyes. "Wonderful. You've got it perfectly. We're going to leave now, Abby. And I must say you're doing splendidly so far. Especially for your first time out."

Abby smiled. "Thanks."

*****

In her White Hallway, Abby heard Simon one last time. "Just do it exactly like that and you'll be fine." Then there was the distant noise of a door closing, and she knew she was alone.

Abby cleared her throat and turned so she was facing down the long Hallway. She took a breath deep and announced: "I am addressing the spirit in this room, which dwells in the body of another. Spirit, do you know my presence?"

On the physical plane, Kelly's mouth formed the words that Abby heard on the spiritual plane. *"Yes. I see and acknowledge you."*

*****

Leanne had her ear pressed firmly to the cell door. When Varr'rak answered back, she gasped and pulled away. She whispered to Simon, "He's awake!"

But Simon shushed her. "Don't panic, Leanne, it's just an unconscious response. Varr'rak's merely talking in his sleep."

*****

In her Hallway, Abby squared her shoulders, took another breath, and looked up to the ceiling. The magic words buzzed in her ear and she knew exactly what to say. She had always known. "My name is Abigail Margaret Henderson, of the line of the Gospels. My father was Donald Richard Henderson, himself the son of Philip Henderson. From these names have I learnt the wisdom of my ancestors. From these names do I draw strength. I offer these names now to that noble witness, the ancient Countenance of the High Celestial!"

According to ancient Vanguard beliefs, the High Celestial was the True Name of God. It was a hive mind—a colossal, spiritual intelligence that represented the supreme power in the universe. All the divine spirits of the earth were a part of the Celestial, and it was the force that controlled them all. Varr'rak snarled and snapped when he heard Abby's invocation, but it was all bluster. He knew as well as Abby did that he was powerless to resist her words. With a final growl, he huffed and grumbled, *"Ask what you will of me, O Gospel. I cannot but acquiesce."*

So far, so good. Abby continued: "Varr'rak the Shadow-walker, I speak to you now as a venerated and recognized agent of the Creator of All Things! I seek the one whose form you unjustly took! She is a prisoner, trapped beyond the veil! I would see her returned to her rightful home! By the Holy Witness, I command you thus: allow me passage; grant me access to the depths of your mind, that I may find the one I seek! In the name of the Earth-maker and the All-seer, I must implore you not to interfere!"

Again, Varr'rak struggled and tried to resist, but there is no force in this life or the next that can deny the High Celestial. Finally, Varr'rak broke down and replied, *"It will be done. I will not impede your search."*

"Truly, you do me a kindness, and for this I give thanks. I command you now to grant me passage, and sleep well and long!"

Varr'rak did not reply again. For a moment, Abby stood alone in the void, wondering if she'd maybe gotten the words wrong, but then she felt a bright light on her back and heard a sound like rolling thunder.

She turned and saw a large black door in front of her, carved from a single piece of beaten-up ebony. Splinters and cracks ran the entire length and there were deep grooves like claw marks around the tarnished, dented brass doorknob. Abby pressed her ear to the door and listened for a second. All she could hear was... nothing. Not nothing like an absence of sound, but nothing like the noise of loss and isolation, of emptiness itself. Abby was listening to the very voice of Hell.

She gulped and put her hand on the doorknob. Then she stepped through into the mind of Varr'rak the Shadow-walker.

The White Hallway disappeared in an instant, and Abby found herself in the middle of a bleak grey forest. She stood on a dirt path lined with gnarled, leafless trees under a black sky. A thick mist drifted over the path at shin height, and faint voices whispered from somewhere beyond the trees. A strong wind howled up from behind her, raising goose bumps on the back of her neck. The wind brought with it that same evil cold that seemed to accompany the Following everywhere they went. Abby spun around, trying to spot the danger, but there was nothing on the path with her. The door had vanished too, its space now occupied by more of the same trail, which ventured off into eternity.

Abby took a deep breath, steeling herself against the dread gnawing away at her insides, and started down the path.

The terrain was easy at first, as the trail was wide and flat, like this was a part of Varr'rak's mind that was visited often. Perhaps this was where his memories were. To her left, Abby saw a white light shining through the trees. She walked toward it, weaving around the jagged branches and clambering over fallen trunks until she feared she would never find her way back to the trail. Closer to the light, and Abby heard a woman's voice.

"Please..." it said. "Please, don't... don't do this..."

Could that be Kelly? Abby quickened her pace and batted low branches out of her face. The trees eventually cleared, and she emerged in an Edwardian-style drawing room. There was a small table in the middle of the room, a big comfy-looking armchair in the corner, and a chaise longue along the wall in front of a big bay window. No question, this must have been one of Varr'rak's memories.

Behind her, the same voice pleaded, "Please, just let him go..." Abby turned.

On the far side of the room, a woman knelt on the floor, her face red and raw from crying. A young boy stood some distance away, ramrod straight but trembling like a leaf. Behind him, a man covered in a shadowy haze held a clump of the boy's hair in one hand and a fireplace poker in the other.

The woman on the floor sobbed. "Please, it's me you want. Just let my son go."

The man with the poker growled in Varr'rak's unmistakeable voice, *"You and your husband both knew what would happen if you went searching for us. The punishment is just!"*

"The boy is innocent!" the woman pleaded. "We're innocent!"

Varr'rak flashed his teeth. *"A whore. A terrorist. A thief. And she proclaims innocence."*

Abby watched helplessly as the Varr'rak of memory raised the poker and sliced it through the air like a fire axe. There was nothing she could do to stop him caving in the poor boy's skull; all of this was merely a playback of events that had occurred who knew how long ago.

As the woman screamed and the boy's skull crunched, Abby turned back. She wanted to run for the forest, but the forest was gone. There was only the wall of the house. The sole door out of the room was way on the other side, and Abby had to shuffle past Varr'rak and his victims before she made it.

She practically jumped through the door and slammed it shut behind her, never looking back. She had re-emerged in the forest, but the wide, flat straightaway was lost. The path twisted and wound through a dense thicket of collapsed trees, rocks, and bracken fern. Boulders as high as Abby's navel jutted out of the ground like tombstones, and the ground beneath was a splatter pattern of mud and dead leaves. Abby resumed her trek, stepping much more carefully than before. Metaphysical constructs or not, the dead foliage and massive stones made the ground incredibly treacherous, and it was all Abby could do not to trip and split her head open on the forest floor.

Soon, the refuse of the forest was so thick as to be almost impassable. A string of jagged, flinty rocks stuck up like sharp teeth in front of a fallen log almost as thick around the middle as Abby was tall. Abby stepped onto one of the larger rocks, fighting for balance as she grabbed a branch on the log. She kicked off from the rock as best she could and swung one leg up, trying to clear the log, but the flat soles of her sneakers were not designed for scaling damp, mossy, rotten bark. She lost her footing almost as soon as she found it, and the branch she was holding snapped off as she fell on her ass.

From the ground, Abby swore violently and tossed the branch aside. She had clumps of earth in her hair and streaked down the back of her shirt, a half-inch cut on the back of her head, and a sharp rock digging painfully into her left butt cheek.

She stood, rubbing her sore posterior, and noticed a hand reaching down toward her. "Would you care for some help?" said a voice attached to the hand.

Abby looked up. The Victorian gentleman with the pince-nez was kneeling atop the log. The woman with the parasol stood just behind him.

"You…" Abby breathed. "How… you…"

"As my brother says," Sister Dearest chirped, "would you care for some help?"

Abby grabbed Brother Dearest's outstretched hand, and he pulled her up onto the log. "It came true…" she stammered. "Him looking like my friend, someone who wasn't whole… It all came true."

"Of course it did," Brother Dearest replied, as if there had never been any doubt.

"You will tend to find that the things we tell you will not be wrong," Sister Dearest said haughtily.

"Well, can you tell me where Kelly is?"

Brother Dearest nodded. "Of course. She is strapped to a cot in the Vanguard's hideout."

"Where her mind is, on the other hand, is not something we can divulge."

Abby groaned, disappointed. "Then why are you here? Who are you two?"

"Who says we are here?" asked Brother Dearest. "For all you know, we could be a figment of your imagination."

"Or lost minds trapped in the Elsewhere with nothing better to do."

"Or fiendish mental constructs that Varr'rak created to distract you."

"All right, well, if you don't have anything else to contribute, I'm going to get going. I don't want to have to spend a second here longer than necessary."

"I can certainly understand that," Sister Dearest said. "Absolutely dreadful place, this."

Brother Dearest concurred. "Mm. Positively ghastly."

"Let us not tarry here a moment longer, Brother Dearest."

"Let's not, Sister Dearest."

Between blinks, the duo disappeared, as did the log Abby had been standing on. It was a shock, feeling the solid ground beneath her feet again, and she wondered aloud what the absolute fuck was going on. The forest did not answer her, and she kept walking in silence.

Several minutes passed, and Abby looked back. The string of teeth-like rocks was a distant memory, and the mist rolled high over the trail, hiding it like a depressing grey curtain. Abby couldn't see anything more than ten feet behind her, and her nervous mind imagined that the trail had simply ceased to exist. She had to keep moving forward, she told herself, otherwise the mist would creep up on her and she'd fall off the edge of the Elsewhere, into a black void of nothingness.

Somewhere deep in the mist, there was a howl. Abby scurried forward a couple steps, taking a combat position and scanning the area for danger. But nothing happened. It wasn't a Varr'rak howl, it was just a lonesome wolf or coyote. Probably just another atmospheric touch to Varr'rak's desolate mind.

Abby closed her eyes and breathed deeply for a few seconds, trying to calm down. *You can do this, Henderson*, she told herself. *You're not really here. You're safe in the Letterbox with the others. They'll be there for you if anything goes wrong.*

Varr'rak's asleep. You are the Gospel. YOU are in control of this situation. Okay? She continued breathing like this for two minutes, until she was quite sure she could keep going.

Then she opened her eyes.

Then she saw the wolves charging toward her.

CHAPTER 22

THE MIND OF EVIL

SHIT! SHITSHITSHITSHITSHITSHIIIIIIIIIIIT!

Abby's inner monologue was having a panic attack, and the rest of her wasn't doing much better. She was running hell for leather down the forest path, ducking low branches and jumping exposed tree roots, trying to stay ahead of the wolves.

Technically, the creatures weren't actually wolves. There were five of them, each about ten feet long from stem to stern and six feet high at the shoulder. They had the grey pelts and long snouts of wolves, but the similarities ended there. Each of these beasts had three heads, and each head bore four bright yellow eyes. Large rams' horns curled out from their heads where their ears should have been, and chitinous black scorpion stings took the place of their bottlebrush tails. Shadows danced around each of the creatures like smoke around a campfire, and Abby concluded that these were the remaining five pieces of Varr'rak's soul. His true form.

Abby looked behind her: the wolf-creatures were aligning themselves in a 'V' formation. The leader of the pack raised its heads and howled a true, bowel-loosening Varr'rak howl.

The wolves kept charging, but the leader's howl was overtaken by a new sound: a human voice, screaming for its life. Abby's own voice had switched to autopilot and was catching up with her inner monologue.

"SHIT! SHIT, SHIT, SHITTY FUCKING SHIIIIIT!"

There had to be a way out. There had to be. Abby's eyes darted around the trail, looking for an alternate path she could take or a weapon she could use to fend off the creatures. Frantically, she groped at her neck, trying to find the silver cross, but then she remembered it was levitating above Kelly's body in the Letterbox.

So overwhelmed was she that Abby didn't initially notice the massive log only a few feet in front of her, blocking the path. When she finally *did* notice it, it did not improve her mood.

The wolves were picking up speed, so Abby did likewise. This log was not nearly as thick as the last one, and she got the idea in her head that she might be able to vault it. A flat stone rose from the ground just before the fallen log, and Abby compressed her core muscles. She screamed again, but not out of fear. This was a scream of determination: the closest Abby could manage to a war cry.

She vaulted from the flat stone and cleared the log with room to spare. But she didn't see the sharp drop-off on the other side until it was too late.

As she landed, her feet slid out from under and she went careening down a 60° incline toward a very nasty-looking patch of thorns some 20 feet below. There were no roots or shrubs she could grab hold of, and the soil was too loose for her feet to gain purchase anywhere. "Well," she told herself as she fell, "none of this is real anyway. It's all just in somebody's head. How much can those thorns actually hurt?"

The answer was quite a lot. Abby landed with a crash, face-down in the thorns and with all the wind knocked out of her. She pulled herself up and picked thorns out of her clothing and hair. She was scraped, cut up, and bruised beyond belief, but at least she was alive.

The wolf-creatures were at the top of the hill just on the other side of the log. They snarled and snapped at her, but it was clear they didn't trust their footing enough to make it down safely. Abby would have gloated if she wasn't in so much pain.

Then all of a sudden, one of the wolf-things climbed up onto the log. All three of its heads turned to look at her. The beast snarled and Abby saw three sets of sharp, crooked teeth pointed in her direction. She saw twelve monstrous yellow eyes staring hungrily at her. And she saw one big-ass scorpion sting whipping dangerously back and forth.

The beast howled again and dissolved into a cloud of black mist. The other four creatures did the same trick, and a black storm cloud came rolling down the hill toward Abby.

She tried to run, but her left ankle gave out after three steps. There were a thousand invisible fire ants jumping up and down on the joint, and Abby knew she must have sprained it when she landed. Behind her, a twig snapped, and Abby turned around to see the storm cloud solidifying once more, spitting out five hungry hellhounds.

Abby scooted backward on her butt as the pack advanced, but the shadows moved before she could blink, and suddenly one of the creatures was right behind her.

The Five Varr'raks snapped their teeth—fifteen jaws strong enough to crush bone—and the one directly in front of Abby licked its lips eagerly. Gobs of black, foul-smelling saliva dangled from its lips and made an oozy puddle on the ground below.

"Stay back!" Abby screamed. "Stay back, goddammit!" She raised one hand in a vain attempt to halt the approaching monster, but it kept coming. Going for the Hail Mary pass, she shouted, "*In the name of the High Celestial*, STAY BACK!"

The last two words came out in a voice that was not Abby's own. It reverberated off every tree trunk and boomed like a thunderclap high above. The effect was immediate: the forest path stretched like a rubber band, and the wolf pack, rooted where they stood, rocketed into the far distance as if on a rogue treadmill. Abby stayed in one place but felt the air swirling around her as it moved and expanded to fill the empty space that had just appeared.

Now a hundred yards from where Abby sat, the five hellhounds shared a few stunned looks before they returned their attention to her. The pack leader led a chorus of fanatic howls, and the beasts charged again. But Abby crawled over to a tree and pulled herself to her feet. Locking eyes with the leader of the pack, she waited until they had closed the gap to a few scant metres and then roared, "**HALT!**"

The beasts didn't just halt, they *froze*. Mid-stride, their bodies locked up entirely, and they stood like statues in the middle of the path. Only their eyes moved, as Abby discovered when she waved a hand in front of one of the creatures' middle faces. "Badass," she observed sagely. Leaning back against the tree to take weight off her ankle, Abby looked at the lead Varr'rak-wolf and said, "Let's try this again. I thought I told you to sleep." Varr'rak said nothing, so Abby snapped her fingers and barked, "**SPEAK.**"

The Prime Varr'rak's three mouths moved in unison with absolutely human dexterity. *"I tried to sleep. I really did. But it's not so easy when a piece of your soul has been burned right. Out. Of your. BODY! Do you know what that feels like, Henderson? How much that hurts? The Munro woman's body sleeps, but the Shadow-walker still dreams."*

"Okay. I guess I can shoulder some of the blame for that. But here's the deal: as soon as I find Kelly, I'm getting her the hell out here, and we can go our separate ways for good. Just stay out of my way, and this whole thing will go a lot smoother. Sound fair?"

"You dare make demands of me? This is my domain, Abigail Henderson!"

"Come over here and say that," Abby retorted. Varr'rak just growled impotently and Abby concluded, "Yeah, that's what I thought. But if you answer me this one question, I promise I will get out of your hair. Where is Kelly?" Again, Varr'rak said nothing, so Abby took another step toward him and snapped, "I'm sorry, I'll repeat the question. **WHERE IS KELLY MUNRO?**"

"Where no light can touch her. The further you stray from the path, Abigail Henderson, the thicker the shadows will get. Your friend is among the thickest shadows, and if you value your sanity in any way, you will not go there."

"Where specifically is she? You know you can't lie to me, Varr'rak."

"I speak no word of a lie. She is in the darkest and most primeval of my thought centres, where even my rational self hesitates to go."

"So, I just have to get myself really, really lost, I guess."

"Be my guest. I promise you: you will never make it home if you continue this foolish quest."

With a wince and a grunt, Abby pushed herself off from the tree. "You said it yourself, Varr'rak. All of this is basically a dream, and Abby Henderson is a natural born dreamer." She closed her eyes and concentrated, wondering just how far she could push the limits of the Bridge. The environment around her was still a part of Varr'rak's mind, but could she control it as she controlled him?

She started with something simple: a tree branch, whittled and smoothed into a five-foot staff. Something to put her weight on. Slowly, the ground at her feet puckered and opened like a leech's mouth. A homemade walking stick rose from the hole, exactly as she had imagined it. She grabbed the stick and leaned on it, and the hole closed up.

"Impressive," Varr'rak muttered, as Abby opened her eyes. *"But what do you intend to do with me?"*

"I won't kill you, if that's what you're asking. That'd be like burning down my own apartment while I was still inside. I need you alive to keep up the psychic link."

"Then what? Break your concentration on me for too long, and I will be free to move again. But if you stay here, you will never find Kelly. What shall become of me, I wonder?"

Abby shrugged and flashed Varr'rak a cheeky smirk. "You're going to do the same as me. **GET LOST.**"

The ground beneath the wolf pack's feet shook with a noise like a boiling kettle, and a large fissure opened in the earth beneath The Prime Varr'rak. A geyser erupted from below and launched The Five Varr'raks high into the air. Abby watched them ascend high over the gnarled trees and far into the distance. She lost track of them as they fell, and she didn't particularly care where they landed. Just so long as they were out of her hair for the time being.

To get herself lost, Abby stepped off the path and onto the steep shoulder. The ground was loose and rocky, and she leaned on her walking stick for balance. Just as Varr'rak had said, the shadows grew thicker and blacker, and Abby started to feel less like she was walking through a thick fog and more like she was swimming in refrigerated molasses. Her forearms prickled with goose bumps, and her breath came out in a thin, silvery haze.

Something fluttered across the back of her neck, and Abby spun around, swinging the walking stick defensively. Whatever it was had felt leathery and membranous, like the wing of a large bat or insect. But it was gone now, and after a moment Abby started to feel a little silly standing there in her combat stance with nothing happening around her.

Back down the hill. The further she descended, the fewer trees there were. Those that did grow here were barely the width of Abby's hips, and half the height of the trees lining the trail. Their bark was an ashen, anemic grey, with ugly blisters of orange-and-brown fungi.

A fallen branch rolled under Abby's foot and she pitched forward down the hill. Her walking stick went flying and she skidded along on her stomach until the ground flattened out. The branch she had stepped on rolled to a stop beside her.

She looked over at it and recoiled in horror. What she'd thought was a branch was a human femur, bleached white with age. With a disgusted shriek, Abby kicked the bone into the distance and scrambled toward her walking stick.

She pressed on, and the forest got still bleaker. Rotten logs littered the ground between the bare, withered trees. The ground beneath was hard and cracked like a clay bed in a sun-baked desert, and dozens of shining white bones dotted the area. For a brief, terrible moment, Abby feared that this was all that remained of Kelly. But as she counted the bones, she realized this was impossible: there were far too many pieces here to be one person.

This was a graveyard. The ground was textbook salted earth, and anything that grew fed on the decay and death of other organisms. Abby kept walking, and the vegetation became still more stunted and pathetic, while the mess of bones on the ground thickened. The shadows got ever denser, and the swim through the molasses was far more difficult. Abby felt the blackness literally pressing down on her, and her feet dragged on the ground. She was lugging around four limbs made of lead, and her walking stick was starting to groan under the added weight. Something, somewhere, had cranked the gravity up to 11 while she wasn't looking.

Among the thickest shadows, Varr'rak had said. Despite the crushing pressure, Abby kept going. The oppressive darkness bent her back and bowed her head, so she stuck her walking stick in the ground to keep herself upright and propel her forward, like a barge pole. It was an exhausting, tedious process, not helped by the fact that everything kept getting progressively heavier. The shadows pressed Abby farther and farther down, until she was forced to crawl on her belly.

She kept one hand in front of her, using her stick to sweep away the bones on the ground in front of her. The other hand dragged her forward in an endlessly laborious cycle of movement. She tore her clothes and scraped much of the skin from her hands and forearms as she inched forward, crawling for what seemed like a solid week.

Suddenly, the trail dropped off. Abby stuck her walking stick out in front of her, barely even looking where she was going by this point, but instead of scraping the ground, the staff swung blindly out into empty space. She finally snapped to attention and saw the yawning pit before her, as well as the sandstone slab planted at its head. The gravestone was curved at the top, with a skull-and-crossbones carved into it and an epitaph that said:

KELLY MUNRO
1993 – ?

Clearly, Varr'rak's sick idea of humour.

Abby pulled herself to the edge of the grave and looked down into impenetrable darkness. She picked up a loose patella lying graveside and threw it down into the pit, listening for the sound when it hit the bottom.

That sound never came. However deep this abyss went, it was clearly not designed to be escapable. But there was no doubt in Abby's mind that Kelly was at the bottom—wherever the bottom was.

She crawled forward until her arms dangled over the side of the grave. The pressure above her increased, like the shadows were trying to push her into the void. No sense in fighting it, Abby reasoned. She scooted forward and tipped over into the black. The pressure eased off, and Abby shut her eyes as the wind rushed past her face. She relaxed her limbs and let gravity take her, keeping her breath steady. "This is all a dream," she told herself. "I am in control. I will land safely without a scratch on me. I will land safely without a scratch on me. I will land safely without a scratch on me. I will..."

Repeating this mantra to herself, Abby began to slow down. Her freefall dialled back from terminal velocity, and she floated down like a feather in the wind.

The grave opened into a wide, flat, stony canyon, where Abby touched down as gracefully as a ballerina. She picked up her walking stick and called out, "Kelly? Are you down here?"

There was a small cave dug out of the canyon wall some two hundred yards away, and as Abby limped toward it, she heard faint sobbing.

"Is that you, Kelly?"

The only reply was the sobbing, which grew louder as Abby neared the cave. She closed her eyes and thought hard for a second, and the ground spat up a heavy-duty flashlight into her hand. Shining the beam into the cave, Abby called once more, "Kelly?"

Kelly was seated on a large stone at the very back of the cave, hugging her knees to her chest and crying into her own thighs. She hadn't seen Abby yet. Abby took two steps into the cave and struck the ground with her walking stick, tapping out a rhythm. She nodded in time with the beat and started singing: "'There must be some way out of here,' said the joker to the thief..."

Kelly looked up. "What?"

Abby took another few steps forward and kept singing, "Businessmen, they drink my wine..."

Kelly looked at Abby and bobbed her head. "Ploughmen dig my earth..."

Kelly jumped to her feet and did a dance atop her slab. In unison, she and Abby belted out, "None of them along the line know what any of it is worth!"

Abby gave a righteous cheer and hobbled toward Kelly as fast as she could. Kelly dropped to the floor and wrapped her arms around Abby in sheer giddy jubilation.

"What the hell are you doing here, Jaws?!" Kelly asked, grinning as the two twirled around the cave.

"I came here to rescue you!" Abby said, lifting Kelly off the ground.

"But, how? How in God's name did you ever find me?"

Abby snorted. "Now that is a story and a half. Do you think we could sit down for a few? My ankle's killing me."

Kelly smiled, her cheeks stained with tears both happy and sad, and beckoned Abby over to her stone. Abby gratefully plopped down and leaned her stick against the wall of the cave.

CHAPTER 23

THE EXORCIST

THEY SPENT the next twenty minutes swapping stories. Abby proudly emphasized her game of Statues with The Five Varr'raks, and Kelly returned the favour by filling in the blanks about her time with the Shadow-walker. She had absorbed most of Varr'rak's memories even while he absorbed hers, and she already knew as much about the Gospels and the Enlightening as Abby did.

"My God," Abby breathed when it was all out there. "Two years... I can't even imagine what that must have been like for you."

"The worst parts were when it started to feel... normal. Like those first couple of days after your mom died. The Deacon was really thrown off his game when she showed up at MacReady's, and he wanted me to keep an eye on you in case there were any more wild cards like that. He let me go through my day-to-day, but I still wasn't really me. Varr'rak was telling me what to say and where to move. I mean, I wanted to say all the stuff I said, but he said it first. Does that make any sense?"

"What about this does?" Abby said.

Kelly sniffed. "True enough." She started to cry again and rubbed her eyes with her hand. "God, Abby, I'm so sorry...

the things he made me do… I never… I never wanted to hurt anybody…"

"It wasn't your fault, Kelly. And I will never hold you responsible for what he did."

"Maybe you should."

"What do you mean?"

"You remember when my dad got sick a couple years ago? And I had to take a semester off to help take care of him?"

"Yeah. Pancreatic cancer, wasn't it?"

"Mm-hmm. He wasn't supposed to live through Christmas."

"And then one day, bam, he was good as new…" A beat. Abby blinked and nodded. "Oh. Oh God."

Kelly swallowed. "Yup."

"What happened, Kel?"

Kelly shuddered and blanched at the memory of it. "It was in Dad's hospital room. I was alone with him, and he was sleeping. I left for two minutes to get a cup of coffee, and when I got back, a man in white robes was standing over the bed. He said he could fix Dad right up if I did him a favour. I took his hand, and the next thing I knew, I was on the floor. He was straddling me and forcing my mouth open. Then there was this black smoke rising from the floor. It jumped down my throat like it was alive, and I screamed for the nurse to come and help me, but I couldn't… I couldn't stop…" She closed her eyes, and a few silent tears trickled down her face. Abby wrapped her arms around Kelly and gave her a kiss on the cheek.

"It's okay, Kelly. We're going to get you out of this. We've got an exit strategy." Abby tapped the crystal around her neck and spoke into it. "Hello, Simon?"

Simon's voice came back simultaneously frantic, excited, and relieved. "Abby?! Oh Abby, please tell me you've found her!"

Abby smiled. "I've got her right here. We're ready to come home."

"Oh brilliant! Absolutely brilliant! If I were human, I would kiss you!"

Abby shook her head and laughed. "So, what's the plan? How do we get back?"

"It's quite simple: all you need to do is—af—si—tur—wa—"

A high-pitched whine filled the air, drowning Simon out completely. Abby gave the crystal a shake and held it closer. "Hello? Hello, Simon? Can you repeat that, please?"

"I—ai—st—gi—"

Again, Abby only caught a few snippets. The whine filled her ears until she couldn't even hear her own thoughts. Then it stopped, just as quickly as it had started. Abby called into the crystal again. "Simon?! Simon?!" She gave it a few hard whacks with the heel of her palm, but the connection was lost.

Kelly looked worried. "What happened?"

"I don't know; it must've shorted out or something!"

"Is it supposed to short out like that?"

"I don't think so."

*****

In the corridor of the Letterbox, Simon was practically shouting into his crystal. "Abby?! Abby, are you there?!"

"What's happening?" Leanne asked.

"I've lost the connection! I don't know how, but I've lost contact with Abby."

"And I'm guessing that's not supposed to happen?"

"No! The relay between Vokarion crystals is supposed to be unbreakable! The only way we could have lost contact is..." He paused just long enough to let the colour drain from his face. "Oh crikey."

*****

"Can you get the connection back?" Kelly asked.

"I... I don't know," Abby admitted.

A deep, smug cackle bubbled up from the darkest corner of the cave, and a voice in the air chirped, "Did you really think it would be that easy?"

Low-hanging black mist trickled into the cave, swirling around the stone block that Kelly and Abby were sitting on. Shadows peeled themselves off of the bare rock and glided into the cloud, flashing with pinpricks of yellow light.

The Five Varr'raks materialized and circled the girls in a slow, measured lope. "I must admit, I am somewhat impressed." The Five Varr'raks spoke in unison, their fifteen mouths ejecting one voice. Kelly's voice. "That 'get lost' trick threw me off. But the game ends here."

"You can't hurt us," Abby asserted. "You can't even touch me."

"Oh, can't I?" The Fifth Varr'rak snapped his scorpion's tale and launched a gob of shadow at Abby's face. It wrapped around her mouth and got tighter the more she pulled at it.

"And you!" Varr'rak barked at Kelly. "You would dare to try and escape who you are?"

The hounds picked up speed, trotting around the stone slab and closing the gaps between them. They kept accelerating until they looked like they would run into one another, and then they melted together into an image of Kelly, draped in the black regalia of the Following, with eyes like yellow lanterns. Varr'rak twisted Kelly's face into a sneer and said, with a flourish of black robes, "This is what you have become, Kelly."

Kelly squeezed her eyes shut and shook her head. "No. No, you did this. You killed all those people, and you made me watch."

"You gave me form. You gave me the lungs I needed to breathe the air of Middangeard. The mouth I needed to pay tribute to the Eldest One. The hands I needed to do His work."

"Shut up," Kelly hissed. "Shut up!"

"The atmosphere of Middangeard is toxic to the demon. We need the flesh of Earth-kind to insulate ourselves against it, to sustain us. Without you, I surely would have perished. You saved me, Kelly Munro."

*****

Simon rushed toward the door of the cell, with Leanne and Natalie hot on his heels. "Vokarion crystals are highly prized for their ability to absorb and transmit telepathic fields. The only way contact between two crystals can possibly be broken is through a terribly powerful psychic block!"

"How powerful are we talking?" Leanne asked.

"*Very* powerful! Even I've never been able to pull it off! Only a heavy hitter like the Deacon could do something like that!"

"But how could the Deacon be doing this? He must be miles away!"

Simon fumbled with the door key, never quite getting it into the lock. The pitch of his voice rose sharply as he spoke. "He must have set up a psychic relay between himself and Varr'rak: anything that Varr'rak says or does, the Deacon can see. There's already a relay between Varr'rak and Kelly, because they're in the same body, so the Deacon—wherever he is—is throwing up a psychic block, which is travelling through Varr'rak and Kelly like they were telegraph wires, cutting us off from Abby! We have to get her out of there immediately." Simon finally got the doors unlocked and yanked on the handles. They didn't budge. Natalie forced him aside and tugged as hard as she could. Still nothing. Something was holding the doors closed from the other side.

"Oh crikey." Simon gulped and ran a hand through his hair, slicking up a few locks with his own sweat. "Oh crikey, crikey, crikey, *crikey*."

*****

"Do you know what kind of torture you put me through?!" Kelly had jumped off her stone, spittle flying from her mouth as she screamed at Varr'rak. "Two years you stole from me, keeping me trapped in here like I was some kind of animal, all while I had to watch you live my life! You don't get to lecture me, you monster!"

Abby jostled Kelly's shoulder and pointed at the mouth of the cave. "Wmmm nmm mm mmm!" was her muffled declaration. Translation: *We need to run!*

"Yes, Kelly, run! Run from what you are!" Varr'rak gloated.

"I am *nothing* like you!" Kelly screamed. Abby tried to pull her away, but Kelly resisted. She snarled and punched Varr'rak in the nose, knocking the demon to the ground.

Varr'rak wiped the blood away and growled in his own voice, *"Big mistake, you little bitch."*

Abby grabbed Kelly roughly and pushed her to the mouth of the cave. "Fmmh Ghhm mmm, rmmm!"

Kelly: "What?"

Abby finally tore the shadow from her mouth. "For God's sake, RUN!"

The two bolted as Varr'rak stood. With a howl, the dark reflection of Kelly split back up into five hellhounds, just as the girls took a hard right and scrambled deeper into the canyon.

"What do we do?" Kelly demanded. "Whatdowedowhatdowedowhatdowedo?"

"Think of a safe place!" Abby commanded. "Someplace you feel at home! Hold the image of that place in your head! I'm going to try something!"

"What, are we just going to dream our way out of here?"

"Pretty much!"

"Abby—"

The wolf pack charged out of the cave behind them, teeth bared menacingly.

"Christ, we don't have time to argue about this, Kelly! Just do as I say!"

*****

Simon had sent Natalie to the armoury to find something that could break down the door. Meanwhile, he remained behind and threw every spell he could think of at the stubborn wood. *"Fyres blæst!"* he shouted, and he hurled a basketball-sized fireball at the door. It bounced harmlessly off the wood and extinguished instantly. *"Bēamas berstaþ! Arquemie! Krakatoa!"* Bolts of red, green, and blue energy flew from Simon's hands toward the doors, but none even made a dent. In desperation, he pointed a finger at the lock and shouted, *"Incantō clāvis!"* Nothing. Then he pointed with the other hand and shouted again, *"Incantō clāvis!"* Again, nothing. He kept repeating the same motion over and over, growing visibly more frantic with each failed attempt. *"Incantō clāvis! Incantō clāvis! Incantō* BLOODY *clāvis!"*

Leanne pulled Simon away from the door and asked, "Simon, be honest with me: if we can't open these doors, what's the worst-case scenario?"

Simon inhaled deeply, trying to calm down. "If we can't open these doors, it means the Deacon is onto us. He's using Kelly as a transmitter to project his psychic energy into the Letterbox and cut us off from her and Abby. Chances are, he's also giving Varr'rak some extra power, and together they'll launch a full mental assault on Abby."

"B-but he won't kill her, right? I mean, she's too valuable to the Following for that to happen, isn't she?"

"They can't destroy her body while they're all Elsewhere, but they could devastate her mind. Remember, the point of the Enlightening is to draw Azna'ghal into a suitable earthly vessel. If they break Abby mentally, it will be that much easier to control the transfer."

The green of Simon's eyes had dulled significantly, and he looked utterly hollowed out. Until Natalie got back, it was futile to tangle with the doors, and by then it might be too late to save Kelly and Abby. Things seemed as bleak as they could possibly be.

And then they heard screaming on the other side of the door.

*****

Abby and Kelly, having agreed on a safe place that they could both picture clearly, joined hands and stopped running. They closed their eyes and thought only of their safe place, remembering its looks, sounds, and smells. The buzz of the fluorescent tube light at the back of the room; the hard plastic chairs that made your ass feel numb if you sat in the same position for too long; the squeak of the chalk as it flew across the board, leaving behind scribblings in that incomprehensible handwriting; the shadows thrown by that big wooden cabinet that no one was allowed to touch.

The ground opened beneath their feet and sucked them below, and they zoomed down a long subterranean tunnel, hand in hand, only to be spit back out into two of the ass-numbing plastic chairs. Abby opened her eyes first, then directed Kelly to do the same.

Kelly did, and performed a double take straight out of a Chaplin film. They were back in Mr. Lockhart's classroom at Frederick Banting Secondary. The blackboard announced that their homework was to read the first three chapters of *Catcher in the Rye*, and the clock on the wall said 3:15 PM.

"How?" Kelly gasped, astonished. "How did we do that? I've never been able to escape the canyon before!"

"I think it's a Gospel thing," Abby said. "The Elsewhere seems to… respond to me."

"Huh. Sweet."

"I like to think so."

A slow round of applause began, and Simon sauntered through the doorway. But it wasn't Simon as Abby or Kelly knew him. His eyes were like two balls of topaz, and black shadows wafted from his waistcoat. Punctuating each word with a sarcastic clap, Varr'rak hissed in Simon's voice, "Top. Of. The. Class. Henderson."

Abby stood and instinctively moved in front of Kelly. Varr'rak looked her up and down with a predatory leer on his face. "You do continue to surprise, Abigail Henderson. Such a large-scale spatial distortion on your first trip to the Elsewhere… well, it's almost unprecedented. You have some real potential, kid. It will be a shame to snuff it out."

Abby didn't have the patience for another pissing contest with this thing. She grabbed Kelly's hand and snapped at Varr'rak to "**Sit down and shut up.**"

Despite himself, Varr'rak's mouth snapped shut and he dropped into a vacant chair. He jerked in his seat and growled furiously as Abby and Kelly legged it out of the classroom. They were past the first row of lockers before he could open his mouth and scream for backup. *"My lord! She is here!"*

The Deacon's hissing reply came over the PA system. *"As I knew she would be…"*

A stretch of eight lockers exploded, blowing a minivan-sized hole in the starboard wall and throwing Abby and Kelly off their feet into the port side wall. The temperature swan-dived off a cliff, and the PA started to sing.

It can take us all to heaven.
It can take us all to heaven.
It can take us all to heaven.
It's good enough for me…

The Deacon glided through the hole in the wall and stopped directly in front of Abby. Her brain shut down immediately, and her throat closed up. It was the first time in twelve years that she and he had been in the same room at the same time, and her brain automatically reverted to her thirteen-year-old mindset for a point of reference.

The Deacon smiled, and Abby's scream punched a hole in the roof of the Elsewhere straight through to the Letterbox.

*****

Natalie sprinted back to the dungeon armed with an antique two-handed battle axe, yelling at Simon and Leanne to get out of the way.

"Are you mad?!" Simon choked as Natalie raised the axe high. "This was a gift from Nicodemus the Narcoleptic after I helped him slay the Goblin King of Lyonesse! It's absolutely priceless!"

Natalie groaned. "Really, we have to do this now?"

"Well, I don't go around smashing up your treasured possessions, do I?!"

"Zeppelin records! Window! Ringing any bells?"

"That was entirely different!"

"Really? Then please enlighten me, Simon. How was that any different than this?!"

Leanne hollered, "GUYS! We have bigger problems right now!"

Simon backed off and gave a heavy sigh. "Very well. Do what you must. Just... try not to break it."

"I make no promises!" Natalie said, and swung the axe.

And then Abby screamed again.

*****

A heavy silence passed as the Deacon surveyed Abby for a moment, beaming like a proud father on the day of his child's convocation. *"You have grown, Abigail."*

Abby pressed against her back against a locker and slowly wriggled to her feet. "How?" she demanded. "How can you be here?"

"Did you think you were the only one with psychic prowess?" The Deacon pointed a bony finger at Kelly and flicked it skyward. She shrieked as invisible force launched her off her feet and pinned her to the ceiling.

Abby's fight-or-flight response came back online, and she pressed the button marked FIGHT. Concentrating hard, she willed a set of brass knuckles into existence on her right hand, closed her fingers, and threw a fierce haymaker at the Deacon.

He zipped to the other side of the hallway like a bullet and barked, *"STOP."*

Abby's shot missed by a mile and every muscle seized up. She stood like a petrified tree and wondered if this was how she had made Varr'rak feel.

"KNEEL, ABIGAIL!" the Deacon bellowed. *"Kneel before your better!"*

Abby's outstretched arm dropped to her side, and her waist cracked and popped as it bent. Her knees gave out and she bashed her shins hard against the floor as her body twisted into a position of submissive genuflection.

"But this is not all I can do…" the Deacon whispered as he ran spidery fingers through Abby's hair. *"I could mesmerise you, bend you to my will… I could show you such images of horror and depravity as you never thought possible, as would drive you to madness..."* Suddenly, he clamped both hands tight around the sides of her head. His fingertips hardened, and Abby felt his black claws digging in. *"Or, I could simply lobotomise you…"*

The Deacon ventilated Abby's skull with his claws and started burrowing into her brain. She was blinded by a scalding lance of pain behind her eyes, and she forced a scream out through her frozen mouth.

*****

KER-ASH! The battered remains of the left door fell into the small cell. Simon and Leanne rushed to the side of the cot while Natalie tried to pull the axe blade out of the shattered wood.

Kelly was lying stock still on the cot, eyes closed, face relaxed and peaceful. But Abby was convulsing on the floor, her face screwed up in a grimace of agony as blood poured from her nose. Her eyes were open, bugging out of her skull and blind to everything around her.

Leanne bent over Abby and grabbed her shoulders. "Oh my God, Abby! Abby, please wake up, please!"

Abby's voice screamed out of the glowing Vokarion crystal on her chest: "LEANNE!"

Leanne screamed into her own crystal. "ABBY! Abby, are you there?"

Abby's voice came out thready and haggard. "Lee… don't know if… hear me… so weak… I can't… much longer…"

Leanne looked up at Simon, her eyes massive and glistening with tears. "Please, Simon. Please do something. I can't… I don't want to lose her like this."

Simon's face betrayed nothing, but there was a storm raging in his eyes. He was terrified and grief-stricken and ashamed that the Deacon had outsmarted him. He was also viciously, vengefully pissed off, and he marched around to the other side of the cot with one hand down his shirt and the other flat on Kelly's forehead. From down his shirt, he extracted a shining silver medallion hanging beside his crystal. It was engraved with the same symbol as on the button that activated the Anointed Gate, and when he gripped it, the storm in his eyes swelled to its crescendo.

With peaceful fury in his voice, Simon commanded Leanne to "Get back."

"But…"

"GET BACK! NOW!" The roar startled her to her feet, and she scurried to the broken door. Natalie, who knew full well what was about to happen, left the axe where it was still stuck in the wood and beat a hasty retreat.

Simon bent over Kelly's still body and held the medallion so tightly it left dents in his palm. "I was really hoping I'd have more time," he whispered. Then he closed his eyes and recited the words as he had been taught them centuries ago. "My name is Ætheriċ, of the line of the Vanguard. My father was Wulfrecg, himself the son of Hroðmund. From these names have I learnt the wisdom of my ancestors. From these names do I draw strength. I offer these names now to that noble witness, the ancient countenance of the High Celestial!"

Along the wall, the torches blazed angrily and the flames doubled in height.

"I offer these words to that divine spirit to show fealty: The High Celestial is our one Father—the Maker of all things. In that aspect, His reign is just! The High Celestial is our one Mother—the Nurturer of Life and the Cosmos. In that aspect, Her Reign is true! The High Celestial is our one Soul—the Breath of Will and the Spark of Wisdom. In that aspect, Its reign is great! I invoke these and all the other Holy Names to compel and bind the spirits which vex this child!"

Kelly jerked on the cot and Simon took a step back, but he never let go of either her or the medallion. The little silver disc hummed and glowed white with energy. It was a Seal of the Vanguard, a relic of Simon's own people which kept him tied to his past and reminded him what they stood for, every second that he wore it. He had the deepest faith in what it represented, and it held as much power for him as the crosses did for Leanne or Abby.

"Varr'rak the Shadow-walker, I thee name! Your sin is known and your crime seen before the true God of the Three Planes! I speak here for the All-Seer: your incursion is unwanted, your trespass unjust!"

Abby went still and Kelly started to shake on the cot. Natalie pulled Leanne around the corner and out of the cell. "We should probably give him some room. This is going to get nasty."

*****

As Abby's brain slowly liquefied, her nose expelled a red river and a bead of drool dangled from her bottom lip. The Deacon knew she couldn't hear him, but he felt like gloating all the same. *"Did you believe it was a coincidence? Kelly.*

Varr'rak. I established the psychic relay days ago. From the moment the second attack began, I have seen and heard Varr'rak's every move. I knew you would eventually learn the truth, Abigail. I knew you would come for your friend. I wanted you to. On the physical plane, you have proved yourself a resilient foe. But in the mindscape, I am superior."

"Simon..." Abby groaned. "Natalie..."

"Your friends cannot help you here... you are in the centre of the Labyrinth, Abigail, and I have cut your string."

But then Abby's vision started to return, and a shallow voice drifted through her ears.

"Varr'rak the Shadow-walker, I thee name! Your sin is known and your crime seen before the true God of the Three Planes! I speak here for the All-Seer: your incursion is unwanted, your trespass unjust!"

Abby recognized the words. They were an ancient Vanguard exorcism rite. As the voice grew stronger, she knew that the cavalry had arrived. She took a deep breath and poured all her strength into her left leg. With the breath-taking speed of a small glacier, she was able to raise one knee. Her body fought against her with burning muscle cramps, but she began to stand up and wrapped her hands around the Deacon's wrists. She opened her mouth and unleased a hearty war cry, coming once again to her full height.

*****

In the Letterbox, Simon planted his feet and began chanting. "Through false witness have you ingratiated yourself upon us, filling the footsteps of your prisoner! I call this deception an abhorrent and blasphemous thing! In the name of the Earth-Maker, the Holy Witness, the Creator, I exorcise you!"

Kelly screamed and snapped her eyes open. They glowed bright yellow, and dense shadows rolled off the cot. Simon gripped her tighter and continued: "Thou servant of the False

Master, the Consumer who did sow and nurture the seed of wickedness and treachery on this Earth, I cast you out!"

A small flame appeared at the foot of the cot and spread outward, forming a perfect circle of fire around Simon and Kelly. Natalie ducked back into the cell just long enough to grab the busted door for an impromptu shield.

*****

Abby tried to focus her vision. Her brain was still burning and she was weeping from the pain, but the Deacon's hazy outline was starting to come into view. She felt his fingers in her head, and her fingers around his wrists.

She smiled. The Deacon looked almost… scared. He had expected her to go down like a bag of wet rice, like the sobbing wreck of a child he still thought of her as. But that Abby just plain didn't exist anymore. The Abby who did exist gritted her teeth and whispered, "Not today, shitheel."

She squeezed the Deacon's forearms until her knuckles were white, and he hissed angrily. *"What?! What is this magic?!"* Abby pulled the Deacon's claws out of her head and forced his arms down to his sides. *"Stop!"* he hollered. *"What are you doing?!"*

"I'm growing up! You're just a bogeyman from when I was a kid, and I'm not afraid of you anymore!"

Abby arched her back and then rammed her skull into the Deacon's nose. He fell to the ground with Abby still atop him, and his hood dropped away from his face.

Never before in her life had Abby seen the Deacon's human visage. In fact, she had sometimes forgotten there was a human visage under that white hood. More than once she had imagined a bald plain of featureless skin connecting his toothy mouth with the regal fabric. But now, the beetle-black eyes of Dr. John Leland drilled into her, shining with intense loathing.

*****

The fire around the cot blazed four feet high as Simon continued with the exorcism, and a black cloud crackling with electricity circulated above. Leanne and Natalie had stuffed their fingers in their ears to drown out the mighty wind now whirling around the cell, over which Simon had to shout in order to hear himself.

"Know the names of your true liege!" he commanded. "He is the Father, She is the Mother, It is the Soul! Know the Names and fear them as your brothers fear them, as the Eldest One fears them! Tremble in humility and flee this place!"

Lightning arced down from the cloud and struck Kelly square in the chest. Two more bolts followed in quick succession, creating a steady chain of electricity between her and the cloud.

Simon was howling at the top of his lungs, his every word flecked with spittle. "Beg forgiveness from the True Lord and torment us no more! Depart this body and return to rest! In the name of the Divine, I command this!"

BOOM! The chain of lightning broke off. Simon blinked and saw a massive hellhound sitting on Kelly's chest. *BOOM!* There was another standing at the head of the cot. *BOOM! BOOM!* More hellhounds appeared in the circle, until there were five in all.

With one hand, Simon removed the medallion from around his neck and raised it high above his head. The hellhounds glowered at him, frozen to the spot.

Simon closed his eyes and chanted in Old English. *"Here metodes miht! Here metodes miht! HERE! METODES! MIHT!"*

As one, the hellhounds looked skyward and bayed mournfully. Then a final bolt of lightning came down from the cloud and struck the first one right on the top of the head.

*****

Leland and Abby stood no more than an arms' length apart, and circled each other like two lions vying for the same mate.

It occurred to Abby that she had seen this white-haired man once before—on her fourteenth birthday, when she dreamed about her mother's deal with the Deacon, this man was the second presence she had detected in his body, switching places with the lion-snake every so often. She saw now from his psychic imprint that he had another name: Leland. Dr. John Leland. And that, she decided, was much less intimidating than 'The Deacon.'

"This is it?" she jeered. "*This* is what I was so afraid of all those years? What are you doing running around with these psychos, old-timer? Don't you have a bingo parlour to get to?"

Leland rolled his eyes. "My acolytes had warned me you might make a fumbling attempt at wit, but I must say I am nonetheless underwhelmed. Banter simply does not suit you, Abigail."

She chortled. "Oh wow, and that *voice*! No wonder you use that creepy whisper! If I had an accent like that, I'd probably disguise my voice too!" She put on a dreadful parody of Leland's Southern twang and tugged at a pair of invisible suspenders. "Now, ah say ah say, now we must prepare for the Enlightening, Abigail Henderson! But first, I must find my seat for the Kentucky Derby and enjoy this lovely mint julep!" She sipped from an imaginary glass and added, "Y'all."

"Mock me if you will," Leland fumed, "but this is far from over."

As if to dispute this, the hallway of Frederick Banting flickered like a hologram. The furthest edges of it began to fade to white, and Kelly was released from her captivity on the ceiling. She floated to the ground as Varr'rak in the form of Simon came stumbling out of the classroom, shaking and spasming. *"M-my lord,"* he stammered, *"O Deacon, I am —"* He never finished that thought, choosing instead to drop to his knees and tear at his shirt with a scream of pain.

Somewhere high above, the real Simon shouted, "Beg forgiveness from the True Lord and torment us no more!

Depart this body and return to rest! In the name of the Divine, I command this!"

The floor opened up beneath Varr'rak and flames tugged at his ankles. His hands morphed into a wolf's paws as he fell, and he sank his claws into the tile floor. *"Please! Please do not send me back there!"*

Abby took a step back and kicked Varr'rak under the chin. He lost his grip on the tiles and the fire pulled him down into the belly of Hell. Abby raised her arms above her head, calling the field goal, and announced, "And the quarterback is toast!"

The last of Frederick Banting faded to white, and then Leland began to dissolve as well as the psychic relay broke. He just had time to curse her name once more before he disappeared completely: "This is not over, Henderson! Mark my words, this is not over!"

"I really hope not, Leland. I'm looking forward to kicking your ass in the real world as well."

And then there was silence, and Abby and Kelly were back in the White Hallway.

*****

When the lightning struck the hellhounds, it triggered a tremendous pressure wave that knocked Simon clear across the room and blew the one remaining door out into the corridor. The hellhounds disappeared amid a roiling fireball, and Kelly lay still once again.

Leanne peeked around the corner. "Is—is it over?"

Natalie yanked her back as the fireball whooshed past them, scorching the walls of the Letterbox. After a few more seconds of waiting, she released Leanne and said, "Now it's over."

When they re-entered the cell, a horror show awaited them. The walls were covered in a thick layer of soot, and the thinner stones were spider-webbed with cracks. The frame of the cot looked like it had been run over by a tank, and the chairs and table were blasted to wood chips. Abby and Kelly lay in a heap on the floor but were otherwise unmarked, and a very dazed Simon sat slumped against one wall.

Leanne eyed Abby nervously while Natalie picked Simon off the floor and dusted him down. "Jesus, Simon, are you okay?"

Simon wobbled and looked right past her like she wasn't even there. In a very confused sort of voice he said, "And hast thou slain the Jabberwock? Come to my arms, my beamish boy!" Then he toppled into Natalie's arms, unconscious.

Natalie checked his pupils and decided, "Yeah, you'll be fine."

*****

In the White Hallway, Abby pointed Kelly to a door and directed her to open it.

"Are you sure this is the way back?" Kelly asked.

"I can hear Natalie and Leanne on the other side."

"I can't."

"Trust me, Kelly. That's the way back home." She opened the door to demonstrate, and they both saw the Letterbox on the other side.

"Yikes," Kelly said. "Looks like a bomb went off."

"Well, Simon said exorcisms were nasty work. Now go! Go and reclaim your life!"

"Aren't you coming too?"

"Yeah, in a sec. I just… I want to take a minute and breathe it in. Like, this is basically everything that being a Gospel is supposed to mean. It's like I'm a violinist, and this is the London Symphony Orchestra."

Kelly nodded, despite not totally understanding the feeling. "Okay, well, I'll leave the door open for you."

"See you in a few."

Then Kelly stepped through and was gone.

Abby waited a moment and then said, "I think the coast is clear. You can come out now."

Behind her, a thick Yorkshire accent asked, "'ow did you know?"

Abby turned and locked eyes with the late 'Grandma' Meg McAllister. "When I was fighting back after the Deacon paralyzed me, I was really struggling at first. My body was resisting what my brain was telling me to do, but then something surged way down deep inside. Like someone was giving me a signal boost. And it was only there for a fraction of a second, right in the back of my head, but I almost swore that I heard someone telling me to FIGHT."

"Well, I might have given you a wee zap," Grandma Meg said, "but you would've got there eventually."

"But how did you find me?" Abby asked. "What the Deacon said about the Labyrinth…"

"Bollocks to 'is Labyrinth. If you'll pardon my French. I'm a spirit, and we're in the spirit world. I sensed ye the moment ye walked in the door, and I fought my way through from Upstairs. Temporarily, mind."

"Sensed me?"

Meg winked. "Kin always knows kin, Abigail."

And then it hit her. The twins' first clue to her: *it happened before, and the eyeless face saw it all.* A face that had no eyes was a clock face. Simon had told her that he and Natalie had stopped the Enlightening once before. The last Alignment had been a century ago in, wait for it, Yorkshire. And two and two makes four…

"You were a Gospel," Abby said. "That was your magic, wasn't it? It was Gospel power."

Grandma Meg nodded. "I was *the* Gospel. First time this all kicked off. That's 'ow it passes down, usually: the mother's line. Sometimes it skips a generation or two, but it never goes extinct. And I'll tell you now, Abby, I'm right proud this is the generation where it resurfaced. You 'andled those ugly sods better than I could have at your age."

Abby beamed and her eyes started to mist. "Thanks, Gran."

"But when you do face the Deacon again—and believe you me, that is a question of when—I don't want you going in unprotected." Grandma Meg reached behind her and pulled something from her waistband, then held it flat on her palm. "Take this with ye when ye go back."

Abby ran her hand over the barrel, eyes shining with amazement. "That's—that's Mom's gun!"

"Aye, and it was mine before it was 'ers. See, the demons teleport by opening doors to the Elsewhere and then walking through to a different point on Earth. When yer mum drove through Varr'rak's portal, the gun fell out into the void. Took me some work to find it again, I can tell ye."

"But, how? I mean, that doesn't make any sense."

Grandma Meg chuckled. "Who ever said Earth-born objects couldn't enter the spirit world? If you know 'ow to open the doors, you can chuck anything you please into another dimension. Even people."

"Huh. I just keep thinking of the Elsewhere as like a kind of dream state."

"It is that, but it's much more besides. Of course, I don't want to spoil it for ye. You'll learn for yourself in time. Meanwhile…" She extended the gun toward Abby, grip first. "It's 'oly fired and everything, so it'll 'ave no trouble against most of yer demons."

"You're just giving it to me?"

"It's yours by birthright, way I figure. You're the last of the McAllisters now, Abby, and last of the Gospels. So, you 'ave to use it well, and make our family name count."

Abby picked up the gun and tucked it into her own waistband. Then she locked her arms around Grandma Meg. "I'll do right by you, Gran. You, Mom, Grandpa Bram, and every generation before you or still to come. I'm sorry I forgot the magic for so many years, but I remember it now, and I promise you—I *promise* you—I won't forget it ever again."

Grandma Meg hugged back without a single whispered word. After a long moment, they both let go, and Meg gestured to the open door. "Now go on. You've a job to do out there. You don't want to waste your time talking to a daft old woman like me."

"'Once more unto the breach,'" Abby announced as she stepped through the door.

The last thing she heard was Grandma Meg's response: "'We few, we 'appy few.'"

And then everything was dark.

CHAPTER 24

NO REST FOR THE WICKED

SHE AWOKE in her and Leanne's darkened bedroom. For a moment, Abby wondered if she had dreamed the whole thing, but then something cold and metal dug into the small of her back. She wriggled around under the covers and slowly worked the Webley out of her pants. She held the gun up to the ceiling and bounced it in her hand a few times, acclimating herself to its weight.

As she laid the Webley on the bedside table, a dark shade stirred in the far side of the room. Abby quickly snatched up the gun once more and trained it on the shadow, resting her thumb on the hammer.

Then the wall-mounted torches burst to life and Abby lowered the gun. Leanne was sitting in an old easy chair with a heavy woollen blanket atop her, just coming out of sleep herself. Now she picked up her glasses, which sat on one of the chair's arms, put them on, and grinned.

"Abby!" she squealed. "Oh my God, Abby, I'm so glad you're awake!" Leanne threw the blanket off and bolted from her chair, jumped onto the bed, and forced Abby down onto the mattress. A hurricane of relieved, passionate kisses jolted Abby awake, as Leanne's soft lips and warm tongue sent 10 000 volts coursing through Abby's body and diverted all the blood from her brain.

Amid all the saliva and hormones, Abby tried to ask a question, but it was muffled by Leanne's lips, still firmly stuck to Abby's own.

"Sorry, what?" Leanne drew back to give Abby a chance to breathe.

"I said, 'How long was I out?'" Abby asked.

"Well, I think it's about 2:30 now, and it was quarter to ten when you came out of the Bridge, so…"

"So, too fucking long, then," Abby said as she kissed Leanne once more.

As Leanne moved in for more face-sucking, the door opened with a groan and Simon and Natalie invited themselves in.

"Is that who I think it is?" Natalie asked.

"It is!" Simon exclaimed as he wrapped his arms around Abby and hauled her out of bed for a rib-cracking hug. "Abigail Henderson, back in the land of the living!" Then, looking at Natalie: "Back in the land of the *mostly* living!"

Under her breath, Abby muttered, "Jeez, couldn't you give us half an hour?"

"Pardon?"

Abby closed her arms around Simon. "I said it's good to see you." Extending one arm, she added, "And you, Natalie. Get in here, for God's sake."

With some trepidation, Natalie joined the hug. Then Leanne hopped off the bed and pressed against Abby.

There was a knock on the doorjamb, and a voice asking, "Am I interrupting anything?"

Abby wriggled out of the group hug and smiled. "Kelly? Is that you in there?"

Kelly grinned and leaped forward to join the love-in. She'd showered and changed her clothes, abandoning Varr'rak's robes for something altogether more tasteful. "It's really me, Abby. Watch this!" She extended a hand to Leanne, who dropped her cross into Kelly's palm. Kelly closed a fist around it for ten seconds and nothing happened. She returned the cross to Leanne and said, "He's gone. Varr'rak is gone and he isn't coming back."

"That's great," Abby breathed. "That's really great, Kelly. Maybe the best news I've had all week."

"There are still a few kinks, though," Kelly admitted. "I haven't been able to stop eating since I woke up, and my left foot keeps falling asleep for no reason, but Simon's pretty confident that'll go away with time."

"Beats the alternative," Leanne observed.

Kelly nodded. "True that." Her smile dropped as she turned back to Abby, but her eyes twinkled with gratitude and relief. "Thank you, Abby. Thank you for everything. I have to say that before we go any farther."

Abby waved her away. "You don't have to thank me, Kel. It's what friends are for."

"No, Abby. Friends are for lending you gas money until your next payday. What you did... I mean, if you hadn't shown up, God knows what might have happened. You saved my life, Abby, plain and simple. I can't even tell you how grateful I am."

Abby nodded toward Simon and the others. "Thank them. Simon, if you hadn't come in with that exorcism when you did..."

Simon shook his head. "Now, really, Abby, I can't take all the credit here. After all, it was your choice to walk into Varr'rak's mind."

Natalie rolled her eyes. "Jesus. Spare us from Canadians and the English. Can we cut the sickening display of humility and agree that we all kicked some major ass tonight?"

Abby shrugged. "Okay, I'll buy that. I mean, what the hell happened in that cell? I got a look before I came back to Earth, and it was like a frigging bomb site."

Simon said, "I'll tell you everything if you tell us what went on in the Elsewhere. It's only a fair trade."

"All right. But let's head to the lounge. It's getting kind of cramped in here."

In the octagonal lounge, the group relayed pieces of the narrative back and forth until they had stitched together a full timeline of events, concluding with Abby's tête-à-tête with Grandma Meg.

"Incredible. Absolutely incredible." That was Simon, who was busily examining Meg's gun. "Well, I always did say your gran was a crafty old bird. Mind you, I would like to run some tests on this gun before long. If it's been sitting in the Elsewhere like you say, there's a chance some cunning spirit will have anchored themselves to it."

"Anchored?" Abby asked.

"Attached themselves," Simon clarified. "You see it all the time: a spirit gets acquainted with an earthly place or object, some of their energy leaks into that place or object, and then the two are stuck together like glue. That's how most hauntings start. The last thing we need is for you to pick up this gun on the night of a full moon and get possessed by the ghost of a Victorian governess or something. And before you ask, that is *not* a random example."

"Took us a week to get rid of the last one," Natalie confirmed. "They're like cockroaches."

Abby slumped on the couch and rubbed her forehead. "Do whatever you have to, Simon. God, my head is killing me. The Deacon nearly turned my brain into soup back there."

"I can't believe that prick!" Kelly fumed. "Using me as *bait*? Where the fuck does he get off?!"

Natalie smiled. "You know, this is actually good for us…"

"How?" Kelly raged. "How is this good? That smug, self-righteous asshole risked my life and played us all like violins!"

"And what did he get in return?" Natalie replied. "This was the ace up the Deacon's sleeve. He risked everything so we'd walk into his trap, and what's he got to show for it? We slaughtered the acolytes, we sent Varr'rak screaming back to Niðerdæl, and we've got what we want: we know exactly where Following HQ is." Looking expectantly at Kelly, she finished, "Don't we?"

Kelly nodded. "Applegate. They're holed up at Applegate Asylum. They have been for years."

"You mean that old mental hospital in the Fraser Valley?" Natalie clarified.

"That's the place. 'The Most Haunted Building in BC,' they used to call it. Too fucking right. I can still picture the front gate. Has these two massive stone angels flanking it. Even a lot of the demons think it's creepy."

"I had a dream about that!" Abby exclaimed. "I just remembered! The day after my mom died, I had a dream Varr'rak was chasing me toward this big iron gate. There were two stone angels and a big capital 'A' carved on the arch above!"

"That's Applegate," Kelly confirmed.

"That settles it," said Natalie. "Now we know where they are, we can take the fight right to the Following. We can make the Deacon sorry he ever messed with us."

"And we will," Abby vowed. "Tomorrow. Tonight..." She stifled a yawn. "Tonight, I think we all need a break."

Simon stretched his arms above him and cracked his back. "That may be one of the wisest things I've ever heard you say, Abby. That exorcism really took a lot out of me."

"Yeah. I'm pooped," said Leanne.

"Okay, fine," Natalie relented. "Tonight, we sleep. Tomorrow, we make the Deacon sorry he ever messed with us."

"Do you even need to sleep?" asked Leanne.

"No, but it feels nice to get my eight hours every few decades."

The Letterbox spat up three more bedrooms for Simon, Natalie, and Kelly, and everyone turned in. As Abby crawled into bed, she couldn't help but notice that Leanne was staring at her and grinning from ear to ear.

"What's up?" Abby asked.

"I'm really impressed with the way you've stepped up to the plate these last couple of days. You know, taking the initiative and everything."

"What do you mean?"

Leanne laughed and wrapped an arm around her partner. "What do I mean? Abby! Mrs. Clifford, Varr'rak, the Bridge, the Hellstrokes… You've sucker-punched the Deacon at every turn!" She laid her other hand over Abby's. "You jumped out a window for me. You saved my life. And Kelly's. You're a genuine hero."

"Thanks, Lee." She tousled Leanne's hair and pressed her lips to Leanne's forehead, the corners of her mouth creeping up into a smile. Everything was so topsy-turvy now, between the demons, ogres, wizards, and astral projection, but this at least still made sense. Leanne always made sense. "What was it you said to me that first night?" Abby asked. "When I kicked you out of bed?"

"You know what I said. And I stand by it."

"I know, but... can you say it again? I just need to hear the words from your mouth one more time."

Leanne nodded and drew Abby's face down to her own. The two pressed their bodies together and kissed. Then Leanne pulled back and whispered softly, "I still believe you. And I'll keep on believing you. I don't know what's going to happen tomorrow, but whatever does, whatever the Deacon throws our way, I will be there for you, Abby Normal. Foreverways."

They stared at each other in silence. Then, just when the moment threatened to get sickeningly heartfelt, Abby's index and middle fingers started tiptoeing across Leanne's left breast. "You know what else we did that first night?" she whispered.

"I thought you were too tired to carry on," Leanne said.

Abby was already wriggling out of her pyjamas. "I'm never too tired for this."

*****

For the next few hours, Abby slept more blissfully than she had in months. She was nude, red-faced, and stinking of sex, but at least she wasn't dreaming about the Following. At one point, she and Leanne were riding a tandem bicycle made of dark chocolate through Stanley Park. Then the chain broke, and they sat under a large apple tree and proceeded to eat the front wheel and a decent portion of the frame. They were presently joined by Sir Isaac Newton, sporting a hard hat and large pink umbrella.

Then a large wrought-iron gate appeared in the middle of the path, which squeaked incessantly whenever it swung open. Isaac Newton was holding a jar of oil which he promised would stop the squeaking, but he wouldn't give it to Abby until she did a handstand while singing "La Marseillaise". Isaac Newton was a weird kind of guy.

It soon started raining. The waters of English Bay swelled dangerously, and tall, foamy waves hammered the Seawall. In the dream, Abby closed her eyes and tightly crossed her legs, trying not to think about it, but her mind kept circling back to lakes, waterfalls, and swimming pools.

She awoke, extremely aware of how full her bladder was. Slowly and deliberately, she slithered out of bed and re-dressed, then tiptoed toward the door with her eyes still half-closed.

She quickly came to regret not putting on her socks. The bare floor of the Letterbox was frigid, and Abby's bladder jolted painfully. Her teeth rattled as she took light, catlike steps down the hall, trying like hell to remember where the bathroom was. In the dark of night, the twisting corridors looked totally unfamiliar to her, but maybe that was just the Letterbox itself. The place clearly had a mind of its own, and Abby got the feeling it liked to move the walls around just to keep things interesting.

At last: relief. As Abby dropped trou and sat on the toilet, she swore she could hear Handel's "Hallelujah Chorus" swelling behind her, but it might just have been in her head.

As she flushed, out came a yawn that made her look like a snake about to swallow a ferret. Screw going after the Deacon tomorrow, she just wanted to sleep through the rest of the Alignment. This had truly been the most exhausting week of her life, and Azna'ghal could go take a flying leap.

After washing her hands, Abby cranked the 'C' tap to full blast and splashed herself in the face. She was so zonked out that she imagined she was hearing the Deacon's voice. But that was impossible. They'd broken the psychic link, and no physical threat could get past Simon's defensive charms. Besides, there was nothing in the mirror.

But the voice kept coming. "Join us, Abigail," it said. "Come to me. Come join us." Abby made a mental correction: it was not the Deacon's voice, but John Leland's. "Come to us, Abigail…" he crooned, with that acoustic guitar voice. "It's what you want… It's what you need…"

Abby closed her eyes and stood there. No running, no screaming for help, no fighting back. She just bobbed her head as Leland purred in that come-hither voice. Bit by bit, her body was deciding it *did* want this, and her brain was too tired and too clouded to argue.

She saw the big iron gate in her head, with its stone angel guardians and the 'A' on the arch above. "You see, Abigail?" Leland whispered. "You know where we are… You must come to us…"

Abby turned, her body now running on autopilot. "Yes. Yes, I know where you are."

She left the bathroom in a deep trance and sauntered barefoot through the Letterbox. In the short time since she'd gone for her pee break, the walls had rearranged themselves yet again. Abby kept her eyes closed and guided herself with a hand along the wall, navigating the new path with surprising ease.

She stopped briefly, when her hand ran over a patch of wet plaster. Abby's rational mind briefly leapt out of the fog clouding her brain and told her to pull the Vokarion crystal out of her front pocket. Fighting the hypnotic lure of Leland's voice, Abby worked one end of the crystal like a stylus, gouging a messy illustration into the soft patch of the wall. She drew the 'A,' and two crude hooded figures that might have been angels (if you squinted at them hard enough). She carved three words below the image before dropping the crystal and carrying on. *Kha'al Azna'ghal ixxi.*

She eventually came to the Anointed Gate. This she stepped through, emerging onto East 6th. She didn't notice that it was 5:00 on a chilly November morning, nor that she was barefoot in a pair of thin cotton pyjamas. Leland's voice assured her it was okay, and she trusted him.

The voice directed her to a big, black Continental Mark III parked on the next block, which briefly reminded Abby's rational mind of a schlocky old James Brolin movie she'd once seen. She got in the back seat of the car, snapping her fingers in time to the song on the radio.

Give me that old-time religion
Give me that old-time religion
Give me that old-time religion
It's good enough for me...

Abby closed the door without needing to be told and buckled her seatbelt. The black-robed acolytes in front of her whispered to each other in that funny nonsense talk they liked to do, while Abby gazed at the pretty patterns the frost crystals made on the window.

The demon in the driver's seat locked the doors and pulled out into the night.

*****

Abby slept for most of the trip. She had no sense of time when she awoke, but it was clear they'd left Vancouver long ago. They were on an empty stretch of two-lane country road lined with tall trees, with taller mountains poking up in the distance. Abby recognized the peaks of the Cascades when she saw them, which must have put them near the Fraser Canyon. There was a fork in the road up ahead, and what looked like a private drive carved right through the thick trees and the hillside. When the car turned up the drive, the demons began to chant. *"Kha'al Azna'ghal ixxi. Kha'al Azna'ghal ixxi. Kha'al Azna'ghal ixxi."*

The top of the hill was clear-cut, and Abby could see the distant outline of a high, gloomy building. Before the clearing, there was the gate and the arch. The two angels stood guard, each one holding a long halberd in one hand and a large key in the other. Carved into the centre stone of the arch, an elegant capital 'A' set in a large circle.

That was when Abby started screaming. All the pieces finally clicked. She was trapped, about to be taken into the lair of the enemy. The Deacon (or Leland, perhaps?) had hit her with some kind of psychic whammy before they parted ways, and she had walked right into his arms.

She screamed and swore and kicked the demons' seatbacks like a fussy toddler on a transatlantic flight. Under its hood, one of the acolytes rolled its eyes and snapped its fingers. Abby's seatbelt tightened and held her against the seat. Nonetheless, she kept screaming. She knew it was futile. She knew she was screwed. But she had to make this as difficult for the Following as she could.

The two demons got out of the car and glided around to the back. The first snapped its fingers again and Abby's seatbelt unbuckled. The second demon reached in and wrapped a hand around her throat, squeezing her windpipe until she stopped screaming.

They hauled her out of the car, and four more acolytes descended in a swarm. Each one grabbed one of Abby's limbs with bone-crushing force, and they marched her in unison toward the brick structure. It was, Abby realized, the same building she had seen in her dream when she was fourteen, but from a different angle. This was where her mother had signed away her life to him.

No robes tonight. No pretence. John Leland had cleaned and pressed his finest white suit for her arrival, and he stood with his hands folded atop a brass-headed walking stick. As the acolytes dragged Abby up the steps, he smiled brightly, looking for all the world like a homicidal William Hartnell.

The acolytes forced Abby to her knees in front of him, and Leland brushed her hair from her face. "I did warn you this was not over."

CHAPTER 25

PRIMUM NON NOCERE

THE STORY of Applegate Asylum—officially the George and Elizabeth Applegate Home for the Mentally Unstable—begins in the spring of 1886. That was the year wealthy Ezra Applegate, together with his wife Winifred and their three strapping sons George, Bertram, and Herbert, settled a parcel of farmland in the Fraser Valley, not far from the town of Hope. The homesteaders had a happy few years on that land until 1893, when Winifred and Herbert were mauled to death by a coyote on the road into town. It was said that Herbert was Ezra's favourite son, and the sudden loss of both the child and his mother had a serious impact on the Applegate patriarch's health. Ezra suffered a nervous breakdown in 1901 and was confined to the family farmhouse under the careful watch of his surviving sons, until he hanged himself in the barn in 1909.

Bertram died during the Spanish flu pandemic of 1919, which also claimed the lives of his wife and two children and George's eldest daughter Annabelle. In 1921, George and his family sold the farm and its lingering bad memories to the government of Canada and migrated east. The farmhouse and barn were razed, and the government clear-cut most of the surrounding 200 acres to make room for a mental hospital and grounds.

Yet even after the Applegates' departure from the area, bad luck continued to plague the old farmstead. When the asylum's East Wing was under construction in 1922, a recently-built staircase collapsed while it was being examined by one of the project's chief architects, killing him and critically injuring two workers.

Shortly after the asylum opened in 1924, a patient escaped his cell on Christmas Eve and murdered two doctors and a nurse. He disappeared from the asylum grounds the same night and was never found.

Despite these and other woes, Applegate Asylum continued to operate until 1961, when a rash of disappearances and fatal "accidents" forced the government to open an investigation into the asylum's operations. The inquest's final report revealed a legacy of systemic abuse and corruption, and allegations even arose that some of the asylum's senior staff had engaged in bizarre pagan rituals on the grounds. But no charges were ever laid, as many of the accused staff members disappeared shortly before the asylum was shut down, and before they could be brought to trial.

But the story doesn't even end there. In the early '90s, a rumour started to make the rounds in the Nocturn. A new Gospel, so the story went, was due to be born before the year was out. And the Applegate staff crawled back out of the woodwork, unaged since the day they went into hiding. They dusted off their black robes and rallied once more around their leader: the man who had spearheaded the campaign of abuse and torture decades before; the man who had overseen all the heinous rituals and summoning rites; the man who had been the first among them to make a pact with a demon. A smooth-talking psychiatrist from Tennessee named Dr. John Zachariah Leland.

*****

Abby sat on the rickety cot, knees drawn up to her chest, trying to melt a hole in the white padded wall with her eyes. She had been humiliated, tortured, and violated by the Following, and she'd only been in the asylum an hour and a half.

From the front steps where Leland lorded his victory over her, the acolytes had dragged her down the asylum's main hall into a room marked RECEPTION/PROCESSING. *Processing*. Like she was a side of beef.

In practice, "Processing" meant stripping her naked, hurling her to the cement floor of a tiny shower stall covered in black mould, and blasting her with a freezing jet of stinking brown water from above. This, Abby had been expecting. Every prejudice she had about creepy mid-century lunatic asylums told her something like this was bound to happen. There probably wasn't a single inmate who'd come through Applegate back in the day who hadn't had the same treatment.

What came next, however, was unique. While she was still wet from the shower, Leland raked his black claws roughly and haphazardly over her scalp, shaving her head smooth and raw.

The next stop on the tour was the SURGERY wing, where she was strapped to an operating table in all her bald, shivering, denuded glory. The claws came out again, and Leland stuck them a quarter of an inch deep into her left side, just above her kidney. With *"Kha'al Azna'ghal ixxi"* on his lips, he carved a series of twisting, spiralling glyphs into her skin between her shoulder and hip. No disinfectant. No anaesthetic. Plenty of screaming.

This, he explained while his hand was still inside her, was meant to "purify" her for the Enlightening. The glyphs were an ancient prayer in the demon language which sang the glory of the Eldest One, and anointed Abby's flesh for His arrival. But even while he told her all this, his face solemn and reverent, Abby saw nothing but pure, fall-over-laughing glee in his aura. This was a power play. This was revenge, plain as that.

They didn't clean or dress her wounds before they dragged her out of the surgery wing. As two hooded thugs frog-marched her to a windowless cell in the most isolated block of the asylum, Abby focused on the stinging, angry pain in her left flank. The Following were trying to break her, to downgrade her from "human" to "meat". But pain was human. The pain made her angry, and angry was even more human. When they locked her in the cell, she shut her eyes and pictured herself holding Meg's Webley. She unloaded five shots into Leland's testicles, and a sixth between his eyes. She tore his head off with her bare hands and diced his body into sashimi with Natalie's machete. This hypothetical filled her with joy, and joy was the most human of all.

She was reflecting on this hypothetical, trying to melt the wall, when the heavy metal door creaked open behind her and an acoustic guitar of a voice strummed, "I hope the accommodations are to your satisfaction?"

Abby kept staring at the wall. "Bite me."

Leland paused to consider the invitation, then shook his head. "No. No, if it's all the same to you, I think I shall leave those duties to Leanne."

She turned and glared at him. "Don't! Don't you *dare* say her name. Your fight was only ever with me, Leland. Messing with my friends, my family, was way over the line."

Leland ambled into the cell, the tap of his walking stick muffled by the padded floor. "Let's not kid ourselves, Abigail. If you had just come when I called, we could have avoided all this unpleasant business. But you defied my will from the first. You insisted on playing the disobedient, petulant child, so naturally I was forced to… break some of your toys, as it were. But you are here now, that is what's important. And I hope that in the brief time you have left, we can be civil with one another."

Leland snapped his fingers with a flourish, and two acolytes floated into the cell, carrying between them a small table, two folding chairs, and a blue tablecloth. Two more acolytes followed them, carrying dishes and silverware for two. Silently and mechanically, the demons arranged place settings for Abby and Leland. As he took a seat, one of the demons pulled the other chair out for her with an expectant bow.

"Well, go on!" Leland gestured to the empty chair. "Have a seat!"

"Why?" was all Abby could say.

"Because it's breakfast time, of course!" Leland snapped his fingers again and a fifth acolyte wheeled a lunch trolley into the cell. It was laden with pancakes, French toast, assorted eggs and breakfast meats prepared a half-dozen different ways, and a large pitcher of orange juice. Leland helped himself to a glass and said, "I wasn't certain what your poison was, so I covered all my bases."

Abby took her seat and eyed the food suspiciously. Leland chuckled: "I know you think me cruel, Abigail, but I wouldn't let you go through something like the Enlightening on an empty stomach! Trust me, you need to build up your strength."

Abby reached for the pitcher of juice. She wanted to throw Leland's peace offering to the floor and tell him to go fuck himself. But she hadn't had a bite to eat since she woke up nearly four hours ago. "It's not poisoned or cursed or anything, is it?"

Leland smiled like a child had just asked him why the sky was blue. "Now why would I poison it if we need you alive for the ritual?"

That was actually a sound point. Abby loaded up her plate and got stuck in, attacking her breakfast like she was just coming off a yearlong fast. Over the sound of her ravenous chewing, Leland asked, "How is it?"

She ignored the question. Secretly, she wished the food was as awful as everything else around here. That way, she could have the satisfaction of spitting it out and still telling Leland to go fuck himself. But the plain truth was it all tasted divine. As she ate, Abby found herself needing more and more of the bounty in front of her, and she hated herself for needing anything from this man.

Leland sighed. While Abby went at it like a pig at a trough, he himself ate very patiently, taking his time with every flavour and despairing at his guest's unladylike behaviour. "Don't you have anything to say to me?"

Abby swallowed a large mouthful of pancake and grunted, "How? How did we get here?"

"I was thinking more along the lines of a 'Thank you.'"

"Sorry," Abby snapped. "Thank you, Doctor, for this lovely breakfast. It really makes up for the kidnapping, stripping, shaving, and involuntary surgery."

Leland chose to ignore the irony. "Now was that so difficult? As to your question: I must confess to a little subterfuge during our battle of wits."

"You mean when you tried to lobotomize me?"

Leland raised his eyebrows and smiled. "Is that what I was doing? Or was I trying to get in close to you? Close enough to implant a telepathic command deep within your mind, an override to bring you here when I felt the hour was right?"

Abby blinked. "Wait… you mean Mrs. Clifford, the Shoppe, Avalon, all of that was to get me into the Bridge?"

"Two out of three. Not bad. It was no accident that Varr'rak revealed himself when he did. I'm sure you know of course that it is sin for a Following acolyte to uncover his head unless he does so on my orders. You were too well-protected when Varr'rak came for you on your birthday, so I knew I had to get you alone. I needed to be close to you. The easiest way to do that would be to lure you into the spirit world. I needed Varr'rak to supplicate to you and I needed you to learn the truth about Kelly's plight. But I couldn't let Varr'rak simply jump you in your apartment the day after your mother died. If he then threw the inevitable fight, it would have looked far too much like a set-up. You or one of your friends would have suspected a trap. Thus, the attack on Leanne. I needed you to see that the stakes were real, because I needed you and your friends to fight tooth and nail to save an innocent life. If you bested Varr'rak then, the victory would have seemed natural, and once you learned the truth about Kelly, you would have done everything you could to free her and one-up me. It didn't really matter whether Leanne lived or died; as long as you were prepared to save Kelly and walk into my arena, I was satisfied. But what happened with your partner's crucifix, and with the imp… that was an unfortunate complication that disrupted our timetable."

"So Varr'rak had to goad Whittaker into getting me to Avalon."

Leland nodded. "The imp's containment circle worked against me. Even my psychic link could not penetrate it. I had mere moments before he raised the enchantment and I was cut off, so I told Varr'rak to get you there by any means necessary and… left him to his devices."

"To Whittaker's torture, you mean."

Leland shrugged.

"But why go to all the trouble? Why did I have to be your sacrificial lamb in the first place? What did you say to my mother to trick her into that deal?"

Leland laughed. "'Trick' nothing! Your mother was *glad* to shake my hand! After what she'd been through, I suspect she would have done anything to save her own hide. No, she was quite willing to give you up."

Abby bunched up her shoulders and pursed her lips. Hearing this was a knife in the heart, but she had to know. She still had far too many questions. "Why'd you wait, then? If she wanted to give me up, why didn't you just take me the day I was born? Why torture me like this?"

"The Dead Man's Pledge," Leland stated, as if that answered everything.

"What?"

"It's one of the oldest known enchantments in True Magic: an unbreakable pact that binds two parties together in the sight of whichever deity you subscribe to. Each party swears fealty to the other, and then they lay down the terms of a contract, and they know that if either one of them break or try to alter the contract in any way, then they will lose that which is most precious to them. In most cases, it's their own life, which is why they call it the Dead Man's Pledge, but with your mother it was... different."

"My dad," Abby said.

"Precisely," Leland nodded. "Your mother invoked the Pledge in my presence, so I was honour-bound to take her up on it. I resurrected your father, and I guaranteed the three of you 25 years of peace starting from the day you were born. In return, they both swore that they would not interfere with my plans come the Alignment, nor would they tell you what you truly were, in case you got some foolish idea about defending yourself. Perhaps I forced your mother's hand by killing your father, but they attacked me first. I was simply defending myself against a rather brazen pre-emptive strike. Of course, we could split hairs about this all day…"

"Man, you really thought of everything, didn't you?"

"That has always been my great secret. Two brains for the price of one."

"I've been wondering a lot about that lately," Abby said. "When I look at your aura, there's still so much of… you in there. John Leland, I mean. Who really runs the show here: the man or the demon?"

Leland leaned forward, deliberately exposing his aura to Abby. "I thought you'd never ask." Something flickered in his eyes, and Abby saw the two entities inside him: the man called Leland and the demon called the Deacon. They danced around each other in a repulsively flirtatious tango, and then started to drift together into one being. Abby was reminded of The Five Varr'raks becoming The One Kelly, as the spirits of Leland and the Deacon melted into one other. Neither one was purely himself, and they both looked at Abby, daring her to guess which was which.

Abby shook her head and averted her eyes before she threw up. The effect was making her nauseous, and she was still only halfway through her breakfast.

Her dining companion, whoever he was, leaned back in his chair and tented his fingers under his chin. "I suppose to properly answer this question, we must venture back to the 1950s. I—that is to say, Leland the man—was Chief Psychiatrist at Applegate back in those days. We had a patient brought in around '57 or '58 who was accused of multiple homicides across British Columbia and Alberta. Have you ever heard of William Joseph McRae, Abigail?"

Abby had. "Wild Bill" McRae was one of Western Canada's most infamous serial killers, formally accused of eight murders between Vancouver and Banff, but suspected of as many as a dozen. The RCMP manhunt that eventually brought him in was the stuff of legend, and the trial was notorious for several reasons, not the least of which being McRae's successful insanity plea, which likely saved him from the gallows and infuriated the citizenry who were demanding his head on a platter.

"From Day One," Leland reminisced, "McRae protested his innocence to anyone who would listen. He claimed that something from outside our world had taken control of him, used him like a puppet, and forced him to commit those crimes on behalf of an 'Eldest One.' His delusion was such a… specific one that when they brought him here, I of course took a personal interest in the case. I worked with Mr. McRae extensively over many long months…"

"Until you realized he wasn't so crazy after all," Abby guessed.

"Indeed. McRae told me of a ritual that would allow me to summon one of these creatures from outside and speak with it directly. It was purely an intellectual exercise on my part, but I performed the rites as he instructed me…"

"And that is where I came in…" the Deacon hissed. *"Leland offered himself as a vessel, so I could continue my work. He offered the asylum as a refuge. His patients… empty-minded lunatics and imbeciles… offered no resistance to my acolytes."*

"And in return for all that I gave him," Leland crooned, "the Deacon graciously allowed me a modicum of control over my own form. I have gained access to powers, to information, that are a million years beyond human understanding. Can you imagine what that is like, Abigail? It has been the endgame of every scientific mind since time began to unlock those mysteries: where did we come from? Why are we here? Where, ultimately, are we going? For 60 years now, I have seen… everything. And it is absolutely spectacular."

Abby's jaw hung loose, and she pushed her plate away with trembling hands. No way she was going to eat another bite now. "Jesus, Leland, listen to yourself! That arcane knowledge, that power, what does it cost you? Mind-raping the mentally ill, indiscriminate murder… have you even stopped to think how many people will die if the Enlightening works? Simon told me Azna'ghal tried to destroy this entire dimension the first time around!"

Leland scoffed. "Typical Vanguard propaganda. Abigail, did dear old 'Simon' ever tell you why the Eldest One rebelled in the first place? Because He had the gall to demand order! The High Celestial gave humans free will not out of infinite wisdom, or the kindness of its heart, but as a social experiment. The Vanguard and the spirits were too tightly bound by their loyalty to the divine, and the divine eventually decided that they were too predictable. Too *boring*. Humanity was created to liven things up a bit. Give these hairless monkeys free will, fire, and pointy sticks, then turn them loose on each other and see what happens! *That* is the true meaning of life! And those chaotic, self-destructive creatures were touted as the superior race! The Eldest One sought to bring the skin-apes in line, to unite them under one law, and for that He was banished?! The Enlightening is not a death sentence, my dear, it is salvation. It is the mechanism by which humanity will finally descend from the trees and join civilization. *True* civilization. And if at this point you still cannot grasp that most fundamental concept, then perhaps you are simply too primitive to appreciate what the Eldest One is offering you. Perhaps you would be better off locked in some dark corner of your own brain while He put your form to better use."

Abby finally snapped. The abuse, the manipulation, and the callous disregard for humanity was one thing. She could excuse that as long as she believed it was the demon making those decisions. But Leland was still in there. He was willing to sell out the human race, and he was rationalizing the decision like he was throwing out a pair of socks with too many holes in them. Taking the knife from her plate, she hollered, "You son of a bitch!" and stabbed Leland in the back of the hand, almost pinning the tablecloth on the other side.

That was a mistake. The acolytes rushed her from every side, dragging her kicking and screaming out of her seat and out of the cell, while Leland just looked very disappointed with her. He shook his head and yanked the knife out of his hand without so much as a wince. The acolytes forced Abby to her knees on the cold cement of the cell block, and Leland came out of the rubber room to meet them, his walking stick *tap-tap-tapping* a circle around her.

"I'm going to tell you another story, Abigail," he said with a wistful glance at the ceiling. "Forgive me if I'm beginning to bore you, but you have me in rather a nostalgic mood today. Once upon a time, there was an old woman who lived with her young grandson in a farmhouse just outside Arlington, Tennessee. These two were dirt-poor, and totally alone in this world apart from each other, so they sought refuge in the arms of the Good Lord Above. The old woman gave her grandson rigorous religious instruction every day of his life, but she was a particular fan of Proverbs 13: 'He that spareth his rod hateth his son; But he that loveth him chasteneth him betimes.' The rod in question was an old hickory walking stick she'd carved in her younger days, and whenever her grandson misbehaved, she would raise her stick up on high just like this and give him a few—solid—*whacks*!" Leland sliced through the air with the hickory, stopping himself an inch from Abby's ear. When she flinched, he smiled. "She would sing while she did it, too. She would sing the hymns she grew up with, loud enough that she wouldn't have to hear the bruises she was giving him. Her favourite was an old nigger spiritual she learned from her nanny: 'Give me that old-time religion! Give me that old-time religion! Give me that old-time religion! It's good enough for me…'

"One day, when the boy was 12, he was roughhousing in the living room while his grandmother was preparing the tea and sandwiches for her bridge game later that afternoon. Perhaps the boy was overly careless, running when he should have been walking, but one thing led to another, and as Granny came out of the kitchen, and her boy ran into the kitchen, bang went her finest tea set right onto the floor. Porcelain in a million pieces, Earl Grey staining the floorboards… The old woman had never been so angry. Before you could think, she came at her boy with her stick in the air, shouting about St. Peter and the little baby Jesus. That first swing took out three of the boy's back teeth. But at some point, during the third or fourth verse, something within that young man broke."

Leland crouched in front of Abby, and his eyes stabbed right through hers into the primal emotional centres of her brain. "The boy realized he'd had enough," he whispered. "The next time his granny came at him, he threw out both hands and caught the stick right across his palms. He pulled it away from the old woman and she lost her balance. Down she goes like a bag of sand, and up he comes with the walking stick, and suddenly he's the one singing. The wrath of God is on *his* side for once, and it takes him longer than he would care to admit to notice when the old woman finally stops screaming. When she just… lies there, never to raise a hand in anger ever again."

"Is there a point to all this?" Abby groaned.

Leland stood and exhaled through his nose. "My point, young lady, is that violence is, and has always been, in my nature. It is not something I hide or attempt to justify to myself; it is a plain truth that I made peace with a long time ago. Now, it is true we need you alive for the Enlightening, but 'alive' is a very loosely-defined term. Technically speaking, I could snap your spine over my knee and pull the blaspheming, whoring tongue right out of your face, and you would still be 'alive' enough for the Eldest One to look the other way."

Abby started laughing to herself. "Go ahead," she hissed.

"I beg your pardon?"

"You heard me! If this is what it takes for you to feel like a big man—beating a defenceless, naked woman who's 40 pounds lighter than you—then you might as well just do it. You geriatric, limp-dicked, dumbshit *redneck*."

The colour rose in Leland's face, and his hand twitched on the head of the stick. One eye did likewise, and Abby half-expected steam to shoot out his ears. "I really wish you hadn't said that."

His arm snapped forward, and the stick rapped sharply against Abby's midsection. She fell to all fours, gasping for breath. "I had hoped you might smarten up," Leland seethed, "given one last chance. But I see now that you are absolutely beyond redemption. You are the most ungrateful, stubborn woman I have ever met. I will not be spoken to like that by anyone, least of all a *degenerate*—"

WHACK! There went the stick across her buttocks, shocking her forward and scraping her knees on the cement floor.

"Lesbian—"
WHACK!
"Skin-ape—"
WHACK!
"Whore!"
WHACK! Abby bit into her own tongue. Her ass and her thighs were raw, red, and starting to bleed. And Leland was starting to sing.

"'It was good for the Hebrew children!
It was good for the Hebrew children!
It was good for the Hebrew children!
And it's good enough for me!'"
Each line was punctuated by the smack of hickory on flesh. Leland crept up Abby's body from one end to the other, sparing her posterior in favour of a hard strike to her tailbone. The small of her back. Her sides: one kidney, then the other.

Come the second verse, he changed up the rhythm. While 'It was good for Paul and Silas,' he flipped the stick around in his hand, and brought the brass head down on Abby's splayed fingers. Her tongue scraped against her teeth and her jaw unlocked automatically, unleashing a wail of pain. Meanwhile, it was still good enough for Leland.

And then: "'It will do when I am dying!'" The brass head came in on her temporal bone, just behind her left ear. Something went *crunch* that wasn't supposed to go *crunch*, Abby's ear started to ring, and blood tracked down her jawline. Then Leland's foot swung up beneath her, and she felt the toe of an Oxford shoe between her breasts, and suddenly she was on her back. It would do when he was dying, and the stick went into her floating ribs. *Crack!* Abby's breath came up short and she started to cry, despite herself. Everything—literally everything—hurt.

"'It will do when I am dying!
It's good enough for me!'" By comparison, the last blow was a love tap. The flat end of the stick—*thok!*—right between her eyes, more to get her attention than anything else. Seconds

later, Abby was on her knees again as the acolytes dragged her back into her rubber room. Leland dabbed his brow with a silk handkerchief as if nothing had happened, then absentmindedly tossed the same to Abby.

"Clean yourself up, Abigail. You have a big day ahead of you." His stick *tap-tap-tapped* down the hall, dribbling fresh Henderson blood on the floor.

CHAPTER 26

IT IS THE BLOODY BUSINESS

WHILE LELAND gave Abby that old-time religion, panic was setting in at the Letterbox. Leanne woke first that morning, and the bottom dropped out of her stomach as she felt the cold empty spot on the other side of the bed. She found Abby's abandoned crystal and the message scratched in the wall only a few feet from the bedroom door, as if the Letterbox itself knew how bad the situation was and was trying to help in its way. Before Leanne could even think about raising the alarm, three doors materialized on the wall beside her, and the Letterbox spat Simon, Kelly, and Natalie out of their bedrooms, all still partly asleep. As one, they realized what had happened and they prepared themselves for the worst. They dressed quickly, Natalie loaded half the Letterbox's armoury into the trunk of her car, and then they were off. The Thunderbird rolled up to the asylum's private driveway around noon, and one look at the weather told them the Following were hard at work.

When Abby's friends had left Vancouver, the sky above had been a thick sheet of tasteless November grey, spitting down a thin drizzle of rain. But the coal-black clouds above the asylum were throwing down the worst rain any of them had seen that year, and a strong north wind rocked the tall trees.

Simon held the rain at bay against a dome of protective magic, and Natalie led the group up the driveway on foot. They turned off about halfway up the drive and looped through the thick trees around to the south end, where ten feet of red brick enclosed the perimeter of the asylum grounds. A two-foot-thick line of concrete was set into the ground about five feet out from the wall, and Natalie suddenly froze and put up one hand as she neared it. "Wait a minute," she said, "I don't like this." She paused for a moment and closed her eyes. "Do you feel that?"

Kelly and Leanne looked at each other and shook their heads.

Simon nodded. "Yes, now you mention it. There's a sort of electricity in the air here."

"I don't feel anything," said Kelly.

"Because it's not meant for you," Simon replied. "But I'm willing to bet…" He pulled a scrap of paper out of his pocket, folded it into a swan, and whispered a magic word to it. The swan jumped to life in his hand and flapped its wings. Simon let it go, and the little paper bird flew over the concrete line. Blue sparks flashed on the swan's wings as it passed over the line, and it suddenly froze in mid-flight. Then it burst into flame and fine white ash drifted to the ground.

"Damn," Simon said. "The Deacon is clever."

Off Leanne's puzzled look, Simon elaborated. "That line is the edge of a magic circle. The Deacon has raised a barrier of protective magic around the asylum to repel opponents. Just like Whittaker had at Avalon, only stronger. Looks like a Level 12 Deterrence Curse."

"What does that mean for us?" Kelly asked.

Simon frowned. "It means this is as far as Natalie or I go, unfortunately. A Deterrence Curse detects and neutralizes any magical energy source stronger than a Vokarion crystal. If Natalie or I crossed that line, we'd be incinerated in seconds."

"Could you break the circle?" Leanne asked.

Simon shook his head. "There's no way of knowing how deep the concrete is set. I'd have to break the circle completely on the first try to collapse the barrier, and then we'd have to move fast. It's like popping a water balloon: if you break a magic circle, the energy it's containing has to go somewhere. The most likely direction is right into your own face. And the noise would surely bring every demon in the asylum running."

Kelly looked past the line, up at the sheer brick wall. "You said this thing responds to magical signatures. But Leanne and I should be okay, right? We're both human, and all my magic got zapped away with the exorcism."

"The Curse won't be wired to deter humans," said Natalie. "If it was, Abby would have been fried the moment they got her here. The two of you should be okay. As long as you steer clear of the guards."

I guess we're on our own then." Kelly dug in her bra and extracted the Vokarion crystal Simon had given her that morning, then looped the string around her neck. "But we'll keep you guys updated if things get dicey."

"What about weapons?" Leanne asked. "I'm not going in there without a safety net."

"I'll fix you up," Natalie said.

"Simon, do you really think this will work?"

"Frankly, I have my doubts," Simon answered. "But if it doesn't, none of us will live long enough to regret it."

Leanne looked at the high wall and gulped. "You're right," she whimpered. "What have we got to lose?"

*****

"Almost… there…" The top third of Leanne's body was just over the wall, but the rest of her hung in the air, struggling to get a foothold on the rain-soaked bricks.

"Come on, Lee!" Kelly whispered. "You can do it!" She was already on the other side, crouching in a low hedge.

Leanne swung one leg over the top of the wall. "Great!" Kelly said. "You're almost there!"

Leanne brought her other leg over and sucked in a sharp breath. Ten feet seemed a lot higher from the top than it did from the bottom, and she shut her eyes tightly. "Don't look down, don't look down, don't look down…"

"You're going to be okay, Lee! I'm right here!"

Leanne jumped, tucking her legs in and landing in a roll. She opened her eyes and exhaled. "Okay, that wasn't so bad."

Kelly opened the cloth gym bag slung over her shoulder, and the pair checked the supplies Natalie had given them. Her own sheathed machete accounted for most of the bag's bulk. The Webley was laid atop it, next to a box of cartridges. Then there were two little holy-fired combat knives—one for each of them—and a small bottle of Bonnesante Potion tightly wrapped in brown paper for its own protection. To this last item, Simon had affixed a label reading "FOR EMERGENCIES". All of this was bundled up in Varr'rak's robes.

The southwest part of the asylum grounds had once been home to a lush garden tended by the lower-risk patients. Now, it was a dense tangle of chest-high grasses, creeping vines, weeds, and thorn bushes. Leanne and Kelly crouched low and scurried through the high foliage toward a creaky utility shed about a hundred yards up the hill, which was being guarded by two Following acolytes. "That's where we need to go," Kelly said, pointing. "There's a hatch in the floor that goes down to a network of maintenance tunnels under the asylum. We take out those two sentries, and we should be able to find our way right to the heart of the Enlightening."

"And how do we do that?"

Kelly looked over Leanne's shoulder. "I may have an idea. Wait here." She retrieved one of the knives from the bag and snuck off in a line to the northeast, where another acolyte was patrolling out of sight of the shed. Leanne held her breath as Kelly crept up to the demon, grabbed it from behind, and drove her knife into the back of its neck where the spinal cord and brainstem met.

Leanne bit back a gasp as Kelly pulled the demon to the ground and disrobed it, even while the body was starting to burn. As the demon's corpse caught fire, Kelly scurried back to Leanne with the robes bundled up in her arms.

"There," Kelly said. "Now we can both blend in." She looked up at the shed. One of the guards had noticed the smoke rising from the third acolyte's corpse and was on his way to check it out. "Quick, we should get dressed while they're distracted."

Kelly set down the gym bag and pulled out Varr'rak's robes, which she handed to Leanne.

"Wait, shouldn't you have these?" Leanne said. "They are your—his."

Kelly shook her head. "Varr'rak had me wearing those things for two years. I never want to fucking look at them again."

"Fair enough." Leanne pulled Varr'rak's robes over her head and drew up the hood, while Kelly did the same with her pilfered robes. "How do I look?" Leanne said after a moment.

Kelly scowled in mock-indignation. "You pull them off better than I did."

A dry-throated screech went up in the distance, and the second guard departed from his post at the shed. Kelly looked again and took off as fast as she could. "Dammit, he must have found his buddy! Come on!"

When the first guard joined the second, he too started screeching out an alert. The demons rose into the air and scanned the grounds for the threat. When one of them spotted the tell-tale rustle in the high grass, he stuck two fingers in his mouth and whistled.

The door of the shed creaked open, and Leanne and Kelly stopped about thirty feet away. A chilling growl filled the air, and then Samson the demon-dog charged out of the shed, barking and snapping his teeth.

"Jesus Christ!" Kelly and Leanne stood up straight and ran in two different directions as the monster dog came at them. He paused for a moment, confused, and then ran after Kelly. At the same time, one of the Following acolytes dropped out of the sky and swooped toward Leanne.

Leanne's Vokarion crystal hummed against her chest and Kelly's voice echoed. *Lee! Circle around to the shed! If we get down in the tunnels, we can lose them!*

Leanne yelped and ducked as the pursuing acolyte swooped over her head, swiping at her with both hands. As it passed, she reached up and grabbed its trailing robes, and then threw herself onto her back. The acolyte snarled and hissed as it hit the ground, and Leanne stuck the blade of her knife up under the creature's chin.

The demon gurgled in surprise and coughed out two short breaths, then quickly expired. Leanne pulled her blade out of the demon's head and ran as it started to burn.

*****

Kelly made a wide loop around the shed. Samson was still behind her. As Leanne struggled with the first demon, Kelly reached into the gym bag and fumbled around for the Webley. She loaded it by feel alone and heard Samson closing the gap behind her.

Kelly pulled the revolver out of the bag and fired. The shot hit Samson with a thud and he crumpled into a pile at Kelly's feet. She didn't stick around to check on him, and ran for the shed as the remaining acolyte came toward her.

*****

The two met at the door of the shed and quickly shut themselves in. An old wheelbarrow with no wheel was rusting quietly in the back corner, and a few bags of fertilizer lay beside a tool rack with only half its tools. In the middle of the floor was a thick, heavy trapdoor with a brass ring set into it.

Kelly grabbed the handles of the wheelbarrow and dragged it over to the door. "Grab some of that fertilizer," she said. "Dump it in here. I don't want those things getting in." She shoved the wheelbarrow right against the door.

Leanne nodded and picked up one of the heavy bags. "Good idea."

BOOM! The entire shed shifted as something hit the outer wall. The acolyte chanted and Samson started barking again.

Kelly heaved another bag of fertilizer into the wheelbarrow and groaned. "How much frigging punishment can that dog *take*?"

Leanne dropped the next bag of fertilizer and grabbed a pitchfork from the rotting tool rack. "Forget the door! Let's just get into the tunnels!"

The door burst into a cloud of wood chips. The last acolyte pointed at Kelly and roared, *"Kill her! Kill the traitor!"*

Samson leaped over the wheelbarrow and Leanne swatted him away with the pitchfork. He snarled at her as he got up, and she jabbed at him with the business end of the fork. "Kelly! Tunnels!"

Kelly grabbed the brass ring with both hands and pulled. The door hardly budged an inch. "I'm… working… on it!" she hissed.

The demon raised its hand and a telekinetic blast knocked Leanne off her feet. She crashed into Kelly, who let go of the trapdoor.

Samson jumped over the wheelbarrow. As he rushed the girls, Leanne swept the pitchfork under his feet and knocked him down. She got up before he did and rammed the tines of the fork into his belly.

Samson howled and scratched at the handle of the pitchfork. Leanne pushed harder as he writhed under her weight and barked furiously.

"Jesus, is he *still* kicking?" Kelly spat.

"Literally! I don't know how long I can hold him back!"

The last acolyte punched a hole in the back wall of the shed. *"Munro! You will die for your sacrilege!"*

Kelly reached through the hole and grabbed the acolyte by its collar. "You sound like my old Sunday School teacher." Then she stuck the Webley against the demon's chin and pulled the trigger.

Samson was still fighting against Leanne. "Can I get some help over here, please?"

Kelly stuffed the Webley back in the gym bag and ran to Leanne's side. She grabbed the pitchfork handle with both hands. "Get the trapdoor! I have an idea!"

Leanne left Kelly with Samson and heaved the trapdoor open. The rusty hinge screamed and a baleful groan rode the gust of stale, chilly air that emerged from the shaft below. Leanne couldn't tell if the noise was demons, or if the ghost of an unfortunate patient was coming up to say 'Hello.'

"Out of the way!" Kelly shouted. The dog kicked as she pushed him toward the trapdoor, and his long claws sliced into her forearm. She stifled a cry of pain and kicked Samson into the yawning shaft.

The dog was swallowed by darkness about ten feet down, but he kept howling for another twenty feet after that. Then there was a distant thud and he stopped howling.

Kelly put her hands on her knees and took a breath. "Okay. That could've gone smoother. Good news is, we haven't seen reinforcements yet. They're probably busy prepping for the Enlightening. If the tunnels are clear, we might still have a chance at this."

Leanne sniffed and made a little choking sound. Kelly looked up and blinked. "Leanne? Are you okay?"

Leanne swallowed and took off her glasses. With the back of her hand, she scrubbed a tear out of each eye. "Where's the line, Kelly? Where do they stop?"

"Who?"

"Who the hell do you think? The Following!" She wiped her eyes again and let out one nervous sob. "I knew since the Shoppe that this was going to be rough. Abby and the others, they warned me that the Following don't play games, and they were right. But I thought there would at least be a line for them! What did Samson ever do? He was harmless! And they turned him into *that* for no reason!" Her shoulders heaved and she started to cry. "If they won't stop at hurting a… a dumb dog, they just won't stop!"

"No, they won't." Kelly went over to the tool rack and picked up two dusty flashlights. She pressed one into Leanne's hand, then hugged her friend tight. "So we can't either. Rescuing Abby is just Step One. Step Two is destroying this fucking cult. That way there won't be another Samson or Mrs. Clifford or Karen Henderson."

Leanne nodded and put her glasses back on. "You're right. Sorry, I just had to… I had to unload."

"Don't be sorry. These assholes have given us plenty to cry about, so let's go return the favour." She turned on her flashlight and shone it down the maintenance shaft.

*****

The ladder took them down thirty feet into a concrete box of a room. Samson lay in a pile at the bottom of the ladder, finally and unquestionably dead. Directly opposite the ladder, there was a metal security door leading into the tunnels. On the right-hand wall, there was a large fuse box that was missing its front panel. Thick cables rose like creeper vines from the fuse box up to the ceiling, where they snaked through a hole drilled above the doorway. A few speakers were mounted high up on the wall, patched haphazardly into the wiring system with faded electrical tape. Along the left-hand wall, there was a stack of long wooden crates with EXTREME CAUTION stamped on their sides. One crate was partially opened, with an abandoned crowbar lying on the lid, and Leanne had a peek inside.

Hellstrokes. Three dozen at least, laid out end to end in individual nests of straw and packing peanuts. There was enough firepower in one crate to bring down the whole asylum, and Leanne counted eight crates. She stepped back and held her breath, keeping her hands well above her head. Kelly had a look over her shoulder to see what the trouble was, and let out a low whistle. "Yikes. Good thing Samson landed where he did."

Leanne took another step back and slowly exhaled. "Yeah. We would have been cooked."

Kelly's eyes widened, and Leanne could almost see the lightbulb flashing above her friend's head. "Wait… that's an idea…" Kelly whispered. She reached for her Vokarion crystal and thought hard. *Hey, Simon?*

Both their crystals hummed and Simon chirped, *Hello? What news from the front lines?*

We're just in the maintenance tunnels now, Leanne answered. *There was some… trouble on the grounds.*

Yes, I thought I heard a bit of a fracas out there. Is everything okay?

All clear now, said Kelly. She winced as the gash on her right arm started to sting.

Leanne looked at Kelly's wound and frowned. "Don't be a martyr, Kelly. That looks bad."

"It's fine," Kelly insisted through gritted teeth. She bit into the sleeve of her robes and tore off a strip for a bandage. As she bound her arm, Simon asked if something was wrong.

Nothing, Kelly thought. *It's a scratch. It's fine. Look, Simon, they're storing a whole bunch of Hellstrokes down here. You know how you were wishing you could take out that magic circle? Well, how do you think it'll stand up to some condensed Hellfire?*

Crackly feedback hummed out of the speakers. *I'm sorry, Kelly, say again?* Simon said. *I'm picking up rather a lot of interference.*

Yeah, that'll be the PA, said Kelly, tying off her improvised bandage. *I asked how your magic circle would stand up to some Hellfire.*

There was a beat before Simon replied, in a scheming tone of voice, *Not very well… Kelly, what was that you said about a PA system?*

The whole asylum is wired for sound, even down here.

Another beat. When Simon's voice came back, the girls could almost hear the mad grin on his face. *Oh,* he hissed. *Oh yes, that is BRILLIANT.*

It seemed that every second or third thing was 'brilliant' to Simon, and Leanne asked if he could narrow it down. *I think I have a plan,* he announced. *I know how we can rescue Abby and snuff out the Following with one blow.*

Great! Leanne exclaimed. *How do we do that?*

Unfortunately, it will require a certain amount of sleight-of-hand. One of you will have to infiltrate the Enlightening rites, I'm afraid, and get right in close with the Deacon.

I'll do it, Leanne said. *I want to see the look on his face when his precious Enlightening falls apart.*

Bravo, Miss Waller, said Simon. *In that case, Kelly, I'll need you to double back to the perimeter wall. Put a couple Hellstrokes on top of the wall near where we came up. Then get back to the tunnels and see if you can find the asylum's main power supply. Can you do that for me?*

I think so. What are you planning, Simon?

Their crystals hummed as Simon beamed the plan to them telepathically. When they understood, they smiled at each other and said their goodbyes to Simon. Then they started gingerly lifting Hellstrokes out of the open crate. They each took as many as would fit in their robes before their bulging pockets became obvious. Leanne shifted her robes so the little bottles wouldn't clink off each other and turned to Kelly. "You going to be okay?"

Kelly was already heading back toward the ladder. "Power supply's a piece of cake. Way I remember, the fuse box is a couple hundred yards down the hallway. Left, right, left again, and down one flight of stairs."

"I meant your hand." Leanne pointed at Kelly's bandage, which was already turning red.

Kelly looked at the scratch and shrugged. "I think a lot of that's Samson's blood anyway."

"But not all of it?"

"I'll be fine, Lee. You're the one you gotta worry about, walking into the lion's den."

"I have to, Kelly. You had it right the first time. The Following won't stop, so we can't either. And if the roles were reversed, if it were me being sacrificed instead of Abby, I know she wouldn't hesitate for a second to come after me. I have to be the one who brings her home."

Kelly nodded. "Like my grandpa used to say: 'You dance with the one that brought you.'"

"Let's go with that."

Leanne's flashlight flickered, and she gave it a hard whack to stabilize the beam. Wishing Kelly good luck, she opened the door and set off into the darkness. Kelly shouted good wishes back, stuck her flashlight in her mouth, and climbed back up the ladder.

*****

The tunnels were built like a rabbit warren, and it wasn't five minutes before Leanne got lost for the first time. She was careful not to make any noise that might alert the Following. She kept her jaw clenched tight so her teeth wouldn't chatter in the cold, and she rubbed or itched her nose periodically to discourage herself from sneezing.

Sneezing was a real concern, too. Leanne had never realized so much dust could exist in one location before today. It danced in the beam of her flashlight and painted the pipes and cables grey. Cobwebs hung in every corner, tickling her face and the backs of her hands when she had to walk through them. Low scraping and squeaking noises occasionally slipped through the cracks in the wall, and Leanne imagined whole colonies of rats on the other side, packed so tight that they were slithering and crawling over each other. She had once read about something called a 'rat king,' which was what happened when a bunch of rats got their tails tangled up together in an impenetrable knot, and she quickly convinced herself that was what she was hearing.

Upon reaching the next corner, she was snapped out of this grim reverie by a flicker of light on the floor. Leanne switched off her flashlight and hugged the wall, drawing her knife from within her robes. Probably better not to risk a Hellstroke in a confined space like this. The hairs on the back of her neck pricked up as a chill crept around the corner. She heard the hiss of demonic voices and risked a peek.

There was a snot-green door about ten feet down on the opposite side, and the light was coming from beneath it. As Leanne watched, the door opened and six Following acolytes glided out in single file, conversing in hushed tones.

"It is ill fortune that Varr'rak cannot make tribute for the Enlightening," said the acolyte at the head of the pack.

"Ill fortune for Varr'rak, perhaps," replied the creature beside it. *"After him, I have taken the most lives for the Eldest One. Now Varr'rak is gone, I shall make first tribute after the Deacon."*

"You have a thousand blessings on you. I look forward to seeing it."

"Not long now. The Deacon is blessing the relics at this moment."

The acolytes continued down the corridor away from Leanne, and she couldn't hear any more. She waited until the acolytes faded into the darkness and slinked after them. She caught up with them several minutes later as they entered a stairwell leading up to the asylum proper. It wasn't difficult to keep her distance, as the acolytes floated up the four flights without effort while she had to use her stubby human legs. Tapping the crystal under her shirt, she thought, *I hope you guys are all set up. I'm pretty sure the ritual's about to start.*

Natalie and I are in position, Simon replied. *I have a clear visual on the perimeter wall, and the Hellstrokes are in place. How are you coming along with the power, Kelly?*

*****

Kelly stood looking at a massive fuse box the size of a plasma TV. She'd jimmied the front panel off with her knife, and she'd pulled all the wires that Simon had told her to pull. Now she was looping two of the loose wires around her Vokarion crystal and tucking it against the fuses.

You should have told me getting back to the wall would be the easy part. I am definitely no electrician.

You don't need to be, that's the whole point. So long as your crystal is hooked into the wiring, its magic will leach into the asylum's power supply and disrupt the system's normal functions. Now, when you've got the crystal in with the fuses, I want you to look for the main power switch. Turn that off, then on again.

Won't someone notice if all the power goes out? Leanne asked.

I doubt it. Magic and electricity are not supposed to mix. When they do, nothing ever works the way it's supposed to. With all the magic the Following are kicking up, they'll surely be expecting a few outages.

Kelly left her crystal in the fuse box and gripped the big red power switch with both hands. She flipped it to the OFF position. She waited ten seconds, as Simon had told her to do, and then flipped the switch back to ON.

Okay, she said at last to Simon, *that's that done.*

Perfect. That will have rebooted the asylum's entire electrical system. Now, the point of this exercise is to establish a psychic link that can feed into the PA system up top. Given the size of the building and the age of the wiring, it may take a few minutes for the crystal to link up with the speakers in the main cell block. Leanne, when you get up there, you may need to cause a distraction.

I've got six Hellstrokes and the Word of God with me, Leanne said. *I can probably handle that.*

What do I do? asked Kelly.

Leanne said, *Go, Kel. Get the hell out of here and get to safety. There's no reason for you to put yourself in any more danger.*

I owe Abby my life, Lee. I can't just walk away from her.

I'm not asking you to. I'm saying you just got your life back, so why throw it away?

Okay. I'll cut back the way we came. See you in a little while.

Here's hoping, Leanne said.

Kelly stepped back. Simon had warned her she'd have to leave her crystal behind, so she said a final goodbye to her friends and started down the hall.

The shadows flickered in the corner of her eye, and she shuddered as she closed the door. Her right hand trembled on the handle, and wisps of black smoke rose from under her bandage.

She made a fist and jammed her shaking hand under her left armpit. "Come on," she whispered. "Stop it. He's gone."

She looked at her right hand again. It had stopped shaking, and her fingers weren't smoking. She kept moving. "He's gone," she repeated.

*****

Leanne followed the six acolytes into a corridor with a sign reading TO CELL BLOCK A. Tattered posters on the walls shouted inspirational quotes and messages about wellness and positive thinking. They were in surprisingly good condition, and Leanne wondered if the Following kept them up as a cruel joke to their victims. *Satanism with a smile.*

The group passed through a large security gate, and they were in Cell Block A itself. But it didn't look like much of a cell block anymore: all the individual cells had been knocked through, and the walkways and staircases had been torn down. There was a raised stage in the middle of the room, currently occupied by a large obsidian altar and lit by torches at every corner. Every flat surface was a canvas of arcane pictograms and hieroglyphs either carved into the very tile or painted in something red and sticky. Not counting the group Leanne had joined, there were nearly 100 acolytes watching the stage in rabid anticipation. She buried her hands in the pocket of her robes and took a Hellstroke in each one, just in case. As the group of six took up positions in the crowd, Leanne cut to the front, hewing close to the stage. Somehow, she had to get herself in the Deacon's line of sight.

Speak of the devil, and he shall appear, said a little voice in her head as the man himself marched up to the stage from the other end of the room. As the acolytes bowed their heads and chanted, the white-robed figure that Abby always described with such horror spread his arms wide and basked in the glory of the moment.

Leanne bowed her head like the others and tried to match their rough, dissonant chant, but the syllables hurt her throat and a knot built up in the pit of her stomach, like the dialect itself was unclean. She quickly gave up on the chant and mouthed the words. Overhead, the PA squawked and sang "Old-Time Religion".

The Deacon took a position beside the altar and raised his hand for silence. Even the PA wound down as he addressed the crowd.

"Brothers! Sisters! Let us rejoice, for the hour of our glory is at hand! The flesh is cleansed and the blood is willing. We shall join them in their holy union and our master shall walk free!" A cheer exploded through the room and the demons applauded. The Deacon continued: *"The Eldest One shall be among us once more, and he will cleanse this earth of the filth who have stolen it! The*

lesser races shall tremble and fall in his wake and the demon shall reign supreme!"

The demons bowed and crossed their hands over their hearts, chanting, *"Kha'al Azna'ghal ixxi. Kha'al Azna'ghal ixxi. Kha'al Azna'ghal ixxi."*

The Deacon traced a symbol in the air with the first two fingers of his left hand. The demons all made the same gesture over their own hearts. Then the Deacon turned back the way he had come and pointed a bony finger at two acolytes standing guard at the door. *"Bring forth Abigail Henderson!"*

The cheering began anew as the two acolytes stepped out of the room, then returned dragging a pale, naked figure between them. Abby was bound in iron manacles, with an array of grotesque cuts and purple bruises marring her tableau of tattoos. She kept her face neutral and her eyes on the floor, but the bunching of her shoulders and the twitching of her hands screamed that she was furious.

*****

Abby bit her tongue and tasted blood. She was certain that Leland's stick had broken a rib, and every step made her want to scream. She'd crafted a little jar in her heart and stuffed all her emotions into it—all the pain, all the hatred—then slammed the lid on tight. When her friends came, and not a second before, she would get right in close to Leland and open the jar, and rain all her pressurized loathing down on his head. She would burn this whole fucking cult to the ground.

If she kept her eyes on the floor, she couldn't see the auras. She couldn't see the true Following doing their war dance inside these meat suits. But she could feel it. She felt the disdain they had for their skin-ape puppets, how they chafed at the gassy, hairy sacs of blood and mucus they had been forced into. And the Gospels were the worst of the skin-ape bunch, because they were the demons' responsibility. One of their kind had gotten freaky with a human way back when before the War, when the demons still had flesh of their own, and the first Gospel squirted out nine months later. Humanity plus. That would be the first mistake the Eldest One fixed in his Second Age of Magic.

But somewhere in that boiling, frothing sea of hate, there was an island. One speck of hope and love in a crowd of angry demons in false skin. In a room where the verse was *"Kha'al Azna'ghal ixxi"*, one mouth was saying, "I will be there for you, Abby Normal."

Abby looked up, and her eyes bored into one short, stout acolyte near the front of the crowd, whose jeers and taunts seemed less enthusiastic than the rest. She gave the small figure an imperceptible nod. *Foreverways.*

The small figure nodded back. *Foreverways.*

Abby cast her eyes back to the floor as they brought her to the altar. They tied her down in a spread-eagle position, her eyes toward the ceiling, but her face remained an expressionless mask. An acolyte stepped onto the stage holding a long ceremonial dagger with a golden hilt and a simple goblet made of varnished oak. In the pit of Abby's heart, the lid on the jar rotated a quarter-turn.

*****

The Deacon said a prayer to Azna'ghal, and the first two rows of acolytes began to jostle for position and work out the pecking order for the tributes. As the shuffling crowd knocked her around, Leanne squeezed the Hellstrokes in her pockets so they wouldn't make too much noise or bump against each other and detonate prematurely. One wrong move, and she could blow herself and Abby to Kingdom Come along with the Following.

The rank-and-file acolytes all stepped back to make room for the tributes, who formed a semicircle around the stage and eagerly rolled up their sleeves. Leanne wound up trapped near the far end of the formation and couldn't see a way out that wouldn't draw undue attention. Reluctantly, she took one hand out of her pocket and rolled up her sleeve as well. Onstage, the Deacon rolled up his sleeve and began to speak.

"Ag'haz Kha'al, dol ek-el lakash ag'rava, o'u-oy kadraz ak aki."

Every demon in the line-up repeated his words in perfect unison.

"Dol ek-el koda resu, o'u-oy ter'ik hael ak aki."

Leanne did her best to follow along as the demons repeated the blessing.

"Dol kalees tak, o'u-oy dol kxx eci draz!"

The Deacon finished the blessing and the Following repeated it to him once again. They chanted as he held his arm over the goblet and pressed the dagger to his wrist. A hush of breathless anticipation fell over the room, and then the Deacon sliced his arm open down to the elbow. Leanne gasped and cut off a scream as the Deacon's blood poured into the chalice.

When the flow tapered off, the Deacon raised his forearm to his lips and licked away the last few drops. He punched the air, showing off the wound to the Following, and they cheered as the cut closed itself up. Meanwhile, Leanne couldn't decide whether to faint or throw up. The chalice and the dagger were passed to the first demon in the semicircle, who cut himself open with great zeal and laughed as the blood dripped into the chalice. Leanne gulped. Elective surgery had not been part of the plan. She was squeamish enough about getting shots when she went to the doctor. How was she supposed to do this?

Oh God. The chalice was halfway down the line now. Make or break time. Leanne started sweating. *Oh crap. Oh crap. Oh crapcrapcrapcrapcrapCRAP!*

Suddenly, the Deacon raised his hand and the acolytes stopped what they were doing. The one holding the dagger put its arm down and unrolled its sleeve, and the one holding the chalice backed away.

"Wait..." he growled. *"Something is… amiss..."* He pulled his hood away, revealing his face to the room. The demons gasped and averted their eyes. John Leland sniffed the air for a few seconds and snarled. "There is... a *human* amongst us."

In the crowd, Leanne slowly took a Hellstroke from her pocket. Abby, seeing this, looked up as best she could and tried to get Leland's attention. "Yeah, sorry, that's probably me. I've been feeling kind of gassy all day. Must have been that big breakfast..."

Leland didn't even look at her. "When spoken to, Abigail." Then he sniffed the air again and pointed at Leanne. "There!"

Leanne screamed as a wave of telekinetic force rolled down from the stage and encircled her. Every muscle in her body froze, and she felt herself rooted to the spot like a tree. One of the acolytes beside her yanked her hood down, knocking her glasses askew, and the other prised apart her fingers and took the Hellstroke from her hand.

Then Leland hopped off the stage and sauntered toward her, shaking his head like he'd caught her sneaking cookies before dinner. He pointed to the floor, and Leanne sank to all fours with the weight of a freight train pressing down on her. Nervous sweat steamed her glasses and dripped down her nose.

Her glasses slipped off her face, and she heard Leland laughing above her. "Come to watch the fireworks, have we?"

CHAPTER 27

NON EST ASYLUM

KELLY TRIPPED going up the stairs and banged her head on the top step. "Mother*fucker!*" She put her right hand to her forehead and gritted her teeth. Her fingers came away bloody and her hand started shaking again.

Kelly shut her eyes and smacked her palm on the concrete steps. "Stop it, stop it! Fucking stop it!" Puffs of black smoke blew off her hand with every smack. "The exorcism worked. It *worked*, goddammit!"

She looked up. A hazy silhouette stood on the top step. Two bright yellow eyes stared down at her from the middle of its blank head.

Kelly stood and lurched toward the silhouette. "It worked! It worked and you're not here!" The silhouette disappeared as she walked through it, and her hand stopped shaking.

She looked around the empty tunnel and made a tight fist with her right hand. This she held in her left hand, down near her side. "You're not here," she said. "You can't be here."

*****

Leanne blinked. The floor and the bottom of the Deacon's robes were hazy in her field of view. "Really, Miss Waller," he hissed, "I am always happy to accept new patients, but I do wish you had made an appointment." Leanne cried out as a tremendous pressure drove her down into a low bow. She jerked to a sudden stop, and her cross necklace bounced out the loose neck of her robes. When the little icon came into view, the demons hissed and began to back away. The pressure on her disappeared, and Leanne put her glasses back on and stood. She held the cross out toward Leland and it glowed white as her faith poured through it.

Leland backed up to the stage, shielding his eyes from the light and uttering a serpentine hiss. "You would dare to bring these idols into the house of our god?"

"There's only one God, Deacon, and I think He'd have some pretty harsh things to say about all this."

Leland ground his teeth in silent anger for a moment. He looked at the acolytes, saw them looking at him for guidance, and realized that he was very close to losing face if he didn't act fast. As much as it hurt to do so, he straightened his back and looked Leanne in the eye. "Be realistic, Leanne. Do you suppose that even Jesus Christ Almighty can see you safely out of this place? Break your concentration for one second, and my acolytes will be upon you. Then you will never walk out of here."

"True." With her free hand, Leanne pulled Plan B out of her pocket. "But if I break my concentration, I might drop this. Then none of us walk out of here." She smiled and gave the Hellstroke a little shake. The acolytes all took another step back. "I found your stash downstairs. And who knows how many I smuggled in with me? Who knows how many of you I'll take out when I drop this?" She turned to the altar. "Or maybe Abby and I will play Catch! Then what happens?"

The acolytes were still watching Leland. They needed their orders. He raised his hands and preached to the masses: "Do you see this, my children? This woman—this nervous, myopic, pathetic excuse for a skin-ape dares to come into our home and transgress upon our venerated rituals, to try and rescue her lover! She deceives us, the way all skin-apes deceive us! She has turned our weapons against us! She has stolen the sacred vestments of one of our own! She dares to think she can fill the footsteps of our brother the Shadow-walker. Leanne, if you must commit such heresy against us, at least have the honour to do so openly. Don't hide your face like a coward and enter this place under false pretence, deceiving us like some pitiable scavenger."

From up on the altar, Abby laughed. "Oh, that is rich! Two minutes ago, you couldn't wait for Azna'ghal to body snatch *me*! Hey, quick show of hands: who in this room is actually showing their true face right now? Come on, don't be shy!"

Leland rolled his eyes. "I said *silence!*"

Leanne turned back to him and wound up her throwing arm. After that, Leland shut up pretty quickly. "She's right, though. Just because you're in league with the Man Downstairs doesn't mean you get to be a hypocrite. Now back off. All of you, back off!" She shook the Hellstroke again and the demons retreated. Watching the Following with a dangerous eye, Leanne climbed the stairs to the stage and looped the cross around her wrist. Then she started sawing through Abby's robes with her knife.

*****

Kelly came to a fork in the tunnel. She blinked and leaned against the wall. Which way had she come from? Left or right? Fuck, she couldn't remember. *Side effects,* she told herself. Side effects from the exorcism. She couldn't concentrate on a thought for more than five seconds before it fell out of her brain. The dark corners of the tunnel were making her anxious. And was it her imagination, or was it getting colder?

She blew on her hands and rubbed them together. Black smoke poured off her shaking right hand, and she slapped the wall desperately. Varr'rak the Shadow-walker whispered in her ear, *"Don't fight it, Kelly."*

Kelly tucked her hand behind her back and pressed herself against the wall. "But Simon exorcised you!" she screamed. "I saw you get dragged below! How—" She started crying into her free hand. "How can you be here?"

"You know it's not just a scratch. Samson infected you, didn't he? His blood is in your blood now. Taking over. Waking up the demon inside you…"

Kelly opened her eyes. One of Varr'rak's hellhounds stood before her, watching her.

"Or maybe I'm just fucking with you," the hellhound said. *"Maybe I'm your guilty conscience. The blood you can never wash off your hands."*

Behind her back, Kelly's hand suddenly felt wet. She looked at it and screamed as the blood ran down her palm and seeped under her fingernails.

"Come to think of it, I might be the PTSD," Varr'rak hissed. *"I lived in you for two years, Kelly. Every lecture you went to, every movie you saw, every boy and every girl you fucked, I was right there beside you. You can't tell me that won't mess with your head."*

Varr'rak opened one of his three mouths and bit into Kelly's right arm. Her ulna snapped and she screamed as her shirt sleeve grew wet with blood.

Kelly grabbed a pipe on the wall for support and raised one leg. "Get the fuck *off of me!*" She kicked Varr'rak right in the snout. He snarled and barked, but he let go of her arm.

Her blood was still dripping from his jaws as she ran down the right fork of the tunnel.

*****

Leanne cut through the last of Abby's ropes. Abby sat up on the altar and hugged Leanne with tears in her eyes. "Thanks."

Leanne hugged back, careful to keep her Hellstroke where the Following could see it. "You realize this means you're making dinner tonight."

"Small price to pay," Abby said with a grin.

Leland groaned. "This is a most heart-warming reunion, but what is your plan now? We still outnumber you 50 to one! You know the moment you step through the front gate, I will send an army after you! There is *nowhere* you can run!"

Leanne pulled the Vokarion crystal out of her robes. "Come on! You didn't really think I was going to be alone, did you?" She tossed the crystal to Leland, who caught it with a knowing smile.

"Of course, a Vokarion crystal… Now who do I know that still subscribes to that dusty, antique form of magic?"

While Leland turned the crystal over in his hands, Abby leaned in and whispered, "Lee, what the hell are we still doing here? Let's *go!*"

"Trust me," Leanne said. "We need to keep him talking for just a little bit longer."

Leland held the crystal at eye level and hollered into it. "Is that you on the other end of the line, Ætheric?"

The crystal glowed in time with Simon's voice. "Ah, hello, Deacon, so glad I caught you at home! It's been far too long since we saw each other! But, that voice… you're not still rattling around in that fusty old Dr. Leland, are you?"

"Choose your words carefully, old friend. There's still enough of me in here to take offence at that. But I must say, this gambit does not seem to be quite up to your usual standards of chicanery. If this is your preposterous idea of a rescue attempt, then I hate to tell you, but you might be losing your touch."

*****

Out in the freezing storm, Simon glanced at the little sheets of paper on the Thunderbird's dashboard and confirmed his calculations. He spoke into his own crystal and gave Natalie a thumbs-up. She revved the car's motor and tightened her grip on the steering wheel. While Kelly had been laying out the Hellstrokes on top of the wall, Natalie had brought the car up through the trees to where she could see the wall and Simon had done some quick math. He'd dug down on the safe side of the magic circle to determine the depth of the concrete—eighteen inches—calculated the blast radius of the Hellstrokes in current weather conditions, and determined the angle and velocity he'd need to hit the circle at. "On the contrary, Deacon! If, after all these years, I can still get you talking like this, then I must be in the best shape of my life!"

"What?"

"Oh, come now! If you think this is the best I can do, then you really are more arrogant than I remember! You see, Deacon, this is merely my preposterous idea of a distraction!" He stood up in his seat and pointed at the Hellstrokes atop the wall, fifteen feet away. He screamed, *"Ðracu glæsene!"* and the three little glass bottles jumped off the wall and threw themselves at the concrete circle.

FWACKOOM! The trees rocked in the explosion and a wide section of the magic circle disintegrated into gravel. With the circle broken, the Deterrence Curse fell, and bursts of blue magic shot through the gap in the concrete. A wave of Hellfire and lethal defensive magic spilled toward the Thunderbird, and Natalie put the pedal to the metal.

As the Thunderbird rushed toward the deadly wave, Simon yelled, *"Duru onhlīde on lyfte!"* A blue-green portal yawned open in front of the car, and Natalie drove right into it seconds before the fire reached them.

*****

In Cell Block A, the PA system crackled and buzzed overhead. Everyone had heard the explosion, and Leland was now barking orders at his acolytes to secure the perimeter and raise the Deterrence Curse again. The acolytes looked around in a panic as blue-green sparks flashed in the centre of the room, and Simon's voice boomed out of every speaker across the asylum. "*THIS* IS MY PREPOSTEROUS IDEA OF A RESCUE ATTEMPT!"

The car exploded out of a portal in the middle of the crowd and skidded to a halt. The bones of a dozen acolytes crunched under the wheels and cracked against the bumpers and windshield, and Simon raised his head and screamed, "My name is Ætheriċ, of the line of the Vanguard! My father was Wulfrecg, himself the son of Hroðmund! From these names have I learnt the wisdom of my ancestors! From these names do I draw strength! I offer these names now to that noble witness, the ancient countenance of the High Celestial!"

The lights snapped on and off and a strong wind kicked up around the stage. Simon's voice was magnified ten times by the speakers, and the asylum began to shake as flames erupted from the floor. "I offer these words to that divine spirit to show fealty: The High Celestial is our one Father — the Maker of all things! In that aspect, His reign is just! The High Celestial is our one Mother — the Nurturer of Life and the Cosmos. In that aspect, Her Reign is true!"

The demons all covered their ears and screeched as the PA blasted the exorcism rites into every room of the asylum. The cell block crackled with electricity and black clouds churned beneath the ceiling. The acolytes nearest the car were having fits on the floor, but many more were trying to fight through the pain. Leland stuffed his fingers in his ears and egged them on. "He's one man! There's more than enough of you!"

"Servants of the Eldest One! Your sin is known and your crime seen before the true God of the Three Planes! I speak here for the All-Seer: your incursion is unwanted, your trespass unjust! You dwell in the bodies of those wrongly displaced!" The acolytes lurched toward the car, hissing and screeching, but determined all the same. Their master was right: there was a hundred of them and one of Simon. The energy it would take to exorcise them all was beyond his ken, and the energy he did have at his disposal would be diluted if it had to reach them all.

And that was where Soviet engineering came into the picture. As the demons swarmed the car like a hive of horrible insects, Natalie hit the trunk release, stood up, and whistled. The loaded AK-47 jumped up into her hands, and she opened fire. There was a scream, a crash, and a gurgle as the demon holding the chalice fell to the floor with three bullets in its head, and the blasphemous contents of the wooden vessel seeped into the cracks in the tile. The demon holding the confiscated Hellstroke fell to the next shot, and the bottle in its hand tumbled along the floor to the foot of the stage.

Leland was on all fours digging his claws into the floor, screeching and spitting as Defeat triumphantly leapt out of the jaws of Victory. "No! It can't end like this!" he raged. "It won't end like this!"

On the stage, Leanne nodded to Abby. "Now, we can go." She picked up her Vokarion crystal and started to run, but Abby pulled her back.

"Wait, can we do something about this first?" Abby gestured up and down, and Leanne remembered her partner was still butt naked.

"Oh yeah, sorry." Leanne pulled off the robes and passed them to Abby. While Abby dressed, Leanne looped the cross around her neck once more. Then she looked back and asked, "Are you decent?"

Abby gave her a thumbs-up. Leanne returned the gesture, then threw her Hellstroke into the crowd of demons.

*****

Kelly turned a corner and fell into the wall. She looked at her arm. It was shaking worse than ever and smoking black, but there was no blood. No dirty great tooth marks. And when she poked at it, it felt like the bone was in one piece.

Jesus Christ. Had she imagined it? No, it wasn't that. The pain was too real. She still felt it, even now. You couldn't imagine pain like that.

Above her head, one of the PA speakers crackled and warbled. Kelly's ears rang and an invisible hand jammed a knife into her brain. She put her head in her hands and screamed as Simon shouted: "Servants of the Eldest One! Your sin is known and your crime seen before the true God of the Three Planes! I speak here for the All-Seer…"

Kelly hadn't thought it could work. She'd thought for sure that Leanne would be discovered or the circuit would just short out. But it actually was working. If her head didn't hurt so bad, Kelly would have jumped for joy.

Her hand shook uncontrollably, and she felt her skin tingling like something was burrowing beneath it. She held her wrist with her other hand, but she couldn't stop the tremors.

"You feel me in you, don't you, Kelly?" said Varr'rak. *"You know I'm coming. Why fight it?"*

Kelly's skin crawled as dark shadows oozed out of her pores. She made a fist, screamed, and punched the wall. The strength of Varr'rak the Shadow-walker flowed through her and made a hubcap-sized crater in the concrete, and the speaker fell from its anchor point above. The wires tore loose as it descended, and it hit the floor with a *clang*.

"Yes! Yes! Feel my strength inside you! Let me make you more than you are, Kelly!"

Simon had gone quiet. The only speaker for a couple hundred yards, and Kelly had just disconnected it. But she had a plan. The exorcism was beyond stopping now, and the tunnel was shaking from the energy it released. If Varr'rak was still in her, he probably wouldn't survive another round. She just had to find the next speaker. As her hand continued to smoke and tingle, she listened for the sound of Simon's voice and ran.

*****

In Cell Block A, the storm was like nothing Abby could have imagined. A ring of fire six feet high had encircled the Thunderbird, and Natalie kept firing her gun blindly at the demons on the other side. Leanne's Hellstroke exploded near the edge of the crowd and engulfed six demons in one go. Some had already succumbed to the exorcism rites, and lightning arced down from the ceiling as they were ripped from their host bodies. Geysers of burning Hellfire erupted from the floor as Abby threw two more Hellstrokes into the crowd. But there were still too many acolytes to take on all at once. Some of them had turned away from the car and were now advancing on the stage where Abby and Leanne still stood.

Lightning descended from the ceiling above the stage and struck the obsidian altar, splitting it almost in two with an almighty CRACK! A shockwave went out that knocked the advancing acolytes off their feet and hurled Abby, Leanne, and Dr. Leland clear off the stage. The pressure ruptured the Hellstroke at the foot of the stage, and another wave of Hellfire ripped through the demons in the front rank.

"In the name of the Earth-Maker, the Holy Witness, the Creator, I exorcise you! Ye servants of the False Master, the Consumer who did sow and nurture the seed of wickedness and treachery on this Earth, I cast you out!"

John Leland struggled to his feet. A wall of Hellfire was spreading across the entire cell block, cutting him and the girls off from the Thunderbird. He could hear his acolytes dying, their screams mixed with sounds of gunfire, Hellfire, lighting and thunder, and a heathen exorcism rite. He could feel the Deacon struggling inside his body, trying to flee before he was ripped forcefully from his host and dragged screaming back to Hell.

"Don't you quit on me now, you coward!" screamed his human side. "We have too much left to do!"

From the PA, Simon shouted, "Beg forgiveness from the True Lord and torment us no more!"

Leland doubled over, clutching both hands to his heart, and the Deacon hissed, *"It hurts, Leland! It hurts too much! I feel every part of me burning!"*

As Abby and Leanne made for the exit, Leland dragged himself toward them. "Then burn for all I care! Those girls have undone us, and you would let them walk out of here? Would you disgrace the Eldest One, Deacon?!"

The Deacon was incensed. His loyalty would not be questioned. The demon struck John Leland with his own hand and roared, *"Never!"*

Leland's lip had split when the Deacon slapped him. Now he swallowed the blood that trickled into his mouth and said to his other half: "Then grow a pair."

The tile floor cracked and split. As Abby and Leanne jumped over the widening fissure, Leland and the Deacon pounced. The sum greater than their parts landed on Leanne with a knee in her chest and two hands around her larynx. Leland's cheeks were pink with rage and foam collected in the corners of his mouth. "Don't you dare try to run from me, you little harlot! I will burn this place to the ground before I let you or anyone else interfere with my plans!"

Leanne's eyes rolled back in her head and her cheeks went blue. She frantically slapped the floor with one hand and gestured repeatedly to her pocket, but it took Abby a couple moments to notice the black knife handle poking out.

As Leanne's eyes bugged out of their sockets, Abby pulled out the knife and got behind Leland. She screamed at him, "GET OFF HER, YOU FREAK!" and drove the blade into his thigh.

Leland howled like a wildcat and looked at Abby. His unstabbed leg ploughed heel-first into her face and she fell back swearing and spitting out blood.

Leanne got her hands around Leland's wrists and bit down on the back of his hand. He screamed and turned back toward her, raising his other hand in a fist, but Leanne kept her teeth in his flesh. She clamped down harder and harder until she tasted blood, and then she whipped her leg up into his groin.

"Depart these bodies and return to rest!"

As Leland rolled off of her, Leanne stood up and kicked him in the ribs. Then she kneeled over him, shoved her cross into his mouth, and held his jaws tight while he screamed and his face burned.

A thin plume of smoke rose from between Leland's lips, and an outline of the cross appeared on one cheek. While Simon finished the exorcism rite, Leanne looked into Leland's eyes and whispered, "Hail Mary, full of grace, the Lord is with thee; blessed art thou amongst women…"

Abby stood transfixed, watching the struggle in Leland's aura. His two halves, who had cooperated so well for over half a century, were at each other's throats. The demon was beating his wings in a vain attempt to flee, but the man had both hands around the demon's tail and held him back. The demon was enraged at the man's presumptuous arrogance: a skin-ape, telling a servant of the Eldest One what to do? And the man was disgusted at the demon's weakness: a servant of the Eldest One, scared of a little religion?

*****

The soul of John Leland pulled the Deacon to the ground and straddled him, grinding his heels into the Deacon's wings.

"Why?" the Deacon roared. *"Why do you still fight?"* His snake's skin was burning and angry red blisters burst under his scales. *"Why are you like this?"*

"You promised me a kingdom," Leland hissed. "I will not let you go until I have it."

"But it is impossible! Our acolytes are broken! Our ritual is destroyed! The Alignment is nearly over!"

"Then we will find another Gospel. We will regroup. If it takes another century, we will wait for the next Alignment.

But before we do that, we will kill the ones who have done this to us!"

A chill froze the burning in the Deacon's chest, and he screamed as Leland's hands turned blue. A sheet of frost expanded from beneath his fingertips and he exhaled icy mist in the demon's face.

"What are you?" the Deacon cried.

The old legends say that demons have the coldest hearts in Creation. The hate in one demon's heart could freeze a man's hand off in seconds, so they say, and the fires of Niðerdæl must burn as hot as they do to counteract this. If the fires ever went out, Hell would freeze over from the sheer force of its inhabitants' hate.

Imagine, then, how cold one's heart must be to make a demon shiver. What manner of hate must a man carry with him to give a demon frostbite? Whatever kind of hate that is, John Leland had it in spades. The Deacon struggled beneath the weight of his host's soul, feeling the advance of ice on his skin wherever Leland touched him. It was hate like the Deacon had never seen, and it scared the daylights out of him.

"You cannot do this!" he screamed. The frost crept up his lion's mane. *"I made you what you are!"*

"I will do whatever I want," John Leland vowed. "Let's not forget whose body this is." Then he squeezed the Deacon's head in his hands, and the demon's eyeballs froze in their sockets.

*****

"...Blessed is the fruit of thy womb, Jesus!" shouted Leanne.

"In the name of the Divine, I command this!" roared Simon.

Abby gave her head a shake and broke off from the vision of her foe's aura. The gap in the floor kept growing, and whole chunks of tile and concrete broke off like pieces of a melting glacier. A horrible grinding noise signalled the collapse of the stage, and Abby watched as the two pieces of the obsidian altar slid into the maintenance tunnels below. She jostled Leanne and pulled her away from the struggling Leland mid-prayer. "We have to go *now!*"

Leanne didn't need telling twice. She pulled her saliva-slicked cross out of Leland's mouth and put it around her neck. Then she and Abby bolted out the door the demons had led Abby through. It was the only route not blocked off by the storm.

Abby and Leanne shielded their eyes as fire and lightning ripped through the cell block. The Following howled in their death throes and half the ceiling collapsed. A towering column of fire punched a hole through the other half and raced into the stratosphere, and most of the cell block's floor fell into the tunnels.

A second after the girls were out the door, an avalanche of rubble came rolling out after them and sealed off the entrance. Abby coughed and fanned away the dust, then called into Leanne's crystal. "Hello?! Simon, Natalie? Are you there?"

Natalie's voice came back. *Abby. Good to hear from you. How are you and Leanne?*

Abby looked at Leanne and squeezed her hand. "We're alive. Just. What about you guys?"

We're okay. Simon teleported us out… couple seconds before the ceiling came down… then he passed out…

"Jesus… is he…?"

He's breathing. The strain of it just knocked him out. You know, I think he only managed to properly exorcise about ten of them. I told him he couldn't take them all down, but he just had to try.

"Well, the rest of them won't be getting up anytime soon. Even if any are still alive, there's no way they're digging themselves out of this shit."

You can say that again. Can you get back through?

Abby looked at the mound of concrete straining against the doorway. "This way's blocked. Have to find another path."

Okay. See if you can find your way to the front gate. And whatever you do, be careful. There's no telling what this has done to the rest of the building.

"We'll watch our backs. Is Kelly there?"

No. If she's not back when you are, we'll check the tunnels together. Sound good?

"Okay," Abby said. "Okay. Yeah, she probably just got turned around or something."

Exactly, Natalie said. *We'll find her.*

They said their goodbyes, and Leanne and Abby started limping down the long hallway. "The first thing I'm gonna do," Leanne said, "Very first thing I'm gonna do when we get home is have a nice, long bubble bath."

"And the second thing?" Abby asked.

"Sleep for about a year," Leanne replied.

"I can dig that."

The air cracked and hissed as a portal opened behind them. A voice asked, "Did you honestly think it would be that easy?"

CHAPTER 28

THAT OLD-TIME RELIGION

"YOU SERVANTS of the False Master, the Consumer who did sow and nurture the seed of wickedness and treachery on this Earth, I cast you out!"

Kelly turned in the tunnel and looked up. The speaker wasn't but twenty feet away now. She could feel the thing inside her, whatever it was, fighting for a grip.

Kelly threw herself against the wall as the exorcism continued. "Hear that, you motherfucker? I will burn you right out of my fucking head before you take me back!"

Her right arm spasmed and grabbed the gym bag slung around her shoulders. Moving independently of Kelly's will, her hand threw the bag to the floor and pulled her down after it.

"Like fuck you will, Munro!" shouted Varr'rak the Shadowwalker. Kelly's right hand pulled the Webley out of the bag and reloaded it. She grabbed her right wrist with her left hand and forced her rogue arm to the ground, but Varr'rak's strength resisted her best efforts. Her right hand came up beside her ear, the barrel of the gun pointed at the ceiling. Then Varr'rak pulled the trigger.

Kelly opened her mouth, but she couldn't hear herself screaming. She let go of her wrist and cupped her left hand to her ear. A thin trickle of blood leaked out her ear canal and wetted the palm of her hand. She took a couple of deep breaths that she couldn't hear and listened for Simon's voice. It was hollow, muffled, and it only came in on her left side.

Varr'rak wasn't done. While Kelly was distracted, her possessed hand jerked up across her chest to a spot beside her left ear. The Webley fired again, and Kelly's good ear shut down with a *pop*.

She blinked, hyperventilating as her ears rang. She couldn't hear the exorcism. Thus, Varr'rak couldn't hear the exorcism. She was stuck with him.

The tunnel rumbled mutely around her. The walls cracked and chunks of concrete fell from the ceiling without a whisper. Over the ringing, Varr'rak's voice reverberated in her head, whispering to her at the speed of thought.

"Give up, Kelly," he said. *"It'll make this so much easier."* He laid the muzzle of the gun against the side of her head, and slowly traced a line down her jaw, under her chin. The movement was delicate and deliberate, like the caress of a lover's fingers. *"Remember what we had. Remember what I made you. Never sleeping. Never aging. As strong as ten men. Would you give that up for the life of a skin-ape?"* With Kelly's right thumb, Varr'rak drew back the Webley's hammer.

"You're fucking bluffing!" she snapped. She couldn't actually hear the words she spoke, but she could think them clearly. "You'll kill yourself as quick as you kill me!"

"If I were aiming for your head, I might! Two weak spots are the heart and the brain, remember?" The Varr'rak hand shoved the Webley into Kelly's thigh. *"What about the femoral artery? Leave you to bleed to death over the next few hours?"* Then the gun pressed into her navel. *"Or I shoot your guts out! Would you like that? Lying here, rotting in your own shit while I regenerate?"*

Kelly reached her left hand behind her back and pulled the knife out of her back pocket. "Or! Or! When I say leave me alone, you leave me the fuck alone!"

And she stabbed herself in the back of the hand. Her teeth shook in her mouth as Varr'rak howled, and her right hand dropped the gun.

"That was the last mistake you will ever fucking make," Varr'rak hissed. He howled again, and a thick black tentacle erupted from Kelly's right palm. It wrapped around her throat and squeezed. The blood pounded in her ears and dark spots danced in her field of vision. She imagined she saw Varr'rak the Shadow-walker walking toward her out of the dark tunnel. As the blood vessels in her eyes burst, Varr'rak smiled under his black hood and said, *"Sleep tight, little girl."*

Kelly's left hand found the gym bag and reached inside. She pulled out Natalie's machete, looked at her right wrist, and blinked away tears. Maybe it was the oxygen deprivation talking, but she couldn't see another way. As her head got lighter, she raised the machete above her head. Then she closed her eyes and screamed.

*****

The first thing Abby noticed was Leland's aura. The Deacon was still in there, but Abby didn't think he'd be much of a problem.

A thin coating of ice enveloped the demon. His eyes blinked, but his face was frozen in a frightened roar. John Leland leaned against the Deacon's flank, smiling at Abby.

It wasn't possible. It just wasn't. A human host, superseding and dominating the will of the demon possessing them. In her free time at the Letterbox, Abby had read everything she could about possession, and all the sources agreed: when a demon joined with a human, the demon ran the show. It didn't, *it wasn't supposed to*, happen the other way around.

But one look in that aura and Abby knew. The Deacon was Leland's prisoner now, as surely as Kelly had been Varr'rak's. The creature she'd feared more than anything else, ever since she was a little girl, now forced into a corner of Leland's brain and compelled to watch, while Leland wielded his magic with abandon.

"I was more than fair to you," he said. The portal closed behind him and he walked toward them slowly, his teeth grinding behind his melted cheek and his nostrils whistling with every heavy, furious breath. His shoulders heaved like a raging bull about to charge.

"I gave you *every* chance. I gave you your father back. I gave you a childhood. Twenty-five glorious years of freedom. Why, if not for the Pledge, you wouldn't have been BORN!"

Abby flinched and grabbed Leanne's hand. She reached into the pockets of the robes and fingered a Hellstroke. It was an insane risk to let one loose in such a tight space, but insane situations called for insane risks.

"Considering the circumstances," Leland fumed, "I'd say you came out of the bargain pretty well. And how do you repay me? How — do you — repay me?!"

His feet left the ground and he stretched his arms wide, relishing in the magic that was now his to control. Abby felt the electricity in the air, and she threw the Hellstroke at him before he got a chance to use it.

He saw the attack coming and threw a hand out in front of him, halting the weapon in mid-air. Then he flicked his wrist and the Hellstroke shot toward the girls.

"RUUUUUUN!" Abby screamed as she pulled Leanne behind her. The Hellstroke exploded into a roiling fireball behind them.

"What the hell happened?" Leanne panted. "How is he still going?!"

Abby pulled her around a corner and made for a stairwell at the end of the hall. She could feel a slight burning sensation on the back of her neck where the heat was getting to her. "I don't know..." she gasped. "He's strong... too strong for the Deacon..."

"Did you see them?"

"They fought… Leland won… that's not supposed to happen… Goddammit, I'm getting sick of this stupid rib!" she screamed as she clutched her side. "He's got total control now… I think he's… he's using the Deacon like a battery!"

Leanne huffed and puffed as they climbed the stairs. "That doesn't make any sense!"

"Really, Leanne?" Abby snapped through clenched teeth. "I hadn't fucking noticed!" When they reached the top, Abby turned left and barged into an old classroom. She picked up an overturned wheelchair and pushed it into the hall.

"What are you doing?" Leanne panted between deep breaths.

"Buying us some time!" Abby shoved the wheelchair down the stairs. She and Leanne didn't stick around for the show, but they heard the impact when the wheelchair collided with Leland. While he was down, Abby pulled the other Hellstroke out of her robes and threw it behind her. It exploded and engulfed the stairway in flames.

What the hell are you two doing in there?! Natalie shouted over the Vokarion relay.

Leanne was so scared, even her thoughts were stuttering. *Leland… alive… magic!*

What?

Abby grabbed the crystal from Leanne. *Leland's alive, he's got magic powers on his side, and he is royally pissed off! I may or may not have set off a couple Hellstrokes to keep him off our backs!*

Are you insane?! We already made the building unstable enough! Do you have any idea —

Natalie, let me talk to them. That was Simon. He sounded exhausted, and Natalie told him as much. He needed to rest right now, not play the —

Natalie, Simon insisted, *give me the crystal.* There was a beat before he said, *Explain the situation to me.*

Abby did so. Another beat, and then Simon said, *Right. I think I have a plan. You two have to get to higher ground. Head for the top floor of the centre block, above the front entrance. I think that's Leland's old office, but it's the highest ground I can see from here.*

We'll be there, said Abby. Has Kelly shown up yet?

No. I'm sorry, Abby, but I don't know if we can wait for her much longer.

You'll wait, Abby said. You'll wait until we get to the office, and not a minute sooner! I'll call you again when we're there!

As she gave the crystal back to Leanne, she whispered, "Please be okay, Kel."

*****

Kelly put the machete and the Webley back in the gym bag and slung the whole thing over her shoulder. Her right arm was jammed tight into her left armpit, and she could feel hot, sticky blood soaking into her shirt and her bra.

In her delirium, Kelly looked down at her right hand. It lay on the floor, amid a puddle of more blood, with six inches of forearm hanging off it. No shadows came from her fingers, so that at least was some good news.

The tunnel shook, and a chunk of concrete the size of a dinner plate fell by her side. Her hearing was starting to return in drips and drabs, and some muffled rumbles and cracks in the asylum above made her think of artillery fire. She expected that Simon must have reached *"Here metodes miht"* by now.

Kelly looked at her severed hand, then at the bloody stump cradled under her other arm. *Okay, Munro, first things first: the bleeding. The bleeding has to stop.*

She reached into the gym bag and pulled out the Bonnesante Potion. She bit into the cork with her teeth and pulled. A chunk of the ceiling caved in behind her and she fell on her side. She held the bottle up so it wouldn't break on anything, and it occurred to her that this might not be safe.

Closing up the gym bag again, she took it and the bottle and ran. The tunnels were constantly shaking, and she never went more than ten steps without tripping or hitting a wall (although, that might also have been because of the blood loss). The jostling of the tunnel made her want to throw up, but she forced herself to swallow it. She'd read somewhere once that feeling thirsty was a sign you'd lost too much blood, and wasn't vomiting supposed to dehydrate a person? Yeah, probably wouldn't do to mix the pair.

Kelly rounded the next corner. The tunnel shook, and she heard another ceiling collapse ahead. This was followed by the thump of warm bodies and the crackle of flames.

A hand grabbed Kelly's ankle, and she went down hard. She held the healing potion above her head and screamed as her elbow hit the concrete. She looked back. It was her own severed hand that had pulled her down. It had grown a long tail of shadows that looked like an arm in progress. The hand was growing another body.

"Jesus Christ!" Kelly yelled. "Why can't you take the hint already?"

"Call me sentimental," Varr'rak growled. *"I kind of liked what we had."*

Kelly's shadowy hand let go of her ankle and jumped for her throat. She put the green bottle down and caught it by the wrist. Her right hand thrashed and wriggled in her left hand, groping and scratching at her with ugly yellow fingernails.

She stood and saw light coming from above about thirty feet down the tunnel. The bodies of three acolytes had fallen through where the ceiling had collapsed, and the bright fire rising from their robes suggested they'd fallen victim to a Hellstroke or three. The tunnel shook and the fire swelled. Her right hand sunk its nails into her arm and scratched her deep. Kelly screamed again. "Okay, you fucker! You want to play rough? I can play rough!" Caution to the wind, Kelly sprinted toward the bonfire of Hellstrokes and threw her demonic hand right into the blaze.

Varr'rak shrieked and howled one last time. Her hand twitched in the fire and then went still.

Kelly blinked sweat out of her eyes and limped back to grab the gym bag. She retrieved the machete and held it at the edge of the fire until the blade turned orange. Then she pressed the flat of the blade to the stump of her right arm and screamed.

When the wound had cauterized and she knew she wasn't going to lose any more blood, Kelly finally allowed herself to throw up.

*****

Abby slipped on the wet floor as the fire alarm went off and the sprinklers activated. A large section of the floor collapsed behind her and Leanne, and a massive gout of orange flame rocketed up through the ceiling. Abby kicked open the door to the next stairwell and shouted abuse at the asylum itself. "Oh, you total whoremonger! This is just… *all* we fucking need!"

They finally reached the top floor of the asylum and Abby pulled Leanne down a long hallway that cut straight through the middle of the building. At the end of the hallway, there was a large, mahogany door with a brass nameplate on it: JOHN Z. LELAND, M.D. – HEAD OF PSYCHIATRY. Leanne sprinted ahead in a final mad dash and kicked the door open, but Abby pulled her back as a section of the wooden floor collapsed and Hellfire erupted toward the ceiling.

"Shit, now what are we going to do?"

Leanne grinned and pointed to a narrow strip of floor along the left wall, which stretched all the way across the office to the large bay window overlooking the front gate. Abby looked where Leanne was pointing and shook her head. "Seriously?!"

"It's the only way across! Come on!"

"But I thought you were terrified of heights!"

"I'm more terrified of what Leland will do to us if he catches us!"

"Good point," Abby conceded.

The two squeezed into the room and crept along the lip of the floor toward the window. The wood was hot under

Abby's feet and thrust tiny slivers into her skin like acupuncture needles. She ignored the sensation and held her hand out for Leanne. "Come on, Lee! Come on, come on!"

Leanne squeezed Abby's hand as she inched toward safety. Her eyes were shut tight and she pressed herself hard against the wall. "Don't look down, don't look down, don't look down…"

"Come on, Lee! You're doing great!"

CRACK! Leland stepped through a portal on the other side of the desk and raised his hands. Leanne screamed as she and Abby were lifted into the air and dropped hard at Leland's feet. Leland raised one hand and his walking stick materialized from nowhere. Abby coughed and covered her nose and mouth with her robes to protect against the smoke, and Leland started to unscrew the head of his walking stick. "Do you know why I've kept this thing for all these years?" he asked. "It's only partially out of sentiment. You see, I've made some… improvements to Granny's stick over the years. Originally it was a defence mechanism against unruly patients, but now… now it's mostly for my own enjoyment." In one fluid motion that Leland must have practiced a thousand times, the stick came apart in two segments. The hickory shaft whistled through the air down into the inferno and the brass head remained with Leland. On its inside was 36 inches of shining, razor-sharp steel. He grabbed Abby by the front of her robes and hauled her to her feet. He held her out over the very edge of the hole in the floor and pressed the blade to her neck, his grin a sickening, melted rictus.

"It's funny," he whispered. "Granny always warned me about mixing with 'the wrong sort of woman.' I don't think this was quite what she had in mind."

The Thunderbird's engine revved somewhere nearby. Abby looked over Leland's shoulder, and her jaw damn near hit the floor. She could see the car just outside the office window, hovering sixty feet in the air. Simon was cross-legged on the hood, his pale, sweaty face screwed up in concentration as he maintained the swirling cushion of air that held the car aloft. In the driver's seat, Natalie looked like this flying 1950s death trap was the most exciting thing that had ever happened to her. She gunned the motor, and then the Thunderbird zoomed toward the window like a Formula 1 racer.

Leland followed Abby's eyes, and his jaw landed right beside hers. His grip on her robes slackened and his sword arm fell to his side. "No…" he murmured. "No, you cannot be serio—"

Abby jinked to one side and hit the deck at the last possible second. The Thunderbird ripped an eight-foot hole in the wall and threw several tonnes of chrome and rubble directly at Leland. He went across the office like a ragdoll and flopped down on a small patch of undamaged floor in the opposite corner.

In her best Waylon Jennings impression, Abby said to no one in particular: "Well, looks like ol' Roscoe's bit off a touch more than he can chew."

Leanne blinked her eyes open and groaned, "Whus— whusgonon?"

Abby shook her head in disbelief. "You wouldn't believe me if I told you."

Natalie slapped a hand on the car door and hollered at the two to get in. Deciding not to question this bizarre quirk of fate, Abby hauled Leanne to her feet and got her into the back seat. Leanne held the door open and reached back for Abby.

Too late. While his bones were still putting themselves back together, Leland soared across the office with a roar and grabbed Abby by the ankle. Without stopping, he spun around and did a sharp upward turn in mid-air, pulling her up through the ceiling.

He threw her onto a flat section of the roof and she felt another rib break. She struggled up to her knees, one hand now permanently clamped to her side, and Leland dropped to the ground in front of her. He pointed his free hand at her, and pure will pulled her up to her feet. "This is where it ends,

Henderson! No tricks, no Hellstrokes, no Word of God! No more childish games." The roof beneath them suddenly cracked and tilted to a sharp angle. Leland's invisible grip relaxed and Abby stuck her arms out for balance as they both lurched to one side.

"You're insane, Leland! This whole place is coming down! Give it a few minutes and we'll both be dead!" The roof shook again, and a section the size of the Thunderbird collapsed thirty feet from where they were standing.

"Then we'll burn together! I spent 60 years working for this, Abigail! You have destroyed *everything* I believe in, and that will not go unpunished!"

Two gunshots *pinged* off the edge of the roof near Leland's foot. He and Abby both looked down as a third shot shattered a tile.

Kelly had emerged from the tumbledown shed and circled around to the front driveway. Her right wrist was cradled in her left armpit, and she was pointing Meg's Webley right at Leland. She adjusted her aim to fire again, but Leland thrust his sword arm toward her and hissed, "Absolutely not." All his telekinetic reserves coursed down the blade toward Kelly, and she was pulled screaming from the ground as he swept his arm. She thudded down onto the roof beside Abby and the revolver skidded out of her hand. Then Leland pointed at Abby and she fell to her knees. An invisible clamp gripped her by the throat and squeezed the air out of her as Leland's eye twitched and he ground his teeth.

The Thunderbird's horn honked as Natalie finally extricated the car from Leland's office. The car zoomed up past Abby and Leland and he whipped his sword defensively at the undercarriage. There was another crack as the roof shifted again, and Leland lost his balance.

Abby dragged herself toward Kelly and checked her pulse. Kelly was alive, but only half-conscious. Abby gave her friend a light smack on the cheek and Kelly opened one eye.

"Hey, Jaws…" she croaked. "You look like shit…"

"You too. What happened to your hand?"

"Long story… I'll live…" Her head lolled to one side and Abby gave her another rousing smack.

"Hey, hey, stay with me, Kel. Please, stay with me."

Kelly closed her eye and murmured something under her breath. Abby leaned in closer and heard the words "potion" and "bag". Kelly pointed with her good hand and then lost consciousness.

Abby followed Kelly's direction and saw the gym bag lying several feet away. Kelly had lost her grip on it when Leland threw her, and as he picked himself up, Abby scrambled toward it and looked inside. She found the bottle of Bonnesante Potion and opened it, draining the contents in one go. She winced as her ribs cracked and snapped back into their proper place and then a sense of painless euphoria washed over her. Abby felt like she could run a marathon or wrestle a bear. Or perhaps both. She stuck her hand in the air and whistled to Natalie, who cranked the Thunderbird's steering wheel for another pass.

Unfortunately, this grabbed Leland's attention as well. He balled his free hand into a tight fist and swept it toward the Thunderbird, hauling Kelly off the ground. She and Abby screamed in unison as Kelly pinwheeled through the air and hit the driver's door, crushing Natalie's mirror and sending the car lurching to one side. Kelly plummeted back to the roof and Simon lost his balance. He grabbed the hood with both hands and tried to correct the spell as Natalie cranked the wheel this way and that. But the Thunderbird was already going down, and the best Natalie could do was steer away from the asylum and find some place to land, with a bloodstained dent in her door.

Kelly went still. Abby picked up the Webley and squeezed the trigger. The muzzle flashed, and then everything stopped.

Ding-dong-ding-dong. The Westminster Chimes clanged and the flames and smoke froze where they were. The Webley's muzzle flash just sat there, like a flare on a still photograph.

The Thunderbird hung against the clouds like a mobile in a child's crib. Abby reached out and flicked a stationary raindrop suspended in front of her eyes. "What the…?"

"Oof. Ye've been in the wars, 'aven't ye?"

Abby looked behind her. Grandma Meg was standing there, swirling a glass of scotch in her hand.

"Meg? What the hell is this?"

"My last bow," said Meg. "I 'ad some time alone with the Webley 'fore I gave it to ye. I fixed up a psychic link, same as the Deacon did. Only I didn't attach t'other end to a person."

"The gun." Abby looked at the revolver in her hand and then at Meg. "You anchored yourself to it, like Simon said."

"Bang on, luv. Before that to-do with Varr'rak, I attached part of me psychic imprint to yon firearm. Yer 'and on the trigger makes for a psychometric link to the Elsewhere. Time's standing still for a mo' so we can talk."

"What do we need to talk about?"

"I don't know if ye noticed, luv, but there's a madman about fifteen feet that way wants to kill ye."

"I can handle Leland."

"Not on yer own, ye can't, an' we both know it. 'E's got the Deacon's full power, an' no reason to 'old back. But if we take 'im together…" She extended her hand.

"What? Like, let you possess me?"

"More like channel me. I'll 'op into yer mind an' give ye me fightin' strength. I can whisper in yer ear an' keep ye safe from 'is attacks, but it'll be yer 'ands on the wheel, I promise."

"Two brains for the price of one?"

"Why should Leland 'ave all the fun?"

Abby slung the gym bag over her shoulder and extended her other hand. "Let's go to work, Gran."

They joined hands and Abby shut her eyes. She felt Meg pulling her, then she felt a cold shock like she was jumping through a waterfall. Her heart skipped a beat, and when she opened her eyes, Meg was gone.

A voice in her ear whispered, *Are ye with me, Abby?*

"Yeah. Yeah, I'm here." She picked up the machete. It felt light in her hand, and it cut through the air with ease when she swung it. Meg's voice was whispering to her, and Abby knew instinctively how to keep her centre of gravity and strike without warning.

'Ow do ye feel?

"Good. Really good. I feel… stronger. Faster!"

Meg chuckled. *We can rebuild ye. We 'ave the technology.*

Thunder rolled and the Chimes clanged again. Time unfroze, and the Webley's muzzle flash flared out and died. Leland screamed as the shot hit him in the left shoulder, and Abby remembered the Victorian twins again: *when the parts will not mesh, the sum is vulnerable.*

Leland. The Deacon. Two halves, no longer cooperating. If she wanted to end him for good, it had to be now. Leland staggered toward her and raised his sword in a duelling stance. She swung the machete to show him she meant business. Then, in the worst, most over-the-top Southern accent she could muster, she drawled, "You, suh, have insulted, ah say *insulted*, mah honuh!" She pointed the machete at him. "Ah demayand satisfaction, suh!"

Leland frowned. "Cute." He planted his feet and thrust his sword toward the hole in the roof where he and Abby had come through. He extended his psychic will and a great plume of fire jumped out of the hole and raced to the tip of his blade. He swept the weapon at Abby and the flames banked hard.

"Oh shit!" She dove out of the way and rolled as the fire landed and punched another hole in the roof. The tiles beneath her feet cracked and shifted and she stuck her hands out beneath her for balance.

Leland jumped nearly twenty feet straight up and flew toward Abby. She rolled onto her back, lifted the Webley, and closed one eye to aim as he descended. Meg was whispering to her: *Line up the shot. Let 'im get close. Let 'im present the target. Don't rush it…*

When Leland was eight feet away, Abby fired. The bullet went straight through his other shoulder, and he jinked to one side as he fell. He landed badly on Abby's right, and she fired again.

Leland raised his free hand and the bullet stopped dead. Then it reversed course and flew at Abby's head.

She ducked. He leaped and thrust his blade at her. She parried the strike, and Leland jumped around behind her. She turned as he made another thrust, and Meg's invisible hand guided her to another clean parry.

"Beginner's luck," he snapped.

"You think?"

Leland looked in her eyes for a moment and smiled. "No… no, I have that wrong, don't I? You're not alone in there, are you, Abigail?" His eyes went to the Webley in Abby's left hand. "I've seen that gun before." He met Abby's eyes again and laughed. "A psychometric link, is it, McAllister? You just can't stay away, can you?"

Abby opened her mouth. It was her voice that came out, but the words were Meg's. "This whole shooting match started with me and your better half! I'll be goddamned if I walk away before the pair of you are in the ground. If you'll pardon my French."

"Then fight, you two. *Fight*!" Leland drove the point of his sword into the tiles and the whole roof shook. Abby stumbled and scrambled away from him as a wide hole collapsed where she had been standing and fire roared up through the gaps. Her feet blistered with every step as chunks of the roof fell away beneath her.

As Abby ran, Leland extended his sword into the fiery pit again. When he withdrew the weapon, red flames crackled and danced on the blade. He swung the sword above his head in a circle, and a narrow tongue of fire extended from the tip like a lasso. He pointed the weapon at the fleeing Abby, and the fire raced toward her.

The roof beneath her suddenly gave way. Abby screamed as she plummeted toward the inferno and she instinctively let go of her weapons so she could grab the edge of the roof. As she fell, Leland's shot missed her by a mile.

The roof tiles were hot beneath her fingers, but Abby didn't dare let go. Her legs kicked wildly in empty space, and a thought cut through the euphoria of the Bonnesante Potion: how bad were her burns going to be if she got out of here? Could the Potion repair her skin as it cooked, or was she doing permanent damage to herself by running around on the hot roof?

Leland leaped out of a portal before her and raised his sword. At the same time, Abby grabbed his ankle and pulled. The roof shifted with another crack, and he tumbled over her head into nothingness.

Despite all his talk, Leland's first instinct when death came rushing toward him was to put some distance between it and himself. At his command, a six-foot-wide portal opened a couple inches above the flames. This was what Abby had been hoping for, and she let go of the roof. She heard another crack and saw more of the roof come tumbling after her, along with the Webley and the machete. The falling debris followed her and Leland into the black void, and then the portal closed.

The long, black tunnel on the other side seemed to go on forever, and it wasn't long before Abby and Leland were separated. Soon after that, she lost sight of him entirely among the tunnel's myriad twists and turns. Obviously, Leland hadn't bothered to prepare an exit portal when he opened this one. Remarkably, despite all the bends and loops in the tunnel, Abby never hit a solid wall. She didn't think there was a single solid surface in here. Come to think of it, she didn't even know how long she'd been falling. Six seconds, six decades, what was the difference at this point?

Abby closed her eyes. *Meg. Are you still with me?*

Aye, said the voice in her head. *Till the bitter end.*

Okay. I don't know what's going to happen next. Just be ready.

You as well, luv. You as well.

They banked hard around the last corner and Abby saw another hole in the tunnel. From this distance, it was about the size of a coffee mug. Abby rolled in the air and closed her eyes. "I'm in control," she whispered to herself. "I am in control. The Elsewhere is the domain of the Gospel. It will obey me… I am in control. I am in control. I am in control…" She bounced a little when she landed, and bedsprings squeaked beneath her. Abby opened her eyes and hopped to the ground. She patted the stack of queen-sized mattresses that had cushioned her fall and looked up.

The machete and the Webley landed on the top mattress with a soft *whumf.* Abby grabbed them both and reloaded the gun with the last few bullets from the box.

Impressive, said Meg. *It's not easy to manipulate the environment like that. We'll make a Gospel of you yet, luv.*

Abby turned and scanned the white void for Leland. It didn't take long to find him, as he landed heavily behind her and raised his sword. "When you say you want a fight," he hissed, "I expect you to fight. Not run away with your tail between your legs!" The blade burst into flames and he shot a wide cone of fire at Abby.

She didn't run this time. She closed her eyes and concentrated, imagining the tremors in the ground below. She thought about the hardest, most resilient substance she could think of. Something that would make a Congolese diamond look like wet toilet paper.

The fire roared as it struck home, and Abby opened her eyes. A ten-foot metal wall rose before her, made of long links of chain pressed together like an accordion. Cold iron, treated with dragonfire. "Looks like you were good for something after all, Whittaker." As the fire dissipated, Abby stared at the chains and imagined them uncoiling, snaking along the ground, binding Leland tight. All of this they did promptly.

Sparks flew as he struck the large chains with his sword, but he couldn't even nick them. Abby didn't know exactly how hard Whittaker's cold iron was, but the stuff she was imagining was pretty fucking hard.

Leland struggled as the chains entwined him and pulled him to the ground. Abby pointed the gun at his head, and he shut his eyes.

She paused and looked up. A large object whistled through the air toward her, and a dark shadow spread beneath her feet. Abby shrieked and leaped out of the way as the Following's obsidian altar crashed to the ground and narrowly missed her. The chains rattled and became transparent as they turned to glass. Leland extended his psychic will and the glass shattered into dust. "Clever!" he gasped. "Very clever! But you're not the only one who knows how to shape the matter of the spirit world." He extended a hand and the ground beneath Abby's feet suddenly split. Tongues of fire jumped out of the widening gap and Abby had to fall to one side before she tumbled into the pit. She struck the blade of the machete once on the edge of the gap and imagined that her and Leland's roles were reversed.

The cracks in the ground spread toward Leland and Abby picked herself up. Fire burst from beneath him and the ground shook hard enough to knock him off his feet. Abby imagined a cork fired from a champagne bottle, and a geyser of molten lava suddenly propelled Leland sixty feet into the air. The ground kept shaking as the topography changed, but Abby didn't notice. She was in control, of course. The Elsewhere dared not move without her permission and she knew exactly where to step to avoid the tremors.

The once flat plane sloped downward as Leland landed, and a rushing stream of lava bubbled up. The ground crumbled beneath him as he scrambled forward to the land's edge, and the heat from the lava ignited the hem of his trousers. His aura wavered and Abby could see he was badly injured. As his strength ebbed, Leland fell to all fours on the impromptu riverbed, and Abby said something she'd always wanted to say.

"It's over, Leland! I have the high ground!"

Leland looked at her, his eyes wide, bloodshot, and desperate. He plunged the end of his sword into the hillside and screamed a demonic prayer. In the sky above Abby's head, two pairs of gigantic wings beat the air, and she saw the stone angels from the asylum's front gate winging their way toward her.

She turned and ran up the hill as the first angel landed halfway between her and Leland. It lunged forward and swept its long halberd. There was the sound of ripping fabric and she felt a sudden breeze on her lower back. The angel had sliced her robes open from one side to the other, missing her flesh by barely an inch.

The second angel landed in front of her and raised its halberd above its head. Abby stumbled backward as the long end of the blade smashed the ground before her, and the angel prepared to strike again.

As the sharp point of the halberd sped toward her face, Abby concentrated hard and tried to convince herself it was no danger to her. Really, honestly, the six-foot polearm stabbing at her head was safe as houses, and may God strike her down if she was lying.

She deflected the thrust with the machete, and the halberd's long blade exploded with a loud bang. There was a beat as the angel looked in confusion at the popped balloon it was now holding, and Abby rolled out of the way.

Leland pointed at the second angel, and suddenly the balloon was a shining broadsword nearly as long as Abby was tall. He spoke a word, and white-hot flames erupted along the broadsword's blade. The same thing happened to the first angel's halberd, and the two looming figures attacked.

Abby concentrated hard and a wall of cold iron rose between her and the angels. But Leland concentrated harder and convinced himself the wall was made of plywood. The angels smashed through it without stopping, and Abby fled.

They're only statues, Meg reminded her. *And not even real statues. They're Elsewhere constructs. A bad dream ye can wake up from.*

I know! I know! But did you see the size of the fucking things?!

Alright, I'll give ye that.

Abby circled around and ran down the hill. The bubbling river of lava suddenly ran clear as she convinced herself it was a babbling brook, and had always been a babbling brook.

The angels followed her with their weapons raised. Abby skidded and turned to face them as she reached the river bank. She closed her eyes, concentrated hard, and the waters swelled behind her. As the angels closed the distance, Abby dropped to her knees, planted her hands on the ground, and extended all of her imagination, all of her will, into the river. She felt a tremendous force suddenly pulling on her heart, sapping the energy that the Bonnesante potion had granted her, and she cried out in pain and anger.

The river rose in a gargantuan wave behind her and rushed toward the stone angels. It passed over her, freezing cold and deafening to hear, but she anchored herself firmly to the spot. The wave crashed down on the angels and roared up the hill toward Leland. He screamed and swept his blade in a wide arc, convinced that the river was parting for him like the Red Sea, and it did so. But Abby kept urging the river on, and it hammered the stone angels into oblivion. Finally, after several minutes of this, she released her psychic hold on the water and collapsed to the ground. The wave died away and the water on the hillside began to flow downstream again. Abby took great, gasping breaths as her pulse slowed to a normal rate. She looked at the spot where the angels had stood, and where there were now two large piles of black sand and rusty metal that might once have been weapons.

Leland staggered down the hill and gritted his teeth. "I think that's plenty of fun for one day." He stabbed at Abby's head, and she had just enough foresight to grab the Webley and the machete before she rolled away. The stab morphed into a wide slash, and Abby jumped to her feet. She swung the machete with both hands, but he hooked the hilt of his sword into the gap between her wrists. With his free hand, Leland opened another portal behind him. Then he spun and threw Abby through it.

She sailed backwards across the roof of the asylum and slammed into a tall ventilation duct. She felt the impact even through the Bonnesante potion, and when she landed, she dropped the Webley.

Ooh, bloody 'ell! Grandma Meg exclaimed. *Even I felt that! 'Ow are you, Abby?*

"Fine," Abby wheezed. "I'm just fine. First, I've got to catch my breath, then I've got to throw up."

Leland jumped out of the portal with his sword raised and bounded right toward her. Abby held the machete tight and rolled away as he landed. He brought his sword down where her head had been and cleaved the air duct nearly in half.

Abby rose in a low crouch and attacked Leland's middle, but with one flick of the wrist he got his blade atop hers and swept the machete clean out of her hand.

She gulped as the machete clattered along the roof and Leland kicked her onto her back. He pressed his foot onto her chest and nestled the point of his sword between her eyes.

"Impressive tricks," he hissed, "but tricks all the same. You have no true power against the Eldest One." He shifted his hips in preparation for the killing blow, and Abby grabbed his foot and wrenched it to one side. Leland lost his balance, and Abby rolled out from beneath him.

"Oh no, you don't!" Leland wrapped a hand around her ankle and pulled her to the ground. Without a look back, she kicked away his fingers with her other foot and ran for the machete.

"That's right, Abigail! Run! Run and hide!" He pulled himself up and hobbled after her. "Run from me, just like Karen ran!"

Abby grabbed the machete and squeezed it with both hands. Deep inside her, the lid came off the jar containing her emotions, and all her rage, all her hate, poured into the blade.

Abby spun and launched a relentless *blitzkrieg* of attacks. Leland smiled and deflected them effortlessly, one after another after another. When she swung low, he jumped over the machete and raked his blade across her shins, drawing blood. When she lunged, he parried up and opened a cut on her cheek. Even with Meg's fighting knowledge, Abby couldn't keep up.

Slow down, Abigail! shouted Grandma Meg. *Save yer energy before 'e kills ye! Ye keep this pace up and ye'll burn yerself out!*

Abby fell back a step, breathing hard. Leland took the opportunity and slammed his elbow into her cheek.

To her dying day, Abby never knew for certain if what happened next was her own adrenaline, or Meg taking the wheel. She would try a hundred times to replicate the move in training with Natalie, and a hundred times she would fail.

As Leland raised his sword for the final blow, Abby hooked the blade of the machete through his bent elbow and grabbed the blunt edge with her free hand. Then she dropped her hips and the machete ripped through Leland's arm like a paper cutter. He screamed and pressed his remaining hand to the stump of his elbow, and Abby got back up and drove the machete through his chest. They fell together and the blade of the machete pinned him to the roof.

She rolled off of him, gasping for breath. He started laughing, but it turned into coughing pretty quick. He spat blood onto the roof tiles and wheezed, "Credit where it's due, Abigail… that was one heck of a move. Karen couldn't have done better."

Abby got up and limped over to the bifurcated ventilation duct. She picked up the Webley, thumbed the hammer, and staggered back toward Leland. "I'd say 'Tell her yourself,' John, but I don't think you're going the same direction." She dropped to her knees, pressed the gun to his head, and pulled the trigger.

The Westminster Chimes began to ring again. Abby sat down and closed her eyes as the first flames danced across Leland's body. "You off?" she asked.

Got to catch me bus, said Meg.

"Will I see you again?"

Ye might. Rank 'as its privileges, Abby. Not many folk upstairs will object to a Gospel goin' walkabout.

"Do me a favour, Gran? When you get upstairs, give my mom a hug."

I'll give 'er one from both of us.

Then the Chimes stopped. Meg was gone.

As Abby pulled the machete out of John Leland's burning carcass, she heard a frail moan in the distance. "Abby… Abby, please…"

Kelly's head lolled from one side to the other as she tried to push herself up.

"Kelly? Oh my God, Kelly!" Abby ran around the great gaps in the roof and landed at Kelly's side. "Oh God, Kelly, oh thank Christ! I thought you were—"

Kelly lay back down and grabbed Abby's wrist. "Abby, please… I can't… my legs…"

Abby knelt beside here. "Shh, shh, shh. It's going to be okay, Kel. It's going to be okay."

In the sky above them, a car horn beeped. It had taken nearly two whole laps of the asylum's perimeter, but Simon finally had the Thunderbird stable again. Leanne opened the back door and Abby flagged the car down, assuring Kelly that it would be okay.

And call ye on the name of your gods, and I will call on the name of the LORD: and the God that answereth by fire, let him be God. And all the people answered and said, It is well spoken.
*

1 Kings 18:24

SIX WEEKS LATER

CHAPTER 29

…AND MANY MORE

IRONICALLY, IT was Karen who had bought the dress.

It had been a gift last Christmas—a long-sleeved, knee-length black number with a small white frill around the collar. Karen had given it to Abby after spending the better part of a year hinting that Abby should start dressing more maturely. Now, as Abby gave herself a once-over in the mirror, fixed her lipstick, and smoothed out the skirt, she started to wish she'd swallowed her pride and actually put it on once before now. She had to admit: it covered the scars pretty well.

Most of the wounds Abby had received at Applegate were mere dull aches and occasional twinges at this point. She'd had X-rays taken just the other day and the doctors had confirmed that her ribs had healed as well as they were going to. But while Abby had her shirt off, one of the nurses had commented on the ugly pink scars creeping up her left side, a reminder of the pound of flesh that Leland had carved out of her before the ritual. In the New Year, she'd ask around the local tattoo parlours and see if she could get the marks covered up. Maybe with an elaborate floral pattern. Or a raven in flight. Or a psychiatrist with one arm and a bullet hole in his skull.

She leaned in close to the mirror and checked her teeth. She'd flossed vigorously after breakfast, but you could never be too careful. Not if the caterers were serving up fresh BC smoked salmon. She didn't want a chunk of fish stuck in there when she was giving the eulogy.

They should have had the funeral earlier. Abby was kicking herself for leaving things so late, but circumstances had conspired against them. Karen's car had been found at a Petro-Canada near Hope, which put her in the Upper Fraser Valley RCMP's jurisdiction at the time of her death. They'd treated it as a suspicious death from Minute One, and held her body as evidence until they could find who killed her. But Applegate Asylum was in the same jurisdiction, and the equally-suspicious nature of the fire had meant an inquest had to be launched between the RCMP and the Hope Fire Department, which had brought the investigation into Karen's death to a screeching halt. Then some bigwigs from Ottawa had swooped in and quietly pulled the investigators away from the Applegate case. The asylum had been connected to a lot of suspicious activity recently, and it seemed the High Heid Yins didn't want anybody digging too deep because they didn't like the questions being raised. It was nearly three weeks between the time Karen died and the time the cops finally released her body to her family. They had her cremated before the government could change its mind, but as they were all still recovering in their own way, scheduling a proper funeral proved monumentally difficult.

There was a knock on the bathroom door. Abby looked over her shoulder and said, "Come in."

Leanne walked in. She'd thrown a sweater on over her sleeveless black dress to keep the winter chill at bay. The sweater was technically a very dark blue, but it was close enough that she'd be able to get away with it at the church. She nodded toward the door and said, "They're here."

Abby took a deep breath and squared her shoulders. "Okay." She turned and presented herself to her partner. "How do I look?"

Leanne reached up and adjusted Abby's earrings. For the sake of decorum, Abby had removed all but one pair of her more obvious piercings today. "You look good." She ran a hand through Abby's hair, which had finally grown back out to a length Abby was comfortable with. Unfortunately, Abby hadn't had the free time to get it dyed yet, so it was currently in its natural mousy frizz. "It's funny," Leanne said, "it's been so long since I've seen your natural hair colour. It makes you look…"

"Dowdy? Dorky? Plain?"

"It makes you look like your mom," Leanne said. She sniffed and wiped away a tear. Abby held her for a moment and rested her chin on Leanne's head.

"Your parents are meeting us at the church, yeah?"

"Yeah," Leanne said. "I think Mattie and Nick are coming too." These were the youngest of Leanne's four brothers. The other two, Jonah and Stephen, had sent Abby their condolences when they heard about Karen but were both out of the province and thus unable to make the funeral.

"And remember, if you can get your dad alone…"

"Abby, I don't know if today's really the best time…"

"Look, the mourning suits are just for the funeral. We've got the reception in the afternoon, and the wine's going to start flowing pretty fast. My mom always said she wanted people to smile when she went. So, you're going to sit down with your dad and you're going to ask him straight out: 'The bank won't talk to me. Can you give me a hand with this?'"

Leanne smiled. "I can't believe I let you talk me into this. My own business? Me? At my age?"

"This is what you've always wanted, isn't it?"

It was, and Leanne didn't currently have a lot of options career-wise. Bookselling was the only thing she was any good at, but ever since the Following had ripped apart the Olde Curiosity Shoppe, no other bookstore in town would so much as look at her résumé. Independent booksellers, it turned out, were a close-knit bunch. Every one of them knew by now that Lydia Clifford, one of their own, had disappeared under mysterious circumstances shortly after her store was ransacked, and that her assistant clerk had given the police some wild story about violent drug addicts in weird robes. That kind of thing tended to attract stigma. Two rival coffee chains were currently bidding for the land on which the Shoppe sat, and Leanne was scrambling to come up with enough funds to outbid them. Working for Mrs. Clifford hadn't always been easy, but Leanne dearly loved the Shoppe itself, and she refused to let another indie bookstore get bulldozed for a Tim Horton's.

They left the bathroom hand-in-hand. As they emerged into the apartment proper, Don Henderson looked up and smiled. He reached out for the walker in front of his chair and got slowly to his feet. He stumbled slightly as he got up, but Abby caught him with one swift motion that flowed seamlessly into a warm hug.

"You look good, Dad," she whispered.

"I sh—I sh-shaved. M-myself. Started that new book this m-m-morning."

Abby smiled and kissed him on the cheek. "That's the new Edward Finney one, right? I got dibs after you."

Don patted her on the back and nodded. Since the fire at Applegate, he and Abby had been making efforts to get in touch nearly every day. She would keep him updated on work at the newly re-opened MacReady's, various hospital visits and doctor's appointments, and training at the Letterbox, and he would talk—as best he could—about his new physical fitness regimen. He'd come a long way in a fairly short time. He was gaining back a fair amount of weight, both fat and muscle mass, and he'd hired a private trainer to help him get out of the wheelchair. He could manage short to moderate distances on the walker now, and he was hoping to move up to a cane by the New Year. His capacity for speech was returning slowly but surely, and he hadn't told Abby to "Go to sleep" in nearly a month. It was as if a wall in Don's brain had crumbled when the Following were destroyed, and everything the Deacon had blocked was now coming back.

And brother, talk about *destroyed*. Abby and the others had watched the asylum's centre block collapse from the safety of the Thunderbird, and the rest of the compound had followed it not long after. There hadn't been a single whisper of Following activity since then. Whatever had been left alive after the exorcism, the fire had swallowed it up without complaint.

Abby settled her dad back into his chair and looked over at the person he'd been talking to while she was in the bathroom. Kelly Munro reached up with her left hand and Abby gave it a squeeze. "How you doing, Kel?"

Kelly smiled. It was a small, tired smile that didn't quite reach her eyes. "I'm… managing. I don't have to wait in line at the movies anymore." She patted the arm of her motorized wheelchair with the lump of moulded plastic that now passed for her right hand. When Leland had thrown her into the Thunderbird, Kelly had suffered an incomplete injury to her ninth and tenth thoracic vertebrae. She had spent a week after the fire in a medically-induced coma, and most of the next month being ferried from one wing of St. Paul's Hospital to another for a battery of tests and sessions with the resident trauma counsellor. To her family, her doctors, and the rest of her and Abby's friends, Kelly had explained the injury as a bad car accident, but there had been a couple nights in the hospital where Abby had sat up late with her and talked her through some nasty panic attacks. On a few occasions, Kelly had suddenly frozen up and demanded that Abby or Leanne hold their crosses against her skin to make sure there was no demonic presence lurking in her body.

Abby kneeled in front of Kelly's wheelchair and hugged her. She spoke low so that only Kelly could hear. "I hate seeing you like this. I *hate* it. He just… he just had to ruin one more life, didn't he?"

"I'm still alive, Abby. We're all still alive. In my book, that means we won. And Simon and I have been talking. You know, that thing in the Faroe Islands?"

By the 'thing,' she was referring to a coven of Old-World folk healers whose matriarch owed Simon a favour. He had mentioned them the last time Abby and Kelly had been at the Letterbox and, while he admitted that their magic was not as powerful as Vanguard magic, many of the techniques they used had been adapted from Vanguard practices of the Early Middle Ages. If Kelly was willing to make the trip and put in the time, said Simon, the coven might be able to help her regain some mobility.

"You think you'll go out?" Abby asked.

"Probably not till next year," said Kelly. "My lease is up at the end of January. I'm going to stick with my current job till the end of the Christmas season, and then I'm putting in my two weeks. You might not see me for a while."

"Well, keep in touch."

Abby got up and looked to the last two seats at the table. Simon and Natalie rose and hugged her as one. Simon wore the long black frock coat and top hat of a Victorian undertaker, but he was insistent that it had served him well enough as funeral attire for the last 150 years and he wasn't about to give up a perfectly good Henry Poole original, thanks very much. Natalie's dress was more subtle and modern, although Abby was a bit surprised to learn they made dresses in that size.

"Haven't heard from you two in a couple of days," Abby said. "No major disasters, I hope?"

Simon gave her a smile. "Things have actually been relatively calm in the Nocturn. We're currently keeping tabs on a situation involving a gremlin, a shoelace, and a banana peel, but I don't think it'll be anything really serious. Actually, I was hoping you might have a look in, give us your opinion."

"I've got tomorrow off. Leanne and I could swing by the Letterbox after lunch?"

"I'll have the tea on when you get there."

"Sounds good."

Leanne squeezed in and put her hand on Abby's arm. "Are we all ready to go?"

"Just gotta get my eulogy. One sec." Abby jogged toward the bedroom. She'd been putting some finishing touches on her eulogy—and drafting another, more personal project—before she went to bed last night. She checked both her and Leanne's bedside tables, the dresser beside the door, and the closet. She even looked under the bed. The eulogy wasn't anywhere. "What the hell?"

Leanne poked her head in. "Problem?"

"I swear my eulogy was in here! You haven't seen a little stack of index cards with a green paper clip, have you?"

"Did you check your bedside table?"

"Yeah."

"Both drawers?"

Abby blinked and sheepishly opened the second drawer of her bedside table. There were no index cards, but there was a black-bordered envelope with a green wax seal. The design stamped into the wax was an oak leaf in front of what appeared to be a rising sun. Abby broke the seal and read the handwritten note inside.

Chickadee,

I found your eulogy. Beautiful stuff. I'm not ashamed to admit I got a bit choked up. I wish you'd signed it, but you can't win them all. I hope you don't mind if I 'borrow' it, but you did say you would owe me one. I figure I'll take this as the one.

I didn't want to leave you completely high and dry, so I left you a copy to take to the funeral. Check under your front mat. No need to thank me.

Yours, &c.,

R.G. Whittaker

PS: I am sorry about your mom, kid. I knew her, once upon a time. Hell of a woman, our Karen.

Abby folded the note back up and chucked the whole thing in the drawer. "You son of a bitch," she whispered. The back of her hand started to itch. She looked at it and watched as the little oak-leaf-shaped welt between her thumb and forefinger slowly disappeared. It had been sitting there, neither bothering her or changing in size, for the last six weeks now, but now it was gone, and she knew her account with Whittaker was balanced.

"What's up?" Leanne asked. "Who's an ess-oh-bee?"

"Never mind," Abby said. "I'll tell you in the car. As long as you're up there, you can turn off my computer and we can get out of here."

Leanne picked Abby's laptop up off the bed. A Microsoft Word document was open on the screen, and Leanne couldn't resist having a peek. The last two days, Abby had been spending a lot of time writing something on her computer, but she'd always become very secretive whenever Leanne asked what she was working on.

The document was nearly six pages long, and the page Leanne was on began like so:

It's been six weeks now, and everybody I've talked to is still asking questions about Applegate Asylum. Hell, CBC ran an hour-long retrospective on the place last Friday. (And I swear, you have not seen strange until you have seen Ian Hanomansing utter the words 'satanic rituals' on national TV. But I digress...)

Nobody can agree on why the asylum burned down last month, and that's got a lot of people thinking about the old ghost stories. Some are saying it happened because the ghosts got angry, or God got angry because somebody was performing rituals again, or the Devil swallowed everything up because a ritual went a little too well.

None of these people are right. But they're not too far off, either. My name is Abby Normal, and I was at Applegate Asylum on the day it burned down. I saw what really happened.

Leanne adjusted her glasses and read the page a couple times. Then she looked down and asked, "Abby, are you writing a blog?"

Abby shrugged as she got to her feet. "Yeah, okay, you got me. But after what we saw at Applegate, I just... I had to get all of this stuff off my chest. And I mean not just to you or Simon or Natalie. I feel like people should know what's out there. I feel like I should warn them, you know? I mean, if even one person reads this and starts looking a little more carefully at the shadows, then... I don't know, I'll just sleep a lot better."

Leanne nodded. "You don't want what happened to you to happen to anyone else. You want to be the last Abby Normal."

"It's funny you should say it like that... I was actually going to call it 'The Abby Normal Blog.'"

"Are you sure about that? What if somebody recognizes the name? Do you really want to go back to being the crazy *Sixth Sense* chick nobody talks to?"

Abby crossed her arms and stuck her chin out. "Yeah, I thought about that. And you know what I've realized? I don't care anymore. I. Do. Not. Care. All this stuff: Gospels and Vanguard and the Following and Azna'ghal, it's so much bigger than me. It's so much bigger than anyone on this planet. Compared to the Deacon, compared to the Enlightening, all those kids who picked on me in high school are nothing. Their taunts, their nicknames, all nothing. And it's time I realized that and stopped letting them dictate who I am. That shy, scared little girl who used to sit in the corner with no one to talk to is gone. Leland beat her out of me at Applegate, and this is what came back. Abby Normal, gay psychic warrior of justice. I might not have had a say in whether I got these powers or not, but I sure as hell am going to have a say in how I use them. I'm not going to hide this part of me any longer, and if anyone's got a problem with that, they can shove it you-know-where."

Leanne digested this for a moment. "You're sure about this."

Abby nodded. "I've never been this sure about anything. This is me. This is who I really am. There's a whole world full of nasties out there who don't like skin-apes, and somebody has to stand up to them when they get rough. Somebody has to knock the bullies down a peg or two."

Leanne put down the computer and squeezed Abby's hand. She looked her partner in the eye and saw a glint of steel there. It was something Leanne had never seen before, and she tried to reflect it in her own eye. "Okay. If you're going to live in this world, if you're going to go after these things, then I'm going with you. Every step of the way. I will be there for you, Abby Normal."

Abby smiled and wrapped her other hand around Leanne's. "Foreverways?"

"Foreverways."

They kissed. Abby closed her eyes and took a moment just to hold her partner. It was nice holding Leanne, she thought. She really should do it more often.

Leanne smiled. "Ready to go?"

"Ready to go." She grinned and took Leanne's hand. Their fingers interlocked. Then they walked out to face the world together.

ABBY NORMAL

WILL RETURN IN

THE NOWHERE HOUSE

WITHOUT WHOM

IT IS commonly held wisdom in filmmaking circles that "movies are not finished; they escape". I think the same can be said of most creative works. It was certainly true in the case of Abby Normal. I began writing the first draft of this book in October of 2014. In the intervening five years and change, I have spent I don't even know how long agonising over all the tiny details, writing and re-writing whole chapters until I got everything just perfect. But that's ridiculous. No creative work can ever be perfect. No story can ever be finished. It can only escape.

Over the years, there have been many people who assisted me in this process, or who gave me advice that ultimately aided Abby Normal's escape. It is time I took a step back and gave those people the recognition they deserve.

Thanks first of all to Raquel Segal for her magnificent cover design. My ridiculous little penny dreadful seems a bit more prestigious with her artwork in front of it. Thanks to Gabby Helmin-Clazmer of Easy Song Licensing for helping me navigate the choppy waters of international music copyright. Special and heartfelt thanks to Shayla Lazenby. Without her blunt and brutally honest critiques and edits, this story likely would not have made it past its horrible first draft.

Beta readers, I've had a few. Thanks in no particular order to Sandor Kovacs, Ted Nulty, and Marinus Opperman for their comments and suggestions. Thanks to David Chariandy and the Spring 2016 ENGL 374 class at Simon Fraser University. I tricked them into workshopping the first chapter for me, and they graciously did not rebel and stick my head on a pike. There may be others who tweaked one or two lines here and there, and if I'm forgetting their names, I apologize. Thanks to all you betas, and hopefully you remember who you are.

Thanks must also go to the teachers. No one person directly inspired the character of Simon Lockhart, but he was influenced by a mixture of feelings that I've had toward various educators I have known and studied under. I acknowledge in particular Dr. Matt Hussey, whose lectures on the Anglo-Saxons helped shape a large chunk of the backstory here; Roderick 'Mithter' Greene, who encouraged storytelling and experimentation, and who introduced me to one of my favourite bands; and Kevin McKendy, fondly remembered and sorely missed, who guided me to a second home in the theatre.

Thanks to my family, who have patiently put up with these strange creative whims of mine far longer than is necessary. Colin, Jen, Robbie, Josh, Louie, and dearly departed Whisky: I love you all.

Finally, all the thanks in the world to you. Yes, you, the person sitting there and reading these words right now. Thank you for setting aside some hours of your precious time. Thank you for letting me in to tell you this story. I hope you enjoyed it.

Samuel Thomas Fraser
February 6, 2020

ABOUT THE AUTHOR

Samuel Thomas Fraser is an actor and author from the rainy mountains of Vancouver, BC, Canada. A lover of literature both medieval and mysterious, Sam is currently pursuing his MA in English at the University of British Columbia Okanagan, with a focus on the relationship between language and magic systems in speculative fiction. His short fiction and poetry has appeared in numerous anthologies and magazines. *Abby Normal* is his first novel.

www.ingramcontent.com/pod-product-compliance
Lightning Source LLC
Chambersburg PA
CBHW051434050726
47593CB00005B/1773